## LOGAN DRAGGED HIS SLEEVE OVER HIS DAMP FOREHEAD.

His body was stiffly aroused, aching with his intense awareness of Madeline. He wanted to reach for her again, bear her to the hard stage floor and take her right there. It was insane, impossible that he could be so obsessed with a naive girl when he'd taken his pleasure with some of the most desirable women in Europe.

"Enough of this damned nonsense," he muttered.

"Nonsense? You . . . don't find me attractive?" Madeline asked in pained confusion.

"Damn." It was proof of her inexperience that she would ask such a question, when the buttons on his trousers were straining to contain his arousal. "I find you attractive," he said gruffly. "Hell, I'd like to do things to you that— It's a bad idea, Maddy. I would end up changing you. Hurting you."

"I understand," she said.

"No, you don't. Which is why I'm going to try like hell to avoid you. I don't need you on my conscience."

"I don't care about that. All I want is for you to kiss me again."

# LISA KLEYPAS

# Because You're Mine

AVON BOOKS
*An Imprint of* HarperCollins*Publishers*

This is a work of fiction. Names, characters, places, and incidents either are the product of the author's imagination or are used fictitiously. Any resemblance to actual events, locales, organizations, or persons, living or dead, is entirely coincidental.

AVON BOOKS
*An Imprint of* HarperCollins*Publishers*
10 East 53rd Street
New York, New York 10022-5299

Copyright © 1997 by Lisa Kleypas
Cover art by Boris Flotsky
Inside cover art by Max Ginsburg
Inside cover author photo by Larry Sengbush
Published by arrangement with the author
Library of Congress Catalog Card Number: 97-93008
ISBN: 0-380-78144-1
www.avonbooks.com

First Avon Books Printing: September 1997

Avon Trademark Reg. U.S. Pat. Off. and in Other Countries, Marca Registrada, Hecho en U.S.A.
HarperCollins® is a trademark of HarperCollins Publishers Inc.

Printed in the U.S.A.

WCD 10 9 8 7 6

To my parents,
Linda and Lloyd Kleypas,
for showing me that love has no limits

# Prologue

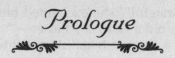

*London, 1833*
*Autumn*

"*I can't* marry him. I just can't." Madeline's stomach churned with revulsion as she watched Lord Clifton stroll the outside grounds with her father. She didn't realize she had spoken aloud until her mother, Lady Matthews, replied.

"You will learn to care for Lord Clifton," she said crisply. As always, her narrow face wore a dour, disapproving expression. Having led her life with an attitude of self-sacrifice that approached martyrdom, she made it clear that she expected the same of her three daughters. She stared at Madeline with cool brown eyes, her features elegant and pale. All the Matthews women shared the same colorless complexion except for Madeline, who tended to blush easily.

"I expect that someday, when you have matured," Agnes continued, "you will be grateful that such an excellent match was arranged for you."

Madeline nearly choked on her resentment. She felt traitorous color climbing up her cheeks, turning them bright pink. For years she had tried to be everything her parents required—docile, quiet, obedient—but she could no longer contain her feelings. "Grateful!" she exclaimed bitterly. "Marrying a man older than my father—"

"Only by a year or two," Agnes interrupted.

"—who shares none of my interests and thinks of me only as a broodmare—"

"Madeline!" Agnes exclaimed. "Such a vulgar choice of words is beneath you."

"But it's true," Madeline said, striving to keep her voice calm. "Lord Clifton has two daughters from his first marriage. Everyone knows he wants sons, and I'll be expected to produce them. I'll be buried in the country for the rest of my life, or at least until he dies, and then I'll be too old to enjoy my freedom."

"That is enough," her mother said tautly. "Apparently you must be reminded of a few facts, Madeline. It is a wife's place to share her husband's interests, not the other way around. Certainly Lord Clifton is not to blame if he doesn't happen to enjoy frivolous pursuits such as novel-reading or music. He is a serious man with great political influence, and I expect you to address him with the respect he deserves. As for his age, you will come to value his wisdom and seek his guidance in all things. That is a woman's only course to happiness."

Madeline twisted her fingers together and stared unhappily out the window at Lord Clifton's bulky figure. "Perhaps it would be easier for me to accept the betrothal if you had allowed me to have at least one season. I've never danced at a ball, or attended a dinner party or soirée. Instead, I've had to stay at school while all my friends have come out. Even my own sisters were presented at court—"

"They were not so fortunate as you," Agnes replied, her back as straight as a fireplace poker.

"You will be spared all the anxiety and inconvenience of the season, as you have already been betrothed to the most eligible and admirable man in England."

"Those are your words for him," Madeline said under her breath, tensing as her father and Lord Clifton entered the room. "Not mine."

Like any other girl of eighteen, she had fantasized about marrying a handsome, dashing man who would fall madly in love with her. Lord Clifton was as far from those fantasies as it was possible to get. He was a man of fifty, with a stocky build and flapping jowls. With his deeply furrowed face, balding head, and moist, heavy lips, he reminded Madeline of a frog.

If only Clifton had a sense of humor, a kind nature—anything that she could find remotely endearing . . . but he was pompous and unimaginative. Rituals guided his life: the entertainments of the hunt and the racetrack, the concerns of estate management, the occasional speech at the House of Lords. Worse still, he had an unabashed disdain for music, art, and literature, all the things that Madeline hungered for.

Seeing her from across the room, Clifton approached her with a thick-lipped smile. The corners of his mouth gleamed with moisture. Madeline hated the way he looked at her, as if she were a thing to be possessed. Inexperienced she might be, but she knew he wanted her because she was young, healthy, and presumably fertile. As his wife, she would exist in a more or less constant state of pregnancy until Clifton was satisfied with the number of boys she had produced. He wanted nothing of her heart, mind, or soul.

"My dear Miss Matthews," he said in a deep,

croaking voice, "you grow lovelier every time I see you."

He even sounded like a frog, Madeline thought, struggling to contain a slightly hysterical laugh. His clammy hand enclosed hers, and he raised it to his lips. She closed her eyes and steeled herself against a shiver of disgust as she felt his bloated lips brush the back of her wrist. Mistaking her reaction as one of maidenly modesty—perhaps even excitement— Clifton regarded her with a deepening smile.

He asked her to walk outside with him, and her objections were swiftly overcome by her parents' enthusiastic agreement. They were determined to have a man of Clifton's means and influence in the family. Whatever Lord Clifton wanted, he could have.

Reluctantly taking her fiancé's arm, Madeline strolled through the garden, a formal, precise arrangement of Maythorn hedgerows, tidily sanded paths, and boxed-in flower beds. "Enjoying your holiday from school?" Lord Clifton asked, his small but heavy feet crunching on the gray-white path.

Madeline kept her gaze on the ground before them. "Yes, thank you, my lord."

"No doubt you have a desire to leave the academy, as your companions have done," Clifton remarked. "Your parents kept you there two years longer than the other girls, at my request."

"Your request?" Madeline repeated, startled that he had such influence over them. "But why—"

"I felt it would be good for you, my dear," he said with a self-important smile. "You needed polish and discipline. A perfect fruit must be allowed to ripen. Now you are not so impetuous as you were then, hmm? As I intended, you have learned patience."

*Hardly,* Madeline wanted to snap at him, but somehow she kept her lips clamped shut. Two extra years of the rigid confinement of Mrs. Allbright's Academy for Young Ladies had nearly driven her mad. It had allowed her rebellious, overimaginative nature the time to ferment into something wild and unmanageable. Two years ago, she had been too timid and easily led to have objected if her parents married her to Clifton. Now, however, the words "patience" and "obedience" didn't belong in her vocabulary.

"I have brought something for you," Clifton remarked. "A gift you've been anticipating, I am certain." He drew her to a stone bench and sat with her, his soft body pressing against her side. Madeline waited wordlessly, finally meeting his gaze with her own. Clifton smiled like some indulgent uncle with a mischievous niece. "It's in my pocket," he murmured, indicating the right side of his brown wool coat. "Why don't you fish it out, like the clever kitten you are?"

Clifton had never spoken to her that way before. They had been carefully chaperoned on previous occasions. "I appreciate your kindness, but it isn't necessary for you to give me anything, my lord," Madeline said, her hands tightly folded, fingers knitted together.

"I insist." He waggled his coat pocket at her. "Fetch your present, Madeline."

Stiffly she reached into the pocket, locating a tiny circlet. Her heart thudded in a sickening rhythm as she withdrew the object and beheld it. A small gold ring fashioned in a braided pattern, adorned with a tiny, dark sapphire. The symbol of her future bondage as Clifton's wife.

"It has been in my family for generations," Lord

Clifton remarked. "My mother wore it until the day she died. Does it please you?"

"It is attractive," Madeline said dully, loathing the object.

Taking the ring from her, Clifton pushed it onto her finger. It was far too loose, and she had to close her hand into a fist to keep it from slipping off. "Now you may thank me for it, my pet." His heavy arms snaked around her, and he pulled her hard against his short, barrelled chest. He had a foul, stale smell, like game birds hung out to ripen for too long. Obviously Lord Clifton believed frequent baths to be an unnecessary indulgence.

Madeline drew in a breath of suffocated misery. "Why must you refer to me as a 'pet' or a 'kitten'?" she asked in a voice that trembled with defiance. "I don't like to be called such things. I'm a woman, a *person*."

Lord Clifton laughed, revealing large yellow teeth, and she winced from the rush of his foul breath against her face. He squeezed her tightly as he replied. "I knew that sooner or later you would try to challenge me . . . but at my age, I know all the tricks. Here is the reward for your impertinence, my spiteful little pet—"

His blubbery lips pressed over hers, smothering and grinding her mouth in the first kiss she had ever been given. His arms were as tight as barrel stays. Madeline held silent and still, quivering with revulsion . . . using all her strength to endure his touch without screaming or crying.

"You will find that I am a very masculine sort," Lord Clifton said, breathing heavily, appearing satisfied with his conquest. "I don't spout poetry or pander to women's ridiculous notions of what they want. I do as I please, and you will learn to like it exceedingly." His pudgy hand stroked the side of her pale, strained face. "Lovely," he murmured. "Lovely. I've never seen eyes the color of yours, like amber." His fingers twisted in a stray wisp of her golden-brown hair, rubbing the silken strands repeatedly. "How I look forward to the day when you'll be mine!"

Madeline set her jaw hard to keep it from trembling. She wanted to scream at him, to tell him that she would never belong to him, but the sense of duty and responsibility that had been instilled in her from birth kept her silent.

Clifton must have noticed her involuntary shiver. "You're getting cold," he said in a tone he might have used with a very small child. "Come, let us go inside before you catch a chill."

Relieved, she rose with alacrity and stepped with him into the parlor.

As soon as Lord and Lady Matthews saw the ring on Madeline's finger, they erupted in smiles and congratulations—they, who made a point of never showing enthusiasm because they considered it unrefined.

"What a generous gift," Agnes exclaimed, her normally sallow face glowing with pleasure. "And such an exquisite ring, Lord Clifton."

"I think so," he said modestly, jowls flapping with gratification.

Madeline watched with a faint, frozen smile as her father ushered Lord Clifton to the library for a celebratory drink. As soon as they were out of hearing, she tore the ring from her hand and flung it to the carpet.

"Madeline," Agnes exclaimed, "retrieve that at

once! I will not abide such childish tantrums. You will wear that ring from now on—and you will take pride in it!"

"It doesn't fit," Madeline said stonily. Remembering the feel of Clifton's wet mouth on hers, she scrubbed her sleeve across her face until her lips and chin were raw. "I won't marry him, Mama. I'll kill myself first."

"Don't be dramatic, Madeline." Agnes bent and picked up the ring, holding it as if it were priceless. "I hope that being married to a man as solid and earthbound as Lord Clifton will rid you of such wild outbursts."

"Earthbound," Madeline whispered with a bitter smile. She found it incredible that her mother could sum up all the repulsive qualities in Clifton with such a banal word. "Just the quality every girl dreams of in the man she marries."

For once it was a relief to return to the academy, where there were no males except for the dancing instructor who came to tutor the girls once a week. Madeline walked along the narrow hallway with a hatbox in hand. The rest of her belongings would be brought upstairs later. Reaching the room she shared with her best friend, Eleanor Sinclair, she came upon a crowd of a half-dozen girls settled on the beds and chairs. As Madeline was the oldest student at Mrs. Allbright's academy, and Eleanor was the second-oldest at seventeen, they were frequently visited by the younger girls, who considered them mature and worldly.

The girls appeared to be sharing a tin of biscuits and exclaiming over some colored print that Eleanor held. Noticing Madeline's arrival, Eleanor gave her a welcoming smile. "How was Lord Clifton?" she asked, having known before Madeline's departure of the planned meeting with her betrothed.

"Even worse than I expected," Madeline replied shortly, walking to her own narrow bed, which was placed opposite Eleanor's. She dropped the hatbox to the floor and sat on the edge of the mattress, wishing that the girls would leave so she could talk privately with her friend.

*Soon*, Eleanor's friendly gaze promised, while the other girls continued to huddle in their excited circle.

"Just look at him," one of them exclaimed breathlessly. "Can you imagine what it would be like to actually meet him?"

"I would faint," someone else declared, and they all giggled.

"He's the most handsome—"

"He looks like a highwayman—"

"Yes, there's something in the eyes . . ."

Madeline shook her head at the flurry of feminine sighs. "What in heaven's name are you looking at?" she asked, her glumness replaced by growing curiosity.

"Let Madeline see—"

"But *I* haven't gotten a proper look yet—"

"Here, Madeline." Eleanor brought the colored print to her. "My older sister gave it to me. It's the most difficult-to-find print in London. Everyone wants a copy."

Madeline's gaze fell on the picture. The longer she stared at it, the more fascinated she became. The man's face could have belonged to a king, a sea captain, or an outlaw . . . someone pow-

erful . . . someone dangerous. He was not classi-
cally handsome—his features were too bold. There
was a lionesque quality about his lean face, his
gaze narrow and piercing, his wide mouth set with
the hint of an ironic smile. The color of his hair was
indeterminately brown in the print, but it appeared
to be thick and slightly rumpled.

The other girls waited for her to blush and giggle
as they had been doing, but Madeline kept all sign
of emotion from showing. "Who is he?" she asked
Eleanor calmly.

"Logan Scott."

"The actor?"

"Yes, the one who owns the Capital Theatre."

A strange feeling came over Madeline as she
continued to stare at him. She had heard about
Logan Scott, but she had never seen his likeness
before now. At the age of thirty, Scott was an actor
of international fame, surpassing the standards set
by David Garrick and Edmund Kean. Some even
said he had not yet reached the height of his
powers. Among his attributes was a voice that was
reputed to stroke the ears like velvet or set fire to
the air with its crackling intensity.

It was said that women pursued him everywhere, enthralled not only by his skillful stage
performances as the romantic hero, but even more
by his portrayal of archvillains. He excelled as Iago
or Barabbas . . . he was the consummate seducer,
betrayer, and manipulator, and women adored him
for it.

A man in his prime, attractive, cultured . . .
everything Lord Clifton was not. Madeline was
wrenched with sudden longing. Logan Scott inhabited a world she would never be part of. She
would never meet him or anyone like him . . . she

would never flirt and laugh and dance, never be seduced by a man's tender words or a lover's touch.

As she stared at Logan Scott's face, a wild, mad idea came to her—one that made her fingers tremble.

"Madeline, what's the matter?" Eleanor asked in concern, taking the print from her. "You're so white all of a sudden, and you look very strange—"

"I'm just tired," Madeline said, forcing a smile to her face. She wanted to be alone; she needed time to think. "The weekend was a strain. Perhaps if I rest for a while—"

"Yes, of course. Come, girls—we'll meet in someone else's room." Considerately Eleanor herded the crowd out the door and paused before closing it. "Madeline, is there anything you need?"

"No, thank you."

"I'm certain that seeing Lord Clifton this weekend was an ordeal. I wish I could help in some way."

"You already have, Eleanor." Madeline lay on her side, drawing her knees up to her chest, the skirts of her simple school frock bunched around her. Her mind raced with thoughts, and she scarcely noticed her friend's quiet departure.

Logan Scott . . . a man whose appetite for women was nearly as legendary as his acting talent.

The longer Madeline considered her own dilemma, the more convinced she became that Scott could provide the solution. She would use him to make herself so undesirable to Lord Clifton that he would have no choice but to call off the engagement.

She would have an affair with Logan Scott.

The sacrifice of her virginity would solve every-thing. If she had to live out the rest of her days in disgrace, regarded by society as used goods, so be it. Anything was preferable to becoming Clifton's wife.

Feverishly she began to make plans. She would forge a note from her family, requesting her to return from boarding school a semester early. During the following weeks, her parents would assume that she was safe at school, while Mrs. Allbright would think she had returned home, leaving Madeline free to accomplish her task.

She would go to the Capital Theatre and ac-quaint herself with Mr. Scott. After she indicated her willingness to sleep with him, Madeline ex-pected that the matter would be quickly resolved. It was a well-known fact that all men, no matter how honorable they seemed, wanted to seduce nice young girls. And a man with Scott's reputation would show no hesitation in matters of sin and debauchery.

When she was ruined beyond redemption, she would return to her parents and accept whatever punishment they meted out. Most likely she would be banished to the home of some relative in the country. Lord Clifton would have a complete dis-taste for her, and she would finally be free of his attentions. The course she had set for herself would not be easy or pleasant, but there was no other way.

Perhaps it wouldn't be so bad, living as a spinster after all this was over. She would have ample time to read and study, and after a few years Mama and Papa might allow her to travel. She would try to involve herself in charitable works and do some good for people in circumstances worse than hers.

She would make the best of things. At least, Madeline thought with grim determination, she would choose her fate rather than have it handed to her.

# Part One

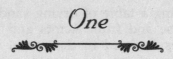

# One

*Gripping the* leather handle of her valise, Madeline paused at the back entrance of the Capital Theatre. It had been frightening and yet exhilarating to make her way through London alone. Her ears were assaulted with the noise of carriages, horses, and street sellers, while her nostrils were filled with a confusing mixture of the aromas of manure, animals, and garbage; the yeasty scent of a nearby bakery, and the hot waxen odor of a candle-maker's shop.

Earlier in the day Madeline had pawned the ring Lord Clifton had given her, and the pocket of her dress was filled with the satisfying weight of coins. Wary of pickpockets, she had kept her plain gray cloak wrapped tightly around herself, but no one had seemed inclined to approach her. Now she had arrived at the Capital, and her adventure was about to begin.

The theater appeared to comprise four or five buildings that must house workshops and storage facilities. Entering the main building, where the stage was located, Madeline walked through a maze of hallways and rehearsal rooms. She could hear people talking, singing, playing instruments, and arguing, and the temptation to peek through the half-open doors was nearly overwhelming.

She reached a large room filled with worn furni-

ture, including a table of drying sandwiches and
wilted cheese and fruit. Actors and actresses of
varying ages lounged in the room, talking and
drinking cups of tea. Apparently accustomed to
frequent comings and goings, they took little notice
of Madeline. However, a shopboy paused and
stared at her inquiringly, his eyes friendly in a
foxlike face. "Is there something you want, miss?"
he asked.

She smiled, trying to cover her nervousness.
"I'm looking for Mr. Scott."

"Oh." He looked at her speculatively and jerked
his head toward the far door. "He's rehearsing
now. The stage is that way."

"Thank you."

"He doesn't like to be interrupted," the boy
advised as Madeline walked toward the stage door.

"Oh, I won't bother him," she replied cheerfully,
gripping her valise handle with one hand as she
opened the door with the other. She pushed her
way past set pieces and flats, and found herself
standing in the right wing of the stage. Setting her
valise on the floor, she drew close to the edge of a
green velvet curtain and looked across the stage.

With its seating capacity of fifteen hundred, the
Capital Theatre was a grand and spacious building.
Massive gold columns inlaid with emerald glass
lined the walls. Tiers of boxes and seats filled the
auditorium in velvet splendor. Crystal chandeliers
shed brilliant light on delicately painted scenes that
adorned the ceiling.

The floor of the stage was built at a slant, so that
actors downstage could be seen as well as those in
the front. The heavy boards were scarred from
thousands of performances, boots and shoes and
scenery leaving indelible marks. There was a re-

hearsal in progress; two men were walking around the stage with foils in hand, discussing the choreography of a fight scene. One of them was fair and blond, with the slender, springy build of a cat. ". . . not certain what you want . . ." he was saying earnestly, tapping the rubber-tipped foil against the side of his shoe.

The other man replied in the most distinctive voice Madeline had ever heard—dark, deep, worldly . . . the voice of a fallen angel. "What I want, Stephen, is for you to put some fire into your performance. Your intention, if I'm not mistaken, is to kill the man who nearly seduced your fiancée. Instead you're handling that foil like an old woman with a knitting needle."

Madeline stared at him, riveted. Logan Scott was taller than she had expected, more charismatic, more . . . everything. His rangy, muscular body was clad in a simple white shirt that was open at the throat and a pair of dark trousers that closely followed his lean hips and long legs. The print Madeline had seen hadn't begun to do justice to him . . . the color of his hair, dark brown touched with fire; the sardonic curve of his wide mouth; the rosewood hue of his skin.

Somehow his polished appearance was tempered by a hint of brutality . . . the sense that the princely facade could disappear at any moment and reveal a man who was capable of almost anything. Madeline blinked uneasily. She had expected Scott to be something of a rakish dandy, a charming skirt-chaser, but there was nothing lighthearted or dandified about him.

The blond actor protested. "Mr. Scott, I'm afraid that if I don't hold back during that last bit of choreography, you won't have time to parry—"

"You won't get through my guard," Scott said with stunning self-assurance. "Give it everything you've got, Stephen—or I'll cast someone who will."

Stephen's mouth tightened. It was clear that Scott's barb had found its mark. "All right, then." He raised his foil and lunged, evidently hoping to catch Scott off-guard.

Responding with a short laugh, Scott parried expertly, and the foils scissored and clashed as the two men moved in a lightning-swift exchange. "More, Stephen," Scott said, his breath quickening from exertion. "Haven't you ever lost a woman before? Wanted to kill someone for it?"

The other actor's temper seemed to flare, as Scott clearly intended. "Yes, damn you!"

"Then show me."

Stephen exploded in a flurry of movement, his face intent beneath a veil of sweat. Scott praised his efforts with a few terse words, retreating and moving forward with his own volley of feints and thrusts. Madeline wouldn't have expected a large man to move with such grace. The sight of Scott literally took her breath away. He was powerful, commanding, and chillingly self-controlled. Fascinated by the intense battle, Madeline drew closer for a better view.

With a shock of dismay, she felt her foot catch on the valise she had set on the floor, and she fell against a small table piled with props. A candelabra, a few pieces of china, and an extra foil dropped to the floor, shattering and clanging noisily. The actors' concentration splintered, and Logan Scott's head whipped around toward the right wing. At the same time, Steven lunged forward with his foil, unable to halt his momentum.

Scott gave a muffled grunt, and his taut rump met the hard floor, his large hand clasped to the opposite shoulder. The ensuing silence was disturbed only by the actors' rapid breathing.

"What the hell . . . ," Stephen murmured, staring into the shadows of the wing, where Madeline struggled to her feet. He glanced back at Scott, who wore a strange expression.

"Stephen," Scott said, his voice slightly raspy, "it appears that the tip came off your foil." As he spoke, a rush of scarlet spread between his fingers and over his shirt.

"My God!" Stephen exclaimed, his face blanching with horror. "I didn't know . . . I didn't mean to—"

"It's all right," Scott replied. "It was an accident. Your performance was exactly what I wanted. Do it that way every time."

Stephen stared at him incredulously. "Mr. Scott," he quavered, seeming torn between despair and laughter, "how can you sit there *directing* me while you're bleeding all over the floor? At times I wonder if you're human." He tore his panicked gaze from the spreading bloodstain on Scott's white shirt. "Don't move. I'll get someone to help . . . send for a doctor . . ."

"There's no need for a damned sawbones," Scott called tersely, but Stephen had already fled the stage. Muttering beneath his breath, Scott tried to lurch to his feet and fell heavily again onto the floor, his face whitening.

Madeline threw off her cloak and snatched at her woolen scarf. "Here," she said, rushing out of the wing and dropping to her knees beside him. She wadded up the scarf and clasped it hard against his shoulder. "This will help stop the bleeding."

Scott inhaled sharply at the painful pressure.

Their faces were very close, and Madeline found herself staring into the bluest eyes she had ever seen, shadowed with thick dark lashes. The irises were lined with sapphire and seemed to contain every shade of blue, from the darkest depths of the ocean to the palest midwinter sky.

Madeline discovered that she was oddly short of breath. "I'm sorry about . . . ," she paused and cast a sheepish glance over her shoulder at the pile of broken stage props, ". . . all that. It was an accident. I'm not at all clumsy, not usually, but I was watching the rehearsal from the wing, and I tripped—"

"Who are you?" he interrupted coldly.

"Madeline Ridley," she replied, using her grandmother's maiden name.

"What are you doing here, aside from disrupting my rehearsal?"

"I'm here because . . ." Madeline met his gaze again, and all of a sudden there seemed to be no choice except to declare her intentions in a bold, straightforward manner that wasn't like her at all. She had to get his attention somehow, to separate herself from the numbers of women who must throw themselves at him all the time. "I want to be your next lover."

Clearly caught off-guard, Scott stared at her as if she had spoken in a foreign language. He took his time about replying. "I don't have affairs with girls like you."

"Is it my age?"

There was a flare of laughter in his eyes . . . not friendly, but mocking. "Among other things."

"I'm older than I look," she said swiftly.

"Miss Ridley." He shook his head in apparent

disbelief. "You have a unique way of introducing yourself to a man. I'm flattered by your interest. However, I wouldn't touch you if my life depended on it. Now if you'll excuse me—"

"Perhaps you need more time to think about my proposal," Madeline said. "In the meantime, I would appreciate it if you would consider giving me a job. I have many skills that could be useful in the theater."

"I'm certain you do," he said dryly. "But none that I require."

"I'm educated in literature and history. I also speak fluent French, and I can sketch and paint quite well. I would be willing to sweep, mop, scrub . . . anything that needs to be done."

"I'm light-headed, Miss Ridley. I'm not certain if it's from loss of blood or sheer amazement . . . but in any case, you've been quite entertaining." Scott got to his feet, the color having returned to his face. "I'll have someone recompense you for the loss of your scarf."

"But I—" she began to argue.

A small crowd of people swarmed onto the stage as various members of the theater company were alerted to the accident. "It's nothing," Scott said, seeming annoyed by their worried exclamations. "No, I don't need help walking. There's nothing wrong with my legs." He went toward the green-room, surrounded by carpenters, musicians, painters, dancers, and actors, all of them determined to help him.

Madeline stared after him. What a remarkable man he was. He seemed like royalty, although most monarchs and princes probably weren't blessed with his good looks and magnificent build. She was positive that Scott was the right man to

have an affair with. Surely it would be nothing less
than extraordinary: a once-in-a-lifetime experience.

True, he hadn't seemed overly eager to bed
her . . . but she wasn't finished yet. She would
wear him down with her persistence. She would
devote every minute of every day to making herself
indispensable to him. She would become whatever
he wanted in a woman.

Thoughtfully Madeline went toward the wing,
where broken china lay scattered next to the over-
turned prop table. There was probably endless
work to be done at the Capital Theatre. She
wondered if there was someone else she could
approach about a job. After straightening the table,
she began to pick up a few shards of china.

A woman's light, melodious voice drifted to her
from a few yards away. "Be careful, child. You'll cut
yourself. I'll have someone sweep that up later."

Madeline placed the china on the table and
turned to behold a golden-haired woman several
years older than herself. The woman was stun-
ningly beautiful, with an aristocratic face, blue-
green eyes, and a warm smile. She was also several
months pregnant. "Hello," Madeline said, approaching her curiously. "Are you an actress?"

"I have been in the past," the woman admitted
readily. "However, I'm currently limited to the
position of comanager, until after the baby's
birth."

"Oh . . ." Madeline's eyes widened as she realized that the woman could only be the Duchess of
Leeds, the well-known actress who had been
paired on stage with Mr. Scott in everything from
lighthearted comedy to Shakespearean tragedy.
Although the Duke of Leeds was reputedly quite

wealthy, he apparently did not choose to stand in the way of his wife's love of the theater and her flourishing career. "Your Grace, it's an honor to make your acquaintance. Please forgive the trouble I've caused—"

"I wouldn't worry," the duchess reassured her. "Accidents happen all the time around here." She stared at Madeline speculatively. "I believe I over-heard you asking Mr. Scott for employment."

"Yes, Your Grace." Madeline blushed, wonder-ing what else the woman had overheard, but her expression was bland and guileless.

"Come with me to my office . . . what is your name?"

"Madeline Ridley."

"Well, Madeline, you're not the usual kind of girl who comes looking for work in the theater district. Well-dressed, obviously educated . . . have you run away from home, child?"

"Oh, no," Madeline said. It wasn't strictly a lie, since she had run away from school, not home, but she still felt uncomfortable at the deception. She struggled to word her reply carefully. "Circum-stances have made it necessary for me to find work somewhere . . . and I hoped it could be here."

"Why the Capital?" the duchess asked, leading her backstage to the administrative offices.

"I've always had an interest in the theater, and I've heard and read a great deal about the Capital. I've never actually attended a play."

"Never?" The woman seemed astonished by the idea.

"Only amateur productions at school."

"Have you aspirations to be an actress?"

Madeline shook her head. "I'm certain I have no theatrical talent, and I wouldn't like to perform in front of anyone. The very thought makes my knees weak."

"A pity," the duchess commented, entering a small office containing a gleaming mahogany desk piled high with folios and notices. Boxes filled with books and papers lined the wall. "A girl with a face like yours would be quite a draw for the Capital."

Madeline blinked in confusion at the compliment. She had always considered herself to be moderately attractive, but nothing more. There were many girls with better figures than her slender, modestly endowed one . . . girls with far more striking features than her light-brown eyes and honey-brown hair. Her mother, Agnes, had always said that her eldest daughter, Justine, was the beauty of the family, whereas Althea was the most clever. Madeline, the youngest, had no special distinction.

Madeline had always been aware that she should have been a boy. Childbirth was difficult for Agnes, and the doctor had made it clear that her third baby would be her last. In spite of willing the child to be a son, Agnes had experienced the greatest disappointment of her life when a third daughter had appeared. Madeline had always felt that it was her fault. If only she had possessed some extraordinary gift that might have made her parents glad to have her . . . but so far she had been very ordinary.

The duchess gestured for Madeline to sit in a chair near hers. "Tell me what skills you possess, and I'll consider the matter of your employment."

They talked for a few minutes while a tea tray was brought from the greenroom. The duchess spoke quickly and smiled often, her boundless energy contagious. It would have been easy for a woman of her celebrity to intimidate others, but instead she was warm and unaffected. In Madeline's sheltered life, she had never met a woman like the Duchess of Leeds. There had only been her mother, and the teachers at school with their lectures on propriety, and her friends who knew no more of the world than she.

"Madeline," the duchess said, "you can see from my condition that I'll be limited in my activities during the coming months. I would like an assistant to fetch and deliver things for me, and keep my office neat . . . there are so many tasks that no one ever seems to have time for. Your skill at needlework may also be useful to Mrs. Lyttleton, the woman in charge of creating and maintaining costumes. And although Mr. Scott steadfastly denies it, we have needed someone to reorganize the theater library for years."

"I could do all of that and more!"

The duchess laughed at her enthusiasm. "Very well. Consider yourself part of the company."

Madeline's gasp of pleasure was cut short by the thought of Mr. Scott's reaction when he discovered her working there. "Won't Mr. Scott object?"

"I'll discuss the matter with him. I'm perfectly within my rights to hire anyone I like. If you encounter problems with Mr. Scott or anyone else, come to me."

"Yes, ma'am. That is . . . Your Grace."

There was a flicker of laughter in the duchess's blue-green eyes. "Don't let the title intimidate you, child. In spite of my position outside the Capital, here I'm only an assistant manager, and Mr. Scott reigns supreme."

Madeline had never heard of such an unorthodox arrangement: a noblewoman actually working in the theater. The worlds of the aristocracy and the theater were irreconcilable. She wondered how the duchess managed to traverse them.

The duchess laughed, reading her thoughts. "Most of my peers believe I do an injustice to my rank by continuing my work here. The duke, bless him, would be quite happy for me to leave the theater, but he understands that I couldn't do without it."

"If I may ask, Your Grace . . . how long have you worked at the Capital?"

"It's been five or six years now." The duchess's face softened in reflection. "How elated I was when Logan hired me to be a member of the company! Every actor and actress in London wanted to be trained by him. He had developed a more natural style of acting than had ever been practiced before—now it's widely imitated, but then it was extraordinary."

"Mr. Scott has quite a presence," Madeline commented.

"And he knows it," the other woman rejoined wryly. She poured more tea into Madeline's cup and gave her a speculative glance. "There is something I should warn you about. Most of the women who work at the Capital sooner or later imagine themselves in love with Logan. I advise you not to fall prey to the same temptation."

Madeline's cheeks burned. "I suppose it would only be natural . . . a man with his looks . . ."

"It's not only his looks. There is a remoteness about him that excites women—each imagines that she can be the one to finally make him fall in love. However, the theater means more to Logan than any real person ever could. Of course, there is a constant parade of women through Logan's life. But never an affair of the heart."

That would certainly make things convenient. If Madeline's plan succeeded, she could sleep with Mr. Scott and leave with no emotional entanglement.

"Enough about Logan," the duchess said briskly, interrupting Madeline's thoughts. "Tell me, child . . . have you found lodgings yet? If not, I can recommend a place for you to stay."

"I would appreciate that, Your Grace."

"I have a friend, an elderly woman who was once a well-known actress. She lives alone in a fine house on Somerset Street, but she takes in boarders occasionally. She likes to have young people around her, and it is quite entertaining to hear her reminisce about the past. I'm certain she'll let a room to you for a small weekly sum."

"That sounds perfect." Madeline flashed her a smile. "Thank you."

A troubled expression crossed the woman's face. "I try not to pry into other people's concerns, but it's clear that you don't belong here, Madeline."

She was silent, uncertain how to reply. She lowered her gaze to avoid looking into the duchess's perceptive eyes.

"You're not very good at hiding your feelings," the other woman remarked. "If you're in some kind of trouble, child . . . I hope you'll decide to confide in me. I may be able to help."

"I can't think why you would be so kind to a stranger," Madeline said.

"You seem so very alone," the duchess murmured. "There were times in my past when I felt that way. No matter what you're running from, the situation may not be as dire as it seems."

Madeline nodded, although she had no intention of confiding in anyone. After thanking the duchess sincerely, Madeline left the theater and summoned a hack to take her to Somerset Street.

Mrs. Nell Florence was an elderly woman with silvery-peach hair that must have been a vivid shade of red in her youth. Her skin was pale and gently worn by time, her bone structure elegant. She seemed warm and kind, with a charming touch of vanity.

"So my dear Julia sent you to me, did she?" Mrs. Florence asked, welcoming Madeline into her home. "I'm certain we'll get along famously. You're an actress, I take it? No? I can't imagine that, not with a face like yours. If I'd possessed half such beauty when I was your age . . . but then, I did quite well with what I had."

Busily she showed Madeline around the two-story house, each room filled with mementos from her acting career. "I was the toast of London," Mrs. Florence declared, taking her past a wall of portraits done some thirty years earlier. Each painting depicted her in a different pose or costume, some of them shockingly revealing. She seemed to take great satisfaction in Madeline's blush. "You're an easy one to read, aren't you? What a refreshing quality."

Intrigued by the collection of memorabilia, Madeline inspected framed play notices, engravings, and colored fashion plates of old costumes. "How wonderful, to have led such a life!" she exclaimed.

"I've had my ups and downs," Mrs. Florence said. "And I've enjoyed all of it. Never regret anything, that's my advice. Come, I'll show you the room you'll be staying in, and then we'll have a long talk. You must tell me everything about your-self."

Madeline had never before realized how obvious her thoughts were. It seemed that Mrs. Florence could read them as easily as Julia did. "Ah," she said, regarding Madeline's face. "You don't want to discuss your past, I see. Well, we can find other things to talk about."

Madeline was gratified by the elderly woman's understanding. "Thank you, Mrs. Florence," she said, accompanying her on the rest of the tour.

After unpacking her few belongings, Madeline changed into a dove-gray wool gown trimmed with plum cording. She was going to the theater tonight, to see Logan Scott on stage and decide for herself if he was as talented as everyone claimed. Standing before the mirror, she finished fastening her gown . . . and frowned at the result.

While the garment was well made, the style was all wrong, modest and practical with a primly high neckline. How was she going to seduce any man, least of all Mr. Scott, without some alluring clothes? Wistfully Madeline smoothed her hands over her figure. If only she had a beautiful gown made of silk and lace flounces, and slippers trimmed in pearls, and fresh flowers for her hair. . . .

After brushing out her long golden-brown hair, she coiled and pinned it carefully on top of her head. She wished she had curling irons, to make artful wisps dangle against her temples and cheeks. "Not even a drop of perfume," she said, shaking her head ruefully.

After a few moments, however, her naturally high spirits asserted themselves. She would solve such problems later. Tonight she had only one

thing to accomplish, and that was to see her first
London play.

The Duchess of Leeds was kind enough to show
Madeline to a place in the wings where she could
stay and watch the play. "You'll be all right here,"
she said to Madeline. "Just make certain you keep
out of everyone's way. They'll be rushing through
scene and costume changes—you wouldn't want
anyone to trip over you."

Obediently Madeline shrank to the side and
found that she could see most of the action onstage, albeit from an odd angle. The play, called *A
Lover Denied*, was preceded by a musical performance and a one-act farce that sent ripples of
laughter rolling through the audience. The curtains
were drawn, and set pieces, flats, and people flew
across the stage in apparent chaos. Miraculously
everything fell into place in less than a minute.
Two young men near Madeline pulled expertly at
ropes and pulleys, and the curtains opened to
reveal the beautifully crafted interior of a London
mansion.

Applause and exclamations of pleasure ema-
nated from the audience at the sight of the display.
Then two characters, a husband and wife, began to
discuss a list of suitors for their marriageable
daughter. Madeline was enthralled as she watched
the story unfold. She felt acute sympathy for the
heroine, an ingenue who was being prevented
from marrying her childhood sweetheart and instead was betrothed to a villainous man who
refused to relinquish her to the arms of her true
love.

To Madeline's surprise, Logan Scott had not
been cast as the girl's true love, but as the villain of

the piece. The moment he strode onstage, an electric thrill shot through the audience. Like everyone else, Madeline was riveted by his self-assurance, the threatening charm of his character. He wanted the girl for himself, and not even her love for another man would stand in his way.

To Madeline, each minute that passed was a revelation. She stood silently in the wings, her fingers gripped in a fold of velvet curtain, her heart pounding so hard that she could feel it down to her toes. Each time Mr. Scott spoke, she could barely breathe. He inhabited the character with ease, conveying the man's selfishness and intense longing. Like the rest of the audience, Madeline began to hope that he might win the innocent girl's love.

Mr. Scott remained onstage for most of the first act, manipulating, bargaining, driving wedges between the two lovers until it seemed that true love would never have its way. "What happens in the end?" Madeline couldn't help whispering to a scene-mover who had stopped next to her. "Does Mr. Scott marry her, or does he let her go to the other man?"

The sceneshifter grinned as he saw the rapt attention Madeline paid to the action onstage. "I can't tell you," he informed her. "Wouldn't dream of spoiling the surprise."

Before she could entreat him again, the first act concluded and it was time for intermission. Madeline skittered to the side as the curtain was dropped. A troupe of dancers filed onstage to entertain the audience until the second half of the play began.

Wistfully Madeline waited in the semidarkness, hidden behind the edge of velvet curtain. It would seem an eternity until the play resumed. Anticipation filled her, and she was conscious of a tingle of happiness. There was no other place she would rather be than here, breathing in the scents of sweat and paint, and the acrid smell of calcium lights.

A large, dark shape moved past her, a man striding from the stage to the cluster of dressing rooms. Their shoulders brushed as he walked by, and his steps slowed. He stopped and lifted his hand to the place where they had touched. Slowly he turned to look at her. Their gazes met, and Madeline felt a throb of alarm in the pit of her stomach. It was Mr. Scott.

A shimmer of perspiration highlighted every angle of his face. Although the color of his eyes was muted in the shadows, the glitter of dawning anger was unmistakable. "You . . ." he said. "What the hell are you doing in my theater?"

No one had ever cursed at her before. Surprise made her slow to reply. "Mr. Scott . . . I can see that Her Grace hasn't yet spoken to you about me. . . ."

"I told you there was nothing for you here."

"Yes, sir, but the duchess didn't agree. She hired me as her assistant—"

"You're dismissed," he snapped, coming forward until he loomed over her.

She could smell the sweat on his skin and the damp linen of his shirt. It was not at all unpleasant . . . it was fascinating. He made the other men she had known in her life seem like soft, tame creatures.

"No, sir," she said, hardly believing she had dared to refuse him.

There was a brief silence. *"No?"* he repeated in a

thick voice, as if the word had never been said to him before.

"The duchess said that she could hire me if she pleased, and that if you objected, I should come to her."

An unpleasant laugh came from his throat. "Did she? I'd like to know who owns this damned theater! Come with me." He took her upper arm in a punishing grip.

Stumbling, gasping, Madeline was pulled toward his dressing room. Her ears were assaulted by his muttered curses. "Sir . . . I would appreciate it if you wouldn't use such words in my presence."

"You come to my theater uninvited, cause an accident in the wings, go behind my back to plead for a job . . . and now give me a lecture on my manners?"

The door slammed shut, and they stood staring at each other—he with palpable fury, she with quiet stubbornness. She would not let him send her away from the Capital.

"I would have thought such language beneath a man like you," Madeline said with extreme dignity.

Mr. Scott opened his mouth to reply, then muttered something under his breath.

In the small, brilliantly lit room, every detail of Mr. Scott's face was vivid. The bronze of his complexion made stage paint unnecessary. His gaze was so piercing that it almost hurt to look at him, and his wide jaw was granite-hard. "You've made a mistake, Miss Ridley. There's no room for you here."

"Mr. Scott, if you're still offended by my clumsiness earlier, I'm sorry for that. I'll be quite careful from now on. Won't you give me another chance?"

Logan was infuriated by his own reaction to her. The memory of her had distracted him all day. The girl's appealing speech would have melted a glacier, but it only strengthened Logan's resolve. "It has nothing to do with this morning," he said brusquely. "The fact is, you're not needed here."

"But the duchess said there were many things I could help with . . . the costumes, the theater library—"

"Julia has a soft heart," he interrupted. "You managed to take advantage of her. I'm not so easily manipulated."

"I haven't manipulated anyone," she protested.

A manservant arrived to help Logan change for the second act, bearing in his arms a fresh white linen shirt and vest. "George," Logan acknowledged him curtly and began to unfasten his damp shirt. There were only a few minutes left before the second act commenced.

Madeline had never seen a man undressing before. As each button was released, more gleaming muscle was revealed. Shocked, she edged toward the door. "Mr. Scott, I . . . believe I should go now. . . ."

"You're going to leave the Capital?" he inquired coldly, shrugging out of the limp garment.

Hastily Madeline lowered her eyes, but the image of his broad, naked chest was permanently seared into her brain. "I will stay if the duchess allows it."

"Then stay if you choose, but you'll pay for it. I'm going to make your life hell. Do you understand?"

"Yes, Mr. Scott," she whispered, fleeing the dressing room as he began to unfasten his trousers.

Logan paused as the door closed, willing his fierce arousal to recede. Tactfully George averted his eyes, scooping up the discarded shirt. "Will there be anything else you require, sir?" he murmured.

A bucket of ice-cold water would have been useful, not to mention a drink. But Logan shook his head and turned away, continuing to undress. The manservant straightened a few articles in the dressing room and left quietly.

Facing the mirror, Logan sighed, trying to bring his thoughts to the work ahead . . . but his mind was filled with the girl. Madeline.

Who was she, and why in God's name did she want to work at the Capital? She was obviously too well-bred for such a place—she had no business associating with the rough theater crowd. What had Julia been thinking to hire her? He dearly wished he could corner his comanager and wring an explanation from her, but there was no time. He had a performance to finish, and nothing was more important than giving the audience at the Capital exactly what it wanted.

Somehow Madeline made her way back to her vantage place in the wings. She put her hands to her hot cheeks, certain they had been branded a permanent scarlet. Had she been wrong to insist on remaining at the Capital in spite of Mr. Scott's displeasure? She was certain this was not the way to go about seducing a man.

Why did he dislike her? She had always found it easy to make friends. She supposed she was not the kind of woman Mr. Scott preferred. How difficult would it be to change his feelings toward her? . . . how long would it take? Troubled, she stared into the darkened backstage area, where actors waited patiently amidst the set pieces.

The curtain rose, and the story of the belea-guered young lovers resumed. It was a testament to Mr. Scott's talent that Madeline soon forgot every-thing but the character he played.

After an intricate maze of plot twists, the villain finally realized that even if he succeeded in marry-ing the beautiful girl, he would never win her love. Assuming the part of an anonymous benefactor, he helped them elope with each other, never letting them know that he was the one responsible for their happiness. Mr. Scott played the role without a touch of self-pity, never letting down the cynical mask he wore, but somehow his rigid control let the audience know that his heart was broken. The play's ending was satisfyingly bittersweet.

Hearty shouts and claps of enthusiasm filled the theater, persisting until the actors had returned to the stage to receive their due. Scott was greeted with the most applause, which he accepted with a faint smile and bow. The program for the next night was announced, and the curtain closed for the last time, despite the fact that the audience clamored for more.

Madeline took care to slip away before Mr. Scott saw her again. She caught sight of his dark head backstage just as he was surrounded by a crowd of admirers. They all wanted to be near him. Sighing, Madeline went to retrieve her coat from the duch-ess's office.

"Madeline." She looked up to see the Duchess of Leeds. "Did you enjoy the play?"

Madeline struggled to find the right words. "Oh,

it was the most wonderful thing I've ever experienced!''

"My goodness," the duchess said, laughing at her enthusiasm.

"No wonder they call Mr. Scott a living legend. He . . . he . . ." Madeline paused, not knowing how to describe her reaction to him.

"Yes, I know," the duchess replied, a smile remaining on her lips.

Madeline's exhilaration faded suddenly. "I'm afraid Mr. Scott saw me backstage tonight. He still objects to me. He made that very clear."

Julia's brows lifted in surprise. "That isn't like him. He's never taken issue with anyone I've hired. I don't see why—" She broke off, staring at Madeline with a perplexed expression. "Don't worry, my dear. I'll meet with him tomorrow morning before rehearsal, and everything will be resolved."

"I hope so, Your Grace." Madeline paused. "I want to work at the Capital very badly."

"Then you shall," the duchess assured her. "Unless Mr. Scott can produce a very good reason to the contrary—and I expect that will be very unlikely."

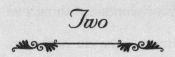

# Two

*Logan stood* at the back of the Capital Theatre's carpentry shop and regarded the double flats critically. The newly constructed stage pieces, made of canvas stretched over ribbed timber frames, would soon be sent to the scene painters.

"We've never made ones this large before," Logan commented to the pair of carpenters who had propped up the hinged flats for his inspection. "How will they be supported?"

"We thought it best to weight the braces in back," the main carpenter, Robbie Cleary, replied. "That should keep them steady during the performances."

Logan reached out with a broad hand to grasp a timber beam and test its sturdiness. "You'd better hook the back flat to a wooden rod and screw it to the floor. I don't want any chance of it falling on anyone. It's a damned heavy piece."

Robbie nodded in agreement and walked behind the flat, surveying it closely. The double flats had been constructed so that the front piece could be collapsed under its own weight to provide a quick scene change, revealing the second painted flat just behind it. It was a tricky bit of work, requiring the right combination of skill and timing to avoid errors.

Standing back from the set of hinged flats, Logan tugged absently at the front of his hair. "Let's see how the first one collapses," he said.

"All right, Mr. Scott," Robbie said doubtfully. "Though I should warn ye, I've yet to test the procedure."

"Now's as good a time as any."

Jeff, the shopboy, darted forward to assist the carpenters, lending his slight weight to help hold the double flats in place.

"Let the front down," Robbie instructed, and his assistants began to collapse the first scene.

Out of the corner of his eye, Logan saw someone enter the shop, a slender girl carrying a broom, a dustpan, and an armload of cleaning rags. The new girl, Logan realized with a pang of irritation. She seemed to be unaware of the demonstration taking place—and she was walking directly into the path of the collapsing flat. "Watch out, damn you!" Logan said sharply. She paused and looked at him with the inquiring eyes of a newborn fawn, while the timber frame toppled toward her.

Automatically Logan rushed forward and seized her, turning to shield her with his own body. The heavy flat landed on his injured shoulder, resulting in an explosion of pain that made him curse and stagger. For a moment he couldn't breathe. Somehow he managed to remain on his feet. He was dimly aware of Robbie and the others scurrying to lift the flat and drag it away, while the girl stepped back from him.

"Mr. Scott?" she asked in confusion. "Are you all right? I'm so terribly sorry."

Logan shook his head slightly, his face white, his

every bit of strength devoted to fighting back a tide of nausea. He would not disgrace himself by losing his breakfast in the middle of the carpentry shop. Always conscious of maintaining his authoritative image, he was never sick, never weak, and never indecisive in front of his employees.

"Oh, your shoulder," Madeline exclaimed, staring at his shirt, where a few spots of blood from the reopened wound had begun to appear. "What can I do?"

"Stay away from me," Logan muttered, finally winning his battle against the nausea. He took a deep, reviving breath. "Why in God's name are you here?"

"I was going to sweep up the wood scraps and shavings, and clean the carpenters' tools, and . . . is there something you would like me to do, sir?"

"Get out!" Logan snapped, a scowl pulling his face into harsh lines. "Before I throttle you."

"Yes, sir," she said in a subdued tone.

Any other girl in her position would probably have burst into tears. Grudgingly he gave her credit for keeping her composure. Everyone else at the Capital was terrified of his temper. Even Julia took care to give him a wide berth when he was in a foul mood.

Madeline glanced apologetically at Robbie. "I'm sorry, Mr. Cleary. I'll come back later to sweep the floor."

"That's all right, lass." The head carpenter waited until Madeline had left before turning to Logan. "Mr. Scott," he said chidingly, "surely there was no need for ye to speak to the lass that way. She was trying to help."

"She's a walking disaster."

"But Mr. Scott," Jeff, the shopboy, said, "Maddy only seems to have accidents when you're around. The rest of the time, she's just fine."

"I don't care." Logan held a hand to his shoulder, which burned like fire. His head throbbed and ached. "I want her out of here," he muttered, and left the shop with determined strides.

He went to Julia's office, intending to vent his annoyance. It was her fault for insisting on hiring the girl—therefore it would be her responsibility to dismiss her. He found Julia at her desk, her face wreathed in a frown of concentration as she revised the weekly schedule. She glanced up at him, and her face turned blank with surprise.

"Logan, what happened? You look as though you'd just been trampled beneath a team of six."

"Worse. I just had another encounter with your little protégée."

"Madeline?" Julia frowned in concern. "What happened?"

Grimly he told her about the scene in the carpentry shop. Instead of reacting with the concern and dismay he expected, Julia seemed to find the story vastly entertaining.

"Poor Logan," she said, laughing. "No wonder you're in an ill temper. Well, you can't blame Maddy."

"Can't I?" he asked sourly.

"It's only her first day. It will take some time for her to find her footing around here."

"Her first day," Logan said, "and her last. I want her gone, Julia. I mean it."

"I simply don't understand why you find Madeline Ridley so objectionable." Julia settled back in her chair with a speculative expression that infuriated Logan.

"She's a green girl who knows nothing about the theater."

"We were all green at one time," Julia replied, and gave him a glance of gentle mockery. "Everyone except you, of course. You must have sprung from the womb knowing everything about the stage—"

"She doesn't belong here," Logan interrupted. "Even you can't argue that point."

"Perhaps not," she conceded. "But Madeline is a sweet, intelligent young woman who has obviously landed in some sort of trouble. I want to help her."

"The only way to help her is to send her back where she came from."

"What if she's run away from a dangerous situation? Aren't you the least bit concerned? Even curious?"

"No."

Julia sighed in exasperation. "If Madeline doesn't work here, who knows what circumstances she'll find herself in? I'll pay her salary out of my own pocket, if you prefer."

"We're not running a charity, damn you!"

"I need an assistant," Julia said. "I have needed one for quite some time. Madeline is exactly what I require. Why does that pose such a problem for you?"

"Because she . . ." Logan closed his mouth abruptly. The problem was, the girl bothered him for reasons he didn't understand. Perhaps it was because she was so ridiculously open and unguarded . . . the antithesis of his own nature. She made him damned uncomfortable, reminding him of everything he didn't want to be, of all the things he had struggled to change in himself. However, he wasn't about to provide such information for Julia's entertainment. It had always irked her that he managed his life and his emotions with apparent ease.

"Logan," Julia said impatiently, failing to read his thoughts in the silence, "you must be able to offer *some* explanation."

"The fact that she's a clumsy fool should be enough."

Julia's mouth fell open. "Everyone has an occasional accident. It's not like you to be so petty!"

"I say she goes, and I'll hear no more about it."

"Then you be the one to dismiss her. I'm sure I would choke on the words."

"I'll have no such problem," Logan informed her. "Where is she?"

"I sent her to help Mrs. Lyttleton with the costumes," Julia snapped, turning away from him to riffle through a pile of papers on her desk.

Logan left Julia's office, determined to find the girl immediately. The costume shop was located in a building set a small distance from the others, as it constituted more of a fire hazard than any other part of the theater. There was a better chance of containing a fire there and preventing the rest of the Capital from burning.

Mrs. Lyttleton was a cheerful mountain of a woman topped with a pile of brown curls. Her massive hands moved with dexterity as she created the most exquisite costumes seen on any stage. She employed a half-dozen girls to help in the task of sewing and maintaining the huge collection of garments that filled rack after rack. The look of a production at the Capital Theatre was uniquely lavish, and the actors and audience alike were aware that no expense had been spared to create the effect.

"Mr. Scott," the seamstress said jovially, "what may I do for you? Is the shirt you wore last night still too short in the sleeves? I'll let them out again if necessary."

Logan didn't want to bother with small talk. "There's a new girl—Miss Ridley. I want to see her."

"Ah, she's a pretty slip of a thing, isn't she? I sent her out to the back with some baskets of costumes to be specially laundered. The silk on the gowns is too delicate to hang in the city air with all its soot, so the baskets will be taken to the country, and the washing and drying done there—"

"Thank you," Logan interrupted, having little interest in the intricacies of laundry. "Good day, Mrs. Lyttleton—"

"After she takes the baskets to the laundry cart," the seamstress said, "she's to go to your office with the costume sketches for *Othello.*"

"Thank you," Logan said through his teeth, experiencing a stab of annoyance—or perhaps alarm—at the notion of Madeline Ridley visiting his office. With the disasters that seemed to occur whenever she was in the vicinity, he would be fortunate if his office hadn't been reduced to a pile of rubble by the time she left.

However, when he reached the small room he considered his sacred territory, he found it empty—and considerably cleaner than it had been in years. Books and stacks of paper had been consolidated into neat piles, shelves and furniture had been dusted, and his chaotically cluttered desk had been straightened and wiped clean. Logan entered the office and looked around bemusedly. "How the hell am I going to find anything now?" he muttered. His attention was caught by a spot of color in the room, a half-opened red rose that had been placed in a glass of water on his desk.

Taken aback, Logan touched the velvety hothouse blossom.

"It's a peace offering," came Madeline's voice from behind him. He swiveled around to find her peeking around the door frame with a friendly smile. "Along with my promise not to cause you any further injuries."

Perplexed and silent, Logan stared at her. The curt dismissal he had been so eager to give her faded on his lips. He had thought himself far beyond any twinges of guilt by now, but the girl's sweet, hopeful face made him distinctly uncomfortable. Moreover, there was no way he could fire her without appearing to be an ogre in front of the entire company. He wondered if she were really as innocent as she appeared, or if she were a clever manipulator. Her large brown eyes gave no clue.

For the first time Logan realized that Madeline Ridley was pretty—no, beautiful—with delicate features, skin like porcelain, and a mouth that was both innocent and sensuous. Her figure was slender and trim, without the voluptuous sleekness that he preferred in a woman, but attractive nonetheless.

Logan sat in his chair and stared at her steadily. "Where did you get this?" he asked, gesturing to the rose.

"At the Covent Garden flower market. I went

there early this morning. It's the most remarkable place, with all the puppeteers and bird dealers, and such an amazing selection of fruits and vegetables—"

"It's not safe for you to go there alone, Miss Ridley. The thieves and Gypsies would make short work of a pigeon like you."

"I had no trouble at all, Mr. Scott." Her smile brightened. "It's very kind of you to be concerned about me."

"I'm not concerned," he said flatly, tapping his fingers on the desk. "It's just that I've witnessed how trouble seems to follow you."

"That's not true," she replied without rancor. "Until now, I daresay I've never caused any trouble for anyone. I've led a very quiet life."

"Then tell me why an apparently well-bred girl like you would seek a job at the Capital Theatre."

"To be near you," she said.

Logan shook his head at the shameless statement. Coming from a girl like her, it made no sense. Her innocence, her inexperience, couldn't be more obvious. Why did she want to have an affair with him?

"Does your family know where you are?" he asked.

"Yes," she said, a touch too quickly.

His lips twisted skeptically. "Who is your father? What is his occupation?"

"He's a . . . farmer," came her careful reply.

"Evidently a successful one." His dubious gaze swept over the soft wool fabric and the fine cut of her gown. "Why aren't you at home with your family, Miss Ridley?"

Her replies became increasingly hesitant, and he

sensed her sudden uneasiness. "I've had a falling-out with them."

"Of what kind?" he asked, not missing the blush of deception that crept over her cheeks.

"I'd rather not say—"

"Does it involve a man?" He saw from the flicker of surprise in her brown eyes that the guess was accurate. Leaning back in his chair, he surveyed her coolly. "We'll leave it at that, Miss Ridley. I don't need—or care—to know anything about your personal life. However, let me advise you once again that if you are somehow harboring hopes that you and I will ever—"

"I understand," she said matter-of-factly. "You don't want an affair with me." She retreated from his office, pausing at the door to add, "People change their minds, though."

"I don't," he said, scowling as she disappeared from sight. For God's sake, didn't she understand the meaning of the word "no"?

Madeline was busy all day, mending tears and snags in a multitude of costumes, cleaning the clutter from the actors' dressing rooms, sorting stacks of freshly printed handbills, and copying the duchess's scheduling notes for Mr. Scott and other members of the company.

The theater company was like a large family, with all the internal squabbling that could be expected of an extended group. Especially intriguing was the colorful assortment of contract players. It seemed to Madeline that actors were far more interesting and flamboyant than normal people, talking and joking with a frankness that shocked her. No matter what the subject of their conversa-

tion, it always seemed to include some mention of
Mr. Scott. Clearly they all admired, even wor-
shipped him, using him as the standard by which
they measured everyone else.

As Madeline swept the floor of the greenroom
and cleared away dirty teacups and plates, she
listened to a discussion between some of the Capital's most popular players, about what made people fall in love.

"It's not what you project," said Arlyss Barry, a
petite, curly-haired comic actress. "It's what you
*don't* show. Mr. Scott, for example. Watch him in
any role he plays, and you'll see that he always
holds something back. It's the mystery of a person
that makes you want him, or her."

"Are we talking about the stage or real life?"
asked Stephen Maitland, the blond gentleman who
had accidently stabbed Mr. Scott during the fencing match.

"There's a difference?" Charles Haversley, another young contract player, asked in pretend
confusion, and they all laughed.

"In this case, no," Arlyss Barry said. "People
always want what they can't have. The audience
falls in love with a leading man because he'll never
belong to any of them. In real life, it's the same.
There's not a man or woman alive who wouldn't
fall in love with someone who is out of their
reach."

Madeline stopped nearby with the broom and
dustpan in hand. "I'm not certain I agree," she said
thoughtfully. "I'm not very well-versed in such
matters, but . . . if someone were very kind to you,
and made you feel safe and loved . . . wouldn't
one find that attractive?"

"I don't know," Charles said with a rakish grin.

"Perhaps you should test your theory on me, Maddy, and we'll see if it works."

"I believe Maddy is already testing it on someone else," Arlyss said slyly, laughing as she saw Madeline blush. "Forgive me, dear . . . we all like to tease each other. You'll have to get used to it, I'm afraid."

Madeline returned her smile. "Of course, Miss Barry."

"On whom are you testing your theory?" Charles asked with great interest. "Don't say it's Mr. Scott?" He pretended to be indignant as he saw Maddy's blush deepen. "Why him and not me? Granted, he's rich, handsome, and famous . . . but what does he have besides that?"

Searching for a way to escape his teasing, Madeline began to employ the broom vigorously, sweeping her way out of the room and along the hall.

"Poor thing," she heard Stephen say in a low tone. "He'll never take notice of her . . . far too sweet for him, anyway . . ."

Troubled, Madeline stopped sweeping and leaned against the doorway of an empty rehearsal room. After listening to the actors talk—and they were far more worldly-wise than she—Madeline was beginning to realize that she had made a mistake. She had approached Mr. Scott the wrong way, boldly announcing her intentions, making herself entirely available, preserving not a shred of mystery to entice him. No wonder he showed so little interest in her. But it was too late to change things.

Sighing deeply, Madeline wished there were someone, some wise and experienced woman, who could give her some badly needed advice. The duchess . . . but she would never condone Madeline's plans. Suddenly an idea came to her, and her brow cleared. Perhaps there *was* someone she could ask.

The sky was filled with murky clouds as the hired hack delivered Madeline to the house on Somerset. Mrs. Florence sat by the fire in the parlor grate with a supper tray. "My dear, you've returned later than I expected. Did they keep you terribly busy at the theater? You must be hungry. I'll send for another tray."

Madeline nodded in thanks and sat by her, shivering as the warmth of the fire sank into her wool gown. At the elderly woman's bidding, Madeline related the events of the day, then stared into the fire. "Mrs. Florence, I would like to ask your advice about something, but I think you'll be shocked."

"It is impossible to shock me, child. I've lived too long to be surprised at anything." The elderly woman leaned forward, her eyes bright in her softly lined face. "Well, you've piqued my curiosity—don't keep me waiting."

"I thought that with your experience . . . that is, your past knowledge . . . I wanted to ask you how . . ." Madeline paused and forced the words out. "I want to seduce a man."

The elderly woman sat back, her eyes unblinking.

"I *have* shocked you," Madeline said.

"'Surprised' is a better word, my dear. I wouldn't have expected such a question from you. Are you certain you know what you're doing? I shouldn't want you to make a mistake that you'll be ashamed of later on."

"Mrs. Florence," Madeline replied wryly, "in my

entire life, I've never managed to do anything that I've truly been ashamed of."

The elderly woman's eyes suddenly sparkled with amusement. "And you wish to remedy that?"

"Yes! Otherwise I'll have no character or spirit at all."

"I disagree, my dear. You appear to have a good deal more character and spirit than the average person. However, if you're determined to carry out your intentions, I'll be happy to advise you. I know a great deal about men—or at least, I used to. I daresay they can't have changed very much in the last decade or two. Tell me, is there a particular man you want to seduce?"

"It's Mr. Scott, actually."

"Ah." Mrs. Florence stared at her for a long moment, her gaze penetrating and at the same time distant. It was as if some past memory had been recalled to her, one that she savored. "I don't blame you in the least," she finally said. "I would seduce him if I were a pretty young girl like you."

"Would you?" Madeline asked, surprised by the statement.

"Oh, indeed. It seems to me that Mr. Scott is one of the few men in England worth seducing. I wouldn't bother with the effeminate, self-absorbed creatures that pass for great lovers nowadays. I've never had the opportunity to meet Mr. Scott, unfortunately, but I have seen him on stage. The first time was five years ago. He played Iago in *Othello* . . . the most adept performance I've ever seen. Pure, seductive, silken evil. As an actor, he's worth any amount of admiration. As a man, he strikes me as rather dangerous."

"Dangerous?" Madeline repeated uneasily.

"Yes, to a woman's heart. Safe men are for

marrying. Dangerous men are for pleasure. Just make certain you require nothing more of them than that."

Madeline leaned forward. "Mrs. Florence, you won't tell anyone about what I'm planning?"

"Of course not. It's a highly private matter. Besides, there is no guarantee that you will succeed. From what I know of Logan Scott—and that is mostly hearsay from Julia—he doesn't prefer your kind. There are men with certain appetites that can be fulfilled only by very skilled women, and you . . ." She paused and viewed Madeline critically. "Something tells me that your repertoire is extremely limited."

"I don't even have a repertoire," Madeline said gloomily.

Mrs. Florence leaned her chin on a wrinkled hand. "That makes things a little more difficult. On the other hand, you have youth and beauty, and those shouldn't be underestimated."

"The problem is, I've already made a mistake. I should have been mysterious and aloof . . . and instead I've made my intentions all too clear."

"He knows that you desire him?" Mrs. Florence asked, seeming amused.

"Yes, and he's made it clear that he wants nothing to do with me."

"Well, your straightforward approach wasn't necessarily a mistake," Mrs. Florence commented. "One can assume that a man like Scott is entirely familiar with women who make subtle and sophisticated overtures. Perhaps you were right to throw him off balance."

"Not only did I throw him off balance," Madeline said sheepishly, "I ensured that he got stabbed in the process."

"You did what?" Mrs. Florence asked, startled, and Madeline told her about the fencing accident. The elderly woman regarded her with a mixture of laughter and disbelief. "I'll say this, child . . . you've presented me with a challenge. Let me think for a moment."

Madeline waited while the old woman contemplated the problem.

"It's a pity you have no acting skills," Mrs. Florence said. "The place to approach a man like Scott is on the stage, where he's most at ease. I would suspect that he never lets down his guard except while he's acting. It is only during those moments of vulnerability that you would be able to slip past his defenses."

"Perhaps I could offer to prompt some of the actors and actresses when they are learning their lines," Madeline said hesitantly.

"Yes, that's an excellent idea."

"But Mrs. Florence . . . what if I do manage to catch Mr. Scott in one of those 'vulnerable moments'? What should I say to him?"

"Let your instincts guide you. Just bear in mind that you mustn't act lovestruck. Simply make it clear that you're available and willing . . . that you're offering pleasure with no responsibility. No man in the world could resist."

Madeline nodded obediently.

"There's one more thing," Mrs. Florence added, regarding her speculatively. "You'll need to dress for the part. Although you appear to have an attractive figure, one can hardly tell in those missish gowns."

A resigned smile crossed Madeline's face. "I'm afraid that can't be helped, ma'am. I can't afford a new gown."

"I'll give it some consideration," the elderly woman assured her. "I'll think of something."

Madeline smiled, admiring Mrs. Florence's crafty energy and enthusiasm. "I'm glad I asked for your advice, ma'am."

"So am I, Maddy. This is the most excitement I've had in years, taking part in your scheme. With my help, you'll lead Mr. Scott to your bed like a lamb to the slaughter."

"I hope so," Madeline replied. "However . . . I don't imagine he'll be anything like a lamb."

"That's for you to discover, my dear. In my experience, men are often different in bed than they are out of it. Actors are the most unpredictable lovers of all. One never knows when they're playing a part." She turned a placid countenance toward the fire, plotting silently, while the maid brought Madeline a supper tray.

After the servant had left, Madeline spoke again. "Mrs. Florence, is there any way of knowing what to expect?"

The elderly woman looked at her questioningly, having lost the thread of the conversation.

"About how a man might be as a lover," Madeline clarified.

"I think you'll be able to tell a great deal from the way he kisses you." Suddenly Mrs. Florence seemed amused, and she toyed with a loose strand of her silvery-peach hair. "In fact, that's a very good idea. Why don't you surprise Mr. Scott with a kiss? That's a bold, stylish ploy. It will certainly intrigue him."

"But how? . . . when?"

"I'll leave that to your imagination, Maddy. You'll find an appropriate moment."

\* \* \*

*Surprise him with a kiss.* Mrs. Florence's mischievous suggestion hovered in Madeline's thoughts
during the next day. There would *never* be an
appropriate time to do such a thing. If only she had
her older sister Justine's great beauty or Althea's
cleverness. But she was terribly ordinary, and Mr.
Scott was . . . unreachable.

She saw the effect he had on others, the crowds
of aristocrats who gathered around his dressing
room door after a performance, the actors and
actresses who sought his advice. Everyone wanted
something from him. *Even me*, Madeline thought in
sheepish discomfort. She wanted the most personal service of all from him, and with any luck he
would never know why.

In an effort to learn more about him, Madeline
approached Arlyss Barry while she was having tea
alone in the greenroom. Arlyss was a fountain of
information. She knew intimate details about
everyone in the company and loved to gossip about
them all.

"You'd like to know more about Mr. Scott?"
Arlyss asked, popping a sugared biscuit into her
mouth. Although Mrs. Lyttleton grumbled about
Arlyss's overly voluptuous figure, it seemed that
Arlyss couldn't control her own sweet tooth. "So
would we all, Maddy. Mr. Scott is the most fascinating man I've ever met, and the most difficult to
know. He's fanatical about his privacy. He never
invites anyone to his home. To my knowledge no
one in the company has ever visited him there,
except for the duchess."

Madeline frowned. "Were Mr. Scott and the
duchess ever—"

Arlyss shook her head, brown curls dancing.
"They've always been too much alike, I suppose,

both of them so in love with the theater that there was never room for anyone else. Then Julia met the duke, and . . . but that's another story. To answer your question: Julia and Mr. Scott were never romantically involved. She told me that Mr. Scott believes falling in love is the worst possible thing that could ever happen to him."

"But why?"

Arlyss shrugged cheerfully. "That's the mystery of Mr. Scott. He's a bundle of secrets, that one." She lowered her voice and leaned closer over her cup of tea. "I'll tell you something that few people know: Mr. Scott was the son of a tenant farmer. He never even went to school. Can you imagine it?"

"No, I . . . " Madeline was genuinely amazed. "He seems so cultured, so noble—"

"He seems that way," Arlyss agreed. "But he's come from beginnings that would make yours and mine look like royalty. In fact, Julia once hinted to me that Mr. Scott was terribly mistreated—beaten and half-starved by his father. It's why his family never visits the theater or is allowed to watch a performance. He *pays* them to stay away from him."

Madeline pondered the information, while Arlyss delved into the tin of biscuits. She tried to imagine Mr. Scott as a boy, living with poverty and abuse, and it was impossible to reconcile that picture with the powerful, self-assured owner of the Capital Theatre. He had assumed such godlike dimensions in the public's eyes—and her own—that she found it hard to believe he had escaped a past as humble as the one Arlyss had described.

So that was where Mr. Scott's talent came from, she thought with a stirring of compassion. A man couldn't leave his old life and invent a new one for himself without having an extraordinary amount of imagination—and determination.

"Excuse me, Miss Barry," she murmured. "I have work to do."

Arlyss winked at her and picked up a play folio, silently mouthing her lines as she memorized them.

Madeline went down the hall to Mr. Scott's office, her heart quickening as she approached the threshold. The door was open, revealing his back as he sat at his massive mahogany desk. His white linen shirt, once crisp and freshly pressed, was now creased as it clung to his broad shoulders. He had discarded the pale gray waistcoat he had worn all day, as well as the black silk cravat.

It was odd to see Mr. Scott still and quiet when he had been so relentlessly active all day. He seemed to have the energy of ten men, striding about his theater like the captain of a ship. One moment he had been directing the actors during rehearsal, alternately cajoling and demanding until their performances satisfied him . . . and the next he was in the scene painter's shop, moving heavy set pieces and flats, explaining how he wanted them painted until it seemed that he might pick up a brush and do the job himself.

Every member of the company knew that his or her work would sooner or later come under his scrutiny, and they labored to please him. When they were given a word or two of praise, they glowed with satisfaction. Madeline longed to win similar attention from him, so that he would take notice of her as someone other than a troublesome employee.

As Madeline paused in the doorway, Mr. Scott stiffened, the heavy muscles moving across his

back. Although she hadn't made a sound, he
turned in his chair and glanced over his shoulder,
his blue eyes questioning.

"Mr. Scott," she said, "I thought I might be able
to help with your correspondence. I noticed how
much of it there was, and . . . I could write letters
as you dictate." She saw the lack of response on his
face, and she added hopefully, "I have very good
penmanship."

It took him an unaccountably long time to reply.
He contemplated the stack of unanswered mail on
his desk before his gaze returned to her. Slowly he
reached over to a nearby chair and removed a few
books that had been piled on the seat. "Why not?"
he muttered.

Madeline seated herself and took up a pen and
paper, using the corner of his desk to write on. Mr.
Scott pulled a page of notes from the top of the pile
and read silently, tugging at a forelock of his hair.
Madeline had never seen such beautiful hair on a
man. There must be many women who were
tempted to smooth the rumpled locks.

Guiltily enjoying the novelty of being alone with
him, Madeline continued her discreet inspection.
His long legs were taut beneath his gray trousers,
the muscles long and well-honed. Many of the
roles he played required great athletic skill. The
rigors of fencing and fighting scenes, played night
after night, kept him in superb physical condition.

"Direct this letter to Monsieur Jacques Daumier,
*rue des Beaux Arts*, Paris." To Madeline's surprise,
Scott began to dictate in French. She realized that
he was testing her, to see if she really did know
French. Rising to the challenge, she began to write
diligently.

As Mr. Scott dictated, Madeline grasped that he

was helping a manager of the Comedie Française to engage a London theater for a brief time, to showcase his performers for English audiences.

"Pardon, sir," she interrupted in the middle of a sentence, "but I believe that verb should be conjugated in the past subjunctive—"

"Leave it."

Madeline frowned. "Mr. Scott, I'm certain you understand how particular the French are about their language—"

"I'm certain I know a hell of a lot more about the French than you do," he shot back. "And I'm going to conjugate the damned verb any way I please."

"Very well." Madeline bent her head over the page. "But you're still wrong," she muttered.

Suddenly Logan's annoyance was washed away in a rush of amusement. Sternly he forced back the laughter that rose in his throat. No one ever dared to speak to him so freely. The aristocrats he associated with were usually patronizing, except on the occasions when they wanted something from him. The people he employed were always telling him what they thought he wanted to hear. The only one who spoke to him as an equal was Julia, but she had a title and a noble ancestry to lend her confidence. This girl . . . Madeline . . . had nothing. Her well-being depended entirely on his goodwill, and still she dared to contradict him.

"Then change it," he said, and continued to dictate before she had time to react. He was certain her hand was aching as the letter was concluded, but she didn't ask him to adjust his speed.

They proceeded to the next missive, addressed to the manager of an insurance company. Logan's letter described a proposed fund for the support of retired performers as well as the benefit of actors'

widows and children. The fund was to be padded
with annual contributions from actors' salaries and
occasional benefit performances.

"That is very kind of you," Madeline commented at the close of the letter. "I suspect most
theater managers can't be bothered with their
former employees' welfare."

"I'm not kind," he replied. "It's a way of attract-
ing the best people to the Capital and keeping
them here. The higher the quality of my productions, the more money I make."

"Then your only motive is profit?"

"Precisely."

"I don't believe that, Mr. Scott. You *are* kind . . .
it's just that you don't want anyone to think of you
so."

He gave her a sardonic glance. "Why do you
think that, Miss Ridley?"

Madeline met his gaze without blinking. "You
didn't fire me even when you were perfectly justified in doing so. And now it seems that you have
made arrangements to take care of your employees
when they are too old to work. Those are the
actions of a kind man."

"Miss Ridley . . ." He shook his head as if
unable to comprehend the extent of her naivete. "I
never do anything out of kindness. My God, it's a
wonder you've made it this far unscathed. You
know nothing of what I've done in the past, or
what I'm capable of. For your own sake, don't trust
anyone—including me."

"What could I have to fear from you?"

His hands gathered into large fists that rested on
the desk. His eyes were the color of blue-violet
flame as he stared at her. A heavily charged silence

filled the office, while Madeline's heartbeat escalated to an alarming pace.

"Let's hope you don't find out," he said softly.

With each word he said, Logan Scott was dispelling her girlish fancies. He was a flesh and blood man, complete with flaws. If she did manage to lure him into bed with her, the experience might change her forever, emotionally as well as physically. The thought sent a ripple of unease through her.

Breaking their shared gaze, Madeline stared into her lap until she heard his quiet, almost contemptuous laugh.

"That's all for now," he said.

"Shall I return tomorrow?" she asked.

A long silence passed, while Logan scowled at his overloaded desk. Julia, damn her, knew exactly how badly he needed secretarial assistance. For months Logan had intended to hire someone for that purpose, but he hadn't yet found the time to interview appropriate candidates.

With Madeline's help, he could clear the work from his desk in half the time it would take to do it alone. Perhaps it wouldn't be a bad arrangement, having her work in his office an hour or two each day. Except . . . he realized with a jolt of surprise that sitting so close to her had made him . . . uncomfortable. Aroused. He frowned and shifted positions, staring at her with narrowed eyes. It was inappropriate, having such a reaction to her. She was too young and naive, and he wasn't the kind of man to go about violating virginal girls, no matter how tempting they might be.

And Madeline *was* tempting, despite his efforts to ignore her. She had freshness and warmth that were unique in his experience. His hands itched to close over the nape of her neck and stroke the silken hairs that had slipped from their pins. Perturbed, he gestured impatiently to the door.

"Yes, come back in the morning," he muttered.

Madeline smiled at him. "Good day, Mr. Scott."

Gradually the sound of her footsteps faded, while Logan sat staring at the empty doorway. The impatient, pulsing warmth in his loins faded very slowly. It had been too long since he'd had a woman, he thought. Months. He had been too busy to find a replacement for his last mistress, and no one had caught his interest . . . until now.

A wry, whimsical smile curved his lips. The idea of bedding an untried girl, or at least a very inexperienced one, had never appealed to him before. However, he couldn't help wondering about Madeline Ridley . . . how she would feel in his arms, what she would look like naked in his bed, how it would feel to lose himself inside all that impetuous energy. . . .

Perhaps he would seduce her. It was only a matter of time before someone took advantage of her in this bawdy environment . . . why shouldn't it be him? At least he would make certain she enjoyed it, and compensate her for it—

"Damn," he said aloud, alarmed at the direction his thoughts had taken, and he forced himself to concentrate on his work. Doggedly he read contracts, revised schedules, and made notes about musical selections and stage settings. While he worked, he heard the sounds of employees leaving the theater. Actors and musicians concluded their rehearsals, while carpenters and painters organized their shops in preparation for the morrow.

Logan took pleasure in the activity around him,

knowing that were it not for his efforts, the Capital wouldn't exist. It had been created from his own ambition, put together scrap by scrap, and painstakingly nurtured. Failure had been out of the question—he had never allowed himself to consider the possibility. Failure would have meant returning to the life he had been born to as the son of Paul and Mary Jennings.

Suddenly a familiar voice broke the silence. "Working at this late hour, Jimmy? You've made your fortune—why not enjoy it?"

# Three

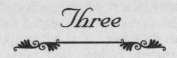

*Turning in* his chair, Logan regarded the familiar face of Andrew, Lord Drake. Andrew was a tall, well-built young man with wicked blue eyes and dark hair worn in a long, windswept style. He was handsome, although signs of his self-indulgent lifestyle had recently begun to appear . . . a fleshiness of the cheeks and chin, the ruddy complexion of a perpetual drunkard, and the dark-circled eyes of a man who was frequently awake for most of the night.

Logan and Andrew had been close companions for most of their childhood. Andrew was the only son and heir of the Earl of Rochester, and Logan had been the son of a local tenant farmer. Together the boys had roamed the estate, fishing, swimming, and hunting small game. For Logan it had been like having a younger brother. Although Andrew was the heir to a great fortune, Logan had always felt sorry for him. From what Logan had been able to observe, the earl hadn't been a much better father than Paul Jennings. Rochester was cold and rigid, far more concerned with rules and discipline than with his son's welfare.

Remaining at his desk, Logan smiled slightly. "I never expected to see you again so soon, Andrew. Not since I told you to stop making advances to my actresses."

Andrew grinned. "There isn't a great deal of difference between a theater and a bordello, you know. Actresses are just like prostitutes, only more expensive." He cast a deprecating glance around the small room, his gaze lingering on the overloaded desk. "I wonder that you haven't gone mad by now, spending so much time in that dusty corner."

"I enjoy working." Logan leaned back and propped his feet on the edge of his desk, resting his hands on his flat midriff.

" 'Enjoy' and 'work' don't belong in the same sentence, Jimmy." Andrew watched his face and smiled as he saw the flicker of reaction in Logan's eyes. "You don't like it when I call you that, do you? I assure you, I don't intend it as an insult. I admire what you've done, turning yourself from humble Jimmy Jennings into the great Logan Scott. When we were boys, I always supposed that you would marry some local dairymaid or shopgirl, and become a farmer like your father. Or perhaps you would have come to London and worked as a clerk for some piddling merchant. Instead you're one of the richest self-made men in England, with beautiful women twitching their skirts to gain your attention, and dinner invitations from the Duke of Wellington. Sometimes I feel as if I'm the only one who remembers who you really are."

"You're not," Logan said. Even if he had been able to forget his own humble beginnings, there were many who never passed up a chance to remind him. No upstart, no matter how talented or wealthy, could ever break into their exclusive circles. Certainly he was fit to entertain them, but not to move among them as an equal. He would never

be allowed to marry their daughters and mix his
red blood with blue.

"Why are you here, Andrew?" he asked. "Have
you come to reminisce about the past, or is there
something you want?"

Seeming annoyed by Logan's bluntness, Andrew shrugged. "All right, if you insist on going to
the point . . . I'm in a pickle."

"You've been gambling."

"Of course I have. What else is there to do with
my bloody time?" Andrew exploded in frustration,
his face reddening. "For the last two weeks I've
spent nearly every night at the club, and I've been
pigeoned out of every shilling I have. Every time I
thought my luck would turn, it got worse. Now the
news is all over London. I'm denied credit at every
turn, and a pair of brutes from the club are
following me wherever I go. I can't seem to give
them the brush, and they're threatening to break
my legs unless I come up with the money I owe.
God help me, I actually think they'll do it."

"Have you gone to your father?"

Andrew made a sound of disgust. "Bugger the
old man, he won't give me a shilling above the
paltry sum he calls my allowance. He could repay
my debts a hundred times over!"

"I believe that's what he's afraid of," Logan said
dryly. "How large is the debt this time? Four
thousand? Five?"

Andrew picked idly at the sleeve of his green
wool coat. "Ten," he mumbled.

The amount was enough to stun Logan into
silence. Ten thousand pounds was a fortune,
enough to keep dozens of families comfortably for
a year, enough to mount several spectacular productions at the Capital. He knew why the Earl of

Rochester wouldn't pay off his son's debt, no matter how great the threat to his safety. If Andrew didn't change his habits, he would run through the family fortune immediately after assuming the title.

"I need the money," Andrew said. For the first time there was a thread of desperation in his tone. "Everyone knows what a wealthy bastard you are. You can afford to loan me ten thousand. You know you'll get it back someday with interest."

"Will I?" Logan asked sardonically, rummaging through his desk. He began to write a bank draft. "This will be the last time, Andrew. I'm not inclined to pour more down a bottomless well."

Andrew peered over his shoulder and made a grudging sound of thanks. "I knew you wouldn't refuse me. It must give you satisfaction to know how my father would react if he knew."

A rueful smile touched Logan's lips as he finished the draft. "It does, actually." He extended the bank draft toward Andrew, then withheld it as Andrew reached out eagerly. "I'm going to offer this with a piece of advice."

"As you well know, I never take advice."

"For ten thousand pounds, you'll damn well take mine. Pay your debts, Andrew, and find some less expensive occupation. You don't have the temperament to gamble successfully—you're too easily lost in the emotion of the moment."

"Then you must be the best gambler in the world," Andrew muttered. "You never have an emotion unless you can display it on stage for profit."

Logan laughed and leaned back in his chair again. "Tell me, how is your father?"

"The same as ever—demanding and impossible

to please. He's done everything short of committing murder to acquire some group of sketches by Rubens or Rembrandt—"

"The Harris collection," Logan said, his eyes brightening with interest. "Ten original Rembrandt sketches, including one for *The Polish Rider.*"

Andrew lifted his hands in a gesture of mock alarm. "Don't tell me *you* want that collection too? . . . I warn you to stay clear, or there will be blood spilled."

Logan responded with a deceptively lazy shrug. "Far be it from me to stand in the earl's way."

"Strange that you and my father both share the same passion for art," Andrew commented.

Logan gave him a mocking smile. "There are many people who appreciate art, Andrew. Even people in the lower classes."

"But how many farmers' sons can afford to collect it? My father insists that you bought that Van Dyck he wanted in order to spite him."

"Why would I do something like that?" Logan asked smoothly.

"I believe the earl's theory is that you're trying to impress him. He claims it comes from your having grown up in the shadow of the estate mansion. You want to prove to him how well you've done for yourself."

All at once Logan was fiercely annoyed, and he didn't bother to conceal it. The words struck a chord of truth that he longed to deny. He didn't know why he felt such a keen sense of rivalry with the Earl of Rochester. It had something to do with the way Rochester looked at him, at everyone, with superiority and disdain. That assessing gaze had always made Logan determined to prove that he was in no way inferior to the earl except by birth.

"The only people I want to impress are the ones who pay to sit in my theater. Your father's opinion has never meant a damn to me. Tell him I said that."

"Egad, what a black mood you're in! Let's change the subject to something more appealing. Are you still keeping that lovely dark-haired wench at your London house?"

Logan shook his head. "I asked her to leave."

"How could you tire of such an exquisite creature? Where is she now? I'm not too proud to accept your leavings."

"I wouldn't do her the disservice of sending you to her doorstep."

Andrew laughed. "Fine, then. There are many other pretty wenches to be had." He sauntered to the doorway and pocketed the bank draft with a grin. "My sincere thanks, Jimmy. I knew you wouldn't turn your back on me."

"Stay out of trouble," Logan said meaningfully.

Andrew gave him a look of pure innocence. "I'll try."

With a rueful grin, Logan watched his childhood friend leave. In spite of Andrew's faults—and they were considerable—there was a streak of goodness in him. Andrew had never deliberately tried to harm anyone or anything in his life. Much of his rebelliousness came from a desire to gain his father's attention.

Logan's thoughts turned to the Earl of Rochester, and his smile turned grim. It had been a pleasure to purchase the Van Dyck from under Rochester's nose last year. The old man had always prided himself on his knowledge of art, and it seemed to annoy him considerably that the son of one of his tenants was a respected patron of the Society of Artists.

For the past several years Logan had acquired knowledge diligently, asking questions of artists and collectors, frequently traveling the Continent with *virtuosi* until he had developed his own sense of taste. The art gallery in his country mansion had become recognized as an important collection. Not only had he befriended most of the leading artists in London, but he was a patron of lesser-known painters who showed promise.

"I suppose you think that owning the Van Dyck makes you a cultured man," Rochester had said the previous year, after Logan had outbid him at the auction.

"No, my lord," Logan had replied, smiling at the earl's frosty annoyance. "Just a fortunate one."

Rochester had struggled to find a scathing reply. "You've done quite well for someone who makes a spectacle of himself to entertain the masses."

"It's called 'acting,'" Logan had said gently, his smile remaining. Nothing had been able to diminish his triumph at acquiring the painting Rochester had wanted so badly.

The old man had snorted. "Actors, singers, circus performers . . . they're all the same to me."

"Just why does my profession gall you so?" Logan had asked. "Would you prefer that I'd stayed on your land and become a farmer like my father?"

"Farming is a far more honorable occupation than performing on stage like a trained monkey."

"But not nearly as profitable," Logan had replied, going to collect his painting.

There had been few satisfactions in his life to compare with the knowledge that he had finally become a thorn in Rochester's side. It had been a long uphill climb, using his theater earnings to make some risky investments, some of which had paid off handsomely. Logan had educated himself about financial matters just as he had about art, though it had been considerably less interesting. The pursuit of money was unquestionably vulgar, bourgeois, but there was no other choice. The kind of life he wanted required a great deal of money, and he had steeled himself to ignore the disdain of aristocrats who had inherited their fortunes rather than earned them. Let Rochester sneer and call him a *parvenu* . . . the fact was, Logan owned the Van Dyck and any other damn painting he wanted.

Bringing his thoughts to the present, Logan rubbed the back of his neck and wandered out of the office. He headed toward the painter's shop, intending to inspect the latest work on a set of flats. The sound of voices drifted into the hallway, making him pause. One of them was unmistakably Andrew's, while the other . . . the feminine tone sent a ripple of sensation down his spine.

Logan felt his fingers curling until his fists were balled at his sides. He should have known that Andrew would take notice of Madeline Ridley if she were anywhere in the vicinity. *It doesn't matter,* he tried to tell himself, but suddenly he felt close to exploding. Following the sound of their voices to the library, he entered without knocking.

Andrew was leaning against a bookcase, talking affably while Madeline sorted through stacks of volumes on the library table. She looked very small in comparison to Andrew's height. Wisps of her golden-brown hair had come loose from their pins, falling against her face and throat. Standing before the worn books and dusty shelves, she seemed like a ray of light in the windowless room.

"Mr. Scott," Madeline said with a smile, "I decided to begin an inventory of the library collection."

Logan ignored her and focused a level gaze on Andrew. "I thought you were leaving."

"I was . . . but then I happened upon this charming creature." Andrew paused before adding, "She's not an actress, by the way." It was a pointed reminder that Logan's edict had been to stay away from the Capital Theatre's *actresses*—not any of the other employees.

The desire to wrap his hands around Andrew's fleshy throat was very strong. "Let me make it clear. Don't go near anyone who works for me in *any* capacity. Do you understand?"

"Oh, I understand very well." Andrew grinned at Logan. "Excuse me, I believe my presence is *de trop*." As he made his exit, he murmured to Logan, "She's not in your usual style, is she?"

Logan didn't reply, only kept his gaze on Madeline. When Andrew had gone and all sound had faded, he spoke in a soft growl. "Go home, Miss Ridley."

Madeline was puzzled and defensive. It seemed that once again she had unwittingly displeased him. "Mr. Scott, I didn't invite Lord Drake's attentions. He happened to see me as he passed the library, and he was very courteous. His only intention was to assist me."

A bright, cold flare appeared in Scott's blue eyes. "He was trying to assist you out of your clothes and into his bed. If you're too simpleminded to realize that, let me explain further. Lord Drake devours pretty young girls like you on a regular basis. You'll get nothing from him except a session of slap and tickle, and most likely a belly swollen with his bastard. If that's your desire, pursue it by all means—but you won't do so at my theater."

Madeline flushed. "Why isn't it possible that he was merely being polite?"

"Because a girl like you doesn't inspire *politeness* in a man." He put a stinging emphasis on the word.

Madeline stiffened and walked away from the library table, brushing by him as she headed to the door. "If you're saying that I've behaved in an improper manner—" She stopped with a gasp as he reached for her, his large hands seeming to burn through her sleeves. Roughly he pulled her to face him.

"I'm saying that when a man looks at you, he can't help thinking . . ."

He fell silent, staring at her for a long moment. Madeline swallowed, and his gaze flickered to the tiny movement. She wondered if he desired her, and what she should do to encourage him. Her heart skipped several beats as she realized that he was staring at her as if he intended to devour her just as he had accused Lord Drake of doing.

Her fingers trembled with the urge to touch his face, to explore the scratchy surface where his beard had begun to grow . . . the bold shape of his nose, the arches of his brows . . . the hard, wide mouth. She wanted to coax his lips to soften and press against hers . . . she wanted to lose herself in his arms.

Scott let go of her with a suddenness that nearly caused her to fall backward. His face turned blank. "Forgive me," he said in a monotone. "My behavior was uncalled for."

Madeline's knees were weak. There was a throbbing sensation in the pit of her stomach. She inched toward the table and gripped the side to keep herself steady. "I . . ." Her lips were strangely dry, and she moistened them before trying again. "I won't speak to Lord Drake again, Mr. Scott."

"Do what you like," he said flatly. "I have no right to object to your choice of companions."

Bewildered, Madeline stared at his profile. One moment he had been in a fury, and the next he was completely indifferent. She must have done something wrong, missed some opportunity that a woman of more experience would have taken advantage of. As a seductress, she was an utter failure.

She waited for him to leave the room, but he was silent and unmoving. It appeared that every muscle of his body was tightly bunched. It seemed as if he were fighting some tremendous inner battle.

"Mr. Scott?" she asked softly. "If you don't mind . . . would you finish what you were going to say?"

His head turned. His searing blue eyes stared into hers.

"You said that when a man looks at me," Madeline prompted, "he can't help thinking . . ."

The tension grew until Mr. Scott shook his head with a muffled laugh. "My God," he muttered, striding from the room. "I'd like to know what I've done to deserve this."

For the next two weeks Logan discovered himself to be the object of the strangest persecution he had ever experienced. Every time he turned a corner, Madeline was there, unrelentingly helpful, nearly driving him mad with her attentions. When he entered his office in the morning, she had already been there, leaving a napkin filled with iced buns or a steaming pot of tea on his desk. She ran to fetch things before he was even aware that he needed them . . . she studied his habits—how much sugar he liked in his tea, how much starch he preferred in his shirts.

Madeline's eager devotion both annoyed and embarrassed Logan, but at the same time . . . he couldn't remember when, or if, anyone had ever been so quick to meet his needs. She made certain that his costumes were always clean, mended, and pressed; brought reference books from the theater library when he needed them; and kept his office and his dressing room organized.

It was constantly on the tip of Logan's tongue to tell her to leave him alone, yet he couldn't seem to get the words out. It was convenient to have her close at hand . . . and oddly pleasant to watch her small, expressive face as she took dictation or sorted stacks of notices freshly arrived from the printer's shop. On the odd days when she was too busy to come straight to his office, he found himself watching the clock for her arrival.

"You took your time," he said when she came to help with his correspondence one morning. "I've been waiting for you."

"I'm sorry, sir," she said breathlessly, "but Mrs. Lyttleton needed my assistance with some costume fittings—"

"You spend too much time at the costume shop. If Mrs. Lyttleton is overburdened, tell her to hire another seamstress. I have mail that needs to be answered."

"Yes, sir," she said obediently, a small smile touching her lips.

Realizing that he had sounded jealous and possessive, Logan scowled. "My correspondence is a

damned sight more important than Mrs. Lyttleton's fripperies," he said, feeling the need to justify
himself. Madeline smiled and sat beside him in her
accustomed place.

Logan kept her working in his office a good deal
of the time, rationalizing that it was the safest place
for an accident-prone girl like Madeline to be. She
had a fearlessness that provoked him mightily, as
he found her engaged in activities that ranged from
hammering nails in the carpenter's shop to crawl-
ing across the fly-floor built high above the ground.
This last instance was too much for Logan, as he
walked onto the stage one day and discovered a
small group of stagehands watching Madeline
work far above them. She held a rope in one hand
and was busily threading it through a pulley that
was nailed to the grid ten feet below the roof of the
theater. "Good work, lass!" one of the men called,
while another laughed admiringly. "Agile as a
monkey, that girl."

Logan's breath seemed to leave his body. One
misstep, and Madeline would plummet to the
boards far below. He clenched his jaw to keep from
shouting, which might startle her and result in a
fatal accident. Breaking out in a heavy sweat,
Logan swore silently and strode to a spiral staircase
built behind the proscenium. He ascended rapidly,
taking the narrow steps three at a time, until he
had reached the catwalk, a two-foot-wide bridge
suspended just below the fly-floor and slung on
iron stirrups from the iron grid.

"I've finished," Madeline called, swaying
slightly as she looked over the edge of the fly-floor.
"My goodness, it's a long way down!" She started

as she saw Logan beneath her. "Mr. Scott," she said in surprise, "what are you doing up here?"

"What are *you* doing," he countered grimly, "aside from letting everyone have a glimpse up your skirts? No wonder you're so damned popular around here."

For the first time she looked at him with anger, her mouth tightening. "That's unfair, Mr. Scott. I'm only doing my job, which is to help wherever I'm needed—"

"Not at the risk of your life," he snapped. "Although at the moment I'm tempted to break your pretty neck myself and save you the trouble. Now give me your hand."

"I can climb down myself—"

"*Now,*" he said between his teeth. She complied reluctantly, and his hand closed around her wrist in a bruising vise, hauling her off the fly-floor and into his arms. The catwalk vibrated from the force of the motion.

Madeline yelped at the indignity of being slung over his shoulder like a sack of flour. "Put me down," she scolded as Logan made his way down the spiral staircase. "I don't need your help!" Ignoring her protests, he continued to carry her until they had reached the stage, and he deposited her roughly on her feet.

Glaring at the sheepish stagehands standing nearby, Logan spoke with ominous softness. "I'd like someone to explain why Miss Ridley was performing a job that I pay my stagehands to do."

"Miss Ridley volunteered," one of them said abashedly. "She pointed out that as she is so small and spry, she could get it done in half the time—"

"From now on," Logan interrupted, "if anyone asks Miss Ridley to set one finger on a rope,

scaffold, or set piece, I'll dismiss him on the spot."
His forbidding gaze moved to Madeline, who was
flushed and furious, one small hand rubbing her
sore wrist where he had gripped her too hard. "I
won't apologize for that," he said curtly. "I was
tempted to do something far worse, believe me."

Mr. Scott's unaccountable anger seemed to last
long into the day, continuing through the rehearsal
of the Capital's newest production, *Haunted*. Madeline fumed silently as she prompted the actors
during their line readings. She avoided looking at
Mr. Scott, thinking angrily that in spite of all she
had done for him, he snapped at her more frequently than he did anyone else. It was obvious to
the entire company. In fact, the stagehands, crew
members, and actors all went out of their way to
show their friendly sympathy. They murmured
words of encouragement as she passed by, and
made great shows of thanking her for helping with
the rehearsal.

"Maddy knows my lines better than I do,"
Arlyss remarked to everyone in general, standing
in the middle of the stage. "She's the best prompter
I've ever had."

"She is," Stephen Maitland agreed loudly. "And
it's a wonder that Maddy has time to study the
play, considering the way she's always running
errands for everyone."

Julia smiled indulgently and patted Madeline's
shoulder as they sat together in the first row of
theater seats. "Maddy has enough energy for ten
people."

Madeline blushed uncomfortably.

"Pardon me," came Logan Scott's cutting voice
from the stage, "but I was under the impression

that we were conducting a rehearsal." He sat in an armchair in front of a set of flats, rolling a whiskey bottle between his large hands. "Shall we get on with it?" he asked acidly.

"As soon as I find out what my line is," Arlyss replied sweetly.

Logan glowered at Madeline. "Give her the bloody line, Miss Ridley."

The displeasure of the company wasn't lost on Logan. Sardonically he reflected that everyone was protective of the girl and regarded him as a bully. To hell with them all. He had built this place, and he would treat his employees any way he saw fit. Grimly he plowed through the afternoon's work, ending the rehearsal nearly an hour earlier than usual.

Julia approached him in his office afterward, her brow knitted with consternation. "I heard about what happened between you and Maddy this morning," she remarked. "Don't you think you're being rather hard on her?"

"You're right," he said sarcastically. "The next time she volunteers to put herself in danger, I won't interfere."

"It's not that," Julia said. "For heaven's sake, Logan, I know how protective you are of your employees. I understand why you were cross with her earlier in the day. What I *don't* understand is your constant harshness with her. She's always at your beck and call—in fact, she's more your assistant than mine. The Capital is running far more smoothly because of her. You should be delighted with Madeline, and yet you act like a surly child whenever she's near."

Logan glared at her, infuriated. "That's enough, Julia."

"I'm sorry," she said, immediately softening her tone. "It's just that you haven't been yourself lately. I'm concerned about you."

"There would be no need for concern if you hadn't hired the girl in the first place."

Julia looked at him in dawning wonder. "I'm beginning to think you don't dislike her at all. I wonder if the problem isn't quite the opposite. Nearly every man at the Capital imagines himself in love with her. Is it possible that you're afraid of falling for her yourself?"

Logan concealed a sudden flare of outrage behind a mocking glance. "Of all the cracked notions you've ever had—"

"I'm right," Julia said, staring at him keenly. "You're fighting an attraction to her. Why not admit it?"

"I don't have time to discuss your addled theories," Logan muttered. "If you wouldn't mind leaving, I have work to do."

Julia didn't move. "I'm aware of your belief that you can turn your emotions on and off at will. You're always the master of your heart, and never the other way around. But emotions are terribly inconvenient, Logan . . . they don't always behave as one would wish."

"Go to hell," Logan said, and strode from the office.

After the rehearsal had concluded and everyone had left the stage, Madeline swept the floor vigorously, stirring up a cloud of dust that billowed around her knees. "Arrogant . . . ungrateful . . . tyrant . . ." she muttered, venting her anger with each stroke of the broom. As she worked her way to stage right, she stopped near a loosely wrapped canvas package filled with foils used earlier in the day.

Reaching down, Madeline extracted one of the swords and grasped the handle. It was light and well balanced, whistling as she swished it through the air. Enjoying herself, she tried to imitate some of the movements she had seen that morning, lunging and thrusting with the foil in her hand. "Take that . . . and *that* . . ." she said, stabbing at an imaginary Mr. Scott.

"You look as though you're swatting flies," came a sardonic voice from nearby.

Startled, Madeline saw Mr. Scott emerging from backstage, and she wanted to sink through the floor. Why did he have to be the one to witness her making a fool of herself? She expected him to make some remark that would cause her eternal humiliation . . . but his blue eyes gleamed with amusement.

"Whom are you attempting to skewer?" he asked, smiling in a way that revealed he was well aware of her invisible opponent's identity. When she didn't reply, he surprised her by taking her wrist in a gentle grip. His hand was very warm on her skin. "Here, this is how to handle the thing properly. Loosen your grip." He adjusted her hand, his fingers pressing over hers. Madeline tried to relax, but it wasn't easy. He was standing so close, and her pulse was racing madly. "Imitate the way I'm standing," he continued, "and keep your knees slightly flexed."

Madeline risked a glance at him. His hair was rumpled, as if he had been tugging it distractedly, and she longed to smooth the thick locks. "You're always directing, aren't you?"

"You're not the first woman to accuse me of

that," he said wryly, and nudged the sword to the
proper angle. "Now lunge forward with your right
foot, bend your knee and extend the sword . . .
yes, exactly like that. A stageworthy move if I've
ever seen one."

He was so close that Madeline could see the fine
texture of his skin, the dark stubble that roughened
his jaw, the gleam of auburn in his long lashes.
With his face relaxed and his lips curved in a smile,
he seemed a little younger than usual, a little more
approachable.

"I understand why you were so harsh with me
before, Mr. Scott," she said.

"Oh?" His brow arched sardonically.

"You were worried about my safety. That's why
you lost your temper. I forgive you." Before he
could react, she pressed her mouth to his chin, her
lips tingling from the scrape of close-shaven bristle.

His entire body stiffened. Drawing back, Madeline waited apprehensively for his reaction. His
face was a blank mask.

Awkwardly Madeline bent to set the sword on
the floor and straightened to look at him. "Was
that . . . stageworthy?" she asked.

Scott wore a strange expression. It took a long
time for him to reply. "Not quite," he finally said.

"Why not?"

"Your back is to the audience. If we were in a
play . . . you would have to turn this way." He
began to reach for her, paused, then finally caught
her arms in his hands. Lightly his fingers skimmed
her shoulder and slid to her throat and jaw.

"You would show your emotions through your
posture and the angle of your head . . ." Carefully
he adjusted her chin a notch downward. His voice
turned hoarse. "If you were ambivalent about the

kiss, you would hold your head like this. And you might put your hands on my shoulders as if you were thinking of pushing me away."

Madeline obeyed, her hands trembling a little as she pressed her palms against the hard surface of his upper body. He was so much taller than she, his shoulders looming high above her, his chin nearly brushing the top of her head.

"If you wanted the kiss," he continued, "you would lift your chin higher . . . you would stand closer . . ." He fell silent as her arms slid around his neck, her small hand touching his nape.

He smelled of starched linen and sweat and sandalwood soap. Madeline had never known such an appetizing scent—it filled her with the impulse to bury her face against his throat, and breathe.

A mist of sweat had broken out on his forehead. "Maddy . . ." he said with obvious difficulty, "you don't know what you're asking for."

Madeline curled her fingers against his chest, gripping his shirt. "Yes, I do." Swallowing hard, she stood on her toes, straining to reach him. His self-control seemed to snap, and suddenly his head lowered, his lips pressing against hers.

His mouth was hard and warm, demanding things she didn't know how to give. His arms closed around her, bands of solid muscle crushing her against his body. Gradually his mouth gentled, and he rubbed his lips over hers until they parted. His large hands closed around the back of her head, holding her steady for his skillful exploration. Nothing in her life had prepared her for this. All her ideas of poetry and romance burned to cinders, replaced by the solid reality of his body against hers.

She groped for his hair, the rumpled locks silken and thick beneath her fingers. The nape of his neck was as taut as a board as she clasped her palm over it. She was caught fast within his embrace, returning kiss for kiss, her heart thundering so hard that she thought she might faint. His mouth left hers, and she felt his lips slide down her throat, hungrily exploring the thin, vulnerable skin. Her legs wobbled beneath her, and she leaned against him for support.

He touched the firm curve of her breast, shaping with his hand until the soft peak tightened into a point beneath the fabric of her bodice.

"Oh . . ." She gasped and jerked backward, holding her own hand to her throbbing breast. Her eyes were wide in her flushed face, her lungs striving for air.

Logan dragged his sleeve over his damp forehead. His body was stiffly aroused, aching with his intense awareness of her. He wanted to reach for her again, bear her to the hard stage floor and take her right there. It was insane, impossible that he could be so obsessed with a naive girl when he'd taken his pleasure with some of the most desirable women in Europe. "Enough of this damned nonsense," he muttered.

"Nonsense?" she repeated in pained confusion.

He prowled around her in a half-circle. "I'm thirty years old, Maddy. I've never been interested in girls your age, even when I *was* your age."

"You . . . don't find me attractive?"

"Christ." It was proof of her inexperience that she would ask such a question, when the buttons on his trousers were straining to contain his arousal. Logan stopped pacing and forced himself to look at her. "I find you attractive," he said gruffly.

"Hell, I'd like to do things to you that—" He stopped and dragged his hand through his hair. "It's a bad idea, Maddy. You couldn't play the game as I like it to be played. And I would end up changing you. Hurting you."

"I understand," she said.

"No, you don't. Which is why I'm going to try like hell to avoid you. I don't need you on my conscience."

"I don't care about your conscience. All I want is for you to kiss me again."

The bold statement hung in the air between them. Madeline was stunned that she had actually said it. Scott stared at her in disbelief, and then he turned away with a laughing groan. "It's not going to happen. For my sake, if not yours."

"Mr. Scott—"

"I won't require your assistance in my office any longer. And I'd prefer that you stay away from rehearsals, although my partner may object." He paused and added curtly, "Just do your best to keep out of my sight."

Madeline was stunned by his callousness. The glow of passion faded from her body, leaving her cold and empty. How had everything gone wrong so quickly? Her mind swam with confusion. He had rejected her . . . he had said he wanted her, and yet . . . he had told her to stay away from him. "Mr. Scott—"

"Go on," he said, gesturing for her to leave. "I came here to have a look at the set pieces. I don't want your company."

Had it not been for Mrs. Florence, Madeline would have sunk into melancholy. Instead, she was profoundly puzzled by the elderly woman's interpretation of the scene. "I call that progress," Mrs. Florence declared after being told of the day's events. "You've almost got him on the hook, child. It shouldn't be long until you reel him in."

"Perhaps I haven't explained well enough," Madeline said, regarding her doubtfully. "Not only is Mr. Scott *not* on the hook, he's swimming as fast as possible in the opposite direction. He wants nothing to do with me."

"Didn't you listen to him, Maddy? He told you to stay away from him because your presence is too much temptation for him to withstand. That's the best encouragement I can think of."

"I suppose," Madeline murmured. "It's just that he seemed so very *definite*—"

"This is no time to falter," Mrs. Florence assured her. "He's weakening." She picked up a book and extracted a slip of paper tucked between the pages. "This is for you, Maddy. If you are able, leave your job at the theater early tomorrow and go to this address."

"Mrs. Bernard," Madeline read the name aloud and looked at Mrs. Florence questioningly.

"One of my dear friends, who owns a shop on Regent Street. Mrs. Bernard isn't the best dressmaker in London, but she's far from the worst. I told her a little about you, and she assured me that she has a bolt of fabric here and there, not to mention some clothing samples, that can be made into a few attractive gowns for you. She won't charge a shilling—one of her assistants will do the work as part of her training."

"Oh, Mrs. Florence! You're so kind. I wish I could find the words to thank you. . . ."

"It's thanks enough for me to have a new project," the elderly woman declared. "Lately there are few pursuits to keep me interested. Helping you attain your goal is quite an enjoyable hobby." She paused and regarded Madeline speculatively. "Not that it's any of my concern, child . . . but have you given a thought to afterward?"

"Afterward?"

"After you've succeeded in seducing Mr. Scott. I imagine you'll have a delightful time with him . . . but you must be prepared for the moment when he desires the affair to end."

Madeline nodded. "My family will take me in," she replied. "They won't be pleased by what I've done . . . but I'm prepared for that."

"And seducing Mr. Scott is worth that?"

"Well . . . yes," Madeline replied uncomfortably. She paused for a long moment. "I'm one of those people who was meant to have a very ordinary life. I have no special talent, no great beauty, nothing that distinguishes me from a hundred thousand other girls. But I can't go through an entire lifetime without at least one night of magic."

"Don't expect 'magic,'" Mrs. Florence counseled, her lined face touched with concern. "That's a difficult order for any man to fill, Maddy, even a man like Mr. Scott. To put it crudely, two bodies in a bed can be a very nice experience . . . but 'magic' happens only once in a lifetime. If at all."

Madeline approached Mr. Scott's dressing room, carrying a stack of freshly washed and folded costumes that had been delivered from the laundry cart. In the mornings the dressing room was always empty, but to her surprise, she heard voices inside. The door was ajar, requiring only a nudge from her elbow to swing open with a quiet squeak. She saw in consternation that Mr. Scott was half-standing, half-leaning against the dressing table, absorbed in conversation with a female visitor. She was slender and elegant, with pale blond hair and attractive features. She wore a rich blue velvet walking dress with intricately pleated skirts. An apparently worldly woman, cool, confident of her place in the world . . . all the things Madeline was not.

Although it was hard to conceal her dismay and jealousy, Madeline managed to keep her expression blank as the pair glanced at her. "Mr. Scott," she murmured, "I didn't expect to find you here at this time of day—"

"I came here for privacy." His tone was flat and dismissive.

"Yes, sir." Flushing, Madeline set the stack of clothes on the chair in the corner. "I'll return later to put these away."

"Let the girl do her work," the blond woman said lightly, taking no more notice of Madeline than she would a servant. "I must be off anyway, and I've no desire to interfere with the running of your theater."

Logan smiled, pushing away from the table and touching her elbow lightly. The gesture was small, but to Madeline's growing discomfort, it seemed to contain an inference of close and intimate friendship.

"Any interference from you is entirely welcome, milady."

The woman's ungloved hand smoothed over the linen that covered his forearm. "Then you shall have more of it."

"I hope so." Their gazes held for several seconds.

Madeline busied herself with the clothes, taking them to the armoire and hanging them methodically. She felt betrayed, although she had no right. After all, Mr. Scott was free to pursue anyone he desired . . . *But why couldn't it have been me?* she thought, seething inwardly.

Mr. Scott murmured a soft question, and the woman smiled and shook her head as she replied. "In the interest of discretion, I'll see myself out." Staring into his eyes, she pulled on her gloves and adjusted each finger precisely. Mr. Scott swung a fur-trimmed cloak over the lady's narrow shoulders, taking care to fasten it snugly at her throat to ward off the winter wind. The woman slipped past the door, leaving behind a delicate flowery scent that lingered in the air.

The dressing room was silent. Mr. Scott stared contemplatively at the door while Madeline finished hanging the costumes in the armoire. She closed the cabinet door a little too firmly, causing Mr. Scott to turn toward her, his dark brow arched inquiringly.

"She wears a rather strong perfume," Madeline remarked, waving one hand about as if to dispel a noxious odor.

"I thought it rather pleasant," Mr. Scott replied, his gaze following her intently as she moved about the room, rearranging the articles on his dressing table, straightening the chair against the wall, picking up a small coin from the floor.

Although Madeline tried to be silent, she couldn't prevent the impulsive question that sprang from her lips. "Is she your paramour?"

Mr. Scott's face was smooth and implacable. "My private life isn't open for discussion."

"She was wearing a wedding ring."

For some reason her disapproving expression seemed to amuse him. "It means nothing," he informed her dryly. "She and her husband have a well-known understanding."

Madeline puzzled briefly over his meaning. "You're saying that he wouldn't mind if his wife . . . and you . . . he wouldn't object?"

"Not as long as she's discreet."

"How very odd."

"Hardly. Many wives of the upper classes are allowed to have 'friendships' outside their marriages. It keeps them from complaining about their husbands' infidelities."

"And it doesn't bother you, the idea of making love to another man's wife?" Madeline dared to ask.

"I prefer married women," he replied evenly. "They're rarely demanding or possessive."

"If that woman weren't married, would you still want to have an affair with her?"

"That's not your concern, Miss Ridley."

Faced with his abrupt, dismissive manner, Madeline left the dressing room. "Oh, yes, it is my concern," she said too softly for him to hear. Her determination to have him was stronger than ever. If it was humanly possible to divert his interest from the blond married woman and turn it toward herself, she would do it.

In the next few days, an illness struck four employees of the Capital, two of them actors and two from the carpenter's shop. The symptoms were high fever, coughing, and congestion, and in the case of one patient, a delirium that had lasted for two days. The duchess sent servants to inquire about the well-being of her employees.

"Illness tends to travel through the entire company before it's finished," Julia commented to

Madeline with a frown. "It's too much to hope that no one else becomes ill."

"Your Grace," Madeline said, her gaze falling to the duchess's obvious pregnancy, "in your condition, you must be careful—"

"Yes, of course." Julia sighed impatiently. "But I can't stay home when there is so much to be done here."

"Your health is more important than any play, Your Grace."

The duchess snorted. "Don't say that in Mr. Scott's hearing. He doesn't believe in illness. For as long as I've known him, he's thought that nothing, not even scarlet fever, should interfere with the theater schedule."

"But people can't help getting sick," Madeline protested, wondering if Mr. Scott were really so unreasonable.

Julia rolled her eyes. "Logan has little tolerance for human frailty. How can he understand weakness when he doesn't have any himself?" Bracing her hands on the edge of her desk, she stood up and quirked her mouth. "I'll have to tell him about the situation. I expect he'll start roaring like a bear."

Contrary to the duchess's statement, there was no audible roaring from Mr. Scott's office . . . but there did seem to be a simmering current of annoyance in the air for the rest of the day, and the members of the company were unusually subdued. Madeline asked the duchess for permission to leave early, and it was given without hesitation.

Clutching the slip of paper in her hand, Madeline walked along Regent Street. She tried to appear confident among the milling crowds of people, carriages, and animals that congested the grand thoroughfare. There were rows of shops containing furniture, china, foodstuffs, milliners' wares, and fabrics. Just as Madeline despaired of ever finding Mrs. Bernard's establishment, she came upon a shop-front identified by a small green sign and a display of fabrics in the window.

Tentatively she entered the shop, causing a brass bell to jangle on a string. A neatly dressed girl not much older than herself approached at once. "May I help you, miss?"

"I'm here to see Mrs. Bernard . . . my name is Madeline Ridley."

Hearing the exchange from the corner of the shop, a tall woman stood up from a table burdened with sketches and fabric swatches. She appeared to be in her late forties and was dressed in an elegant blue gown, her graying hair pulled back in a stylish braided twist.

"Mrs. Bernard?" Madeline murmured while the shopgirl took her cloak and gloves.

"So you're Nell Florence's protégée," Mrs. Bernard remarked, surveying her keenly. "Nell sent me a letter about you, saying you wanted to catch a certain gentleman's eye but hadn't the proper attire. . . ." She gave Madeline's modest gown a disparaging glance. "Well, you won't be landing any well-heeled protectors with *that*, for certain." Gesturing to the shopgirl, she directed Madeline toward the back of the establishment. "Ruth will help you try on some things. I'll be along soon."

Madeline glanced over her shoulder as Ruth ushered her away. "Mrs. Bernard, I must tell you how much I appreciate—"

"Yes, yes. I was going to have Ruth remodel

some clothes in any case—she needs the practice. You must be a worthy cause if Nell has taken such a liking to you. I owe her several favors, as she has steered many good clients my way." She paused and called after the shopgirl. "Ruth, make certain to bring out the brown velvet and the yellow Italian silk. I think they'll do nicely for Miss Ridley."

Madeline had never visited a dressmaker before. Her mother had always summoned a local seamstress to their country estate, where they planned and designed five or six new gowns for each upcoming season. Often they had referred to the most recent ladies' periodicals for questions of style . . . but in Madeline's case, that never seemed to make much of a difference. She hungered for stylish gowns, but her mother had deemed them inappropriate. "After your marriage to Lord Clifton, you may select your own gowns," her mother had told her. "Although he is a conservative man, and I am certain he will not want his wife to flaunt herself."

"I don't wish to *flaunt* myself, Mama," Madeline had replied in exasperation. "I just want the kind of clothes my friends have, gowns with pretty colors and perhaps some lace trimming—"

"You have no need for such clothes," her mother had said calmly. "Those are designed purely to attract men's attention . . . and you are already promised to Lord Clifton."

As she remembered her mother's steely insistence and her own despair at being an old man's intended, Madeline's resolve hardened. She would do whatever was necessary to make Mr. Scott see her in a new light.

At the shopgirl's bidding, Madeline removed her

clothes and stood in her wrinkled cotton chemise and long drawers. Ruth gave a dubious glance at the undergarments and murmured something indistinguishable as she disappeared. When she returned a minute later, Mrs. Bernard was with her. The dressmaker recoiled at the sight of Madeline's knee-length chemise.

"Dreadfully out of style," Mrs. Bernard commented, folding her arms and shaking her head. "You can't wear those things under my gowns, Miss Ridley—the lines will be spoiled."

Madeline gave her a glance of mingled alarm and apology. "Everything I have is like this, ma'am."

"Where are your stays?" the dressmaker continued. At Madeline's blank look, she became slightly impatient. "Your corset, dear. Don't you wear one? For heaven's sake, how old are you?"

"Eighteen, but I've never—"

"Every girl your age should wear stays. It's only decent, not to mention healthful. I'm surprised you haven't got a curve in your back, going without support like that."

Anxiously Madeline strained to see her own back in the reflection of the mirror, half-expecting to see a grotesque hunch.

Mrs. Bernard sighed and spoke to the shopgirl. "Ruth, bring me three sets of the personal garments from Lady Barkham's order. We'll run up some new ones over the weekend. And fetch a set of stays from the box on the second shelf."

"Ma'am," Madeline said regretfully, "I'm sorry, but I can't afford—"

"It's all right," Mrs. Bernard told her. "Nell said that if extras were needed, you and she would work out some arrangement. You might run errands for her in exchange for pin money. Is that agreeable to you?"

"Yes, I think—"

"Then let's get started."

With the dressmaker's kindly bullying and Ruth's quiet efficiency, Madeline was divested of her bulky cotton undergarments and given a set of chemise and drawers that didn't even reach her knees. They were made of sheer, fine linen, so light that she had the feeling of not wearing anything. They were even slightly transparent, making Madeline blush as she stood before the mirror. If her mother had any idea what she was doing, she would have apoplexy.

Next came a set of stays, a ribbed silk garment that hooked up the front and laced up the back, drawing in her waist at least two inches. Madeline stared intently at her reflection. Was this indeed what men wanted, and would it make an impression on Mr. Scott? She could hardly wait to find out.

The first dress Madeline tried on was a soft yellow silk with a finely corded surface. Although the garment had been designed for a much taller woman, its simple style suited her. Madeline waited in barely contained excitement as Ruth fastened the concealed hooks at the back.

"Excellent," Mrs. Bernard said, expertly taking up the loose material with a row of flashing pins. "It's difficult for most women to wear that shade of yellow, but it brings out the gold in your hair."

The neckline was low and scooped, baring her throat and collarbone and revealing a hint of cleavage. The lines of the gown followed her cinched waist, making it seem impossibly small. Gleaming folds of yellow draped over her hips and legs, ending at the ground in a hem of deep pleats and simple scalloped work. "I look so different," Madeline said breathlessly.

"You certainly do," Mrs. Bernard replied. "It's a pity you can't afford extra trimmings for the gown, but perhaps that's for the best. A simple style lends a more sophisticated appearance." She supervised the fittings of three more gowns: a brown velvet with long sleeves of banded velvet and lace, a blue twilled cashmere, and an ivory gown cut so low that Madeline doubted she could wear it in public. It was accompanied by an ivory scarf embroidered in pale blue, meant to be draped lightly over her elbows.

Realizing that Madeline had no appropriate shoes, Mrs. Bernard brought out a pair of velvet slippers with narrow ribbons that laced across the ankles. "They were too small for the client who ordered them," she said, declining Madeline's offer of payment.

Declaring the afternoon to be a success, Mrs. Bernard promised Madeline that the new gowns would be ready in a matter of days, depending on when Ruth found time to work on them. Madeline thanked the two women effusively, unable to believe her good fortune.

"It is Nell Florence who should be thanked," Mrs. Bernard told her. "She's a grand old woman. You were a clever girl to choose her as your mentor."

"It had nothing to do with cleverness," Madeline replied. "It was a stroke of luck. Now if I could have just a little more—"

"If you're referring to the man you wish to attract, there's no need for luck. Once he sees you in your new gowns, he'll jump to do your bidding."

"I can't quite picture that," Madeline said with a laugh, thinking of Logan Scott's commanding face, and she bid the dressmaker farewell.

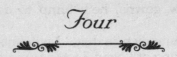

# Four

"*One always* hears the best gossip at the dress-maker's," Mrs. Florence said reminiscently, after hearing Madeline describe her visit to Mrs. Bernard's. "It always seems to be brimming with news of scandal and intrigue. I daresay I was discussed in many a shop—women were always terrified that I would steal their husbands or para-mours."

"And did you?" Madeline couldn't help asking.

"Just one or two."

Madeline smiled and investigated Mrs. Florence's sitting room. A scanty costume made of gauze and clasps of semiprecious stones had been framed and hung in the center of one wall. On either side of the costume were carved trunks fashioned in triangular shapes to fit in the corners. "What do you keep in here?" she asked.

"Mementos from my younger days." Mrs. Florence rearranged herself on a chair upholstered in painted velvet and nibbled from a plate of sand-wiches. "You may look inside, if you wish."

Needing no further encouragement, Madeline knelt on the Aubusson carpet and turned the key of the first trunk. A stale aroma of lavender sachets wafted upward. Carefully Madeline removed a stack of clothing neatly packed in tissue.

"That was what I wore as Hippolita, in *She Would and She Would Not,*" Mrs. Florence said, as Madeline unwrapped a military costume, complete with knee breeches and a plumed hat. "I was always good in tomboy roles—I had a nice pair of legs." She leaned forward with increasing interest and enjoyment. "And that was my Ophelia gown."

Reverently Madeline held up a costume of filmy white and green, adorned with hundreds of tiny embroidered rosebuds. "You must have been stunning in this!"

'There's a matching hairpiece in one of those smaller boxes," Mrs. Florence said.

Opening a leather case, Madeline discovered elaborate jewelry; gloves of lace, silk, and leather; faded shoes painted with flowered designs; and an array of fans. Mrs. Florence commented on many of the items, telling tales of her days in the theater while Madeline listened avidly.

However, when Madeline came to a small green-lacquered case, Mrs. Florence's smile vanished, and an expression of anxiety and sorrow appeared on her face. "Don't open that, child. It's private."

"Oh, I'm sorry—"

"It's perfectly all right. Just give it to me, please." The elderly woman received it in her wrinkled hands, white fingers gripping the case tightly. She stared down at the object, seeming to forget Madeline's presence.

"Ma'am . . . shall I put everything away and leave?" Madeline asked softly.

Mrs. Florence started a little at the sound of her voice. There was infinite regret in her gaze. "It contains a set of miniatures," she told Madeline, her thumbs passing over the lacquered case repeatedly, smudging the glossy surface. Slowly she raised the box and kissed it, then regarded Madeline with bright eyes. "Would you like to see one of them?"

Madeline nodded, drawing closer and kneeling by the elderly woman's feet.

Fumbling a little, Mrs. Florence withdrew one of the tiny gold-framed pictures and handed it to Madeline.

The painting was a portrait of a little girl no more than five or six, with large blue eyes and an angelic face. A huge bonnet was tied over her head, long red curls trailing beneath it. "How lovely," Madeline said sincerely. "Who is she?"

"My daughter."

Surprised, Madeline continued to gaze at the miniature. "I wasn't aware that you—"

"Few people ever were. She was illegitimate, you see." She paused and surveyed Madeline's face, perhaps hunting for a sign of shock or condemnation. Finding none, she continued. "I wasn't much older than you are when my Elizabeth was born. Her father was a wonderful man, handsome and honorable, though not well-born. He wanted to marry me, but only on the condition that I leave the stage forever."

"Did you love him?"

"Heavens, yes. If I ever felt magic with anyone, it was with him. But I turned down his proposal. I didn't want to sacrifice my career; it meant too much to me. When I found out I was expecting, I never told him. Eventually he married someone else, and to all appearances led a happy life.

According to a mutual acquaintance, he died ten years ago."

"Did you ever regret not marrying him?" Madeline asked.

"I don't allow myself to have regrets."

They were both quiet then, staring at the portrait. "Where is she now?" Madeline asked.

Mrs. Florence's answer was barely audible. "Elizabeth died many years ago."

"Oh, Mrs. Florence . . ." Madeline was filled with compassion.

"I never knew her very well," the elderly woman confided, stretching out her hand for the miniature, her fingers curling around it tightly. "I kept her with me during her early childhood, but when she reached an appropriate age, I sent her away to school."

"Why?"

"Life in the theater world wasn't suitable for Elizabeth—being exposed to my gentlemen friends and so forth. I wanted her to be sheltered and educated. I made certain that she had the finest clothes, books, dolls . . . anything she needed. Sometimes I would take her traveling on holidays. We never discussed my profession or the kind of life I led. I had dreams that someday she would marry well and live in a grand home in the country. Instead . . ." Mrs. Florence fell silent and shook her head.

Madeline's mind sifted through various possibilities until the elderly woman's expression of sad irony made the answer clear. "Elizabeth wanted to be like you," Madeline said with quiet certainty.

"Yes. She left school of her own accord and told me that she intended to become an actress. I begged her not to, but nothing would change her mind. The desire to act always seems strongest in people with a great emptiness to fill. No doubt Elizabeth had many needs that were never met, especially the desire for a father and a family. I did the best I could for her. Clearly I should have done more."

"What happened to her?"

"Elizabeth began on stage at age sixteen. She was greeted with ecstatic reviews. Her acting had a subtlety and power that far surpassed mine. I believe Elizabeth would have been one of the great actresses, even greater than dear Julia. Though I had originally disagreed with Elizabeth's choice of career, I had great hopes for her."

Mrs. Florence sighed and slid the miniature back into the case. "Soon after her seventeenth birthday, she met a man. An aristocrat. Handsome, intelligent, and cold-blooded. She loved him insanely, enough to throw away her career and everything of value in order to become his mistress. When she became pregnant, she was radiantly happy. I never knew what *he* thought of the situation, but it was clear that he had no intention of marrying her. One day . . ." She stopped, her mouth twisting as if she found it hard to speak. "His lordship sent a servant to inform me that my daughter had died in childbirth."

"And the baby?" Madeline asked after a long silence.

"I was informed that the baby didn't survive either."

"Who was—"

"I'd rather not speak of him, my dear. The man took my daughter's life and caused me more pain than I ever thought I could feel. I never let his name fall from my lips."

"I understand," Madeline said, reaching out to pat Mrs. Florence's hand gently. "I'm honored that you would share a little of your past with me, ma'am."

The elderly woman smiled at her, folding her hands closely around the box.

"Are there other miniatures of Elizabeth?" Madeline asked.

"Yes . . . but I can't bear to look at those, or to show them."

"Of course." Madeline regarded her curiously, sensing that there were more secrets about Elizabeth that Mrs. Florence had chosen not to reveal.

When Madeline returned to the Capital the next morning, it was to discover that Arlyss Barry had fallen prey to the illness that had affected so many others. Her husband, who was also the head scene painter, had stayed home to take care of her. The duchess was clearly concerned. "It takes a great deal to keep Arlyss from the theater," she told Madeline. "I want to visit her, but the duke has forbidden it. In fact, he's threatening to keep me at home for the next few weeks, until the illness has run its course through the company."

"That sounds like a wise suggestion," Madeline said. "Perhaps you should consider it, Your Grace."

The duchess gave a frustrated sigh. "There's too much to do . . . and soon I'll be in confinement. I must stay here for as long as I can. In the meantime, both Arlyss and her understudy are ill. I wonder if you might consider taking the role during rehearsals until one of them is able to return?"

"Oh, Your Grace, I couldn't . . ." Madeline shook her head. "I could never act. I have no talent and absolutely no desire. . . ."

"You don't have to act. Just say the lines—you know them better than Arlyss herself—and move about the stage exactly as you've seen her do. You needn't be shy, Maddy. Everyone would understand you were temporarily taking Arlyss's place to make rehearsals easier for the company. Won't you consider it?"

"Mr. Scott won't like it," Madeline said awkwardly.

"You leave him to me. Above all else, Logan wants what is best for his theater."

Madeline didn't see Mr. Scott until the next morning. To her discomfort, she had been told that the rehearsal would be conducted with the players in costume. She was already self-conscious, assuming Arlyss's place; it was even worse, having to wear the character's gown, which was little more than translucent layers of blue and silver draped over her body. Because her measurements were smaller than Miss Barry's, the wide scooped neckline kept slipping down over her breasts, revealing far more than had been intended.

"What a beauty you are," Mrs. Lyttleton said, standing back to view the costume with pride. "'Tis a pity Miss Barry doesn't have your lovely figure. You give the costume an ethereal quality that she doesn't."

"I think Miss Barry has a fine figure," Madeline said quickly.

"She would if she stopped eating sugar biscuits with her tea every afternoon," Mrs. Lyttleton said darkly, swinging her mountainous girth around as she turned to a rack of costumes to be worn that day.

As she joined the players in the greenroom, Madeline went to the nearest corner, trying to remain inconspicuous. Unfortunately, the revealing costume left her open to a predictable amount of teasing. Charles Haversley was the first to notice her, greeting her with admiring whistles.

"My Lord, what a transformation!" he cried, rushing to her and seizing her hands. His avid gaze moved over her body, lingering at her half-exposed breasts. "Dear Miss Ridley, I had no idea what you were hiding beneath your usual attire. I'll admit, during my private moments I did wonder—"

"Charles," interrupted the older actor, Mr. Burgess, who played the part of the bereaved father, "none of us, least of all Miss Ridley, wants to hear about your private moments."

Madeline pulled her hands from Charles' enthusiastic grip. "Mr. Haversley . . ." she began in a chiding tone. Before she could continue, Stephen Maitland had joined them, his gaze locked on her bosom.

"Miss Ridley, I'll escort you to the stage. It's dark, and you might trip on the way—"

Their antics were interrupted by a quiet voice from across the room. "That's enough, gentlemen."

Madeline looked toward the source of the voice and saw Mr. Scott standing across the room, a few pages of notes in his hand. He swept a glance across the assembled players, seeming not to notice Madeline. "Let's get started," he said. "I have a few notes concerning yesterday morning's rehearsal, and then I want everyone to take their places for the first scene."

Mr. Scott ran through the list of comments and changes, while the actors listened attentively. Near the end of his brief talk, he looked directly at Madeline for the first time. "Miss Ridley, I believe everyone is aware that you have agreed to take part in the rehearsal because Miss Barry and her stand-in are both indisposed. Our thanks for your assistance."

Madeline felt her color rise, and she managed a small nod in response. He switched his gaze from her at once, his face unaccountably grim.

Quickly the players filed from the greenroom, Madeline along with them. She—or rather the character of the deceased wife's ghost—appeared in the first scene. As she passed Mr. Scott, who had stayed by the doorway, she stopped and looked up at him.

"Mr. Scott," she said softly, careful not to let anyone overhear, "I know you told me to stay away from you, but the duchess asked—"

"I know," he interrupted.

"You're not angry with me?"

His face was a mask of indifference. "Your presence won't affect me in the least."

"All right," she said, giving him an uncertain smile as she continued toward the stage area. As she passed him, she wondered why his hand was clenched hard around the door frame, the pressure making his fingers white. Dismayed, she thought that Mr. Scott hadn't been telling the truth. He *was* angry with her. She went to the wings with a heavy sigh, jerking up the drooping bodice of her gown.

Why had she picked a man who was so difficult to seduce? She may as well settle for Charles Haversley and be done with it. But Haversley didn't inspire any of the feelings she had for Mr.

Scott . . . the giddy nervousness, the fear and delight that tangled inside her whenever he was near. She wanted to be in his arms and no one else's . . . to know the forbidden pleasure of being with him—

"Maddy," came the Duchess of Leeds's voice as she entered the wings. Madeline ventured from behind the curtain.

"Yes, Your Grace?"

Julia sat in the first row of seats. A smile appeared on her face as she saw Madeline. "You look very nice in costume, Maddy. Before we begin, I want to assure you that no one expects you to do everything perfectly. Just follow along as best you can, and try to enjoy yourself."

Madeline listened to Julia's directions. They were going to rehearse the opening of the play, in which the ghost of a young woman visited the loved ones she had left behind: her brother, played by Charles Aversley; her "parents," Mrs. Anderson and Mr. Burgess . . . and of course, her husband, played by Mr. Scott.

"None of them are supposed to see or hear you," Julia told Madeline, "but they all have an awareness that someone . . . or something . . . is there."

"I understand," Madeline said, retreating to the wings from which Arlyss was to make her first entrance.

The rehearsal went smoothly, with few interruptions. After a while Madeline lost her self-consciousness and imitated Arlyss Barry's previous performances as closely as possible, even matching some of her gestures and inflections.

"Very good, Maddy," Julia said occasionally, as Madeline moved in and out of the scene, speaking to her unhearing companions and witnessing what had become of them since her death.

There was only one break in the action, when Charles Haversley happened to glance at Madeline and stopped in midsentence. Suddenly he erupted in helpless laughter. Puzzled, Madeline stared at him, while Julia asked crisply what was wrong.

Haversley shook his head and looked apologetic, even as he continued to snort with amusement. "I can't help it, Your Grace," he said, gasping. "Miss Ridley stares at me as if she believes everything I'm saying, and she looks so *earnest* . . . it's too adorable."

Julia gave him a reproving stare. "You're not supposed to look at her, Charles. She's a ghost."

"I can't help it," he said again, smiling raffishly at Julia. "If you were a man, you would understand."

"Oh, I understand," Julia replied dryly. "You would do us all a service, Charles, if you could manage to act like a brother instead of a town-bull."

"Town-bull?" Madeline asked, perplexed, having never encountered such a term at Mrs. Allbright's academy. For some reason her question set off another spurt of laughter in Charles. She looked to the wings, where Mr. Scott waited to make his entrance. He was a striking figure as he stood amidst the velvet curtains, dressed in elegant clothes, his posture relaxed yet controlled.

It struck Madeline that a hundred years from now, people would read about him in history books and wonder what it must have been like to see him act. No words would ever accurately describe his voice, with its deep, vibrant quality, or the remarkable range of his talent. It seemed as if

Mr. Scott were two different people: the disciplined man offstage, and the actor whose emotions simmered and exploded during a performance. Mrs. Florence had been right—this was the place to approach him.

Logan watched the rehearsal from the wings, resentment uncoiling in his chest. Damn Julia for suggesting that Madeline assume Arlyss's place . . . damn Arlyss and her understudy for being ill . . . damn himself for being so riveted by Madeline that he could barely remember his lines. Who could blame Charles Haversley for his lack of concentration? Logan doubted he would fare any better, with Madeline dressed in a flimsy costume that made him want to sink to his knees before her and bury his face between her breasts. She looked so young and fresh, her skin like cream silk. It wasn't her sheer prettiness that proved such a potent allure; it was the troubling desire to cover her up and carry her away from the others' admiring gazes . . . to keep her all to himself.

Somehow Madeline had insinuated herself into his life and forced him to take notice of her, and now there was no retreat. Now that he had rejected the idea of taking her into his bed, she had become the thing he most wanted. Every other woman he had considered seemed to lack something, and it maddened him to realize that he was subconsciously looking for her likeness. He couldn't stop thinking about what it would be like to lose himself inside her youthful energy. She made him want to play, to experience a little of the boyhood he'd never had . . . and that was something no other lover had ever been able to do.

He felt hot and annoyed, and ready to chew the scenery into splinters. Hearing his cue, he took a bottle from the propman, holding it loosely between his fingers as he walked onstage. The other actors had made their exits, the boards cleared except for him and Madeline.

As the grieving widower, he was supposed to be drunk. It wasn't easy to portray intoxication well. Most actors tended to overplay it or, worse, underplay it. It was one of the few pieces of stagecraft that required a great deal of technique in order to seem natural. Forcing himself to concentrate, Logan captured the slur, the expansive gestures, and the off-balance walk of a man who had been drinking for a long time.

He sat in a large oak chair, before a box set resembling a library. Clearing his mind of all else, he began a lengthy monologue, revealing the biting irony and quiet despair of his character.

Somewhere in the midst of the monologue, Logan felt rather than saw Madeline come up behind him, her small hands resting on the back of his chair. As the play dictated, she leaned over him and spoke during the pauses of his monologue, her sweet voice falling against his ears.

Logan didn't move. He was feverishly aware of her body just behind him, her scent, the feel of her breath on his skin. He began to sweat profusely. One of Madeline's long golden-brown curls fell over his shoulder, tickling his neck. An aching pressure gathered in his groin. He was rock-hard, his entire being consumed with lust and yearning.

Logan couldn't stand it any longer. He broke in midsentence, just as Charles had . . . only he wasn't laughing.

The theater was silent. Logan tried to collect himself, aware that the cast and crew were watching. Perhaps they thought he had forgotten a line, although that had never happened before. He hoped to God no one suspected the truth—that he was completely undone by one naive girl. Setting his jaw hard, he took several deep, even breaths.

"Mr. Scott," came Madeline's hesitant voice from behind him, "if you would like me to tell you the line—"

"I know the bloody line," he said, his back stiff. God help him, if he glanced at her even once, he was afraid of what he might do.

Julia spoke from the audience seat. "Is there a problem, Mr. Scott?"

Logan responded with a murderous glare, longing to strangle his comanager for putting him in this situation. Julia was genuinely puzzled, staring back at him with knitted brows. She pondered his simmering discomfort, her gaze flickering from him to Madeline, who continued to stand right behind him. Then she seemed to understand. They had been friends for a long time, he and Julia. She knew him too well.

"Shall we break for a few minutes?" she asked briskly.

"No," Logan muttered. "Let's finish the damned scene." He swiped at his forehead and resumed the monologue once more, starting somewhere in the middle. Madeline followed along, a note of uncertainty in her voice.

Without regard to technique, characterization, or any of the nuances of acting, Logan muddled through the rest of the scene. Julia let the performance pass without comment, speculation causing her fair brow to crease.

The second the scene ended, Julia called for a twenty-minute break. The theater company dispersed at once, heading to the greenroom in search of refreshment or to the dressing rooms. Logan remained in his chair onstage, keeping his back to Madeline until he sensed that she had left.

Slowly Julia made her way to the edge of the stage, rubbing the small of her back. "Logan," she said quietly, "I have no desire to interfere—"

"Then don't." He walked downstage to within a few feet of her, staring into her upturned face.

Julia made certain no one was close enough to overhear before she continued, choosing her words with obvious care. "I suspected there was an attraction between you and Maddy, but she's not the kind of girl you've ever been interested in before, and I certainly never dreamed—"

"What is your point, Your Grace?"

She looked stung by his abruptness. "I happen to like Maddy. I hope you won't take advantage of her. You and I both know she would never recover from an affair with you. She's not nearly hardened enough."

Logan felt his face turn to stone. "What I do—or don't do—with her is my business."

"Maddy's welfare is also my concern. And I seem to recall your hard-and-fast rule that you never become personally involved with anyone in the company—"

"She's *your* employee, not mine. I didn't hire her, and therefore I'm free to do whatever the hell I want with her."

"Logan," she warned in frustration, watching as he strode away.

Madeline wandered through the greenroom, summoning a wan smile in response to the other actors' praise for her efforts.

"What's the matter with Mr. Scott?" she over-heard someone asking. "He's been acting strange lately."

"Who knows?" came another's reply. "I just hope it isn't that bloody fever that's going around. All the company needs is for Mr. Scott to be under the hatches."

The rest of the conversation was lost on Madeline as she headed to the practice rooms. She needed to find a place to think. What had happened onstage? She had thought everything was going well. She had even felt a sort of connection with Mr. Scott. But he had turned wooden, his performance strangely mechanical, as if he could hardly bear her presence. She felt close to weeping . . . she wanted to hide somewhere.

She heard rapid footsteps behind her. Someone caught her arm in a biting grip and ushered her into the nearest practice room. Madeline stumbled a little, twisting to stare at her captor with wide eyes as he closed the door. "Mr. Scott . . ."

His face was in shadow, the outline of his head framed by shafts of light coming in from the window. His breathing was rough and unsteady. She stepped back, but he caught her with startling suddenness, his hands closing on either side of her head. It seemed that he tried to say something, then gave up with a muffled sound and kissed her.

His mouth was startlingly hot, almost clumsy with urgency. He explored her as if he couldn't get enough, trying to assuage a hunger that would never be satisfied. Madeline trembled in surprise, meeting his aggression with a surrender that only inflamed him more.

His hand raked down her back, nearly tearing

the fabric of her costume. Madeline couldn't help molding herself to him, craving more, her legs parting at the hard intrusion of his thigh. She wrapped her arms around him, clasping the taut muscles of his back. This was what she had wanted, what she had dreamed of, and it was even sweeter than she had imagined. His mouth was tender and erotic, his body hard against hers, filling her with delicious, giddy weakness.

His lips broke from hers, and he gasped harshly against her ear. Taking a fistful of her long hair, he pushed it aside and pressed his lips against her throat. He found a sensitive place on the side of her neck, kissing, gently biting until she whimpered in pleasure. She was desperately empty inside; she wanted something . . . something . . .

He shoved at the sleeves of her gown and shift, the material tightening until stitches popped and her naked breast was revealed. Madeline caught her breath as she felt him cup the soft weight, brushing the tip with his fingers, pulling gently until the point was taut and aching. She leaned against him, her body shaking uncontrollably.

"Sweet," he whispered, holding her tightly, "Sweet. Don't be afraid." He arched her over his solid arm, and she felt his lips slide over her breast until they closed over the aroused nipple. He brought it to an even harder peak with swirling touches of his tongue, seeming to know exactly how to pleasure her.

Suddenly Mr. Scott lifted his mouth from her breast and let go of her. Stunned by the abrupt release, Madeline stared at him in astonished silence. Her hands came up to cover her nakedness, and she turned away from him, fumbling with her gown. Her fingers trembled violently, making the task impossible. She struggled with her clothes until she felt his hands on her once more, carefully pulling her sleeves and bodice back into place.

As soon as she was safely covered, Mr. Scott retreated to the other side of the small room. He dragged his hand through his hair, letting out an explosive sigh. After a long time, he spoke while pacing away from her. "Maddy, I didn't mean to . . . approach you that way. It's just that I . . ." He stopped with a grim laugh. "I can't seem to stop myself."

She gripped her hands together. "Mr. Scott," she said with difficulty, "I'm not sorry that you kissed me."

He turned at the words, his eyes like blue fire. He came to her in three strides, taking her face in his hands. "Maddy," he whispered. His lips came to the curve of her cheek, and he smoothed her hair back from her face, his fingers curling in the silken locks. "I wish to hell I didn't want you so badly."

Her heart gave a leap of pleasure at the words. "Mr. Scott—"

"Listen to me, Maddy." He let go of her and drew back. "I'm not going to make love to you, regardless of how much I desire you. You would hate me afterward, and I would probably hate myself."

"I could never hate you."

He smiled sardonically. "No? Not even after I've robbed you of your innocence? Any involvement with me would change you, and not for the better."

"I'm willing to take that risk."

"You don't understand." His mouth twisted bitterly. "I use women for physical pleasure, nothing

more. Once I've learned all a partner has to offer
it's not long before I become bored and move on to
the next one. You wouldn't last long in my bed
room."

"Haven't you ever been in love?" Madeline
asked, staring at his set face.

"Once. It didn't work."

"Why—"

"You don't need to know about my past, an
more than I need to know about yours."

Madeline didn't argue, knowing that he wa
probably right. The more she knew about him, th
more difficult it would be to leave him when th
time came. Like so many other women, she ha
been ensnared by Logan Scott's potent mixture c
masculinity and mystery. For her own protectior
she had to keep her heart safe. Suddenly Mrs
Florence's sage advice came to mind . . . *Whateve
you do, you mustn't act lovestruck. Simply make it clea
that you're available and willing . . . that you're offer
ing pleasure with no responsibility.*

"Mr. Scott," she said quietly, "if you're attracte
to me, I don't see why we shouldn't act upon it. A
I want is one night with you."

His expression didn't change, but she sense
that she had surprised him. "Why?" he aske
softly. "A girl like you . . . why would you lowe
yourself to that?" As he waited for a reply, he sli
his fingers beneath her chin and forced her fac
upward. There was a flicker in his eyes, a new
alertness that made her uneasy. Her lashes lowere
in an effort to hide her thoughts.

"I believe I would enjoy it," she said. "Isn't tha
reason enough?"

There was a brief, baffled silence. "Look at me,

he murmured. Slowly she obeyed. He searched her eyes and shook his head as if he were dismissing a not-so-entertaining puzzle. "You're a poor actress, Maddy. I'd like to know what it is you're after, but I have other issues to deal with, especially the fact that nearly a quarter of my company has fallen ill. As soon as the Capital is back to rights again, I want you to leave the theater. I'll get you another job, a better one."

"I want to stay here."

He appeared to be unmoved. "Believe me, it's best for both of us."

Madeline swallowed hard while a sickening tide of disappointment swept over her. What now? Her offer had been made and rejected. The sound of his refusal rang in her ears until she burned with mortified anger. Her hands clenched in her skirts, crushing the gossamer material.

How foolish she had been! She had wasted so much time spinning fantasies about him, about things that would never happen. Now she was left with nothing except the knowledge that soon her absence from school would be discovered by her family.

For a fraction of a second, she considered explaining the situation to Mr. Scott and throwing herself on his mercy. No . . . he would have no sympathy for her. *Marry Clifton and consider yourself well off,* she could almost hear him saying cynically. In truth, she was hardly fit to do anything else.

Clenching her fists, Madeline went to the door with determined strides. She would not spend the rest of her days as a possession of Lord Clifton's. "Very well," she said, pausing at the door. "I'll leave the Capital whenever you wish. You needn't

bother to find another situation for me. I'm perfectly capable of finding something on my own."
She left before he could reply.

Logan wandered to the door and braced his hand on the upper panels. He pressed his forehead to the cool wood and let out a muffled groan.

*One night with you* . . . he would have given up his entire fortune for it. He had never known anything as exquisite as the feel of her in his arms, and the fearless vulnerability that welcomed and drew him near until he felt close to shattering. But he couldn't allow that, couldn't let someone tear out what was left of his heart.

She would be gone soon. He waited for a feeling of relief that did not come.

Wrenching open the door, he went to his office, ignoring the curious stares of the people he passed. He closed himself inside the small room and rummaged in his desk until he found a bottle of Highland whiskey. He sat at his desk and took a swig right from the bottle, letting the subtle flavors of smoke and peat linger on his tongue. Another swallow, and his throat was filled with the warming glow. But it failed to melt the block of ice in his chest.

Logan drank leisurely, resting his feet on the edge of the desk and contemplating the tips of his polished leather shoes. At this point in his life, when he was saturated with success, he had thought himself invulnerable. It was amusing, really, that one small female had been able to wreak such havoc on him.

Perhaps it was because Maddy was unique in his experience. She was certainly a far cry from the women of society's upper circles, who made certain Logan knew they were his superiors even as they slipped him discreet notes to arrange romantic rendezvous.

And there were the creatures he detested most of all . . . the pedigreed daughters of the upper classes, whose only purpose in life was to marry and reproduce more of their kind. He wasn't good enough for them. He had no family or title, and money alone wasn't sufficient.

Had he desired to court one of those privileged young ladies, he would have been informed by her family that she had far more desirable prospects. Just the sight of a chaperoned, white-gowned virgin at a ball or soirée was enough to remind Logan that no matter how great his achievements, there were some things he could never have. He would never be fully accepted. Outside the theater, there was no place he really belonged.

Madeline Ridley seemed equally out of place. She was too warm and unaffected to be a society miss, too idealistic to be a courtesan. She was clearly meant to be someone's wife, but he couldn't imagine a man who would be worthy of her. She needed someone who would take care not to crush her spirit, who would be able to love her as completely as she would love him.

All of the things Logan could never do. He was ill-equipped for such a relationship, having been taught at an early age to despise the words "home" and "family." He had survived only by becoming as callous as the man who had sired him.

Years of beatings and abuse had toughened him and made him a supremely good liar. His father, Paul Jennings, had always committed his acts of violence in the midst of a drunken rage . . . but afterward he had resisted facing the results of what he had done. Logan had been required to pretend that all was forgotten, maintaining the fiction that everyone in the Jennings household was happy and well. The sight of one tear, one wince of pain or resentful glance, had been enough to incur a second beating worse than the first. Unwittingly, his father had been a superb acting teacher.

Once, after a particularly brutal beating, Logan had gone for three days with a broken arm, denying that he felt any pain until Andrew had finally dragged him to the estate mansion and seen that the arm was splinted and bound. "How did it happen, boy?" the earl had asked him, his keen eyes fastened on Logan's battered face. Logan had refused to answer, knowing that if he even hinted at the truth, Paul Jennings would probably kill him.

Years later, Logan had wondered why his mother had never offered him any consolation, no maternal kisses to soothe the hurts. He had come to the conclusion that his mother had been too desperately determined to keep the peace in her house to spare him much attention. He had long since ceased to want softness from a woman . . . he didn't need comfort or caring. Women were to be enjoyed and discarded, but never to be trusted. Never to be needed.

Now that things had finally been settled with Madeline, all he had to do was ignore her until Arlyss was well again. He had no doubt that Julia would protest the girl's dismissal, but he could deal with that. Besides, Julia would soon be occupied with a newborn baby, and all thoughts of Madeline Ridley would fade. Soon it would be as if she had never been there at all.

Logan felt the bracing effects of the whiskey settle in his bones, making him comfortably numb. Just as he preferred. Carefully he replaced the bottle of whiskey in the drawer and closed it.

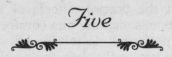

# Five

*Madeline went* to bed early, deciding to forgo her nightly conversation with Mrs. Florence. The pain of rejection was too fresh. Perhaps she would be able to talk about it tomorrow, or the next day, when she was able to compose herself.

Staring into the darkness, Madeline considered not returning to the Capital. The idea of facing Mr. Scott again was unbearable. Unfortunately she had promised the duchess that she would help with rehearsals until Miss Barry was well again. She couldn't break a promise, but to stand opposite Mr. Scott on stage and look into his eyes . . . Madeline winced in acute embarrassment. She didn't know if she could do it.

Just one or two days—surely Miss Barry would be well by then. She would steel herself not to blush or stammer in front of Mr. Scott. She would be cool and utterly self-possessed.

Madeline turned and twisted in the bedclothes all night, trying in vain to escape her thoughts. In the morning she awoke exhausted and apprehensive, wondering if she had ever dreaded a day in her life as she did this one. No doubt she wasn't the first woman to fail at seducing a man—but how many of them were required to face him the very next day and pretend nothing had happened?

She donned her clothes and arranged her hair,

pinning it into a tight coil at the nape of her neck. She managed to leave before Mrs. Florence rose for the day, and took a hackney to the theater.

The theater company seemed unusually lackluster, the practice rooms and workshops much quieter than usual. Discovering that the morning rehearsal had been canceled, Madeline went to the costume shop and was immediately enlisted by Mrs. Lyttleton. "It seems as if half the company is ill," the heavyset woman said breathlessly, her needle flashing as she basted a seam. "A dozen people have sent word that they won't be coming in. But my work has to be done as usual, and I've practically no help."

Madeline worked in the costume shop for most of the morning, grateful for the temporary reprieve from seeing Mr. Scott. It was only when Mrs. Lyttleton commanded her to fetch some costume sketches from the duchess's office that Madeline wandered reluctantly into the main theater building. As she approached the office, she heard an unfamiliar male voice mingling with Julia's light, clear tones. Madeline stopped just outside the doorway, reluctant to intrude on the scene.

"It's enough," the man was saying. "I told you to stay away from this damned theater."

"There's too much to be done," Julia replied. "Just one more day, darling. Perhaps two. I can't leave with so many things unfinished—"

"Your health means more to me than anyone or anything in this entire place."

"I promise you, I'll be fine."

"Come home, Julia."

"First I have to pack some things."

"I'll send a servant later to fetch whatever you desire."

"You're being unreasonable—"

There was a long pause, followed by a muffled sound that Madeline couldn't quite decipher. Then the man spoke softly. "Are you still going to argue with me, Julia?"

"No."

Madeline had never heard such a meek tone from the duchess, who was usually so firm and authoritative. Gingerly she peeked around the corner and saw the duchess standing in the middle of her office, being thoroughly kissed by a dark-haired man. The Duke of Leeds, Madeline thought, her interest immediately sparked. He lifted his head, revealing a lean, exotically handsome face as he stared at his wife with loving exasperation. Evidently sensing that they were not alone, he glanced in Madeline's direction with alert gray eyes.

Blushing, Madeline came forward at once. "Forgive me, I didn't mean to intrude—"

"That's all right, Maddy," Julia said, her cheeks pink as she disentangled herself from her husband's arms. She introduced them, and Madeline sank into a respectful curtsy.

"A pleasure," the duke murmured with a friendly glint in his eyes. "Miss Ridley, I would appreciate your efforts to help the duchess gather any necessary papers and books, as she is leaving immediately."

"Yes, Your Grace."

Julia rolled her eyes and sighed. "It seems I have no choice. Maddy, please tell Mr. Scott that I need to speak with him at once. He's been in his office all morning, trying to rearrange the schedule to accommodate the absences in the company."

Although Madeline dreaded having to face Mr.

Scott, she nodded resolutely. The duke and duchess resumed their conversation as she left, both of them seeming to take great pleasure in a new bout of verbal sparring.

Madeline reached Scott's door and hesitated, listening for signs of activity inside. The office was jarringly silent. Hoping that Scott wasn't there, she lifted her hand and knocked softly.

"I'm working," came a threatening rumble from within.

Madeline twisted her hands together and stared at the door. Gathering her resolve, she finally spoke in a calm, controlled voice. "Mr. Scott, the duchess wishes to speak to you."

He was silent for a moment. "You," he said in an unfriendly tone.

"I believe the duchess wishes to tell you that she is leaving, sir. The duke has come to take her home." Madeline was greeted with more silence. "It's not wise for her to stay at the Capital in her condition. I'm certain you would agree that with all the people who have succumbed to the fever—"

"Good riddance to her. Now get away from my door."

Madeline complied gladly, but after the first few steps, she paused. There had been something odd in his voice, a strain that touched her. He sounded tired. No wonder, she thought, with so much of the company absent. In spite of his orders to stay away, and her own hurt and embarrassment, she was driven to return to the door. "Mr. Scott, is there something I can do? Would you like some tea?"

"Just leave," he muttered. "I have work . . . no mood for distractions."

"Yes, sir." But still she couldn't go. She was filled with the growing conviction that something was wrong. It was so quiet inside the room. It wasn't like him to keep his door closed at this hour, barring himself from the rest of the company. Placing her hand on the worn brass doorknob, she closed her eyes and took a deep breath. If her suspicions proved to be false, Scott would most likely take her head off.

As Madeline entered the room, Scott seemed not to notice her until she was at his side. He sat at his desk amid a pile of blotted and crumpled paper, dragging a sleeve across his forehead before picking up a pen. He wore no coat or waistjacket, and shivers chased down his back as the cold air in the room sank through the thin linen shirt. He smothered a violent cough, dropping the pen and scattering drops of ink over the desk.

"Sir," Madeline said quietly.

Scott's head turned toward her, revealing a flushed face and glazed eyes. It seemed as if he watched her through a dense fog. Without thinking, Madeline reached down to touch the damp ruff of his hair and smooth it gently. Her fingers brushed against his forehead, detecting the dry heat of a raging fever.

"Let me help you," she said as he twisted away with a muffled curse.

"I have to finish the new schedules." Doggedly he groped for the discarded pen.

"You have a fever, Mr. Scott. You must go home and rest."

"I'm not sick. I never—" He jerked as she touched his hot forehead once more, and then his eyes closed. "Your hand is so cool," he said hoarsely, catching at her fingers. "Christ, my head is pounding."

Madeline was wrenched with worry. Was there

no one to care for him, to look after his welfare? Frozen in indecision, she stared down at him while he shook with tremors.

"You must go home, sir," Madeline said firmly, and repeated it over his objections until Scott fell silent, huddling against his desk. He rested his forehead on his closed fist, using his other hand to grip her fingers. Reluctantly Madeline pried herself free. "Don't move," she said. "I'll be right back." He didn't reply, only sat listlessly, using the last of his strength to keep himself upright.

By a stroke of fortune, the carpentry shopboy, Jeff, was passing the office. Madeline called his name, and he stopped at once, his eyes friendly and inquiring.

"I'm afraid Mr. Scott is ill," Madeline said, indicating the half-closed door behind her. "He must leave right away. Would you please tell someone to have his carriage brought around?"

"Mr. Scott . . . ill?" the boy repeated, seeming not to hear the rest. He looked thunderstruck, as if such an occurrence were outside the realm of possibility.

"There's something else," Madeline added. "Make certain that the duchess is told to leave immediately. She mustn't come near Mr. Scott—it would be dangerous for her to catch the fever."

The boy retreated, glancing warily at the office. "What about you?" he asked in concern. "Shouldn't you stay away from him, too?"

"I don't believe I'll get sick," Madeline replied. "I think I would have by now, if I were going to. Please go quickly, Jeff. I'll stay with Mr. Scott while you send for the carriage."

"Yes, Miss Maddy." He shot her a glance of admiration. "If you don't mind my saying, you're an angel, Miss Maddy. As kind and sweet as any girl I ever knew."

Madeline shook her head with an abashed smile. "Thank you, Jeff." Returning to the office, she found Scott's cloak and draped it around him. The heavy wool should have warmed him, but he continued to shiver and cough. As he tried to rise from the chair, Madeline rushed to him.

"Sir, you mustn't! You aren't well enough. The footmen will arrive soon to help you."

"I can leave on my own," he growled, pushing at her small, restraining hands.

"I won't be able to keep you from falling," Madeline insisted. "And if you collapse before you reach the carriage, you may injure yourself . . . and think how it will appear to the others. You wouldn't want them to see you that way."

Scott went still, and Madeline realized she had hit on a vulnerable point. He couldn't tolerate the least sign of weakness in himself. At all costs, he would maintain his image of authority in front of his employees. Leaning his head on his hands, he waited in a subdued manner that almost frightened Madeline. He wasn't at all himself.

It was only a few minutes until a footman dressed in black and silver livery appeared at the office, but it seemed an eternity. Although the footman tried to appear unruffled, his eyes widened as he saw Scott. Madeline asked him to help Scott to his feet, and the servant complied in a dumbfounded manner. She wondered why it was such a surprise to see his master ill. Apparently Scott was so good at being a legend that it was easy for everyone, even his servants, to overlook the fact that he was only a man.

A crowd of actors and crew members had assembled outside the office, their faces registering everything from curiosity to alarm as they strained for a glimpse of Scott. "Perhaps you should all stand back," Madeline said. "It would be terrible if someone else became ill."

The group followed the suggestion at once, retreating to a respectful distance. "What's to be done now?" the property man asked of no one in particular. "With the duchess away and Mr. Scott sick, who's to manage everything?"

"I'll ask Mr. Scott," Madeline said, and ducked back into the office. The footman had eased Scott to a standing position. The blood had drained from his face, leaving it ashen. His gaze careened around the room before settling on Madeline. "Sir," she murmured, "shall I tell the company that you want Mr. Bennett to manage the theater in your absence?"

Bennett was the assistant stage director, usually called upon to manage rehearsals and arbitrate disputes when the duchess and Scott were otherwise occupied. Scott stared at her with fever-glazed eyes, and Madeline wondered if he had fully understood. Then he gave a short nod.

Returning to the group outside the office, Madeline repeated the instructions. Scott emerged, gripping the footman's shoulder, concentrating on the act of walking. It was a testament to his physical stamina that he was able to stand in such a condition.

Madeline led the way toward the entrance at the back of the theater. She heard Scott's rough breathing, the uneven pace of his feet, and knew he couldn't last much longer. The footman showed obvious signs of exertion as he supported Mr. Scott's increasing weight.

"We're almost there," Madeline said, hoping desperately that he wouldn't collapse.

They reached the back entrance and stepped outside, the caustic wind biting through the sleeves of Madeline's gown and numbing her cheeks. A second footman opened the door of a bronze-and-black-lacquered carriage. The vehicle was drawn by a team of perfectly matched chestnuts, their nostrils blowing gusts of steam in the freezing air. The footman lowered a folding step and glanced questioningly at Madeline.

She hesitated, staring at the luxurious vehicle with longing. She had no right to leave with Scott. Still, if there was a chance that he might need her in some way . . .

Madeline hurried into the carriage before she could change her mind. Grateful for the reprieve from the bitter temperature, she settled on a velvet-cushioned seat. The footmen grunted in the effort to load Scott into the space beside her, and he slumped in the corner, his complexion waxen, his eyelids sealed. His cloak had dropped from his shoulders, and Madeline drew the wool garment closer about his neck. Taking another rattling breath, he coughed harshly.

The carriage rolled away, the ride smooth and springy. The interior was finer than anything Madeline had ever seen, with highly polished wood, coffee-colored upholstering, and the intricate motif of the Capital Theatre painted in gold on the ceiling. Even her father, with his well-deserved pride in his own carriages, would have been impressed.

Her gaze returned to Scott, who looked vulnerable and large at the same time, like a felled lion. A jolt of the carriage wheels on the road caused him to groan. Automatically Madeline reached for him, pressing her cool hand to his forehead.

Her touch seemed to bring about a moment of lucidity, and his bruised-looking eyes opened into slits of startling blue. "M-Maddy," he said, clenching his teeth in the effort to keep them from chattering.

"Yes, Mr. Scott?" Her hand drifted to the side of his face, gently touching the dry, bristle-roughened skin.

"You shouldn't . . . have come with me."

"I'm sorry." She drew her hand away. "I know you're very protective of your privacy. You needn't worry, sir. I won't stay long. I just want to make certain you're all right."

"N-no, it's not that . . ." He clenched his jaw against a new bout of shivering. "You'll get sick," he said distinctly.

Madeline glanced at him in surprise. How many people in his condition would have given a thought to her welfare? Touched by the unexpected gallantry, she smiled. "I feel very well, Mr. Scott."

Seeming too exhausted to argue, Scott closed his eyes and lowered his head against the seat back. Madeline's smile faded, and she tried to remember what her nanny had done whenever she and her sisters had been sick . . . kept them warm, applied mustard plasters to their chests and heated soapstone to their feet, and fed them beef tea and milk toast. For a cough, Nanny had made a syrup of lemons and oil of sweet almonds. Beyond that, Madeline's medical knowledge was sadly lacking. She sighed, feeling utterly useless.

The carriage traveled into the quiet court suburb

of St. James Square, past a stone guard gate adorned with bronze griffins. Madeline peeked through the curtain at the carriage window as the vehicle progressed along a tree-lined drive to a mansion fronted with fluted columns.

As the carriage slowed to a halt, one of the footmen jumped from his platform and hit the ground running. He reached the double front doors and hammered vigorously. One of the doors opened, and the scene became a blur of activity.

A lad dressed in a thick coat and cap came to help the coachman stable the team. Two footmen reached for Mr. Scott, half-dragging, half-carrying him from the vehicle. They each wedged a shoulder beneath Scott's arms and brought him into the mansion, while Madeline followed. She felt as if she were treading on forbidden ground, intruding in a way that Scott would never have allowed if he were well.

They entered a magnificent entrance hall illuminated by a crystal chandelier strung in intricate loops. The entrance opened into a main room where a matronly housekeeper gave orders to a troop of housemaids. ". . . Set out fresh linens and water," she was saying in a voice that rang with authority. "Tilda, fetch my medicine case, and tell Gwyn to bring the jar of leeches. The doctor may wish to use them when he arrives."

A gray-haired butler was similarly engaged in giving instructions to the male servants, directing them to procure bottles of brandy and whiskey, and assist the valet in putting Scott to bed. Madeline stood to the side, watching helplessly as Scott was taken up a double-sided staircase of white and gray marble fashioned in a horseshoe shape.

The housekeeper quickly noticed Madeline's

presence and introduced herself as Mrs. Beecham. "Please forgive us, miss . . ."

"Ridley."

"Miss Ridley," the housekeeper repeated. "I'm afraid we're all rather distracted at the moment. This is an unusual situation."

"I understand."

The housekeeper's gaze swept over Madeline. Clearly she was trying to decide who Madeline was and exactly how she was acquainted with Mr. Scott, but she refrained from asking. "It was kind of you to accompany Mr. Scott from the theater," the woman remarked.

Madeline glanced in the direction they had taken him. "I only hope he'll be all right."

"Mr. Scott is being made as comfortable as possible until the doctor arrives. Would you care to wait in the downstairs parlor?"

"Yes, thank you."

Mrs. Beecham led her to a spacious parlor decorated in understated shades of gold and plum, with French armchairs upholstered in silk and velvet, and tables bearing books of poetry and engravings. One wall was covered with the tapestry of a French landscape. Between two floor-to-ceiling windows, a long table displayed Oriental figurines.

Noticing Madeline's interest in a small Japanese statue of a bearded old man holding a golden staff, the housekeeper smiled wryly. "The god of good fortune, Mr. Scott says. I couldn't begin to pronounce its name. He has others in his collection, all of them heathenish things."

"I like this one," Madeline said, touching the little man's beard with a fingertip. "I only hope he lives up to his reputation and brings good fortune to Mr. Scott."

"Some would say Mr. Scott has already enjoyed more than his share of luck," Mrs. Beecham commented, walking to the parlor door.

Left to her own devices, Madeline wandered to the parlor window, staring out at a row of topiaries and a marble fountain in the garden. It was a bright, wintry day, and the dormant trees in the orchard shuddered from gusts of wind.

Madeline shivered a little and retreated to an armchair, where she sat and tapped her foot nervously on the thickly carpeted floor. Noticing a wooden box on the table next to her, she picked it up curiously. The interior of the box was lined in silver, the top carved with the Shakespearean medal. On the bottom was the inscription "Presented to Mr. Logan Scott by the Stratford Corporation."

A voice interrupted her musings, and Madeline looked up to see a pair of housemaids bearing a tray of tea. "That box was carved from Shakespeare's mulberry tree," one of the maids said with pride. "The master is always getting awards an' such, on account of all 'is charity works and benefits."

Madeline smiled, observing that Scott certainly seemed to have the admiration and affection of his servants.

The maid set the tea tray on a low table. "Mrs. Beecham said for you to ring for one of us whenever you want something."

"Thank you, but I won't require anything. Mr. Scott's welfare is all that matters."

"Dr. Brooke is coming soon. 'E'll 'ave the master back in the pink in no time."

"I hope so," Madeline replied, picking up an empty china teacup and fidgeting with the delicate handle. She glanced at the door, wondering when the doctor would arrive and how long it would take him to issue a pronouncement on Scott's condition.

The maids left the parlor, whispering to each other as soon as they crossed the threshold. Madeline couldn't help but overhear a snippet of their conversation. "Do you think she's the latest? . . ."

"Nay."

"She's pretty enow."

"Aye, but she's only a spring lamb . . . not 'is sort at all."

Madeline frowned and set down the empty cup. She rose from the chair and paced around the room. The reference to her youth annoyed her profoundly. Suddenly aware of the straggling locks of hair that had slipped from her pins, Madeline sighed. No doubt she looked like an untidy child who had been romping out-of-doors.

Wandering to the gilded doors at the other end of the parlor, Madeline discovered that they opened into a music room, two long galleries, and a drawing room with a floor patterned in inlaid wood. There were art treasures everywhere: portraits and landscapes, marble statues, works of pottery and porcelain.

As Madeline toured the elegant rooms, she sensed that Scott had chosen the decor and the art himself. It was all a reflection of what he admired and wanted to be. He fascinated her. Madeline wanted to know him, to be trusted with his intimate thoughts . . . to be some small part of the world he had created for himself. But he had made it clear that he didn't want her. Feeling desolate, she made her way back to the main hall. By now the doctor must be upstairs examining Scott. The household was strangely quiet, as if the staff was holding its collective breath.

"Is there something you require, Miss Ridley?" the butler inquired, rising from a chair near the staircase.

"Yes." Madeline approached the marble steps, half-afraid that he would stop her from ascending. "I would like to know where Mr. Scott's room is located."

The butler was expressionless, but Madeline sensed his inner consternation. She knew that he and the servants were unclear about her relationship with Scott, whether she was merely an employee like themselves, or perhaps his latest paramour.

"The doctor is with him, miss," the butler said carefully. "If the parlor isn't to your liking, perhaps there is another place you would prefer to wait—"

"I would prefer to go to his room," Madeline said evenly, imitating the crisp tone she had always heard her mother use with the servants.

"Yes, Miss Ridley," came the reluctant reply. The butler rang for a footman and instructed the servant to show her to Scott's private rooms in the east wing.

The hall was illuminated by a long row of windows that shed light on four alcoves filled with statues, including one of a nude female bathing, which caused Madeline to color. Passing through an arch of gleaming mahogany, she entered a distinctly masculine suite of rooms with rich mahogany paneling, a set of antique German maps framed in carved rosewood, and Persian rugs underfoot.

The footman brought her to a closed door, where Mrs. Beecham was waiting. A housemaid stood nearby, ready to go running for any item that might be requested.

Mrs. Beecham's brows lifted as she saw Madeline. "Miss Ridley . . . didn't you find the parlor comfortable?"

"I wanted to find out if there has been any word yet."

Mrs. Beecham shook her head. "The doctor is still with him. I will inform you as soon as there is any news. In the meantime, the maid will accompany you to the receiving rooms downstairs."

Madeline prepared herself for an argument. "I would rather—"

She was interrupted by the click of the doorknob as the valet opened it from within. Falling silent, she waited as the doctor emerged.

Dr. Brooke was a man in his thirties, with a receding hairline and a pair of round spectacles that gave him an owlish look. He had a kind face and dark, solemn eyes. His gaze fell on Mrs. Beecham, then Madeline.

"I am Miss Ridley," Madeline said, coming forward. "I came to ask about Mr. Scott's welfare. I am his . . . companion."

The doctor took her hand and bowed politely.

"How is he?" the housekeeper asked.

Dr. Brooke's gaze encompassed them both. "Recently I've seen many cases like this. I'm sorry to say that this appears to be one of the worst. Rather surprising for a man of Mr. Scott's usual health . . . but he does nothing in moderation, does he?"

"I'm afraid not," the housekeeper replied ruefully.

"I'll visit again tomorrow, to see how the fever progresses," the doctor continued. "Unfortunately he hasn't yet come into the worst of it. Cool him with frequent applications of water and ice. I suggest feeding him jellies, broth, perhaps a spoonful of milk punch now and then."

"I have an old family recipe that calls for steeping eucalyptus leaves in brandy," Mrs. Beecham commented. "Might I give him a dose in the evenings?"

"I don't see why not." The doctor paused, his gaze lingering on Madeline. "Miss Ridley, may I ask if you intend to help care for Mr. Scott?"

"Yes," Madeline said firmly.

"Then I suggest that you limit your association with people outside the household. The fever is highly contagious. I wouldn't rule out the possibility that you may yet succumb to it."

Mrs. Beecham regarded Madeline with a perplexed expression. "I suppose we'll have to ready a room for you."

Madeline understood the woman's reluctance. None of Scott's staff had had any knowledge of her existence before now. They obviously cared for their master and were wary of allowing someone to intrude on his privacy when he was helpless to prevent it. "Thank you, Mrs. Beecham," she said quietly. "I assure you, my only intention is to help Mr. Scott . . . Logan . . . in every way I can."

The housekeeper nodded, still looking troubled, and gave instructions to the maid. In the meanwhile, Dr. Brooke bid them farewell and departed in the company of the footman. Taking the initiative, Madeline slipped through the half-open doorway into the bedroom.

It was simply furnished and decorated, with no artwork except a view of clouds and sky painted on the ceiling. The room contained a very large bed with a plum silk counterpane and feather pillows piled three deep at the headboard. Scott lay covered with a sheet and light blanket, the counterpane folded back to his feet. He had been dressed in a suit of flannels, the top half unbuttoned halfway down his chest. He slept as if he had been drugged, the side of his flushed face buried in a pillow.

As Madeline entered, the valet placed a jug of water and a pile of folded linens on the bedside table. A small armchair had been positioned nearby, but Madeline chose to sit on the edge of the mattress. The slight shift of her weight caused Logan to turn toward her with an incoherent mutter, his eyes still closed. His breath scraped in his throat.

"It's all right," Madeline said softly, soaking a linen cloth in the water, wringing it out and laying it on his hot forehead. The coolness seemed to soothe him, and he relaxed deeper into the pillow. She reached out and dared to stroke his beautiful hair, as she had so often longed to do. It was soft and thick beneath her fingers, like dark silk burnished with mahogany.

She studied his face, the pallor of his skin emphasizing the stark beauty of his bone structure. His lashes lay in feathery crescents on his cheeks, the eyelids trembling slightly as he drifted through fever-induced dreams. Such a proud, solitary man, rendered helpless in sleep, his lips parted like those of a child. If she were in love with him, it would devastate her to see him this way.

Madeline sat without moving, trying to understand the dull pain that had settled in her chest. If she were in love with him, the ache would never leave. The memories of him would haunt her every day for the rest of her life . . . because there would never be another man like him.

Briefly she thought of her own dilemma. There was so little time for her. Perhaps it was already too late, and her parents had discovered that she had left school. If they had, they would be frantic with worry. They would look for her—and once they found her, they would browbeat and threaten her until she crumpled under the pressure. She would end up as Lord Clifton's bride in spite of her best efforts to resist. Unless she were damaged goods.

She should leave here at once and find someone to have an affair with. No doubt there were far more willing targets than Logan Scott. She had never imagined it would have been so difficult to seduce him, not a man with his reputation. But she hadn't bargained on his complexity or his unexpected scruples. He had refused to dishonor her, and she wouldn't fool herself into thinking she could change his decision.

She wasn't needed here. Scott had servants to care for him, the services of an excellent doctor, more friends and acquaintances than he could count. He would recover without her help. Frowning, Madeline watched him sleep for a long time. She sat by the bed, changing the cloth on his forehead or spooning a few drops of tonic between his lips when the cough became troublesome.

Every now and then a servant came to ask if Madeline required anything, but she refused. Except for those brief intrusions, it seemed that there was no world outside the bedroom. Minutes stretched into hours, until the afternoon sky began to fade and evening shadows approached.

Just as Madeline considered sending for some

beef tea, Scott began to waken. He stirred and blinked, his eyes fever-bright. Gently Madeline removed the damp cloth from his head and resumed her seat on the edge of the bed. "Mr. Scott," she said, smiling at him.

He stared at her as if she were a figure in a dream, his expression curious and slightly detached, and then an answering smile hovered on his lips. He spoke in a rusty voice punctuated with harsh coughs. "It seems . . . I'll never get rid of you."

Madeline poured a glass of water and helped him to drink, keeping her hand on the glass and sliding her arm behind his head. Unsteadily he leaned back against her supporting arm as he took a few listless swallows. He was very heavy, and the muscles in her arm began to strain from holding him. When he had had enough, he turned his face away, and she eased him back to the pillow.

"Would you like me to leave?" she asked softly.

He closed his eyes, taking so long to answer that she thought he might have fallen asleep once more.

"Stay," he finally said.

"Is there someone I should send for to take care of you? A friend or relative—"

"No. I want you." He closed his eyes, the conversation finished. His fingers curled in a fold of her gown.

Despite her worry, Madeline wanted to smile. Even in his sickbed, he was as commanding as ever. For some reason, he wanted her to remain. He trusted her. She had no more thought of leaving. "Logan," she murmured, testing his name on her lips.

Somehow, after her ambitious scheme had failed, she found herself standing watch in a sickroom. Nothing had gone according to plan. Strangest of all, she didn't even care about her own problems. All she wanted was to see Logan well again.

She went to the writing table positioned beneath one of the windows, and wrote a note to Mrs. Florence, explaining the situation. Folding it neatly, she sealed the letter with a stick of brown wax, then rang for a maid and gave her the letter to be delivered to Mrs. Florence's residence on Somerset Street. "Please send a footman to collect my belongings," she added, and the housemaid bobbed in a curtsy before departing.

Madeline returned to her bedside vigil. It seemed that Logan's condition deteriorated by the hour, the fever strengthening its hold and advancing stealthily. He was too groggy to argue as she fed him sips of beef tea. After Madeline's persistent efforts, he had managed to eat perhaps half a cup of the nourishing broth; then he fell asleep once more.

Somewhere in the house a large clock chimed twelve times, its tone deep and sonorous. Despite herself Madeline grew weary, her head bobbing as a wave of sleepiness nearly overcame her. She stood and stretched in an effort to waken herself, turning with a start as she heard someone enter the room.

Mrs. Beecham and the valet approached the bed. "How is he?" the housekeeper asked in a friendlier manner than she had used before. It seemed that she had adjusted to the idea of Madeline's presence and had decided to set aside her suspicions.

"The fever is worse."

"That is what Dr. Brooke said to expect," Mrs. Beecham replied in a matter-of-fact tone. "Mr.

Scott's valet, Denis, is going to assist me in sponging him with cold water. Perhaps that will help to bring the fever down. You may wish to rest for a few hours. I thought you would like to occupy the small bedroom in Mr. Scott's private suite."

"That is very kind of you," Madeline replied. "But I want to be here if Mr. Scott needs me—"

"I'll watch over him until you return," the housekeeper assured her. "You'll need a few hours of sleep, Miss Ridley, in order to be fresh for tomorrow."

The point was well taken. Madeline was exhausted, and there were many long hours, even days, ahead before the fever would run its course. "Thank you," she said, and the housekeeper showed her to a guest room only a few doors away.

Her gowns and other garments had been put away in a mahogany armoire. The bed was covered by a blue silk canopy that matched the embroidered counterpane. Madeline declined the offer of a maid to help her change, preferring to undress herself.

Donning a prim white nightgown with rows of pleats at the neck, Madeline climbed into bed. It seemed that she had never been so tired. Sleep claimed her immediately, the welcome darkness filling her mind.

At the first ray of morning light, Madeline snapped awake, feeling somewhat refreshed. Eagerly she reached for the robe that matched her nightgown and hurried to Logan's room, her bare feet quickly chilled in the cold morning air. A maid was lighting a fire in the grate while Mrs. Beecham collected a pile of damp linens that had been used to cool Logan during the night.

There were smudges beneath the housekeeper's eyes, and her forehead was tracked with lines that had not been there the previous day.

"There is no change," she said in answer to Madeline's unspoken question.

Madeline went to the bed and stared down at Logan. His skin was dry and burning, his lips slightly chapped. The suit of flannels had been removed, and a single sheet rode low on his waist, exposing the muscled lines of his torso, the dark patches of hair beneath his arms, the hollow of his navel. She had never seen a naked man before. Her gaze strayed to the area of his body covered by the sheet, the endless length of his legs, the intimate shape of his loins draped with thin white linen. Her cheeks prickled with a modest blush, and she turned to find Mrs. Beecham's gaze on her.

"You're not his 'companion,' as you claimed," the housekeeper said with quiet conviction. "Whatever you are to him . . . you're not his mistress."

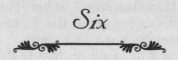

## Six

*Caught off-guard*, Madeline couldn't reply at first. Her heart changed its rhythm, and she tried to think above its rapid thundering. "How can you be certain?"

Mrs. Beecham smiled. "Everything about you proclaims it. Your nightgown, for one thing . . . a garment intended only for sleeping. Your manner, the way you look at him . . . it's clear that you haven't been intimate with him. You're a well-bred girl, barely out of the schoolroom. There is a particular kind of woman that suits Mr. Scott's taste . . . the kind that wears silk peignoirs and sleeps until two o'clock in the afternoon and would never lower herself to the drudgery of nursing a sick man. You are not his mistress."

"I work at the Capital," Madeline admitted. "Not as an actress . . . I'm only an assistant. But I am Mr. Scott's friend. At least, I hope he considers me as such."

"And you're in love with him," Mrs. Beecham remarked.

"Oh, no," Madeline said, feeling the blood leave her face. "As I said, my feeling toward him is friendship . . . and admiration, of course—"

"You've gone to a great deal of trouble, and placed your own health at risk, only for the sake of friendship?"

Stricken, Madeline stared at her. Her throat felt tight, and the dull ache of the night before had worked its way back into her chest.

"Well, there's no need to discuss it," Mrs. Beecham said, seeming touched by whatever she saw in Madeline's face. "Your reasons for being here are none of my concern. You may stay as long as you wish . . . until Mr. Scott says otherwise."

Madeline nodded and sat down, feeling for the edges of the chair before lowering herself into it.

"He hasn't eaten for a while," she heard the housekeeper remark. "I'll send up some milk toast. Perhaps you can coax him to take some."

Madeline was only half aware of the woman's departure. She stared at the sleeping man's profile. This morning there was a shadow of bristle on his face, imparting the swarthiness of a sea captain or highwayman.

Taking his large hand between hers, she stroked the smooth back until she reached his hair-dusted wrist. His hand was strong and well-tended, the nails short and buffed to velvety smoothness. There were no rings on his fingers, only the white marks of a few nicks and scars. She remembered the touch of his hand on her face, her breast . . . the gentle brush of his fingertips.

Madeline wanted him to caress her again. She wanted things from him that she could never have. She wasn't aware that she had lowered her head to his hand until she felt his skin against her lips. Turning his palm up, she pressed her mouth to the creased hollow and tasted the salt of her own tears.

Logan would never want her . . . he had made that clear enough. And she had made any sort of trust between them impossible by approaching him with lies and an assumed name, and making him the object of a sordid plan. How could a man with his pride forgive her for such behavior? He couldn't.

She had never felt this kind of pain—persistent, heavy, crushing out every fragile flicker of happiness inside her. How ironic that she had pursued her goal with such cool determination, and ended up with her heart broken. She had always understood the social and even physical risks she was taking, but never the emotional ones. She hadn't planned on falling in love with Logan.

She whispered into his palm, curling his loose fingers as if to contain the precious words within his hand.

She would leave the minute his fever broke. She would not insult him, or coarsen her own feelings, by using him for the purpose she had originally intended. All at once she was glad that they had not made love, that she hadn't hurt or betrayed him. She wouldn't have been able to live with herself if she had.

There was a tap at the door, and a maid came in bearing a tray with tea and milk toast. Following Madeline's directions, she left the tray on the bedside table and helped prop Logan up with extra pillows. Madeline thanked the maid and bid her to leave, and sat beside Logan as he awakened. His lashes lifted, and he gazed at Madeline for a long moment. It seemed he didn't recognize her at first. After a while his lips formed her name.

"Maddy . . . the Capital . . ." The velvet-and-wine voice had been reduced to an arid rasp.

"Mr. Bennett is managing the company," Madeline replied, hesitating before she pulled up the sheet that had ridden low on his hips. He didn't seem to be aware of his state of undress. "I'm certain he has everything under control."

Logan didn't reply, but Madeline could see the torment in his eyes. She doubted that he had ever entrusted his theater to someone else's keeping before. "Shall I request that he send a daily report until you return?"

Logan nodded, leaning against the stack of pillows, his eyes closing.

"You mustn't fall asleep yet," Madeline said, placing a hand on his bare shoulder to shake him slightly. His skin seemed to scorch her hand. "First you must eat."

"No." He began to turn onto his side, gasping with the effort.

"Then I won't give you any news from Mr. Bennett," she said evenly.

All movement stopped, and his eyes slitted open. He glared at her like a baleful cat.

"Just some tea and a few bites of breakfast," Madeline coaxed, repressing the sudden urge to laugh. If not for her worry, she would have enjoyed having him in her power. Carefully she held the cup of hot tea to his lips, encouraging him to sip the sweet liquid. He complied, seeming to enjoy the warmth of the tea as it trickled down his throat. However, the first bite of buttered toast soaked in hot milk—classic sickroom fare—caused him to turn his head with a sound of disgust.

"Milk," he muttered with scratchy loathing.

"I'm not fond of it myself," she admitted, carving out another spoonful of mush. "However, you're in no position to argue. Here, try another bite."

He refused with an incomprehensible mutter, his face twisting.

"Mr. Bennett's report," she reminded him, and he responded with a hostile glare. "Please," she murmured, changing her tactic. "I promise, someday when I'm sick, you can travel to wherever I am and personally feed me bowls full of milk toast."

The idea seemed to inspire him enough to choke down a few more bites. "Thank you," she finally said, setting aside the bowl. She leaned over him to remove the extra pillows and smoothed his hair. "You'll be well soon, and you can choose your revenge."

He turned his face into the coolness of her hand and promptly fell asleep, his breath coming in rattling surges. Continuing to lean over him, Madeline traced the fine curve of his ear . . . small ears for such a large man . . . and kissed the indentation where his jaw met his throat. For an instant she knew an absurd rush of happiness, being near the man she loved, having the freedom to touch him. She would do anything, go to any lengths to please him. Eagerly she went to ring for a servant, and sat at the writing desk to dash off a missive to Mr. Bennett.

Mrs. Beecham, Denis, and two other servants came in shifts to help Madeline nurse Logan. It was difficult work, constantly sponging and cooling his body until her sleeves were soaked to the elbow and the front of her gown was damp. At first the sight of his nakedness had startled and fascinated her, but there was little enjoyment in staring at his body, no matter how attractive, when he was suffering with fever.

Madeline worked ceaselessly in the darkened room, forcing liquid between Logan's lips, cooling his skin until her shoulders and back ached from bending over him. Stains from beef broth, water, and herbal infusions covered her gown from neck to hem. Occasionally Mrs. Beecham came to urge her to take a bath or nap, but Madeline couldn't bring herself to leave Logan.

Iced sheets and frozen compresses had no effect on the fever, which raged out of control. By early afternoon, Logan had descended into a delirium from which he couldn't be roused. Anxious servants came to the door of the private suite, volunteering folk remedies and family recipes, even bringing powders and amulets that they swore would be effective.

Careful not to offend the givers' dignity, Mrs. Beecham accepted the offerings and deposited them in a box to be discarded later. "Powdered bone dust," she said with a rueful smile, showing Madeline a handkerchief that had been given by one of the footmen. It was filled with a handful of fine gray crumbs. "He bought it at a shop in London—they told him it was ground from a unicorn's horn and would cure any illness. Dear man, to sacrifice his 'magic remedy' for the master's sake."

"They have great affection for him, don't they?" Madeline asked from her position at the bedside, her gaze fastened on Logan's face.

"Mr. Scott is a unique man," the housekeeper replied, filling linen bags with crushed ice and piling them on a tray. "He prides himself on never being ruled by his emotions, yet he can't bear the sound of a child crying or the sight of someone frightened or in trouble. The things he's done for his own servants . . . why, it would amaze you." She paused in her task, looking thoughtful. "Mr. Scott has a way of drawing people close, making them depend on him . . . and yet at the same time he manages to hold them at a distance."

"It's because he has absolute control that way," Madeline said, picking up the ice bags and packing them around the still form. "He's protecting himself."

The housekeeper looked at Madeline with some surprise. "You seem to understand him quite well."

"Not really. I just know that he would choose to deny himself something he wants rather than risk being hurt."

"I see." Realization dawned in Mrs. Beecham's face, and new interest appeared in her gaze. "You are the 'something' he wants, aren't you? And yet he turned you away."

Perhaps it was the mixture of weariness and worry that made Madeline admit the truth. "He said that any involvement would hurt us both," she said, lowering her face until a few strands of hair dangled over her cheeks.

The housekeeper rubbed her chilled hands together as she contemplated Madeline's statement. "He was probably right, Miss Ridley. If I were you, I would accept his word on that."

"I have. The only reason I'm here is that I can't walk away from him while he's sick . . . without saying good-bye."

"Miss Ridley." The housekeeper's tone was gentle. She waited until Madeline looked at her with glittering eyes. "In his heart, I believe he knows that you truly care for him. It's a fine gift you've given him."

Madeline set her jaw to stop its trembling, blinking hard against her tears as she took her place in the bedside chair once more.

\* \* \*

The following day there was an unexpected visit from Lord Drake, who had learned of his old friend's illness and had come to the estate without delay. He was standing in the entrance hall, asking questions of Mrs. Beecham, when he happened to catch sight of Madeline passing by with an armload of soiled linens.

"Ah, the little wench from the theater," Lord Drake exclaimed, gesturing for Madeline to approach him. A grin crossed his face, but it didn't reach his worried eyes. "Trust Jimmy to have a pretty nurse to attend him!"

"Jimmy?" Madeline asked in confusion.

Lord Drake smiled faintly. "He wasn't always Logan Scott, you know."

Mrs. Beecham took the linens from Madeline. "I'll dispense with these, Miss Ridley," she murmured, glancing at Madeline's disheveled appearance. "You might try resting for a little while."

"Yes, I might," Madeline replied, rubbing her aching temples. "If you'll excuse me, Lord Drake—"

"Wait," he said, his cocky demeanor dropping away. As Madeline stared into his face, puffy and pale from too much alcohol and not enough sleep, she sensed that underneath his reprobate exterior, there was sincere worry for his friend. "I came to offer my services . . . to ask if there is something I can do for Jimmy. He's my oldest friend, you know. Never been sick a day in his life. I knew it was serious if it kept him from his bloody theater. Tell me what he needs—anything—and I'll get it for him."

"Thank you," Madeline replied, touched by the earnest note in his voice, "but I don't think there is much that anyone can do for him." She felt her

throat tighten, and she couldn't go on, only looking at him with helpless desperation.

It seemed that from her expression, Lord Drake
understood the seriousness of the situation. "It's
that bad?" he asked, and swore quietly. "I want to
talk to him."

Madeline shook her head. "He's delirious, Lord
Drake."

"I have to see him."

"But you may catch his fever—"

"I don't give a damn. Jimmy's like a brother to
me. Take me to him . . . please."

After a long hesitation, she led him upstairs. The
lamp had been turned low in Logan's room.
Robbed of all expression, his face was masklike,
with fitful breaths passing through his dry lips. He
hardly resembled himself, his body lax and helpless.

"My God," Madeline heard Lord Drake mutter
as he approached the bed. He stared at Logan's still
form and shook his head, seeming bewildered.
"Dammit, Jimmy," he murmured, "you're not going to die." He smiled crookedly. "For one thing, I
owe you a bloody fortune, and it's going to take me
years to pay you back. For another . . . you're the
only anchor I've got." He sighed and scrubbed his
hands through his long dark locks in a gesture that
struck Madeline as oddly familiar. She had seen
Logan pull and tug at his own hair just that way, in
moments of tension or distraction. "I'm warning
you, old boy . . . make plans to recover, or you'll
answer to me."

Lord Drake turned and walked away from the
bed. He paused by Madeline and spoke with
difficulty. "If you're certain you don't need my
services, I'm going out to get stinking drunk."

"That won't help anyone," she replied.

"It will help *me*, Miss Ridley, I assure you." He rubbed his forehead. "I'll see myself out."

Doctor Brooke visited in the evening, and Madeline waited outside the room with Mrs. Beecham as he tended to Logan. After a short time, the doctor emerged. "You appear to have done an excellent job of nursing," he remarked, but his tone was one of consolation, not reassurance.

Although his face was composed and he had the same pleasant manner as the day before, Madeline sensed that something had changed. "Do you think the fever will break soon?" she asked. "It can't last much longer."

"No, it can't, Miss Ridley. Not without killing him. He's in a bad way. You must prepare yourself for the possibility that he may not recover."

It took a moment for Madeline to understand what he had said. She waited for Mrs. Beecham to respond, but the housekeeper was silent. On her face, Madeline saw the same frozen expression that must be on her own.

Madeline looked back at the doctor, while denial welled up inside her. "Prescribe something, then. Tell me what must be done."

"He's beyond mine or anyone's help, Miss Ridley. At this point, I can suggest nothing other than prayer."

"Prayer," Madeline exclaimed bitterly, wanting something far more substantial.

"I'll come by tomorrow morning. Continue to give him liquids and cool him as best you can."

"That's all?" Madeline asked incredulously. "They said you were the best doctor in London . . . they said you would cure him! You can't leave without doing something."

Dr. Brooke sighed. "I don't work miracles, Miss Ridley, and I've far too many cases like this to attend to. Most of them have survived, but there are a few instances in which the fever cannot be overcome. I could try bleeding him, but it hasn't brought about a significant improvement in the patients I've already tried it on."

"But . . . he was perfectly healthy only three days ago," Madeline cried, bewildered and suddenly furious, as if the doctor were responsible for the life that ebbed from Logan's body.

Staring into her pale face, Dr. Brooke sought to give her comfort. "He's a young man with a great deal to live for. Sometimes that makes a difference." He straightened his coat and nodded to the footman who had come to show him downstairs.

"What does he have to live for?" Madeline said scornfully, striding back into the sickroom with her fists clenched. "The theater?" It was only a building, a place where he could lose himself. He had no family, no lover, no one to whom he had given his heart.

She thought of the mountains of flowers and gifts that had accumulated in the receiving room, sent by friends and acquaintances to express their concern. There was even a basket of jellies from Mrs. Florence, tied with a jaunty blue bow. How could a man who knew so many people, a man so admired and celebrated, end up dying alone?

She wasn't aware that she had spoken her last thought aloud until she heard Mrs. Beecham's reply.

"It's what he wants, Miss Ridley. And he's not alone. He asked you to stay, didn't he?"

"I don't want to watch him die."

"Are you going to leave, then?"

Madeline shook her head and wandered to the bedside. Logan twisted and murmured in a delirium, as if he were trying to escape an inferno. "Someone must inform the Duchess of Leeds," she said. "She will want to know." She went to the writing desk, extracted a sheet of paper, and dipped a pen in ink. Her fingers were chapped and stiff as she addressed the note. *Mr. Scott's condition has worsened* . . . she wrote. Her penmanship, usually so neat, was cramped. *According to the doctor, he is not expected—*

She stopped writing and stared down at the letters, which seemed to dance before her eyes. "I can't," she said, and replaced the pen in its holder.

Mrs. Beecham went to the desk and finished the task for her. "I will have it sent at once," she remarked, and left the room as if she couldn't stay a moment longer.

As midnight approached, a new doctor arrived, the personal physician to the Duke and Duchess of Leeds. He was a kindly older man with an air of competence that gave Madeline a flicker of hope. "With your permission, the duchess sent me to examine the patient," he said to Madeline. "Perhaps there is something I can do for him."

"I hope so," Madeline replied, welcoming him into the room. She stayed as the doctor conducted his examination. By now she had become so familiar with Logan's body that she was beyond embarrassment. She knew every line of the long bones, the curves of muscle so close beneath the skin, the latent power that reminded her of a slumbering lion.

Madeline's hopes died quickly as she realized that there was nothing the doctor could recommend beyond what was already being done. Before departing, he left his own elixirs, but Madeline sensed that he didn't have much hope for their efficacy.

"Miss Ridley," Mrs. Beecham said, approaching her, "you've been with Mr. Scott all day. I'll watch him for a while, and then Denis will have a turn."

Madeline smiled at the housekeeper, who looked exhausted. "I'm not tired," Madeline replied, though she ached with weariness. Her eyes felt swollen and gritty, and her arms were raw to the elbow from exposure to ice and poultices. "I'll stay a little longer."

"Are you certain?" Mrs. Beecham asked.

Madeline nodded. "I would like to be alone with him."

"Very well. Ring for me or Denis if you need help."

The door closed, and the room was lit only by a lamp flame and the coals in the grate. The glow touched Logan's face, glazing his profile with burgundy light. Madeline pressed an ice-filled cloth over his forehead, but he dislodged it, his movements increasingly violent.

"Hush," she said repeatedly, stroking his hot skin.

Unguarded in his delirium, he uttered garbled lines from plays and spoke to unseen people. Madeline sat with him in the near-darkness, her face turning crimson. He used words she had never heard before, saying things that shocked and aroused her, until the hair prickled on her arms. He filled the air with obscenities until Madeline felt she would do anything to make him stop. "Please," she murmured, laying a cool cloth on his forehead, "you must be quiet—"

She gasped as he caught her wrist, his hand

closing until the fragile bones threatened to snap. At the sound of her soft cry, his grip relaxed, and he seemed confused. He said a woman's name . . . Olivia . . . his voice turned venomous. He wanted to kill her, he said. She had taken everything from him. He wept and cursed, his suffering so acute that Madeline was wrenched with jealousy.

*Haven't you ever been in love with anyone?* she had asked him not long ago.

*Once,* he had replied. *It didn't work.*

It was clear that Olivia was the woman he had loved, and that she had betrayed him. Madeline stroked Logan's hair and murmured to him, using her slight weight to subdue him until his body relaxed beneath her. "I would never leave you if I had a choice," she whispered, her heart pressed to his. "I would never hurt you. I love you." Passionately she kissed his hot face and dry lips. "I love you," she repeated, wishing desperately that she could pour her strength into him.

He made an incoherent sound and went still, sinking further into the fever.

Madeline lifted herself away and rested her hand on his chest. His breath was only a weak stirring beneath his ribs. She felt the vitality draining from him, and she was terrified to sleep. He was going to die in her arms, she thought, and a knot of cold despair formed in her stomach.

Slowly Madeline knelt on the floor. Despite a lifetime of regular church attendance and weekly religious instruction at school, she had never been a person of strong faith. She was too rebellious in nature, too resentful of what her mother had assured her was "God's plan" for her to marry Lord Clifton. It had always seemed that God's wishes were to make her life as joyless as possible. But if He were truly merciful, He would accept her bargain . . . and she would never again dare to ask Him for anything.

Carefully she folded her hands together and prayed, investing her soul in each word. It was an unexpected relief to pour out her fear and longing. For the first time in her life, it seemed that prayer was not just a useless ritual, but a confession told to a loving friend. ". . . I ask forgiveness for my sins," she whispered in the dim light. "I'll be an obedient daughter and do everything my parents wish. I'll marry Lord Clifton and serve him in every way I must without complaining . . . as long as You make him well. I don't care what happens to me anymore. All I want is for him to live. He doesn't deserve to die so young. You must let him live. . . ."

She wasn't aware of how long she prayed. When she finally arose, her knees were numb and cramped from the floor, and she was slightly dizzy. When she returned to Logan's side, she packed fresh ice bags and placed them around his body.

Many more supplications passed through her lips as the night wore on. She felt as if she were in a dream that would never end. Mechanically she worked without stopping, forcing Logan to drink, calming his delirious ravings until at last he fell utterly silent. She scarcely noticed when the lavender light of dawn ventured through the French glass doors that opened onto a small balcony.

"Miss Ridley."

Madeline jerked and turned toward the voice.

Mrs. Beecham approached with the valet, their faces blank with dread. "How is he?" the housekeeper asked, coming to the bed and looking at Logan's still form. Madeline watched silently, her body swaying, a dripping rag clutched in her hand.

The housekeeper placed her palm on Logan's forehead. After a long moment she turned to Madeline, peace and relief spreading over her face. "Thank God. The fever has broken." Gently she used a dry corner of the sheet to blot the beads of sweat on his skin.

Madeline watched without comprehending. The valet approached her, speaking with the trace of a French accent. "Everything is all right, *mademoiselle*. He'll be well again soon."

Dizzily she turned toward him, not daring to believe the truth. She tried to remember his name. "Denis? . . . " she asked through dry lips, and the room seemed to tip sideways. She felt his wiry arms close around her, and for the first time in her life, she fainted.

As Logan awoke, it seemed that he drifted upward from heavy layers of water and darkness, his body becoming lighter until he finally broke through the surface. He felt sluggish and weak. It would have been easy to sink back into the mist of sleep, but one thought clattered through his brain, forcing him awake. Madeline. Opening his eyes, he waited until the blur had cleared. She wasn't there. His lips parted, but the only sound he made was a harsh croak.

"Ah, Mr. Scott." The housekeeper's familiar face appeared. "We've all been quite worried for the past few days," she said with a smile. "Thank heaven, you're much better now. You must want something to drink." She lifted his head and offered him a few sips of tepid broth. Logan drank the liquid, which had a salty, faintly metallic taste.

He thought of asking about the Capital, but at the moment the subject paled in importance next to the other question in his mind. He remembered Madeline's presence all through the fever. He had felt her hands on him, her gentle breath on his face as she recalled him from torturous dreams. *Maddy*, he thought, wanting her, craving her. But she was gone. Had she been there at all, or had he merely imagined her?

He listened without interest to the housekeeper's chatter, vaguely registering that Dr. Brooke would be visiting later in the day, that the Leedses had been concerned enough to send their own doctor, that the entire household staff was rejoicing in his recovery. His fingers plucked at the freshly laundered bedclothes, and he focused on the rectangle of daylight that came in through the parted curtains at the French doors. Then Mrs. Beecham said something that captured his attention.

". . . Perhaps Miss Ridley will come to see you later in the day, though I suspect tomorrow morning is more likely—"

"She's here?" He struggled to sit up, his gaze riveted on the housekeeper.

"Mr. Scott, you should not exert yourself—"

"Where?" he barked, levering himself upward, cursing as he discovered how weak he was.

"Miss Ridley is sleeping only a few doors away. I doubt I could wake her, sir. She insisted on caring for you the past three days and nights, hardly resting or eating. The poor lamb finally fainted this morning, after she learned that your fever had passed." Mrs. Beecham paused as she saw the look on his face. "Oh, you needn't worry, sir," she said hastily, "she's not ill. 'Tis only exhaustion. I'm sure she'll be fine after several hours of sleep."

Logan's mouth felt pinched and dry. He reached for a glass of water on the bedside table, unsteadily navigating it to his mouth. "Why didn't you make her rest?" he demanded scratchily. "There was no need to let her work herself into exhaustion."

"There was no way to stop her. She insisted on taking care of you—"

"Bring me a robe."

"Sir?" Mrs. Beecham seemed appalled as she realized that he intended to get out of bed. "Mr. Scott, you can't possibly mean to . . . why, it would be madness . . ."

"Ring for Denis," Logan said, with no thought save that he had to see Maddy for himself. "And send for the doctor."

"But sir, I told you he'll be calling later in the day—"

"I want—" He stopped as a harsh cough was torn from his chest. Gripping the glass of water, he took another swallow. "I want him to see Miss Ridley. *Now*." He had to be certain that Maddy was well, that it was indeed exhaustion and not the beginning stage of illness that had brought about her collapse.

Mrs. Beecham retreated to the door. "I'll send for the doctor," she said crisply, "but it will be no service to Miss Ridley, waking her after all she's been through. And before you attempt to leave the bed, I suggest that you eat something. I'll have a maid bring up an egg custard and some toast."

Logan subsided against the pillows as the house-keeper left, though it was hardly by choice. He was as unsteady as a colt. His unmanageable limbs hardly seemed to belong to him. For a man who had always enjoyed unusual health and agility, his weakness was maddening. Cursing beneath his breath, he leaned back until his head stopped spinning.

Despite Dr. Brooke's assurances that Madeline was not afflicted with the fever, Logan was not satisfied.

"My friend," Dr. Brooke said with a laugh, "you needn't expend your energy worrying over Miss Ridley. I assure you, she's quite healthy, only a little tired. Tomorrow morning should see her back to her usual self. It's your own health you should concern yourself with. You mustn't go charging back to your usual schedule, or your recovery will take twice the time it should. Stay in bed for at least a fortnight, and refrain from any exertion." He winked as he added, "That includes any amorous inclinations, though I'll admit I would be sorely tempted if I were in your place. Miss Ridley is a delightful creature."

Logan was annoyed by the doctor's statement, experiencing a rare stab of jealousy. Scowling, he tapped his fingers on the counterpane, signaling his impatience for Brooke to leave.

"Very well," Dr. Brooke murmured, "there's no need for me to return unless you bring about a relapse. Follow my advice, Scott, and try not to overdo."

Logan grunted in assent, continuing to drum his fingers until the man was gone. Then he reached for the bellpull and rang for Denis.

Overriding the valet's objections, Logan commandeered his help to walk to Madeline's room. The amount of exertion it required amazed him.

When he finally crossed the threshold, his lungs and heart were laboring to accommodate the demands he had made on his body. Releasing his hold on the valet's shoulder, Logan went to the bed alone. "Leave," he said brusquely. "I'll ring if I want your help."

"*Oui, monsieur*," Denis replied, his tone littered with skepticism. "But I think with the two of you in such a condition, a *rendez-vous* is not such a good plan—"

"Go, Denis."

The door closed behind him. Logan stared down at the still figure on the bed. Madeline lay on her side like a child, her hands loosely curled, her breasts covered by a modest white gown that reached her throat. Logan sat beside her, touching a lock of golden-brown hair that streamed across the pillow. She stirred and resettled her face against the pillow, her breath resuming its deep rhythm.

He saw that her hands were reddened from the days of nursing him, and a flush warmed his face. The feeling was not one of embarrassment—he had no shame when it came to matters of nakedness and physical intimacy. Rather, it was the sense that she had claimed a part of him that he couldn't retrieve . . . he felt bound to her. While part of him resented the feeling, another part welcomed it.

He wondered what he would do with her. One thing was certain—he couldn't send her away now. She had launched into his life and wedged herself into every private corner, and it seemed that he had no choice but to accept her. Why not take the enjoyment she offered? She was young, beautiful, and fearless, possessing a resilient optimism that he had come to admire. His gaze moved over the outline of her body, cocooned in linen and wool blankets. Lightly he touched her breast, his fingers shaping over the soft mound until it nearly filled his hand. His thumb drew across the tip in a small circle, luring the nipple into a swelling point. Madeline murmured in her sleep, and the bed-clothes rustled as her knees drew up slightly.

Logan smiled, smoothing the silken hair on the pillow. For a moment he allowed himself to think of the things he would teach her, the pleasures they would share, until the heat of arousal began to fill him. Grimacing wryly, he stood up from the bed. Too soon for such thoughts. There would be time enough when they had both recuperated. Then he would indulge Madeline's every fantasy . . . and more than a few of his own.

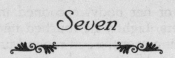

# Seven

*Madeline awakened* and lay still for a few minutes, slowly recollecting all that had happened.
She began to rise from bed and winced at the ache
of her muscles. The worst of it was in her back and
shoulders. Cautiously she stretched, gasping as the
pain brought smarting tears to her eyes.

A housemaid knocked at the door and entered
with a bucket of coal to refresh the grate. "Miss
Ridley," she said, seeming gratified to find Madeline awake. "Mrs. Beecham says we should all
thank you for what you done for the master."

"How is he?"

"Oh, very well, miss! Sleeping most o' the time.
When 'e's awake, 'e rings for someone every few
minutes, wanting food, liquor, books, an' such, but
Mrs. Beecham said not to bring anything like that."

Madeline smiled, reflecting that it wasn't in
Logan's nature to be a good sickroom patient. She
wanted to go to him at once. Self-consciously she
put her hands to her unwashed hair.

"We'll pour a bath for you in the dressing room,"
the maid said. "And I'll bring a breakfast tray. Mrs.
Beecham said you were to have anything you
wanted." She went to the armoire and opened it to
reveal some garments. "These came for you last
evening."

The new gowns . . . Mrs. Florence must have sent them from Somerset Street as soon as they were delivered. Murmuring her thanks, Madeline approached the armoire and lifted out the yellow corded silk, grimacing at the ache in her shoulder. Noticing her expression, the maid quickly deduced the reason. "I'll 'urry with the bath, miss. May'ap the warm water will ease your pains a bit."

Two maids helped Madeline to bathe and wash her long hair, rinsing it with violet-scented water until it gleamed. They wrapped her in warmed towels and brushed her hair before the fire, brought a tray of ham, soufflé, and fruit, and pressed every last wrinkle from her gown.

They arranged her hair in a neat braided coil on top of her head, letting a few waving strands fall on either side of her face, and helped her to dress. The yellow gown was cut with a simplicity that suited her, giving her an appearance that was neither too young nor too sophisticated. She enjoyed the rustle of the scalloped hem around her feet, and the crisp fabric that flowed down to a cuffed wrist. As the maids exclaimed admiringly, Madeline felt a blush rising from the scooped neckline.

"Quite lovely," Mrs. Beecham said, coming into the room with an approving smile. "Are you feeling better this morning, Miss Ridley?"

"Yes, thank you. About Mr. Scott—"

"He's been asking about you every five minutes," the housekeeper replied. "In fact, I've come to tell you that he requires your presence immediately."

Madeline smiled. "It sounds as if he's nearly back to his old self."

"It won't be long," the housekeeper agreed.

Madeline followed Mrs. Beecham to the suite's main bedroom. As they approached, there was a stream of clearly audible complaints.

". . . I don't want any more broth," Logan said, lecturing a hapless servant who had brought him a tray from the kitchen. "I want meat, bread, coffee—how the hell am I supposed to live on paste and broth? And if you bring me anything else with milk in it, I'm going to—"

He stopped abruptly as his gaze fell on Madeline. "Maddy," he said, his voice still raspy.

Like her, he had bathed recently. His hair was still damp, his face gleaming from a precise shave. He was dressed in white flannels that had been buttoned up to the neck, but the memory of what was beneath them, every inch of smooth skin and hard muscle, was forever imprinted in her mind. Now, seeing him fully alert and commanding, it already seemed impossible that she had seen and touched him so intimately.

Discreetly Mrs. Beecham and the servant departed, leaving them alone together.

"You're not a very accommodating patient," Madeline said, coming to the bedside.

"I'm going mad," he said. "I want you to find out from Bennett what the hell is going on at my theater, and bring me something to do—"

"You're supposed to rest," she replied, enjoying his enforced helplessness as well as the signs of his returning temper. "I'm certain the doctor must have told you not to strain yourself."

"It's a strain to sit here and be treated like a bloody invalid."

Smiling, Madeline leaned over until their noses were nearly touching. She stared directly into his eyes, her own gleaming with challenge. "You *are* an invalid, Mr. Scott."

His gaze dropped to her mouth, and time seemed to stop for a moment. "I won't be for long," he said softly.

There was something new between them, a flow of awareness and intimacy that made Madeline breathless. "For now you must stay in bed."

He glanced at the valley of her cleavage, the curves of her breasts barely contained in yellow silk. When his gaze returned to her face, blue flame danced in his eyes. "Make me."

Madeline backed away hastily. "I'll fetch some books and papers, a-and I'll read Mr. Bennett's report to you."

"That's a start," he said. "You can also bring me some decent food."

"I can't do that. Dr. Brooks wouldn't approve. You wouldn't be able to keep it down anyway."

"*Food*, Maddy," he said imperiously, watching as she left the room. "And come back quickly. I've never been so bloody bored in my life."

Madeline remained at the mansion for two weeks, aware that she would always regard this time as the happiest of her life. Each day she considered leaving but decided to stay just a little longer. She knew her behavior was irresponsible, but it didn't matter. The knowledge that her time with Logan was limited made it even more precious. She had not forgotten her vow to God to return home and marry Lord Clifton. Her bargain had been made in good faith, and God had fulfilled His part. She intended to keep her half of it.

Even confined to a sickroom, Logan seemed to live at twice the pace of other people. He badgered

Madeline and the rest of the staff until they re-
lented and allowed him four hours a day to con-
duct his business. From his bed or a nearby chair,
he dictated letters addressed to Mr. Bennett regarding the management of the Capital, and sent
missives to stewards and estate agents regarding
his properties. In between, he corresponded with
aristocrats, artists, and public figures . . . propos-
ing projects, reminding them of promised sponsor-
ships and donations, and accepting or rejecting
social invitations.

"You must be the busiest man in England,"
Madeline exclaimed after a particularly long session. She set down the pen and flexed her aching
fingers.

"I have been for a while," Logan admitted,
fitting his hands behind his head as he leaned back
against the headboard. He was dressed in a robe of
luxurious burgundy-and-brown-striped silk. A
narrow French *déjeuner* table had been placed by
the bed to hold books and other articles he wanted
close at hand. "Having a full schedule has helped
me keep my mind off other things."

"What things?" Madeline asked without
thinking.

His lips curved with a smile that flustered her.
"Lack of a personal life, mostly. It's not easy to find
balance, especially when you're as involved in a
profession as I am."

"It would be easy for you to find a partner,"
Madeline said, switching her gaze to the desk. She
occupied herself with arranging the blotter, paper,
and silver inkstand, aligning them precisely. "I'm
certain any woman would have you."

"But I wouldn't have just any woman."

"Of course . . ." She fiddled with a sheet of paper, repeatedly folding it until it was a small, thick square. "You want a woman of experience. Someone mature and sophisticated."

"That's what I wanted in the past," he said, and waited until she glanced at him. His blue eyes were piratical as he added, "Now I'm not so certain."

Unnerved, Madeline stood and went to the door. "I'll consult with the chef about luncheon."

"You can do that later."

"Would you care for some soup, or some fresh vegetables and a slice of ham—"

"I don't want to talk about food. I want to know why you've stayed so long to take care of me."

She remained at the doorway, keeping a safe distance between them. "There was no one else to do it."

"I have an entire staff of servants who could have managed quite well."

Madeline took a deep breath. "I'm sorry if you would have preferred that."

"Regardless of what I would have preferred, you've been under no obligation to take care of me." His hand moved in a gesture for her to come to him. "I'd like to hear your reasons for staying. God knows it hasn't been easy for you."

Madeline covered her discomfort with a wry smile. "I don't know how this all happened. I started out trying to seduce you, and instead you nearly expired in my arms."

"Did you stay out of pity, then?" he asked, his blue eyes locked on hers. "Or do you still harbor hopes of seducing me?"

"No," she said immediately, flushing. "I wouldn't . . . I don't want that anymore."

"I should probably feel relieved," he reflected out loud, although his tone held a distinct shadow of regret. His gaze continued to pin her in place. "I never understood why you were so determined to climb into bed with me."

Madeline shrugged and cast a desperate glance over her shoulder, longing to flee to the empty hallway behind her. She couldn't begin to think of how to answer him.

Her distress hardly failed to escape his notice. He stared at her contemplatively, while the silence simmered around them. "At times," he said slowly, "women have approached me that way because they consider bedding a well-known actor a sort of . . . trophy. A conquest they could boast to their friends about."

"Yes," Madeline said, seizing on the excuse, though nothing could have been further from the truth. "That's why I wanted you."

Logan regarded her with a puzzled frown. When he spoke, his voice was softer and more tender than she had ever heard him before. "Little one . . . don't you know you're worth more than that?"

She dropped her gaze, unable to look at him anymore. If she didn't leave him now, she would weep and howl, and throw herself at him in a way that would embarrass them both. "But we didn't have an affair," she said faintly. "There was nothing for either of us to be ashamed of. That's all that matters."

Before he could reply, Madeline walked away quickly, pressing a hand to her hot cheek. She knew it was far too late for any kind of intimacy between them. She loved him too much to use him that way.

The only thing left to do now was go back to her former life and assume her position as the Honourable Madeline Matthews. *Honourable*, she reflected with shame, and sighed. She had failed everyone by embarking on this escapade. Worse, all she wanted was to stay with Logan forever and live as a fallen woman. She was certain that her sisters would never have entertained such wicked thoughts. On the other hand, they had probably never met a man like Logan Scott.

Through bullying persistence, Logan finally had his sickroom fare changed back to his usual fine cuisine. Furthermore, he insisted that Madeline share the evening meal in his suite. It was the first night that he felt well enough to keep his usual hours, instead of falling asleep early as he had done the previous two weeks. Madeline agreed reluctantly, deciding that sometime during the private dinner, she would bring herself to tell him that she was going to leave his estate the next day.

She dressed in her blue cashmere gown, the twilled fabric clinging to her body and making her skin look translucent. Her hair was pulled into a simple knot at the back of her neck, with loose strands curling at her cheeks and nape.

At eight o'clock Madeline entered Logan's bedroom. He waited for her beside a table laden with candles and silver dishes. Wearing another of his luxurious collection of robes and a pair of fawn-colored trousers, he seemed like a lion at rest in his den. The air was filled with a silken mixture of aromas: soup swirling with leeks and pepper, salmon simmered in wine, poultry dressed with herbs, truffles, and champagne.

Logan's attentive gaze swept over her as she

stood in the pool of candlelight. "I hope you're hungry," he said, seating her expertly.

The French dishes prepared by Logan's private chef were vastly different from the plain English fare Madeline had eaten all her life. She indulged in one heady flavor after another as the staff served them *à la russe.* In spite of Logan's amused warnings, Madeline overate during the first two courses, filling herself with the delicious offerings until she was unable to take more than a bite of the salads and desserts that came later in the meal.

"Slowly," he advised her, his eyes twinkling as he watched her drink thirstily from a glass of French wine. "A hedonist would savor every drop."

"Hedonist?" Madeline repeated curiously.

"A person devoted entirely to self-indulgence," Logan said, refilling her glass. "Someone who regards pleasure as a way of life."

"Is that what you are?" Madeline asked.

"I try to be."

"But you work so much of the time."

"For me that's a pleasure as well."

Her brow wrinkled. "It seems an odd idea, life being centered around pleasure."

"What is life supposed to be, then?"

"It's about duty, and sacrificing for others. And if we've been good, our pleasure comes later when we're rewarded in the hereafter."

"I'll take my rewards now."

"That's sacrilegious," Madeline replied, frowning at him.

"Hedonists don't hold stock in religion. Suffering, self-sacrifice, humility . . . none of those things would have helped me in my career."

She remained silent and puzzled, unable to find the flaw in his logic.

"Maddy," he said softly, and an irresistible laugh was pulled from him as he stared at her. "You're so damned young."

"You're laughing at me," she chided.

"I'm not. It's just that you're a pleasant change from the crowd of degenerates I usually associate with. All your ideals are intact."

"So are yours."

"I never had ideals to begin with, sweet. I've never believed in pure honesty and kindness—I'd never seen it in anyone. Until you."

Sickening guilt made Madeline's stomach turn over. She hadn't been honest in her dealings with him, and her every act of kindness had sprung from ulterior motives, until the moment she had recognized that she had fallen in love with him. And even then she would have carried out her original plans, except that she was afraid of hurting him and making him even more cynical than he already was.

"What is it?" Logan asked, staring at her keenly, and she realized that her misery was easy for him to read.

"I'm not a kind person, or a good one," she said in a low voice. "It would be wrong of me to allow you to think otherwise."

"I have my own opinions on the matter," he replied, his gaze caressing.

Dessert was brought in, a dish of pears poached in a sauce of red wine and topped with English cream. In between spoonfuls of the sweet, tart confection, Madeline drank from a tiny glass of liqueur. Feeling drowsy from the alcohol, she blinked as she stared at Logan through the veil of candlelight.

"It's late," Logan said. "Would you like to retire now?"

Madeline shook her head. She was filled with the bittersweet awareness that this was their last night together.

"What do you want, then?" There was a teasing edge to Logan's voice. He was relaxed and handsome with the golden light playing over his dark hair, bringing out the rich glints of fire.

"Perhaps you could read to me," Madeline suggested. They shared a love of literature and philosophy, having previously discussed subjects as diverse as the superiority of Keats over Shelley, and the theories of Plato. To Madeline's delight, she had discovered many rare and unique books in the mansion's library, many of them acquired at private auction or presented as gifts from powerful friends.

Logan helped Madeline from her chair and rang for the servants to clear the dishes. He led her to an adjoining room, a private area filled with amber cushions, works of Chinese porcelain, and paintings and bronze moldings on the walls. Sitting before the marble fireplace, Madeline shivered from the pleasant warmth of the blaze. Logan lounged on the floor beside her, leaning an elbow on a velvet pillow as he read from *Henry the Fifth*, his voice a quiet rumble. Mesmerized, Madeline only half-heard the words.

She tried to fill her mind with every detail of his face: the shadows of his lashes as he looked down at the volume in his hand, the elegant planes of his cheeks, the shape of his wide mouth. At times he quoted from memory rather than reading, reciting the romantic passages in which Henry wooed Katharine, the daughter of the French king. The words were wry, tender, touched with ironic humor. Suddenly Madeline felt as if she couldn't stand another moment, listening to entreaties that made her heart ache. The setting was too intimate, the words too close to her own longings.

"Please, no more," she said breathlessly, just as he reached the line "You have witchcraft in your lips, Kate . . ."

Logan set down the book. "Why not?"

Madeline shook her head, beginning to rise from the cushions, but he reached out and caught her. He drew her down beside him, running a hand along her stiff body. "Don't go," he murmured.

Madeline gasped as Logan pressed her against him. They were matched length to length, and he was so large and solid, his shoulders looming over her. She couldn't see his face, but she felt the brush of his lips as he whispered close to her ear.

"Sleep in my arms tonight, Maddy."

The words she had worked for, waited for. Madeline nearly choked on a sudden rush of tears. "I can't," she managed to say.

"You told me this was what you wanted the first time we met."

"It was . . . but nothing's turned out the way I thought it would."

"What a puzzle you are," Logan said, wiping the wet corners of her eyes with his thumbs. "Tell me what you want, then."

He was so gentle, so tender, that for a wild moment Madeline thought of confessing everything to him. But if he knew the truth, he would hate her for it, for lying to him and planning to use him, and making him the unwitting target of her ridiculous scheme. She had no choice but to leave him and hope that he would never guess what she had tried to do.

"Logan," she said, her voice blotted against his silk robe, "I can't stay with you any longer. I'm leaving tomorrow."

Easing her head away from his chest, he stared at her with penetrating blue eyes. "Why?"

"The past two weeks have been like something from a dream. I've been very happy here . . . with you . . . but I have another life to return to. It's time I went home."

His hand moved over her back in a slow, repeated stroke. "Where is home, Maddy?"

"Another world away," she said, thinking bleakly of the remote country estate where she would spend the rest of her life as Lord Clifton's wife, giving birth to his children and striving to please him.

"Is there another man?" he asked, as if he could read her thoughts.

The image of Lord Clifton's smug face rose before her, and she closed her eyes while tears squeezed from beneath her lashes. "Yes."

Logan showed no surprise at her answer, but Madeline sensed a powerful emotion . . . anger? . . . jealousy? . . . stirring beneath the stillness.

"Tell me who he is. I'll take care of everything."

She became alarmed at the steely purpose in his voice. "No, you can't—"

"You're going to stay here, Maddy." He pulled the pins from her hair and smoothed the rippling

locks over his arm. "I've needed someone like you
for a long time. Now that I have you, no one is
going to take you from me."

"I'm not at all what you want," Madeline said,
rubbing the heels of her hands over her wet eyes.
"We're as different as two people can possibly be."

Logan smiled in wry agreement. "I doubt we're
anyone's idea of a perfect match, but I don't give a
damn. I'd forgotten how it felt to want someone
this badly. After the last time, I swore never to go
through it again."

"You mean when you fell in love with Olivia,"
she said.

His smile vanished, and he stared at her quizzically. "How did you know her name?"

"You called out to her during the fever. You were
angry . . . you called her things I never . . ." Madeline stopped and turned scarlet, remembering the
words he had used.

"Yes," he said wryly. "That was because Olivia
slept with Andrew while she was engaged to me."

"Lord Drake? Your friend . . . but why would
she do that?"

"Olivia was impressed with his titles and social
position, far above anything I'll ever aspire to. I was
a fool for thinking I loved her—but she was
beautiful and sophisticated, the kind of woman I
thought I would never have." He paused, his
expression becoming remote. "I don't know what
you've heard about my past. It's not exactly an
illustrious one."

Madeline was silent and curious, waiting for him
to continue.

"My father is a tenant on Lord Rochester's estate.
Andrew is Rochester's only heir. I grew up with

Andrew, and for a while I was allowed to take
lessons with him, until I became so unruly that
Rochester deemed me a bad influence."

"I don't believe that."

Logan smiled wryly. "You didn't know me then.
I was a petty thief, a vandal . . . I prided myself on
being the village bully."

"Why?"

"Youthful rebellion . . . anger. I resented the fact
that there was never enough to eat, that we lived in
a hovel . . . mostly I was angry that no matter what
I did, my lot in life was already determined."

"Yes," Maddy said softly. "I've felt that way
too."

He gave her a penetrating glance. "I believe you
have."

"How did you become an actor?" Maddy asked,
uncomfortable at his scrutiny.

"When I was sixteen, I left home and became an
apprentice to a wine merchant in London. I did
well enough in that trade and might have continued in it, except that I saw a play at Drury Lane on
the night of my eighteenth birthday. That changed
everything. I joined a group of traveling players,
taking bit parts and learning the rudiments of the
craft. Two years later I returned to London to start
the Capital. I met Olivia around the same time."
He smiled bitterly. "I thought that marrying her
would make up for all the things I'd been deprived
of."

"I see." Jealousy stung her, and she lowered her
eyes to keep it from showing.

"While I was occupied in assembling the theater
company," Logan continued, "I made the mistake
of introducing Olivia to Andrew. Evidently she
decided that Andrew's title and inheritance were

preferable to the uncertain future I offered her. She set her cap for him, not knowing that Andrew had no intention of marrying anyone."

"How did you find out that they were . . ." Madeline stopped in consternation, trying to find an appropriate word.

"I found them in bed together."

"How wicked of them," she exclaimed, coloring with embarrassment and indignation.

"I thought so too," he said dryly.

"I don't understand how you could have forgiven them."

Logan shrugged. "As time passed, I realized that Andrew had done me a favor by showing me what kind of woman Olivia really was. And ultimately I couldn't blame Olivia for wanting more than what I could offer her."

"She should have been proud and grateful to have won your heart—"

"She saw me for what I was," he said flatly. "My fortune has been built on entertaining people . . . exhibiting myself like a trained monkey, as Rochester says. An actor is the servant of everyone who pays for a ticket to see him, wastrels and merchants and nobility alike. Olivia understood that, and she didn't like it."

He lifted his large hand from her hair and held it before her. "No matter how often I play kings and princes on stage, I'll always be a Jennings. I have the hands and feet of a laborer. A back meant for hauling and ploughing. For that matter, even my face—"

"No," Madeline said swiftly, her fingers going to his mouth, temporarily silencing him.

He caught at her hand, pressing a kiss into her palm before pulling it away. "You deserve someone

better than me. Someone young and idealistic . . .
someone who can experience things for the first
time along with you. I'm not always kind, and I
have more faults than I'd care to name. All I can
promise is that I'll want you until my last breath."

She realized what Logan was doing, laying bare
his soul with a reckless honesty that broke her
heart. He wanted her to understand who he was,
so that she would have no illusions about him. But
none of it mattered to her, not his past and
certainly not his profession. He was an extraordinary man who deserved to be loved for himself. So
few people had been given that chance. Miserably
she thought that it was going to be the hardest
thing she had ever done to walk away from him.
"Olivia was a fool," she sobbed. "But not half as
much as I am."

Gently he kissed away the tears on her cheeks. "I
don't care who you are or what you've done. Just
tell me why you want to leave. Are you in love with
this other man?"

"Oh, no," she said at once, wanting to laugh
hysterically at the idea. "It's not that, it's . . . I
promised God that I would go back home if you
got well again."

She felt him smile against her shoulder. "That's
not my idea of a good bargain, sweet. Besides, I
wasn't consulted." He lifted his face, and his smile
faded as he stared at her. There was an intensity, a
hunger in his eyes that made her stiffen. It seemed
that the situation had finally slipped from her
control. He wanted her, intended to have her, and
to her despair, she wanted him so badly that
nothing else seemed to matter.

"I love you, Maddy." His lips raked hungrily
over her cheek. "It scares the hell out of me to say

that; I've always thought of love as a weakness. I still do. But I can't be with you and *not* say it . . . and I can't let you go." He cupped her head in his large hands and kissed her on the mouth, searching deeply, exploring with a rough tenderness that devastated her. "Let me love you," he said, his voice turning hoarse. "Let me take care of you." His mouth crushed hers in sweet, raw need, and he kissed her over and over, until every inch of her skin was suffused with heat.

She couldn't stop herself from responding, her arms locking around his long, hard back, her heart thundering with fear and reckless love. "I don't know what to do," she gasped against his lips.

"You don't have to do anything. Just trust me."

Trembling violently, she felt his hand work at the back of her gown until the cashmere loosened across her breasts. Her nipples were tight and aching even before Logan pulled down her bodice and lifted her breasts from the prison of ribbed silk stays.

One last warning shot through her mind, but she ignored it, living only for this moment, this night, no longer caring about what happened later. "Kiss me," she said faintly, wanting his hot, drugging mouth on hers again. Instead his lips closed over her nipple, teasing, pulling, nudging with his tongue and teeth. She struggled upward, trying to push herself deeper into his mouth, and he subdued her easily. His hands slid over her body, undressing her, pulling at laces and hooks, stripping away every scrap that covered her until all that remained were her stockings and drawers.

In her adult life, Madeline had never been naked in front of anyone, not even at school, where the students had been admonished to bathe in their linen undergarments. "Don't," she heard herself whisper, her face flaming as Logan untied her drawers and tugged them past her knees and ankles.

His face was taut with passion. "Sweet love," he said as she tried to cover herself with her hands. "You've seen every inch of my body . . . it's my turn now."

Madeline experienced a feeling of unreality as she let him push her hands away. *It can't be me*, she thought dazedly, laying naked amid a pile of velvet cushions while Logan stared at her and touched her intimately. His fingertips slid lightly over her breasts and stomach and legs, causing shivers and twitches of pleasure to race across her skin. She sensed him studying her, as if he were learning things he needed to know, and she saw the flush of passion spreading across his face.

"Beautiful," he whispered. "More beautiful than I'd imagined. I'm going to be your first and last, Maddy . . . forever."

She quivered beneath him, unable to answer. His hand slid to her taut stomach, fingers stroking the crisp curls, searching the tender division of her thighs. Her heart beat hard in her chest, until she felt the echo of its pounding in every part of her. The effort of holding still made her shiver like a tightly drawn bow.

"Yes, that's right," she heard him murmur, and he bent to brush his mouth over hers. "Let me touch you . . . love you . . ." He explored her with extreme gentleness while she moaned and arched upward, her body consumed with pleasure. Using his fingertip, he gave her the first hint of the invasion to come, pushing until his finger was buried in the moistness.

"Is this what you want?" he asked softly, repeating the question as he stroked inside her. With a stifled cry, she pulled away before the sensations became too intense. She rolled to her side and heard him undressing, the rustle of fine cloth, the raspiness of his breathing.

When Logan was naked, he pulled her to face him. "Touch me," he said, kissing her, his hands tangling in her long hair. Madeline hesitated; his body had changed with arousal, far different than when she had seen him during his illness. Her hand shook with excitement as she reached down to him, grasping timidly, her fingers filled with silk and steel and scorching heat. Logan made a soft masculine sound and his hand closed over hers, guiding, pressing, showing her what pleased him.

He kissed her with delicious roughness, his tongue twisting and diving into her mouth. Madeline searched his body with her hands. She was hungry for the texture of his skin, so taut and smooth, his legs rough with wiry hair, his back rippled with hard muscle. She crushed and rubbed her face against his throat, inhaling his scent—crisp and masculine, almost like cinnamon. "Do you love me?" she heard him ask, and her voice broke as she replied.

"Always."

He pushed her thighs apart and settled between them, and she felt the hard, heavy pressure of him at the entrance of her body. Cradling her in his arms, he thrust forward, and the discomfort turned into searing pain. Madeline writhed in protest at the invasion, her body stretched and burning.

Logan muttered against her ear. "God, Maddy, hold still—"

"It hurts," she gasped.

"I'll make it better," he said thickly. "Hold onto me." His mouth traveled to her breasts, lips covering the taut peaks, sucking and stroking. Her desire began once more, flickering and blazing into life. She clasped his head to hold him closer, the soreness almost forgotten as he began a gentle rhythm inside her, barely moving at first, then increasing the depth of his thrusts. She clung to him, beginning to welcome the slow, repeated penetration. Each movement was luxurious, deliberate, exquisitely controlled.

"Maddy," he said, his breath scraping in his throat, "you're so tight, so sweet—I've never felt—" He broke off, his brow creased as if in pain, his features veiled in sweat.

Locked in the twisting tangle of their bodies, she was overwhelmed with the need to lift her hips, to pull him tightly inside her. Seeming to understand, Logan pushed her legs up and whispered for her to wrap them around his waist. As he continued the slow driving rhythm, Madeline's mind went dark, and she was suddenly suspended in the white-hot center of intense pleasure. Waves of sensation rolled through her, leaving her limp and stunned in their aftermath.

A violent tremor shook Logan, and he held himself within her, releasing a groan from between his clenched teeth. For a moment his embrace was unbearably tight, and then he relaxed, his passion spent. Breathing hard, he held Madeline's slim body in the circle of his arms and rolled to the side to keep from crushing her.

The storm passed and quietness descended, broken only by the crackle of the small fire. They remained locked together, while Logan stroked

Madeline's hair and touched his lips to her damp forehead. He had never felt so contented. For years he had guarded his heart so carefully—perhaps he was a fool for giving it to her so easily. He didn't care. Madeline was different from all the others . . . she was innocent, loving, honest. Feeling drunk with love, he lifted his head to look at her. Her eyes glittered with tears, as if from some secret grief.

"Regrets?" Logan asked quietly, guessing that many women experienced sadness when they passed from innocence to experience. He stroked her cheek with his fingertips, wanting to give her the reassurance she needed.

"No."

"Sweet love . . . I'm going to make you happy. I'll give you whatever you want, whatever you need—"

"There's only one thing I want," Madeline choked, burying her face in his shoulder.

"Tell me," he insisted, but nothing would make her answer. Finally he lifted her naked body in his arms and carried her to the bedroom, settling her on the cold linen sheets. She shivered and bit her lip as he pressed a damp cloth between her thighs. Realizing that she was sore, he experienced a mixture of regret and elation. She had been a virgin—and she would never know another man's touch but his.

"Would you like a bath?" he asked, gathering her in his arms once more. "A glass of wine?"

"My nightgown . . ."

"Not tonight." He rested his forehead on hers. "I want to feel your skin against mine."

Madeline hesitated and then nodded, her head

settling against his shoulder as they lay back to-gether. "I didn't mean for this to happen," she said, her hand resting on his stomach. "I planned to leave tomorrow without ever—" She stopped, her fingers curling into a small, hard fist.

"It's all right," he soothed. "Sleep now." He cuddled her and murmured softly until her breathing turned slow and regular, and her body became limp against his.

Sometime in the middle of the night, Madeline awakened in a fog of guilt and misery, wondering how she could have been so careless . . . so weak. She began to move away from the long body next to hers, and Logan murmured quietly, his hand curving over her hip. She could barely see him in the darkness, only the outline of his head and shoulders as he rose above her. Gently he touched her breast, and her traitorous body responded at once, the nipple contracting in anticipation. She felt the caress of his breath against her skin and his lips closing over the aching peak . . . the swirling pass of his tongue.

"You're everything a man could want," Logan murmured. His hand slid between her thighs. "And you're mine."

Madeline moaned softly as she felt his mouth moving to her other breast.

"I need you, Maddy." He pressed her thighs open. "I would do anything for you."

She tried to beg him not to say such things, but as he made love to her, all thought vanished. There was only Logan . . . his body possessing hers, his soft groan as he pushed himself within her. "I love you," she whispered against his cheek, her arms wrapped around him. Desperately she wished that the moment would never end, and that morning would never come.

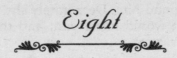

# Eight

*Logan blinked* as a shaft of sunlight moved across his eyes, rousing him from the depths of sleep. Stirring and stretching, he found himself alone in his bed. The relaxed smile left his face as he wondered for an instant if he had dreamed the previous night. No, there were faint rust-colored smudges on the sheet . . . traces of Madeline's blood. A wave of tenderness went through him, and he was suddenly eager to hold her, tell her what pleasure she had given him, how much he loved her.

After rolling from the bed, he pulled on a robe and dragged his hands through his rumpled hair. "Maddy?" he said aloud, striding through the suite. Her discarded gown was gone from the private sitting room. Even the pins from her hair had been gathered from the carpet. Logan reacted with a puzzled smile. Perhaps Maddy had been embarrassed by the signs of their night together and hadn't wanted to cause gossip among the servants. But there was no need for such modesty . . . and furthermore, she wasn't to go about straightening up rooms like a housemaid. She was never to lift a finger again; from now on she would live like a queen.

Logan entered the room she had been using. It was oddly bare and pristine, as if she had never been there at all. Frowning, he went to the armoire and opened it. A few of her gowns were missing, as well as her shoes and bonnet.

He didn't like the suspicions that formed in his mind. Striding from the suite, he went barefoot to the great staircase. To his relief, he saw Madeline's small form in the hallway. She had paused to exchange a few words with the housekeeper. Mrs. Beecham wore a disturbed expression as she evidently tried to detain Maddy.

Maddy was dressed in her wool cloak and carrying a bag that must contain her belongings. She was trying to leave him.

Soundlessly he descended the stairs and approached Maddy from behind. Mrs. Beecham's perturbed gaze flew to his face. Sensing his presence, Maddy turned toward him.

"Good morning," he said, his hands closing over her shoulders. He stared into her tense face, noting her pale cheeks and dark-circled eyes. She looked like she had been through hell. To his knowledge, no woman had ever worn such an expression after spending the night with him. It was hardly flattering.

Discarding false modesty, he knew he was a skilled lover. His partners had always purred with gratitude the morning after. It had been obvious that Maddy had enjoyed his lovemaking—he was too familiar with the signs of a woman's pleasure to doubt it. Why did she look so tormented?

Her lips parted and she began to say something, but he interrupted and spoke calmly to the housekeeper. "Mrs. Beecham, see to it that breakfast is prepared."

"Yes, sir." Understanding his desire for privacy, the housekeeper left at once.

"I won't stay—" Maddy began unhappily, and Logan silenced her with a long kiss.

She resisted at first, her body stiff in his arms, her mouth closed. Logan continued with loving determination, his lips twisting over hers until she shivered and sighed in surrender. Only when he was assured of her response did he lift his head. A touch of color had entered her cheeks, but she still wore the same stricken expression as before.

"Maddy," he said softly, his thumb tracing the line of her jaw, "what the hell is going on?"

"I told you I was going to leave."

Logan stared at her for a long time, while her gaze dropped to the floor. "You were going to sneak away without a word to me? After what happened last night?" His voice roughened. "Dammit, I've had enough of this." Ignoring her protests, he took her wrist in a hard grip and pulled her to the nearby parlor. Closing the door behind them, he held her against his body, his fingers digging into the braids pinned at her nape. "Maddy," he said urgently, "it's never easy for a woman the first time. I should have been more gentle with you last night—"

"No," she said, her eyes glittering. "You . . . you were very gentle."

"I'll make it better for you next time." Gently he nudged her chin with his knuckle. "Come upstairs with me, and I'll show you how enjoyable it can be. I'll make you forget any pain you felt—"

"Just let me go," she choked.

"Not until you tell me what's wrong."

Maddy twisted free of him, backing away to the door. "I can't stand it when you look at me that way, when I know that soon you'll hate me . . . almost as much as I hate myself."

Perplexed, Logan considered her words. "Is it that you're ashamed at the idea of being my mistress?" It was the only explanation that made sense. The self-loathing on her face, the misery in her eyes . . . it must be that she thought it immoral to give herself to a man outside the bonds of marriage. Filled with tenderness, he crossed the distance between them and cupped her face in his hands. "Sweet love, would it ease your conscience if we were married?"

Startled, she looked at him with wide eyes. "You would do that for me?"

Logan smiled slightly, his heart beating fast. He hated to put himself at risk—the very word "marriage" sent a chill of apprehension down his spine—but he was no coward. It had taken him long enough to find a woman he could love. He wouldn't shrink from any commitment she required. "God help me, I told you I'd give you whatever you wanted."

An intensely bittersweet expression wrenched her features. "I wish . . ." she began, and stopped as if her throat had closed.

Before either of them could continue, there was a knock at the parlor door. "Ignore it," Logan muttered, lowering his mouth to Maddy's. But the irritating staccato persisted, and Mrs. Beecham's voice drifted to them.

"Mr. Scott . . ."

Logan's head jerked up, and he looked at the closed door in disbelief. The housekeeper knew better than to interrupt him at such a time. "What is it?" he snapped.

"There is a . . . situation."

"Unless the house is on fire, don't bother me with it now."

"Sir . . ." Mrs. Beecham persisted uncomfortably.

Logan let go of Maddy with a curse and went to the door, flinging it open. "Is there something you'd like to tell me, Mrs. Beecham?"

The housekeeper squared her shoulders and studiously avoided looking at Maddy. "There is a gentleman waiting in the entrance hall."

"I have no appointments for today."

"Yes, sir, but he is in an extremely agitated condition."

"I don't care if he has an apoplectic fit on my doorstep. Tell him to come back later."

Mrs. Beecham looked strained. "Mr. Scott, the visitor identifies himself as Lord Matthews. He claims that he is trying to find his missing daughter. It is his belief that you have her."

"That *I* . . . " Although Logan made no conscious movement, he must have turned to look at Madeline. Her face was in his line of vision . . . she looked horrified . . . her lips silently formed the word "no."

The same word sprang to Logan's mind. *No*, not again . . . another time that he had found happiness, only to have it crumble. He didn't comprehend what was happening, or of what significance the visitor might be. All he knew was that the look on Madeline's face forbode an awful discovery, her paleness suddenly covered with the flush of shame. *God, no*, he thought desperately, *let this be a mistake.*

He summoned all his abilities to make his face impassive, while underneath his emotions seethed. Some rational part of his brain analyzed the situation. If Maddy was the daughter of Lord Matthews—whoever the hell he was—then she had lied to him, not once but repeatedly. The only thing left now was to find out just how deep her deception had gone, and for what reason.

"Send him in," Logan said softly.

As the events unfolded, it seemed to Logan as if he were in some third-rate play. He had been cast as the villain of the piece, while Maddy was the helpless ingenue . . . and Lord Matthews, the aggrieved father.

Matthews came into the room as if fearing what he might see. He wore the expression of a man who had entered what he thought was a respectable dwelling, only to discover that it was a house of ill repute. He was a man in his early forties with an unremarkable face, too short in the chin and round on the sides, and dark hair that had receded far back on his head.

For a moment Logan experienced a twinge of relief at the sight of the man, thinking that he looked like no relation of Maddy's. However, both father and daughter wore identical expressions of mute accusation and dread as they stared at each other. There was no doubt of Maddy's identity.

"Madeline, what have you done?" Matthews murmured.

She stood like a statue, except for the small shake of her head, as if she were trying to deny her father's presence. "I . . . was coming to you today."

"You should have come to me a month ago," Matthews retorted. Attempting to gather his self-control, he turned to Logan. "Mr. Scott, it appears that explanations are in order. You have no idea how sorely I regret meeting under these circumstances."

"I have some idea," Logan murmured.

"I am Lord Matthews, of Hampton Bishop. Two days ago I learned that my daughter Madeline has been missing from school for almost a month. I—" He stopped briefly, his face contorting as he glanced at Maddy. "I should have expected something like this. She is the youngest of my three children, and by far the most willful. Although she is betrothed to Lord Clifton, she had refused to accept my judgment that he is an appropriate husband for her—"

"He's an old man!" Madeline burst out, and her father turned toward her with a thunderous face.

"Refusing to accept my judgment," Matthews resumed, his tone raw, "Madeline came up with just the sort of foolish scheme that I should have anticipated. One of her friends at school, a Miss Eleanor Sinclair, was forced under threat of expulsion to confess the details of the plot."

"What plot?" Logan asked softly.

Disgust and condemnation shadowed Matthews's face as he glanced at his daughter. "Perhaps Madeline would care to explain."

Logan forced himself to look at the girl who stood nearby . . . the innocent who had managed to give him back the hopes and dreams he had relinquished so long ago. Her face was mottled with guilty color, her eyes round with protest. Whatever she had done, she regretted it now. Or perhaps it was merely sleeping with him that she was sorry for. He wanted the truth, wanted to choke it out of her. His gaze remained locked on her as he waited.

Finally she managed to speak. "I never wanted to marry Clifton. I was desperately opposed to the match, a fact that everyone—even Clifton himself—is aware of. While I was at school, I realized that short of suicide, there was only one way to stop the wedding from taking place." She began to stammer, but her gaze begged him to understand. "S-so I decided to r- . . . ruin myself."

Logan's stomach roiled unpleasantly. He heard Lord Matthews's cold, agitated voice as if it came from far away. "Apparently you, Mr. Scott, were my daughter's chosen target. Tell me . . . is there any chance . . . have I, by the grace of God, managed to arrive in time?"

Logan waited for Maddy to reply. *Tell him, damn you!* he snarled inside, but she remained silent. "You're too late," he said flatly.

Matthews rubbed his forehead and eyes as if they ached intolerably.

Logan was surrounded by a red mist as the truth sank in.

It had been a game to her. While he had been tormented with longing and love, she had been winding him around her dainty little finger, making a fool of him. He flushed with humiliation, but that was the least of the emotions that shredded his innards. *Again,* he thought sickly. Once again a woman had betrayed him. But this was much worse than the last time.

He glanced at Madeline, hating her for looking so pale and forlorn. She was nothing more than a high-priced broodmare whose sole purpose in life was to produce thoroughbreds. It wasn't her place to demand more than that. To her kind, marriage had nothing to do with love; it was an arrangement of economics and social advancement. And in a fit of rebellion, Madeline Matthews had used him to avoid her responsibilities.

"Why me?" he asked her, his voice a mere scrape of sound.

She moved toward him, one slender hand turned upward beseechingly. Logan stepped backward instinctively. God help him, he would crumble if she touched him.

Madeline stopped, realizing that he wanted to preserve the distance between them. Nothing about the scene seemed real—not her father's presence, not Logan's controlled expression, not her own sickening sense of loss. If only words could make everything right. If only Logan would understand that what had begun as a schoolgirl's rebellion had turned into love. She would do anything to take away the pain she knew he must be feeling. Anything to spare him one moment of suffering.

"Eleanor had shown me a colored print of you," she said, staring at his beloved face. "I thought you were . . . dashing." She flushed as she realized how shallow she sounded. "No, that's not the right word. I . . . I began to fall in love with you even then, and I wanted . . ." She stopped and shook her head impatiently. There was no way to put her actions in a good light.

"Flattering," Logan said hoarsely, sounding anything but pleased.

"You don't understand how it was." No matter what she said, he would only regard it as insult added to injury. *I love you*, she longed to cry out, but she hadn't the right to tell him that. And he would despise her more for saying it. She turned away as her father approached Logan.

"Mr. Scott, I'm not certain how much responsibility, if any, to ascribe to you, since you were apparently an unwitting dupe in the whole business. I suppose one could have hoped that you wouldn't have touched Madeline, but debauching innocent young girls is no less than I'd expect of a man like you." Matthews closed his eyes wearily. "It is too much to ask for reparations, I suppose."

"What kind of reparation would you like?" Logan asked coldly.

"I'd like her to be made suitable for Lord Clifton once again. Since that is an impossibility, I will have to settle for your silence. I, and my family, will handle the disgrace with as much discretion as possible. We will see to Madeline's future, whatever form it may take. All I ask is that you deny the rumors if you are confronted with them."

"Gladly." Logan didn't look at Maddy. She no longer existed to him.

"Logan, please," she whispered. "I can't bear for things to be left like this."

"Mrs. Beecham will see you out," he said in a monotone. "Good day, Lord Matthews." He walked from the room, not conscious of where he was going, only aware that he had to leave at once.

Soon he found himself in his private rooms, fumbling with the door as he locked himself in solitude. He felt as if he were moving underwater. He stood in the center of the room for a long time, not even daring to think. But Madeline's voice echoed through his mind, saying *I love you, Logan . . . love you . . .*

She was a better actress than he'd ever suspected. She had sounded absolutely sincere. And he had allowed himself to believe it.

His eyes ached in their sockets. Reaching up to clear away an infuriating blur, he felt an insistent trickle down his cheeks. "Christ," he muttered, while self-hatred washed over him.

He heard a despairing groan, felt the exquisitely textured surface of a Tang-dynasty vase in his hands, and hurled it in no particular direction. His ears were assaulted by the shattering of priceless porcelain. It seemed that the sound unleashed a destructive demon within him. Barely conscious of his actions, he tore a painting from the wall, ripped the fragile creation of canvas and oil, and moved to other objects nearby, his hands demolishing works of glass, wood, and porcelain until he had sunk to his knees, his bloody fists resting on his thighs.

The muffled knocking at the door underscored the vicious pounding in his head. "Mr. Scott! Please won't you answer? Mr. Scott—"

A key grated in the lock, and Logan turned with his features twisted in fury to view the worried faces of Mrs. Beecham and Denis. "Get out," he said hoarsely.

Shocked and frightened by what they beheld, they retreated at once, leaving him alone with the ruins of his beloved artwork. Logan dropped his head and stared at the floor. He felt something dying inside . . . all the potential warmth and tenderness that could have transformed his life. He would never be the same. He would never let anyone hurt him again.

# Part Two

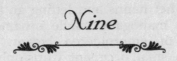

# Nine

"*Logan!*" *Julia* exclaimed in delight, standing up from the long velvet sofa. Her cheeks were slightly fuller than usual, the remaining vestiges of her pregnancy, but with Julia's active lifestyle, the added pounds would come off soon. The extra weight actually enhanced her beauty, giving her a soft and wholesome appeal that would have affected any man under the age of ninety.

As Julia welcomed him into the Leeds family's parlor, there was a flash of concern on her face, but it was quickly buried in an extravagant smile.

Since the birth of the Leedses' son, two months passed before Logan made the journey from London to the duke's luxurious Warwickshire castle. The ancient honey-colored building had been modified to make it light-filled and comfortable. It was a perfect place to display a magnificent collection of tapestries, paintings, and sculpture that Logan greatly admired. However, the duke's greatest treasures were his wife and two beautiful children . . . Victoria, the golden-haired daughter who had been born four years earlier, and Christopher, the latest arrival.

"You took your time coming to see the baby," Julia reproved, gripping his hands firmly.

"I've had to attend to the small matter of running the Capital," Logan replied, returning the pressure of her hands and letting go at once. He strode to a mahogany cradle ornamented with mountains of embroidered cream linen, and peered at the small occupant. Christopher William, the current Marquess of Savage and future Duke of Leeds, lay sleeping with a miniature thumb tucked in his mouth, his features a near-perfect replica of his father's imposing ones.

Seating herself on the velvet sofa, Julia smiled with pride. "It was thoughtful of you to send so many gifts, and especially to include one for Victoria. Most people never think of the first child in all the fuss over a new baby."

She reached to the floor, where her daughter played with the gift Logan had sent, a toy theater commissioned to resemble the Capital, complete with little velvet curtains and an elaborate proscenium. A set of tiny dolls had been costumed as the actors, while a collection of backdrops and set pieces had been included.

"Darling," Julia said to her daughter, "this is Mr. Scott. You remember him, don't you? You must thank him for the lovely gift he sent you."

Victoria remained on the floor near her mother's skirts, half-hidden in the heavy silk folds as she peered out at Logan.

Having no natural affinity for children, Logan regarded the girl with polite interest but made no attempt to approach her. "Hello, Victoria," he said with a faint smile.

She was a beautiful child with a mass of blond curls and large blue eyes, her small hands filled with dolls. "Thank you for my toy," she said shyly, returning his smile with a wary one of her own.

At that moment the Duke of Leeds entered the room. As always, it struck Logan that the man was completely different in private than in public situations. To the outside world Damon presented an aloof mask, while at home with his family he was warm and smiling, cavorting with his daughter in a manner that no one would have believed.

"Papa!" Victoria cried, darting across the room to him, and Damon scooped her up with a soft laugh.

"Hush, imp, or you'll wake the baby. And then I'll have to take you outside and roll you in the snow as punishment."

The child giggled at the idea and looped her arms around her father's neck. "I'll put a snowball down your collar, Papa."

"I'll bet you would," Damon replied ruefully, grinning at his daughter's demure threat. He turned to Logan, his smile fading a degree. "Scott," he acknowledged in a polite tone. They had never been close and probably never would be. They moved in some of the same social circles, yet they occupied very different worlds. Julia was the only bridge between them, serving as a wife to Damon and a colleague to Logan.

It was no secret that Damon would be pleased if his wife never set foot onstage again, but he tolerated her profession because it made her happy. Logan respected the duke for that, knowing that only a rare man of his position would allow his wife to mix in the disreputable world of the theater.

"A handsome child," Logan said, nodding toward the sleeping infant. "My congratulations." Before Damon could acknowledge the compliment, Logan turned to Julia. "When are you coming back to the Capital?"

"When I'm able," Julia replied, smiling at his abruptness.

Logan glanced at her speculatively. "You look healthy enough to me."

"Regardless of my wife's condition," Damon interceded, "the babe is still too young for her to return to London."

Victoria spoke up with childish curiosity, her expression anxious. "Is he going to take Mama away from us, Papa?"

"Of course not, Tory," Damon replied, his expression gentling as he regarded the small face so close to his own. "Come, let's visit the new horse in the stables, while Mama explains to Mr. Scott that his theater is not the center of the universe."

"Don't forget her coat," Julia called after them, laughing as the pair exited. Her smiling regard turned to Logan, and she indicated a seat nearby. "Old friend," she said, half in jest, half in earnest, "I was beginning to think you'd forgotten my existence."

"I told you I've been busy." Logan sat and stretched out his long legs, casually regarding the tips of his polished shoes. "It's not easy managing the theater without you, much as I hate to admit it."

Julia bent to gather up the discarded dolls, each of them no longer than one of her fingers. "I'm sorry I couldn't come to you when you had the fever—"

"I wouldn't have wanted you," he assured her swiftly. "Not at the risk of harming the babe."

"At any rate, it seemed that you were in capable hands."

They both fell silent while the subject of Madeline hung between them like a silent specter.

"I've been reading the *Times*," Julia commented. "The reviews haven't been flattering of late."

"The critics can go hang themselves," Logan said. "The theater seats are filled every night. That's all that matters."

The papers had taken to complaining about what they called a series of blank-souled performances on Logan's part, technically proficient but emotionally bereft. Unfortunately, even he couldn't disagree with their collective opinion. The knack he had always taken for granted—of connecting with the audience, of making them see a play through his eyes—had vanished. He didn't care. He couldn't seem to care about anything now.

Even his keen interest in the company had evaporated, replaced with a sour attitude that seemed to antagonize everyone. The Capital players were resentful of his directions, his sharp manner . . . for God's sake, even his acting.

"I don't know what you intend when you read the line that way," Arlyss Barry had actually dared to complain during rehearsal the previous day. "I don't know how my character should react when I can't tell what you're supposed to be feeling."

"Worry about your own performance," Logan had snapped, "and I'll take care of mine."

"But my character—"

"Have your character react any way you like. I don't give a bloody damn."

And Arlyss had continued the rehearsal with flat, unemotional line readings that fell just short of mimicking his own. Logan had been tempted to fine her, but that might have provoked the entire company into outright rebellion.

Perhaps the atmosphere at the theater would return to normal once Julia came back, with her softening influence and diplomatic ways. Perhaps acting on stage with her would help Logan to rediscover the inner reservoir of emotion he had always tapped for his performances.

Another endless silence passed, and then Julia dared to bring up the subject that lay at the heart of everything. "Any news of Madeline?"

He gave her a guarded look and didn't reply.

"Arlyss told me what little she and the others knew," Julia murmured, her face compassionate. "I've been able to guess the rest."

Reluctantly Logan told her the briefest possible version of the story. "It seems that Madeline decided to make herself less attractive to her fiancé by ridding herself of her virginity," he concluded dryly, "and I was enlisted to help her."

Julia's turquoise eyes darkened in consternation. Carefully she set aside the collection of dolls. "And the two of you actually . . ."

Logan spread his hands in a mocking gesture of appeal. "Who was I to resist such charms?"

A frown worked across Julia's brow. "You must not have realized what Maddy had planned until after . . ." Her voice faded. "Oh, Logan," she whispered.

"No harm done," he said, his back stiffening at her sympathy. "Miss Matthews accomplished her objective, and I had a delightful time assisting her. Everyone was satisfied." As Julia continued to stare at him with searching blue-green eyes, he stood and began to wander around the room as if it were a prison cell.

Most men would have been able to dismiss the matter without difficulty, perhaps even count themselves fortunate to have been given the gift of a beautiful girl's virginity with no obligations. Why, then, was it still twisting him into knots? Why was the knowledge of Madeline's betrayal just as painful—more so—than it had been the day she had left?

Logan was able to fill the daytime hours with work and social commitments, until the thought of Maddy rarely entered his mind. But at night his sleep was broken by dreams of her. She had cared for him so tenderly when he was ill, had fed and bathed and cooled him, and made his suffering bearable. There had never been a need for anyone to take care of him before . . . and that, more than anything, had made him love her.

The realization that Maddy had only done those things in order to serve her own purposes nearly drove him mad. In the dark hours of evening he silently raged and twisted in his bed until the sheets formed tangled ropes around his legs. Each morning he woke up exhausted and angry, hating himself and everyone who was unfortunate enough to cross his path.

"I don't believe there was any malice in Maddy's actions," Julia said quietly. "Only the thoughtlessness of a child. It speaks of her innocence that she would have dared to meddle with a man like you— she couldn't possibly have understood what she was doing."

His hand moved in a silencing gesture. "Enough about her. She's irrelevant to anything we have to discuss."

"How can you say that when it's obvious that you still haven't recovered from what happened?"

"I don't want to talk about her."

"Logan, you'll never have any peace until you find some way to forgive Maddy."

"Mention her name again," he said softly, "and our partnership is over." The threat was in deadly earnest.

Suddenly Julia looked every inch a duchess, her nostrils flaring with hauteur. "I don't like your tone."

"Forgive me, Your Grace," he said with exaggerated courtesy, returning her cool glare.

After a moment Julia's temper died as quickly as it had flared. "When I was her age," she said, avoiding the use of Madeline's name, "I ran away from my family for a very similar reason. I wanted to escape the plans my father had made for me. I can't blame her for that, and neither should you."

"I don't. I blame her for being a liar and a manipulator."

"What's going to happen to her now?"

"I don't care."

"Of course you care," Julia replied, staring at his grim profile. "You can't do your work properly, the acting company is nearly in revolt, and the reviewers are tearing you to shreds. You've lost weight, which means you're not eating, and you look as though you're at the end of a week-long hangover. This is far more than wounded pride. From all appearances, your life is falling apart around you."

There was no hangover. A hangover would come when he stopped drinking, and that wasn't likely to happen for a while. Logan gave Julia a glacier-cold smile. "Nothing is falling apart. Every actor is due for bad reviews at some time during his career. It's merely my turn now. Furthermore, the Capital players will get used to the fact that I'm not going to coddle them any longer. If I've lost weight, it's because I've been doing some extra fencing for an upcoming play. And let me make one thing clear— I *never* loved Madeline. I desired her, I had her, and now I'm finished with her."

The housemaid's tap on the door was a welcome

interruption. She entered the room with a silver tea tray, giving Logan a shy smile as she passed.

"You don't have to be honest with me," Julia said in a low voice, staring at him with exasperation. "But at least be honest with yourself."

It was early evening at Somerset Street, and Madeline's heart drummed as she stepped from the carriage. She stared at Mrs. Florence's house with a mixture of hope and trepidation.

"Shall I tell the driver to bring the bags in?" her maid inquired.

Madeline hesitated before replying. "I don't know if we'll be staying, Norma. Please wait in the carriage for a few minutes while I call on my friend."

"Yes, miss."

Madeline smiled at her gratefully. It was only because of the maid's kind and sympathetic nature that she was able to pay a visit to Mrs. Florence. At this moment Madeline was supposed to be arriving at her sister Justine's home for a month-long stay, but thanks to a forged note sent to her sister and a bribe to the family driver, they wouldn't be expected until tomorrow. "Thank you, Norma," she said quietly. "I don't know how to thank you for keeping this visit to Mrs. Florence a secret. I know the risk you're taking by helping me."

"I've known you for many years, miss," Norma replied. "You're a good, kind girl—the best of the Matthews lot, I daresay. It's made all the staff sad to see you so brokenhearted. If talking with your friend will make you better, 'tis worth the risk." The maid retreated into the carriage, pulling a heavy fur-lined blanket up to her shoulders.

Madeline took care to walk between the thick

patches of ice as she approached Mrs. Florence's
house. It had been over two months since she had
been there, and she had no idea what kind of
reception to expect. It wasn't likely that Mrs.
Florence would turn Madeline away—she was too
gracious for that. Still, Madeline was uneasy as she
knocked at the front door.

Soon after leaving London, Madeline had written a letter of explanation and apology to Mrs.
Florence and had asked her not to send a reply, as
her parents had forbidden all communication with
the outside world. It must have seemed to everyone
who had known her that she had disappeared from
the face of the earth.

Her parents were considering various plans for
her, everything from living abroad to working as a
companion for an elderly relative. Perhaps what
had angered them most was Madeline's statement
that any of these options pleased her better than
their original intention of marrying her to Lord
Clifton.

Lord and Lady Matthews had been devastated
by a visit from Lord Clifton, who had wished to
formally terminate the betrothal arrangement and
retrieve the ring he had given to Madeline. As he
had stood before her, his jowly face quivering with
righteous indignation, Madeline hadn't been able
to prevent a small, hard smile from coming to her
lips. Only the thought of Logan, and the grief she
had caused him, kept her from feeling triumphant.

"I pawned the ring, Lord Clifton," Madeline told
him without a trace of remorse.

He looked like an apoplectic frog. "You pawned
my family ring? And used the proceeds to finance
your fiendish little plot?"

"Yes, my lord."

Clifton's outraged gaze traveled from her resolute face to her parents' stricken ones, and back again. "Well," he huffed angrily, "it appears that I have been spared from making a grievous mistake. A pity I didn't realize earlier that you were never fit to be my wife."

"Lord Clifton," Madeline's mother Agnes cried, "I can't express how deeply sorry we are—"

"No, I am sorry—for all of you." He sent Madeline a contemptuous glance. "There's no telling what will become of you now. I hope you're aware of what you could have had, were it not for your deceit and stupidity."

"I know exactly what I've given up," Madeline assured him with a subtle trace of irony, and her smile was bittersweet. She had succeeded in escaping from Lord Clifton . . . but the price had been a high one. Not just for her, but for Logan.

She also felt sorry for her parents; their misery was all too clear. Her mother was especially distraught. "I can't bear the thought of what people will say," Agnes had declared in a voice as taut as the embroidery thread in her hands. Her thin fingers jerked and tugged at a strand, tangling the colored floss. "I can't abide the disgrace Madeline has brought on us. It is clear that she must go abroad. We'll tell everyone that she wishes to continue her studies on the continent."

"How long must I stay away?" Madeline asked, her cheeks coloring. It was difficult to hear her own mother making plans to dispose of her.

"I have no idea," Agnes said tautly. "People have long memories. It will take years for the scandal to fade. Foolish girl, not to realize how much better off you would have been as Lord Clifton's wife!"

"I told you I didn't want Lord Clifton," Madeline said calmly. "You left me no other choice. I'm willing to accept the consequences of what I've done."

"Have you no regrets at all?" Agnes asked in outrage. "What you did was sinful and cruel."

"Yes, I know," Madeline whispered. "I'll never forgive myself for hurting Mr. Scott. But as for the rest—"

"You didn't hurt that debauched actor; you hurt yourself! You destroyed your entire life and brought shame on all of us."

Madeline had kept silent after that, knowing that there must indeed be something very wrong with her . . . because what tormented her was not the disgrace she had brought on her family, but the pain she had caused Logan. The memory of his face the morning they had parted—so blank, so controlled—sent her into fresh agony every time she thought of it.

If she had it to do all over again, she would behave so differently. She would have trusted Logan enough to be honest with him, and perhaps he might have listened. She longed to comfort him, a ridiculous notion since she was the one who had caused him grief. If only she could see him one more time, to assure herself that he was all right—but common sense told her such ideas were useless. She must let him go, and salvage what she could of her own life.

Unfortunately, that was becoming increasingly difficult.

The front door opened, and Mrs. Florence's maid, Cathy, peered out. "Yes?" Her eyes widened as she beheld Madeline. "Oh, Miss Maddy!"

"Hello, Cathy," Madeline said hesitantly. "I

know it's an odd hour to call, but I've traveled a long way. Do you think Mrs. Florence will receive me?"

"I'll run and ask her, Miss Maddy. She's just finishing her supper."

Standing inside the door, Madeline breathed in the musty vanilla scent of the house, the aroma familiar and comforting. The panicked rhythm of her heart eased as soon as she saw Mrs. Florence approach, her silvery-peach hair arranged in a twist, her hazel eyes soft in her lined face. One of her hands was wrapped around an engraved silver and mahogany cane. It thumped gently on the carpet as she walked toward Madeline.

"Maddy," she said in a kindly way.

"Have you been injured, Mrs. Florence?" Madeline asked in concern.

"No, my dear. It's only that the cold weather sinks into my bones sometimes." She reached Madeline and took her hand, enclosing Madeline's cold fingers in her warm ones. "Have you run away again, child?"

Madeline felt a rush of gratitude. It seemed that Mrs. Florence's face was the only friendly one she had seen in two months. "I had to see you. I need someone to confide in. I felt that you wouldn't turn me away . . . or condemn me for what I wish to talk to you about."

"Have you no grandmother of your own to turn to?"

"Only one, on my mother's side." Madeline thought of her stern, religious grandmother, and winced. "She wouldn't be of any help, I'm afraid."

"Will your family be alarmed to find you missing, Maddy?"

Madeline shook her head. "I told my parents

that I was going to visit my sister Justine. I think they were happy to have me out of the house for a while. I've caused them quite a bit of trouble, and no end of embarrassment." She paused and added in a strained tone, "With more to come, I'm afraid."

Mrs. Florence held her gaze, her alert eyes missing nothing. She reached out to pat Madeline's tense shoulder. "I believe I understand why you're here, my dear. You were right to come to me—more right than you know. Go to the parlor, child, while I tell the footman to bring in your bags. You may stay as long as you wish."

"I have a maid and driver—"

"Yes, we'll put them up as well." She turned to the maid who waited nearby. "Cathy, fetch a supper tray for our guest and bring it to the parlor."

"I'm not hungry," Madeline protested.

"You've lost weight, Maddy . . . and that isn't healthy for a girl in your predicament."

They shared a gaze of mutual understanding. "How did you know?" Madeline asked.

"How could I *not* know?" Mrs. Florence rejoined with a touch of wry sadness. "Nothing else could put that look in your eyes. I gather your family isn't yet aware?"

"No," Madeline said, her voice strained. "And I don't think I'm strong enough to tell them. I feel . . . very much alone, Mrs. Florence."

"Come inside, my dear, and we'll talk."

Enthusiastic cries and applause followed Logan as he strode offstage. It had been a successful performance, though he hadn't played the part to his satisfaction. He had tried to summon the depths of feeling required for the part, but all he had been able to dredge up was a halfhearted effort.

Scowling, Logan ignored the cast and crew members who tried to gain his attention. He entered his dressing room and pulled off his damp open-necked shirt, dropping it to the floor. As he headed to the washstand, a flicker in the mirrored dressing table caught his attention. He turned quickly, startled to see an old woman seated in the corner.

She regarded him calmly, as if she had every right to be there. Although she was a small woman, she had an outsized presence and wore her age with regal pride. One veined hand, laden with jeweled rings, was clasped around an elaborate silver cane. Although her hair was a soft shade of peach, it was clear that at one time it had been a flamboyant red. Her hazel eyes gleamed with keen interest as she stared at him.

"They told me I could wait for you in here," she said.

"I don't receive visitors in my dressing room."

"An adequate performance," she commented, ignoring his brusque statement. "Polished and fairly well-paced."

Logan smiled ruefully, wondering who the hell she was. "This isn't the first time of late that I've been damned with faint praise."

"Oh, you were quite satisfactory as Othello," she assured him. "Any other actor would have called it the performance of his career. It's just that several years ago I was privileged to see you in the same play, in the role of Iago. I must say I preferred your interpretation of that part . . . magnificent. You have a singular talent, when you wish to use it. I've often thought it a pity that you and I couldn't have acted together, but my time was long past when your career was just beginning."

Logan stared at her intently. Her red hair, her vaguely familiar face, her reference to the theater . . . "Mrs. Florence," he said questioningly. She nodded, and his brow cleared. This wasn't the first time that a colleague had desired to meet him, although no one had ever been quite as forward as this particular lady. Taking her hand, he raised it to his lips. "It is a great honor to make your acquaintance, madam."

"You are aware, of course, that we have a mutual friend in the Duchess of Leeds. A delightful woman, is she not? When she started in the theater, she was a protégée of mine."

"Yes, I know," Logan said, pulling a striped brocade robe over his bare chest. He reached for a jar of salve and a towel, and began to wash off the sheen of bronze paint that had given him the necessary swarthiness for Othello. "Mrs. Florence, I'm accustomed to a few minutes of privacy after a performance. If you wouldn't mind waiting for me in the greenroom—"

"I will stay here," she said firmly. "I've come to speak to you about an urgent personal matter. There's no need to be modest on my account. After all, I've been in many men's dressing rooms before."

Logan suppressed an admiring laugh. She was a brassy old woman, to barge into his dressing room and demand his attention. He half-sat, half-leaned against the heavy mirrored table. "Very well, madam," he said dryly, continuing to wipe his face and throat. "Speak your piece. I'll try to overcome any fits of modesty."

She ignored his sarcasm and spoke incisively. "Mr. Scott, you may not be aware that during her brief tenure as a Capital Theatre employee, Miss Madeline Matthews leased a room at my home."

The name, spoken so unexpectedly, sent a shaft of pain through Logan's chest. He felt his face harden. "If that's all you've come to discuss, I suggest that you leave."

"Miss Matthews came to me this evening from her family's estate in Gloucestershire," Mrs. Florence continued. "She is sleeping at my house as we speak. I might add that she is quite unaware of my decision to visit you—"

"Enough!" Logan dropped the face towel and headed to the door. "When I return, I want to find my dressing room empty."

"Do you think you're the only one who's been hurt?" she asked crisply. "You're an arrogant young cur!"

"And you're a meddling old bitch," he responded evenly. "Good evening, madam."

Mrs. Florence seemed amused rather than outraged by the insult. "I have information that is of great significance to you, Scott. Refuse to hear me out, and you'll regret it someday."

Logan stopped at the door with a sneer. "I'll take my chances."

Mrs. Florence folded both hands over the head of her cane and regarded him with blinking eyes. "Madeline is expecting your child. Does that mean anything to you?" She watched him keenly in the ensuing silence, seeming to relish the upheaval she had caused.

Logan fixed his gaze on the wall. The beating of his heart became unnaturally loud. It must be a lie, something Madeline had concocted to manipulate him further.

He shook his head blindly. "No. It means nothing."

"I see." The elderly woman regarded him with piercing eyes. "You know what will happen to Maddy. In a family such as hers, the only recourse is for her to have the baby in secret, and give it away to strangers. Either that, or she'll have to leave her parents and make her own way in the world, providing for herself and the child as best she can. I can't think you would be pleased by either option."

He forced himself to shrug. "Let her do as she wishes."

Mrs. Florence clucked softly. "You would deny all responsibility to Maddy and her baby?"

"Yes."

Her expression took on an edge of contempt. "It seems you're no different from your father."

Logan's shock gave way to a spurt of baffled rage. "How the hell do you know Paul Jennings?"

One of her hands lifted from the cane, and she gestured to him. "Come here, Scott. I wish to show you something."

"Go to hell!"

Shaking her head over his stubbornness, she opened her reticule and unearthed a small green-lacquered box. "It's a gift . . . a piece of your past. I assure you, I have no reason to deceive you. Come take a look. Aren't you the least bit curious?"

"You have nothing to do with my bloody past."

"I have everything to do with it," she replied.

"The Jennings weren't your real parents, you see. You were given to them because your mother died in childbirth, and your father disclaimed responsibility for you."

He stared at her as if she were mad.

"There's no need to look at me that way," Mrs. Florence said with a slight smile. "I'm in full possession of my senses."

Slowly he walked toward her, while uneasiness spread inside him. "Show me your damned trinket."

Carefully she extracted a pair of gold-framed miniatures and placed one in his palm. The subject was a little girl not much older than Julia's daughter Victoria. She was a pretty child with a pink bonnet tied over her long red curls. Logan stared stonily at the tiny painting and gave it back without comment.

"You don't see it?" the elderly woman asked, and gave him the next one. "Perhaps this will prove more illuminating."

Logan stared at a lovely young woman, her features strong but finely proportioned, her luxuriant hair darkened to auburn and pulled to the crown of her head in a mass of curls. Her expression was confident and flirtatious, with intense blue eyes that seemed to stare directly into his. As he examined the miniature, he realized that it was a feminine version of his own face.

"You want me to admit there's a resemblance," Logan muttered. "Very well, I see it."

"She was your mother," Mrs. Florence said gently, taking back the miniature. "Her name was Elizabeth."

"My mother was—*is*—Mary Jennings."

"Then tell me which of your so-called parents you favor. Tell me which of your siblings is most like you. None of them, I'll wager. Dear boy, you don't belong in that family. You were never a part of it. You are my daughter's illegitimate child—my grandson. Perhaps you don't want to accept the truth, but in your heart you must recognize it."

He reacted with a contemptuous laugh. "I'll need a hell of a lot more proof than a set of miniatures, madam."

"Ask me anything you like," she said calmly.

Folding his arms over his chest, Logan leaned back against the closed door. "All right. Tell me why I've never laid eyes on you before . . . Grandmother."

"For a long time I didn't know of your existence. Your father claimed that you had died along with your mother. He kept you a secret and gave you to the Jennings to raise. Your father and I have always despised each other, and he wanted to make certain I had no influence on you. I'm certain he feared that if you knew me, you might be lured into the theater, and he wished to prevent that at all cost. Your mother was an actress, you see."

Mrs. Florence paused, and a grim smile crossed her face. "My pleasure in your success is indescribable, dear boy. In a way, it's a perfect revenge. After all your father did to prevent it, you still found your way to the theater . . . and you've become one of the greatest actors of your time."

Logan's arms unfolded, and he pushed away from the doorjamb. Although he still didn't believe a word she said, he felt the sudden need for a drink. He went to the battered wooden cabinet in the corner and rummaged in a drawer until he located a bottle of brandy.

"What an excellent idea," came the elderly woman's voice behind him. "A drop of spirits would take the chill from my bones."

Logan's mouth twisted, and he managed to locate a clean glass. He poured a brandy, brought it to her, and took a swig directly from the bottle. The comforting glow spread down his throat and into his chest. "Go on," he said gruffly. "I may as well hear the end of your entertaining story. How exactly did you come to the conclusion that I was your daughter's long-lost bastard?"

She shot him a cold look for his choice of words, but continued calmly. "I didn't suspect anything until I saw you on stage, when you were about twenty or so. I was stunned by your remarkable resemblance to my daughter. When I began asking questions about your background, my suspicions were further aroused. I went to your father and accused him of keeping the knowledge of your existence from me. He admitted everything. By then, he didn't care if I knew about you or not. You had already made the decision to become an actor, and there was nothing he could do to reverse it."

"Why didn't you tell me?"

"You had no need of me then," Mrs. Florence replied. "You had a family, and you did not doubt your identity as their son. I saw no reason to put you through turmoil, and especially not to do something that might affect your acting career." She smiled at him over the rim of her glass and took another sip of brandy. "I always kept abreast of your activities through Julia. Privately I've worried over you, taken pride in your success, and entertained the same hopes for you that any grandmother would have."

"Did you ever tell Julia?"

"No," she said immediately. "It wasn't necessary for her to know. I believe the only people who are aware of your true identity are me, the Jennings, and of course your father."

Logan smiled with pure sarcasm. "I can't wait to find out who he's supposed to be."

"Don't you know?" she returned softly. "I should think you'd have guessed by now. You're rather like him in some ways." Her voice remained gentle in the face of his hostility. "It's the Earl of Rochester, dear boy. That's why you spent your childhood on his estate, living in the shadow of his mansion. If you don't believe what I've told you, go to Rochester and ask him."

Logan turned away from her, stumbling against the dressing-table chair. Clumsily he set the bottle of brandy on the table and braced his hands on the flat surface. Rochester, his father . . . the idea was obscene.

It couldn't be true. If it were, then Andrew was his half brother. Even Rochester couldn't be that cruel, watching his two sons grow up side by side, never allowing them to know they were related. One brought up with wealth, luxury, and privilege, the other with hunger and abuse. "It couldn't be . . ." Logan was unaware that he had spoken until Mrs. Florence answered.

"It's the truth, dear boy. I'm sorry if I've destroyed your illusions. I only hope that the Jennings were good parents to you. At the very least, Rochester cared enough to ensure that you lived close by him."

Bitterness welled up in his throat until he nearly choked. All of a sudden he wanted to tell her what kind of life it had been, the fear and pain he had suffered at the hands of Paul Jennings, the indifference of his so-called mother. And Rochester had been aware of all of it. Logan kept his mouth shut, gritting his teeth with the effort. Unfortunately, it seemed that he wasn't able to keep all his feelings hidden.

"Well," Mrs. Florence said, staring at him, "I can see that you had far from a pleasant time of it. That's partly my fault. I should never have taken Rochester at face value—I should have demanded proof that you had died. I was too absorbed in my grief over Elizabeth's death to pursue the issue."

Logan's head was spinning. He fumbled for a chair and lowered himself into it. He heard a knocking at the door and the voice of an employee who had come to collect his costume for washing and mending. "I'm busy," he said in response. "Come back later."

"Mr. Scott, there are some admirers who wish to meet you—"

"I'll kill the first person who comes through that door. Leave me in peace."

"Yes, Mr. Scott." The employee left, and the dressing room was silent once more.

"Julia was right about you," Mrs. Florence finally remarked, finishing her brandy. "She once told me that you are not a happy man. That's one of the reasons I encouraged Madeline to seduce you." She met his stunned, accusing glare without flinching. "Yes, I knew about her scheme, though I wasn't aware of her precise reasons for it. I wanted you to have her. I thought you might fall in love with her—I fail to see how the most hardened man could resist her. I thought a girl like Madeline would make you happy."

"Damn you for meddling in my life!" he said savagely.

Mrs. Florence appeared to be unimpressed by his fury. "Save your passion for the stage," she advised. "I may have made a mistake, but all your snarling and snapping won't change anything."

Somehow he managed to gain control of his temper. "Why now?" he asked through his teeth. "If anything you've said is true—and I don't believe a word of it—why did you come to me now?"

She gave him a smile that held more than a hint of challenge. "History has a way of repeating itself. I find it ironic that you're about to behave exactly as your father did and condemn your child to the same life you had, with no one to protect him or provide for his needs. I thought I should at least make you aware of the truth about your past, and allow you the chance to do the honorable thing by Maddy."

"And if I don't?" he sneered, a flush creeping over his face. "There's not much you can do about it, is there?"

"If you won't take Maddy in, I will. I have the means to ensure that she and her child will lead a comfortable life. That baby is my great-grandchild, and I will do everything in my power to help him . . . or her."

Logan shook his head as he stared at the elderly woman. Frail and small she might be, but she possessed an amazing force of will. "You're a tough old hen," he said gruffly. "I can almost believe we're related."

Mrs. Florence seemed to read his thoughts. Another smile curved her lips. "When you know me a little better, dear boy, you'll have no doubt of it." She rose from her chair, leaning on her cane, and Logan automatically moved to assist her. "I'm going home now. Will you be coming with me, Scott? . . . Or shall you conveniently ignore the mess you've helped to create?"

He let go of her with a scowl. The honorable thing, of course, would be to marry Madeline and legitimize the baby. But it was galling—no, outrageous—to be forced into this position. Besides, he had never been a particularly honorable man.

He looked longingly at the brandy bottle, tempted to drink himself into a stupor.

"You'll have a bald patch if you don't stop that tugging," Mrs. Florence said, her voice touched with amusement.

Logan realized that he had reverted to his habit of pulling the front of his hair when distracted. He let go of it with a muttered curse.

"Your pride is hurt because Maddy deceived you," Mrs. Florence said. "I'm certain it will take a long time for your wounded feelings to heal. But if you could manage to look beyond your own concerns, you would realize that there is a frightened girl who needs your support—"

"I know what my duty is," he said tersely. "I just don't know if I can stand to look at her again."

Mrs. Florence frowned, impatiently tapping her cane on the floor while he went to the dressing table and took a long pull on the brandy bottle. He was filled with the urge to punish Madeline, humiliate her as she had him . . . and yet the prospect of going to her now nearly made him tremble with anticipation.

"Will you come with me?" Mrs. Florence asked.

He set down the bottle, nodding briefly.

"And will you offer for her?"

"I won't know until I talk to her," he growled, fumbling for a fresh shirt. "Now if you don't mind, I'd like to change my clothes . . . *without* an audience."

# Ten

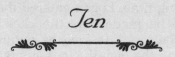

*A clock* chimed as they entered Mrs. Florence's house, signaling the arrival of midnight. "Where is she?" Logan asked.

"She needs to rest," the elderly woman said. "I'll have the maid show you to another room until a decent hour of the morning—"

*"Where is she?"* he repeated grimly, preparing to go through the house room by room until he found Madeline.

Mrs. Florence sighed. "Upstairs. The room at the end of the hallway. But I warn you, if you disturb her in any way—"

"I'll do what I like with her," he said coolly. "And I don't expect to be interrupted."

Rather than look distressed, she rolled her eyes at the bit of theatrics and waved him on his way.

Logan strode alone through the house, which seemed to be filled from floor to ceiling with antique clutter and theater mementos. He ascended the stairs and located Madeline's room. His chest was taut with anticipation as he clasped the brass doorknob. He felt his blood pumping fast in his veins. The power of his reaction alarmed him . . . he was tempted to turn and flee . . . but he couldn't seem to make himself let go of the doorknob. His hand clenched around the polished metal until it turned hot from his skin.

After a long time, Logan entered the room. The only sound he made was the click of the key turning in the lock. He saw the outline of Madeline's body on the bed, the loosely braided rope of her hair on the pillow. Her breasts moved in a deep, regular rhythm. Suddenly he was shocked by the vivid memory of how it had felt to have her breathing against him, her naked body clasped to his.

He sat in a chair by the bed, unable to take his eyes from her. After two months of drowning in numbness, it seemed that life was returning to his body. He thought of taking her now, stripping off her gown and entering her before she was fully awake, burying himself in her tender flesh.

For hours he sat with her in the darkness, watching her sleep. The smallest movement she made fascinated him—the way her fingers curled and twitched, the turn of her head on the pillow. There had been so many women in his life—erotic, talented, passionate women . . . and yet none of them had ever affected him as she did.

He was glad that her condition made it necessary for an expedient wedding. Having her at his convenience would be worth the mockery he would have to endure once all of London became aware that he had been "caught." No doubt he would be the subject of many a caricaturist, portrayed as a meek bull with a ring through his nose, being led by a pregnant shepherdess . . . no, the jeers would be even more fiendish than that. People loved to poke fun at public figures, and he was a highly visible target.

He thought of what his friends would say, especially Andrew, and made an involuntary sound of discomfort. Andrew would take great amusement in the situation, merciless bastard that he was. Before Logan could dwell on the subject of Andrew, Rochester, and the question of his parentage, the small figure on the bed began to move. It was morning.

Although Logan remained silent, Maddy quickly became aware that someone was in the room with her. Her breathing changed, and she rolled toward him with a sleepy murmur. The kitten-sound reverberated through him, making him hard and excited, and most of all resentful. He had discounted his love for her as a temporary madness . . . but it seemed that she still had the same power over him. He craved her physically and, what was worse, emotionally. She had made him lose the easy detachment that had always kept him safe. He would never again hold himself aloof and superior to others. Madeline had shown him that he was all too human, and therefore vulnerable. He intended to punish her for that, in ways too numerous to count.

Madeline's amber eyes opened, and she stared at him in bewilderment. He waited until he saw the recognition on her face, and only then did he move, crouching over her on the bed, pinning her in place.

Madeline caught her breath as she felt Logan strip back the sheets, revealing her meagerly clad body, the hem of her nightgown having crept to the tops of her thighs. His hot blue gaze moved over her shrinking body, and that, combined with the cold air in the room, made her nipples harden. Her mind reeled, and she wondered frantically if she were dreaming. How had he known to come here? It must be that Mrs. Florence had told him.

His gaze raked over her breasts, noting the

shallow rise and fall of her breathing. His large hand moved to one gentle mound, fingertips plucking gently at the tender point, stimulating her through the thin cloth until she fought to suppress a moan. His fingers wrapped around her breast, tightening in a grip that was almost painful. Too stunned to speak, Madeline watched his blue eyes narrow to bright slashes.

Releasing her breast, Logan touched her stomach, flattening his hand on the surface. "As beautiful as I remembered," he said in the low, rich voice she remembered so well. "I suppose that's some compensation for having to be shackled to you for eternity."

His fingers drifted to the soft valley between her thighs, and Madeline's shaking hand caught at his. "Please," she gasped. "Not here."

Logan's hand jerked away from hers. "You're going to be examined by Dr. Brooke today," he said flatly. "If he confirms your pregnancy, I'll take you back to your parents and inform them of our plans to marry. I'll get a special license and make the necessary arrangements. It should all be accomplished before the New Year."

Madeline blinked in confusion. He wanted to marry her in just a fortnight. But it was all wrong . . . it was clear from his expression that he was revolted by the idea. "There's no need for that," she said. "I have no intention of entrapping you into marriage."

"Don't you?" he asked calmly. "Then why are you in London?"

"I . . . I wished to talk with Mrs. Florence."

"And you never thought she would come to me," he said with stinging skepticism.

"No, I didn't. She shouldn't have told you anything."

His mouth twisted derisively, and he let go of her. Sitting on the edge of the mattress, he watched as she drew a sheet over her body. "I wish you'd given someone else the good fortune of bedding you," he jeered. "But since you picked me for that particular honor, and we're in this damnable mess, I have no choice but to marry you. If there is a child, it's the only way I can be certain of his welfare."

"I can manage on my own. You won't have to worry about me or the baby—"

"You don't seem to understand, my sweet. I don't give a damn about what happens to you, but I do want the child. I'll go to hell before I cast him on the mercy of your family."

"I don't want to marry you," she said thickly. "I could never live with a man who hates me."

"We won't be living together. I have several residences. After the babe is born, you may have your choice of them. In the meanwhile, I'll spend most of my time at the theater, as usual."

Madeline tried to envision the businesslike arrangement he was describing. She was chilled by the realization that he was going to exact his revenge for the hurt she had given him. There would be no tenderness, no closeness or shared joy in the baby's birth. And if he knew that she still loved him, he would use it against her without mercy.

"The answer is no," she said. "You don't have to marry someone you don't love merely to ensure the baby's welfare. I'll take good care of him, and I would never deny you the right to see him whenever—"

"I'm not *asking* you for anything, Maddy." He was chillingly matter-of-fact. "I'm telling you what's going to happen. I'm going to have every right imaginable over you and the child—because I'm going to own you body and soul."

"Nothing will change my mind," she said, knowing that it would destroy her to live with his contempt. "You can't force me to become your wife—" She stopped with a gasp as he shoved her back onto the mattress and swung a muscled thigh over her, crouching astride her helpless body.

"Can't I?" he asked, looming over her. He let her feel the hard pressure of his arousal, while his fingers dug into her shoulders until she winced in pain. "You have no idea what I can do, my sweet. I'll get what I want no matter what it takes. You may as well make things easier for yourself and give in without a struggle."

Outraged, Madeline twisted beneath him, but he was at least double her weight, his muscles as hard as iron. With each movement of her body, she felt the heavy ridge of his sex press deeper against her, until she relaxed with a defeated gasp.

"You may as well know that you're going to pay for the trouble you've caused me," Logan said. "You're going to make free with your body whenever I want you. And don't expect it to be anything like before. You won't find it nearly as pleasant."

Madeline kept silent, while all manner of wild schemes went through her mind. She would find a way to disappear before the wedding ever took place.

Logan read her thoughts easily, his mouth curving with a thin smile. "Don't even think about running from me. Because I'll find you, and when I do, you'll be sorry you were ever born."

Her lashes lowered to hide her eyes. It was agony to face the prospect of a marriage that would be a mockery of what they could have had. "Everyone will know you were forced into it," she said, hoping to change his mind.

"Yes, I've no doubt the gossips will flay us alive."

And he would punish her for that as well, she thought bleakly. It was proof of his determination, the fact that a man who was so conscious of his public image was willing to look the fool in order to marry her.

He was gripping her shoulders, making them ache. She lifted her hands to push him away, her palms flattening against his chest. "You're too heavy," she said, arching beneath him. "Please . . . let me go."

Logan made a muffled sound as the movement of her hips set him on fire. He rolled to his side, intending to release her, but somehow his arms caught at her slender body, bringing her with him. One of his thighs nestled between hers, and the pulsing length of his arousal thrust along her stomach. Her breast was close to his mouth, and he could almost feel its delicate weight against his cheek, the velvety tip of it on his tongue.

His senses swam with pleasure. Now . . . *now* . . . his pulse was like a drumbeat, urging him to take her. The sweet elixir of her scent drove him insane. He wanted to taste and touch her everywhere. His hand trembled as it cupped her breast, so plump and firm, yielding deliciously to the pressure of his fingers.

He heard the sound of protest she made, felt the slight jerk of her body, and suddenly the temptation was too powerful to resist. He caught at her nipple with his lips and teeth, wet it through the

thin fabric of her gown, sucked greedily as he
savored the sweetness of her flesh. His fingers
fanned over the side of her breast and slid over her
ribs. She twisted and gave a soft cry, first trying to
push his head away, then curling her fingers into
his hair. They strained together hungrily, writhing
in a wild search for satisfaction.

Trailing his hand down her body, Logan reached
her stomach, then went still, his hand flattening
over the place where she carried his seed. The
thought that his child lay within her was a cold
shock of reality. He rolled away and left the bed.

"Get dressed," he said, making his expression
blank. He headed toward the door. "I'll send for
Dr. Brooke."

"Logan . . ." Her use of his name caused his
back to stiffen. "I've wanted to tell you . . . I'm
sorry for what I did."

"You'll be even sorrier in the future," he said
softly. "You can count on that."

Strangely, it was not Dr. Brooke's examination
that Madeline found humiliating, but rather
Logan's presence in the room. He stood in the
corner and watched the proceedings impassively,
seeming to expect that her claim of pregnancy
would be revealed as a lie. She fixed her gaze on
the ceiling, concentrating on the pattern of Grecian
moldings. Somewhere inside there was a wild
hope that she was mistaken, that there was no
baby. But the awareness of life within her was
undeniable, and she knew what Dr. Brooke's ver-
dict would be.

She wondered if Logan would be a kind father,
or if his animosity toward her would also extend to
the baby. No—she couldn't imagine that he would

hold an innocent child responsible for something that wasn't its fault. Perhaps time would soften him . . . it was her only hope.

The doctor stepped away from the bed and regarded her with a grave, vaguely disapproving expression that made her heart sink. "From what my examination has revealed, Miss Ridley, and what you've told me of your last monthly flux, I would expect the baby will arrive sometime at the end of June."

Madeline slowly pulled the robe around herself. She didn't bother to correct the name he had used, reluctant to explain the situation to him. To her relief, Logan also refrained from mentioning her real name.

"Perhaps fatherhood will be good for you," Dr. Brooke said to Logan. "It will give you something to think about besides that blessed theater."

"No doubt," Logan muttered without enthusiasm.

"If you would like to retain me as Miss Ridley's personal physician, there are a few instructions I'd like to give her—"

"By all means." Logan stepped outside the room, suddenly feeling claustrophobic. He took no joy in the knowledge that Madeline was pregnant. The baby wasn't real to him. In fact, nothing about the situation seemed real. It was strange, however, that the rage he had felt for weeks had faded considerably since this morning. He was filled with a sense of relief that he didn't care to dwell on. Rubbing the back of his neck, he went downstairs, silently making plans. There was much to do during the next fortnight.

Mrs. Florence waited at the bottom of the stairs, staring at him expectantly. "Were Madeline's sus-

picions correct?" She read the answer in his eyes
before he could reply. "Ah, that is wonderful
news." She smiled, her lined face suddenly glowing. "What are you thinking, to put such a sullen
look on your face?"

"I'm wishing that I'd booted you out of my
dressing room last night, instead of listening to
you."

Mrs. Florence laughed dryly. "I imagine Maddy
is none too pleased with my interference, either. I
console myself with the thought that someday
you'll both thank me."

"If I were you, I wouldn't count on that . . .
Grandmother." He put sarcastic emphasis on the
word.

She cocked her silvery-red head and regarded
him with bright eyes. "Have you begun to believe
my story?"

"Not a word of it, until I go to Rochester's
estate."

"What a suspicious man you are," she remarked.
"Clearly it's from the Rochester strain in you. I've
always been something of an optimist, myself."

Logan did not touch Madeline once during the
day-long trip to Gloucestershire. They sat in opposite seats, the conversation sporadic and filled with
long silences. Madeline's maid, Norma, followed
behind them in a second vehicle to allow them
privacy.

"How is the theater?" Madeline asked.

Logan glanced at her in a way that was both
defensive and accusing, as if he thought she was
trying to mock him. "Haven't you read the *Times*?"
he asked sardonically.

"I'm afraid not. I've been closed away from the

world while my parents have tried to decide what to do with me." Her brow creased with concern. "Hasn't the season gone well so far?"

"No," he said curtly. "The critics have been sharpening their pens with glee."

"But why—"

"The fault is mine," he muttered.

"I don't understand," she exclaimed, bewildered. "During rehearsals you were so brilliant, and I thought . . ." Her voice trailed away as she realized that the two plays in question had been launched after she had left London. She remembered the strange, blank look on his face the morning she had left him, and she was wrenched with regret. So this was yet another way in which she had caused him harm. "You were very ill, and so was a large portion of the company," she murmured. "I'm certain that in time you and the Capital will regain your abilities—"

"I don't need you to make bloody excuses for me," he snapped.

"Of course. I . . . I'm sorry."

A sneer swept over his face. "I hate to bruise your vanity, sweet, but my professional difficulties have nothing to do with you. After you left, I found it surprisingly easy to put you out of mind, until your champion Mrs. Florence came to my dressing room last night."

Her cheeks burned with humiliation, as he had intended. Logan felt a stab of satisfaction at the sight.

"I wish I could say the same. But I've thought about you every day and night. I'll never forgive myself for how I behaved. If you could only know how I—" She stopped suddenly, managing to stem the flow of renegade words.

Logan clenched his teeth. She made herself so damned vulnerable that there was no sport in crushing her. It was infuriating, it made him feel ashamed, and he didn't know how to deal with it.

He watched Madeline close her eyes and lean her head back against the seat, her lips parting with a sigh. Suddenly her skin seemed chalky against the chocolate velvet upholstery. "What is it?" he asked abruptly.

She shook her head in a tiny motion and answered without opening her eyes. "I'm fine," she said through stiff lips. "It's just that sometimes I feel a little . . . queasy." The carriage bounced over a rough patch of road, and she pressed her lips together.

Logan regarded her suspiciously, wondering if she were trying to gain his sympathy. No, she was too pale to be faking illness. And now that he thought of it, Julia's morning sickness had lasted during her first three or four months of pregnancy, causing frequent absences at the theater. "Shall I tell the driver to stop?" he asked.

"No. I'm fine . . . really."

She didn't seem fine. There was a pinched look on her face, and she kept swallowing convulsively.

Logan frowned and drummed his fingers on his taut thigh. He had been too preoccupied earlier to make certain that she had breakfast. As far as he knew, she hadn't eaten all day. "We'll reach Oxford soon. We'll stop at an inn there, and you can have an early supper."

Madeline shook her head before he could even finish the sentence. "Thank you, but the thought of food . . ." She put her hand to her mouth and breathed until her nostrils flared.

"We'll stop soon," he said, picking up a crystal

decanter of water from a mahogany sideboard fitted in the carriage. He moistened a handkerchief and gave it to Madeline. She murmured gratefully and pressed the cloth to her face.

Remembering the covered basket that Mrs. Florence had packed for them, Logan reached beneath the seat and dug it out. He found a few pieces of fruit, a wedge of cheese, a few slices of brown bread, a small pudding wrapped in a damp napkin. "Here," he said, extending a piece of bread to her. "Try this."

She turned her face away weakly. "I couldn't swallow anything."

He sat beside her and held the bread up. "One bite, damn you. I won't have you getting sick in my carriage."

"I won't damage your precious carriage," she said, lowering the handkerchief and glaring at him over the edge.

All of a sudden Logan wanted to smile at her defiance. He remoistened the cloth, folded it, and draped it over her forehead. "One bite," he said, his voice gentle as he held the bread against her lips.

She made a sound of wretchedness and complied, chewing as if her mouth were filled with sawdust. Finally she swallowed, making a face as she tried to keep it down. It seemed to Logan that her color began to improve. "Another," he said inexorably.

She ate slowly, seeming to feel better, until she relaxed and let out a deep sigh. "I'm better now. Thank you."

Logan realized his arm was around her, securing her firmly to his side. Her head was close to the crook of his shoulder, her breast pressed lightly

against his chest. The position was so natural, so
comfortable, that he hadn't noticed what he was
doing until that moment. She looked up at him
with eyes like liquid amber. He remembered when
she had taken care of him during his illness. No
matter what else she had done, she had led him
through the fever and nurtured him back to health.
She had given him hope, and a taste of happiness.

And then she had taken it all away.

Overwhelmed with bitterness, he let go of her
roughly. "Take better care of yourself in the future," he said, returning to his own seat. "I'm not
inclined to play nursemaid."

Madeline was sick with dread as the carriage
rolled along the winding drive to her family's
estate. It was situated amid the gentle hills of
Gloucestershire, with rich fields veined by mineral-
laden creeks. The Matthewses' land was far more
impressive than the manor house, which seemed
to huddle awkwardly in the midst of a patch of
smaller buildings. The tiny one- and two-room
cottages had been erected to accommodate the
family's need for extended servants' quarters and
kitchen areas.

Logan glanced out the window at the estate and
made no comment as they approached the manor
house.

"My parents won't like the idea of our marriage," Madeline said, plucking at her skirts. She
was dressed in a plain, girlishly styled gown. It
seemed to him that the bodice was already too
tight across her breasts. He wondered why her
parents hadn't yet suspected her pregnancy.

"I expect they'll be more than happy to have you

married once they learn of your condition," he said.

Madeline didn't look at him as she replied. "My parents disapprove of anyone associated with the theater. I think they would rather die than see their daughter enter into marriage with an actor."

"No wonder you chose me," he murmured, his eyes narrowing as he stared at her. "Not only were you able to rid yourself of your virginity; you also managed to pick a man whom your parents would find particularly offensive."

"I never meant for anyone to find out whom I had slept with," she said. "That was supposed to remain a secret."

Logan scowled and swallowed back a stinging comment, reminding himself that now was not the time to argue. He had only one objective, and that was to inform the Matthews of what would take place in two weeks' time.

The carriage and outriders halted in front of the manor. Logan removed Madeline's lap robe and assisted her with her cloak. After fastening the soft wool at her throat, he gripped her chin in his fingers. He stared into her wide eyes, taking care not to mark her delicate skin with the pressure of his grip.

"There's something I want from you," he murmured. "No one is to know that we're unwilling partners in this marriage. Everyone who sees us, including your parents, is to believe that the arrangement is desired on both sides. One unhappy glance from you, one hint that you're being forced into it, and I'll wring your little neck. Have I made myself clear?"

"I'm not an actor," she replied stiffly. "I don't

know how convincing I can be. If you expect me to
walk into my parents' home and pretend that I'm
happy—"

"That's exactly what I expect." There was a
discreet knock at the carriage door, the footman
ready to assist them, but Logan ignored the sound.
"You look like hell," he said, staring at Madeline's
white, strained face. "Smile. Try to relax."

"I can't." She gave him a glance rife with dread.

As Logan stared into her tense features, it occurred to him that she would belong to him for the
rest of her life. Their blood would mingle in the
veins of their child. It was paramount to the child,
as well as Logan, that no one ever realize the true
state of affairs between them. His pride demanded
that Madeline look and behave like a woman in
love, that she accept his suit with the appearance of
gladness.

He cupped her face in his hands and brought his
mouth to hers. He kissed her with all his considerable skill, slipping his tongue into her softness,
probing and caressing until she responded helplessly. When he lifted his head, she was gasping,
her face flushed.

Pulling back, Logan surveyed her dispassion-
ately. "That's better."

Helping her out of the carriage, he guided her
along the paved circular pathway that led to the
front door. The footman had already rushed ahead
to knock on the cream-painted panels and announce their arrival. A welcome gust of warm air
rushed out from the house's entryway.

Logan kept his arm around her in a solicitous
manner that was guaranteed to shock the Matthewses. Although Madeline knew that his sup-
portive arm was merely for show, she was grateful

for it. She wondered how her parents would react to the impending news. Logan Scott lacked the all-important birthrights of aristocratic blood and family inheritances. Furthermore, they had made it clear that a professional man would never be suitable for one of their daughters, even one involved in medicine or the law. An actor was unthinkable.

Both her parents appeared in the entryway with expressions of horrified amazement. Her mother's aristocratic features were pale, her narrow mouth pinched with outrage. "Madeline, you should be with Justine!"

"There was a change of plans," Logan replied, stepping forward with a slight bow. "An honor to make your acquaintance, Lady Matthews."

Madeline winced as her mother gave Logan a deliberate snub, stepping backward and refusing to make any gesture of welcome.

"Mr. Scott," Lord Matthews said, staring at the pair of them in disbelief, "perhaps we can retire to the parlor, where you may attempt to explain this situation to me."

"Yes, my lord."

Lord Matthews turned to his daughter with a forbidding glare. "Not you, however. You may go to your room, where you will be dealt with later."

Madeline began to stutter in protest, and Logan interrupted quietly. "Madeline will stay with us, my lord. Her presence is necessary, as the matter of her future will be discussed."

"As I once told you, Scott, I will see to my daughter's future. You are possessed of rather amazing effrontery to come here and interfere with a situation in which you are no longer involved."

"I'm afraid it's not that simple, my lord." Keep-

ing his arm around Madeline, Logan followed the
Matthewses into a small parlor filled with straight-
backed English furniture made of "plum-pudding"
mahogany with swirling yellow and brown wood,
and gold upholstery. The only painting in the room
was a nondescript English landscape.

Lady Matthews seated herself and indicated for
the rest of them to do the same. "Madeline, you
may sit over there," she said crisply, indicating a
chair set away from the main grouping of furniture.

Logan felt Madeline stiffen. He caught her cold
hand and drew her to a place beside him on a small
settee. Glancing at Lady Matthews, he silently
challenged her to object. Her nostrils flared, and
she gave him an icy glare.

Some would have called Lady Matthews a handsome woman, but she was utterly devoid of
warmth, with no softening laugh lines around her
eyes or mouth. There were two faint but distinct
horizontal creases on her forehead, giving her a
pinched and resolute appearance. He guessed that
once Lady Matthews made a decision, nothing
would cause her to change her mind.

No wonder Madeline had run away from school
against their wishes. No wonder she had conceived
such a ridiculous plan to thwart the match they had
made for her. He could only imagine what sort of
man Lord Clifton was. Old, Madeline had said . . .
and no doubt very, very respectable.

"Now, Mr. Scott," Lord Matthews said, uncon-
sciously smoothing the top of his balding head and
the graying hair in the back, "if you would care to
enlighten me—how is it that you've come here
with our daughter? I would ask Madeline herself,
but I doubt she is capable of telling the truth."

Deliberately Logan brushed his thumb over the

burning crest of Madeline's cheek. He took pleasure in Lady Matthews's gasp of outrage. "Madeline came to inform me of a very significant fact. She felt it was her obligation to let me know before anyone else did."

"That fact being?" Lord Matthews asked, suddenly sounding suffocated.

Logan fingered a loose curl at Madeline's temple. "She . . . *we* . . . are expecting a child, sir. According to the doctor, it will be born in June." He paused to take in their stunned reactions and continued at a measured pace. "Naturally my sense of honor demands that I do the right thing by Madeline and the baby. Therefore I've come to ask your blessing—"

"Your *sense of honor?*" Lady Matthews broke in, each syllable crackling with outrage. He guessed that if there were a knife in her hand, she would gladly stab him. "After what you've done to our daughter, you have the gall to claim that you have a sense of honor?"

"It wasn't his fault," Madeline broke in impetuously. She would have said more, but Logan's hand settled on the back of her neck, squeezing her into silence.

Logan kept his gaze on Lord Matthews while the atmosphere swirled with hostility. "My lord . . . I believe the situation can be salvaged to everyone's satisfaction. I give you my word that your daughter will be well taken care of. With your permission, I'll arrange for an expedient wedding—"

"You're not fit to marry her," Lady Matthews burst out. "I spent years training her to be the wife of a man like Lord Clifton, only to have her ruined by a theatrical performer. Now her descent is complete, and she's nothing more than a—"

"Agnes," Lord Matthews interrupted brusquely. His wife clamped her mouth shut and regarded Logan with outrage.

Lord Matthews returned his attention to Logan. "Mr. Scott, I appreciate your willingness to do your duty. However, I must give the matter very serious thought. Despite Madeline's unfortunate condition, we must also consider what is in the family's best interest. If my daughter marries you, we will face years of unbearable notoriety. I'm sure that a man like you would not be able to understand the effects this would have on the Matthewses, but our good reputation is central to our very existence. I believe the matter would be better handled more quietly, without your involvement."

A contemptuous smile tugged at Logan's lips as he realized what Matthews was saying. They would rather give the baby away and send their daughter into exile than see her enter into a marriage with a public figure like him. He would go to hell before letting them dispose of Madeline and the baby like some sordid secret.

"Give it all the consideration you like," he said softly. "But I assure you, Lord Matthews, the child is going to be born with a name—*my* name." He stood up from the settee, indicating that the conversation was over. "It's late," he said abruptly. "I'll take my leave now and return in a few days to inform you of the arrangements I've made. Madeline will be my wife in a fortnight."

The couple shot to their feet, both of them spluttering with threats and refusals. Logan interrupted calmly, all pretense of courtesy vanished. "I warn you not to upset her while I'm away. I expect Madeline to be well rested when I return." He glanced into her upturned face as she stood beside him. "Send for me if you have any difficulties," he said.

"Yes . . . Logan." She summoned a tremulous smile.

"Very good," he said softly.

"Mr. Scott," Lord Matthews broke in, his round face burnished with scarlet, "I'll have to ask you not to set foot on my estate again."

"Very well," Logan replied. "After I've come to collect Madeline."

"Do you think to defy me?" Matthews blustered. "I could ruin you at will, Scott. I have very powerful and influential friends—"

"So do I." They faced each other in a silent standoff, and then Logan spoke in a quiet, almost conciliatory tone. "Don't be a fool, Matthews. You have more to gain than to lose by this marriage. In spite of my background, I think you'll find that there are certain benefits to having me as a son-in-law."

"And what are those?" Lady Matthews asked haughtily. "Theater tickets whenever we desire?"

Logan smiled sardonically and kept his gaze on Madeline's father. "I trust you'll want what's best for your daughter, my lord."

Lord Matthews nodded reluctantly and turned to hush his protesting wife.

Nodding a businesslike good-bye, Logan began to leave the room. Madeline followed him, reaching his side in a few steps. "Logan . . . where are you going?"

He stopped and looked down at her impatiently. "To pay a visit to my family."

"Are you going to tell them about me?"

"Among other things." He hadn't yet discussed Mrs. Florence's claims about his parentage with

Madeline. There was no point in saying anything until the story was confirmed—which he intended to do this very evening.

Madeline bit her lip nervously. "You . . . you'll come back?"

A mocking smile crossed Logan's face. "All too soon," he promised, and then he was gone.

# Eleven

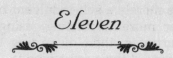

*It was* half past ten when Logan finally reached Buckinghamshire on the way back to London, but he was certain that Rochester would not yet have retired. The earl never required more than a few hours of sleep. He was like a busy old spider, spinning his webs far into the night in hope of snaring some unlucky prey on the morrow.

Rochester had a knack for discovering people's vulnerabilities and taking advantage of them, such as the time he convinced a new widow to sell him her home and property at a fraction of its true value, or sat at a relative's deathbed and badgered him into signing a new will—with Rochester as the principal beneficiary, of course. Andrew had told Logan of those and many other instances, and the two of them had laughed in companionable disgust at the old man's greed.

The carriage drove through the village next to Rochester's estate, passing the churchyard filled with stone monuments and historic landmarks paying tribute to the Drakes' achievements. The thought of being one of the Drakes . . . God, of being Rochester's son . . . made Logan ill. He had always hated the earl for being a calculating, predatory bastard. It couldn't be true that the same tainted blood ran through his veins. It was even more distasteful than being Paul Jennings's son.

Jennings was merely a self-indulgent brute. Rochester was far more calculating, using people to serve his purposes, then discarding them when they had outlasted their convenience.

The carriage passed a large cottage surrounded by curved stone walls, the house he'd had built for the Jenningses several years before. Mary, Paul, and their three children resided there in comfort. Paul still had his allotted land on Rochester's estate to tend. Now, however, he enjoyed the assistance of a hired hand, who saw to his duties while Paul spent the better part of each morning in a drunken stupor. Logan supported the entire Jennings family on the condition that they never attempt to visit him in London. He considered it a small price to pay.

They reached the great country house, its familiar outline barely visible in the darkness. The hall had been built by the Drakes three generations earlier, with an elegant stone exterior and acres of carved oak paneling inside. Like its present occupant, Rochester Hall possessed a stern dignity, seeming unassailable and utterly impenetrable. Even the windows were small and narrow, as if to guard against any intrusions.

Having known most of the servants at Rochester Hall since childhood, Logan entered the place unannounced, forestalling the housekeeper's attempts to alert the master to his arrival. He went to the library, where the earl was engrossed in a book of art engravings.

"Scott," Rochester said, looking up with a narrow-eyed glance. "Of all people to be calling at this hour, I wouldn't have expected you."

Logan hesitated at the doorway, momentarily

transfixed. Outwardly he and Rochester shared no likeness, save a similarity of size and build. But there was something about the old man's jaw, the unyielding jut formed as if by carpenter's tools, the aggressive slope of the nose, and the decisive slashes of his brows . . . dear God, were his own features really that different?

Ignoring the sudden hammering in his head, Logan advanced farther into the library. "I seem to be paying a great many unexpected visits these days," he replied, and made his way to the book of engravings on the table. Noting an exceptionally fine plate by the English portrait engraver William Faithorne, he touched the edge of it.

Rochester jerked the book away with a snort. "Have you come to whine because I managed to acquire the Harris collection despite your oversized bid?"

"I never whine, my lord."

"You did in that ridiculous production of *Richard the Second* that I had the misfortune to attend a few years ago. I hope never to see such a whining, sniveling performance again."

"I played the part as it was written," Logan replied evenly.

"I doubt Shakespeare ever had such intentions in mind when he set pen to paper," Rochester remarked.

"Well acquainted with him, were you?" Logan asked, and the elderly man scowled at him.

"Insolent mongrel. Tell me what you've come about, and be on your way."

Logan studied him for a long moment while he experienced an overwhelming urge to leave without saying another word.

"Well?" Rochester demanded, arching one brow.

Logan half-sat on the library table, casually pushing aside the engraving book to make room for himself. "I have a question for you. Tell me, my lord . . . have you ever made the acquaintance of a Mrs. Nell Florence?"

Rochester showed no reaction to the name except for a tightening of his fingers on a gold-rimmed magnifying glass. "Nell Florence," he repeated slowly. "The name isn't familiar."

"She was once a comic actress at Drury Lane."

"Should I be expected to know such trivial information?" He looked at Logan without blinking, as if he had nothing to hide. His eyes held all the expression of a trout's.

Something crumbled inside as Logan began to understand that Mrs. Florence had told him the truth. He felt a painful hollowness in his chest, and he took a steadying breath. "You're an accomplished old liar," he said hoarsely. "But you've had years of practice, haven't you?"

"Perhaps you should tell me what has caused you to throw a tantrum in my library. Some bit of gossip Mrs. Florence told you, eh?"

Logan clenched his hands to keep from tearing apart the table and everything else within reach. He knew that he had colored with fury, and he longed to have the same impassive expression that Rochester wore. What had happened to the self-possessed Logan Scott of a few months ago? He had always been able to save his emotions for the stage. Now it seemed that they were bleeding into every area of his life.

"How the hell are you able to live with yourself?" Logan asked, his voice unsteady. "How could you have given your own son away to a brute like Jennings?"

Rochester set the magnifying glass aside with undue care. His skin took on a gray pallor. "Have you gone mad, Scott? I haven't a clue as to what you're talking about."

"Let me refresh your memory," Logan said savagely. "Thirty years ago you gave your bastard son to Paul and Mary Jennings, to raise as their own. The problem was, they weren't fit to care for one of your dogs, much less a child. For the next sixteen years, I was beaten to a bloody pulp more times than I can count, by my 'father.' You knew what was happening all that time, and you did nothing to stop it."

Rochester's gaze finally slid from his, and he pretended to inspect the magnifying-glass frame as he considered how best to answer. Logan found himself seizing the old man's shirtfront, half-lifting him out of the chair until they were practically nose-to-nose. "You owe me the truth, damn you," he snarled. "Admit that I'm your son."

Rochester's face turned forbidding. "Take your hands off me."

They remained in a frozen tableau for an endless moment, and then Logan's hands loosened. Rochester settled back in his chair, pulling down his rumpled shirt. "Very well," he said. "I'll admit it . . . you're the bastard I sired by Nell Florence's daughter. And I could have done worse than give you to the Jenningses. I could have sent you to an orphanage and never given you another thought. Furthermore, I did not stand by idly while you were being abused by that lout Jennings. When the episodes became too violent, I threatened him with the loss of his land and the annuity I had agreed to pay him—"

"Am I supposed to thank you?" Logan wiped his hands on his coat as if they had been soiled.

"I have no doubt you feel you deserved more from me," the old man said icily. "Indeed, at one time I had plans for you, until you insisted on taking to the stage. I would have done a great deal for you, had you chosen any other profession."

"Now I understand why you've always hated the theater," Logan muttered. "It reminds you of my mother."

Rochester's eyes flashed with anger. "I gave Elizabeth a better life than she'd ever known before. And she would still be alive today if not for you. You were too large for her—she died because of your confounded size, gluttonous brat that you were."

The accusation rang like a gunshot in the room. Logan nearly reeled backward from the impact. "Christ," he said, feeling ill.

Although Rochester's demeanor was as callous as before, his tone softened as he remarked, "You couldn't help it, I suppose."

Groping for the edge of the table, Logan leaned against it once more, his blank gaze locked on the old man's face. "Have you ever told Andrew about me?" he heard himself ask.

Rochester shook his head. "I never saw the need. And considering his recent round of indulgences, I think it would do him harm to find out now. I haven't seen him sober in months. This could be just the thing to finish him off."

"I don't blame Andrew for drinking. When Mrs. Florence told me that you were my father, I reached for the nearest bottle myself."

"Nell . . . that interfering old cat," Rochester said, stroking his chin and scowling. "I always knew she would make trouble someday. Why did she choose to approach you now?"

Logan wasn't about to explain anything about the situation with Madeline or his impending marriage. He would let Rochester find out from someone else. "I don't know."

"Well . . . what will your next move be? Do you plan to stage some sort of reunion with Andrew and inform him that you're his half brother?"

Logan shook his head. "As far as I'm concerned, that will never come to light."

Rochester seemed surprised. "I hope you're aware that even if I choose to acknowledge you, there is no legal right of inheritance for illegitimate issue—"

"I want nothing to do with you—not one bloody shilling."

"If that's how you want things to be—"

"It's what you've wanted since the day I was born," Logan said bitterly. "I'll be happy to honor your wishes. You have only one son. God spare him from your fatherly attentions."

"I've done perfectly well by Andrew," the old man retorted. "It's *you* who have made him into the drunken spendthrift he is today."

Logan stared at him in stunned belief. "Me?"

"Don't think I'm not aware of all the times you've given money to Andrew. In your misguided attempts to help him, you've made the problem worse. He'll drink and gamble as long as he has someone to assume his debts."

"You'd rather have him crippled by the sharps he owes money to? They'll send someone to break every bone in his body . . . and that's if he's lucky."

"Andrew will have to face the consequences of his actions. Otherwise he'll land in debtor's prison when I'm gone. I'll thank you not to interfere in his life again."

"Gladly." Somewhat dazed, Logan pushed away from the table and headed to the door.

"Scott," the old man murmured.

Logan stopped at the door without looking back. He waited until he heard Rochester speak once more, sounding reflective. "I always wondered why you chose the stage. You would have been successful in anything—you have a great deal of me in you."

"You're right," Logan said, his voice thick with self-hatred. He turned toward his father. To his horror, he realized that he shared more than superficial similarities with Rochester. Self-centered and manipulative, both of them, choosing to invest their time in art and business rather than take the risk of caring for someone. "Given enough time, I'll probably turn out to be a ruthless bastard just like you. And the reason I took to the stage was that I had no other choice. It was in my blood."

"Like your mother." Rochester studied him intently. "I'll admit, you've always resembled Elizabeth too damned closely for my comfort. I can only guess what it does to Nell to look at you."

Logan left without replying, feeling as if the hounds of hell were chasing him.

Madeline sat on the corner of the canopied bed in her room amid piles of neatly folded clothes, surveying stacks of trunks and boxes that lined the walls. Most of her belongings were being packed and sent to Logan's London home before the ceremony. The wedding would take place in a week's time, in the drawing room of Logan's London estate. Despite the Matthewses' assertions that it would be more proper for the ceremony to be conducted in the chapel of their own estate, Logan had refused. Madeline knew that he intended to control every detail of the wedding, with no interference allowed.

"Madeline!" Her older sister Justine appeared in the doorway, her eyes sparkling with excitement. Justine had come to help with the wedding preparations. Althea had sent a warm note of congratulations, but unfortunately wouldn't be able to attend the wedding, as she was in Scotland with her husband, awaiting at any day the birth of their first child.

'He's here!" Justine exclaimed. "His carriage is coming up the drive."

Madeline felt a pang of nerves in her stomach. Although Logan had corresponded with her parents during the past week, she had not been permitted to see the letters. She had found it difficult to eat and sleep, wondering if he would change his mind about marrying her.

"You must finish your supper," her mother had said to her the previous evening. "If you lose any more weight, I believe your fiancé might actually attempt to upbraid us for it—and if he does, I shall certainly set him in his place."

Madeline went to the mirror and checked her appearance, smoothing her skirts and jerking her bodice into place. In spite of her weight loss, her breasts pushed against the material of her gown until the stitches strained to contain them.

"Do something with your hair," Justine advised impatiently. "It looks like a bird's nest."

Pulling the pins from her hair, Madeline brushed and braided it mechanically, and fastened a coiled knot at her nape. Justine joined her at the mirror, delicately smoothing her own golden locks, sticking a few tiny curls to her forehead and temples with touches of saliva. Admiring her own flawless reflection, Justine smiled in satisfaction.

Even in childhood, Justine had amazed people with her porcelain white-and-gold beauty and her remarkable poise. She had been the kind of little girl who never behaved badly, broke a toy, or got her shoes muddy. During her season, she had been pursued by the most eligible men in London, and even a few French noblemen, and had landed Lord Bagworth, a wealthy viscount. Justine was, and always would be, the pride of the Matthewses—whereas she, Madeline, was the shame of the family.

As Justine urged her to hurry, Madeline inserted the last pin in her hair and pinched her cheeks to impart some color. By the time they went downstairs, Logan had already been shown to the parlor, where Agnes had received him with a minimum of cordiality.

Logan stood as the two young women entered the room. He looked exceptionally large in the confines of the parlor, his shoulders broad beneath a perfectly cut black coat, his body lean and taut in a gray brocade waistcoat and charcoal trousers. His hair had been freshly cut, and a subtle glitter of mahogany showed in the dark locks.

"Mr. Scott," Madeline said, uncertain whether or not to approach him. Logan solved the dilemma immediately, coming to her in a few strides and taking her hand. Rather than kiss the back of it, he turned her palm upward and pressed his lips into the soft hollow, making the gesture tender and intimate. It was done for the benefit of her mother and sister, of course. Even so, Madeline felt her heart jolt at the warmth of his mouth on her skin.

Logan straightened and looked down at her, surveying every detail of her appearance. A frown worked between his thick brows. "You haven't been eating," he muttered, too softly for the others to hear.

"Neither have you," Madeline replied. It wasn't lost on her that his body had been honed to a new spareness, with no trace of softness to conceal its raw power.

Logan smiled wryly at her comment, and turned for an introduction to Justine, who waited close by. Dutifully Madeline presented him to her older sister and waited for the look of awestruck admiration that would appear on his face. Men always reacted to Justine that way. Strangely, Justine's incandescent beauty seemed to make little impression on Logan.

"A pleasure," he murmured indifferently.

A touch of pique flashed in Justine's luminous gaze. "Welcome to the family, Mr. Scott. I do hope you'll be kind to my dear little sister."

"I intend to, Lady Bagworth." Logan regarded Justine with a sardonic quirk of his left brow. Obviously the chit expected him to be taken with her. She was attractive, although Madeline was actually the more beautiful of the two, her features more refined, her eyes filled with a warmth and intelligence that her sister lacked.

His attention switched to Madeline's mother, Agnes, who sat at the other side of the room. "Lady Matthews, I'm afraid I won't be able to stay long. I'd hoped that you would allow me a few minutes alone with Madeline."

Agnes looked affronted at the request. "As you must know, Mr. Scott, it is unseemly for the two of you to speak without a chaperone present."

"At this point, it hardly matters, does it?" he asked softly, making Madeline flush and Justine giggle.

Agnes frowned at the shameless comment. "While you are under my roof, Mr. Scott, I insist that you abide by my standards of decency—even if you do find them too exacting. You may indeed speak with Madeline, but Justine will serve as chaperone." Calmly she swept from the room, giving a meaningful look to her eldest daughter.

The three of them were left in silence. Justine made a face and threw them both a rueful grin as she retreated to the far side of the room. She stood at the window and feigned interest in the view outside, while Logan pulled Madeline to the corner.

"I'm sorry—" Madeline began unhappily, wanting to apologize for her mother's coldness, but Logan held a finger to her lips. Madeline fell silent, spellbound by his nearness. His scent was exquisitely familiar, a masculine blend of linen, wool, and skin, laced with tobacco.

"How do you feel?" he asked, glancing down at her prim, high-necked dress and back to her face.

Madeline colored slightly. "Very well, thank you."

"Still having morning sickness?"

"Yes."

"It should last only another month or two. In the meantime, try to keep something in your stomach."

"Why are you so well-informed on the subject?" she dared to whisper.

Logan smiled at the flash of impudence. "My comanager was often absent because of the same malady."

"Then you haven't ever . . ." Madeline asked, unable to conceal her worry.

"No," Logan said, his voice suddenly gentle. "You're the first woman I've ever gotten with child." He reached into his pocket and extracted a small object. "Give me your hand."

She felt him slide a cool, heavy ring over the fourth finger of her left hand, and her gaze fell to the object. It was a canary-yellow diamond at least five carats in weight, surrounded by a row of round white diamonds that glittered with brilliant fire. Stunned by the extravagance of the ring, Madeline looked up at Logan with wide eyes.

"Good heavens," came Justine's exclamation from across the room. "It's as big as an egg!"

"Thank you," Madeline said to Logan with a catch in her voice. "I've never had anything so beautiful."

Logan's shoulders moved in an indifferent shrug. "If you wish, we'll exchange it for something else."

"Oh, no . . . it's perfect." She stared at the sparkling diamond, searching for the right words to thank him, but nothing seemed appropriate.

Unable to suppress her curiosity, Justine hurried over to them. "Do let me see it, Madeline! Dear heavens, what a magnificent stone. May I try it on?" Before the request had even passed her lips, she had tugged the ring from Madeline's finger and was inspecting it with an admiring gaze. "Flawless, and such a spectacular color!" She threw the two of them a sly glance. "I should think a gift like this deserves more than a paltry 'thank-you,' Madeline. Shouldn't you reward Mr. Scott with a kiss? Mama's not here, after all . . . and I would never tell."

Madeline glanced at Logan in consternation, unable to read his expression. "Mr. Scott is very private—" she said, but Logan interrupted with a roguish smile.

"Not *that* private, sweet." His hands slid gently over her cheeks, holding her still as his lips descended to hers. She quivered at the light brush of his mouth, the way he tasted her as if she were a delicacy to be savored. It was merely a display, she reminded herself, to convince Justine that they were in love . . . but she couldn't prevent the glow of pleasure that spread through her. Her knees wobbled, and she swayed against him, disoriented by the sheer delight of his mouth on hers.

Logan finished the kiss with a soft nudge of his lips and drew back to stare at her.

"Well," came Justine's speculative voice, "you seem quite taken with my little sister, Mr. Scott. One can't help but wonder what a man of your sophistication sees in a girl like her."

Logan's mouth twisted sardonically. It was clear that Justine harbored more than a touch of jealousy. "Madeline has the qualities I've always desired in a wife," he replied evenly.

"She's willful," Justine said. "One can only hope

you'll have better luck than my parents at restraining her."

"Justine," Madeline said, glaring at her sister from beneath her lashes, "you needn't talk about me as if I were a disobedient household pet."

Logan laughed suddenly, and there was a flash of approval in his gaze as he guided Madeline to the settee. "Save your squabbling for later," he murmured. "I don't have much time, and there are details about the wedding that I'd like to discuss."

"Won't you stay for dinner?" Madeline asked.

He shook his head immediately. "I have no desire to put anyone—least of all myself—through the trial of making small talk at the Matthews table."

"That's probably wise," Justine remarked with sly amusement. "Our mother's disapproval of you is hardly a secret. It's a pity, though . . . I've a feeling you would be a most entertaining dinner companion, Mr. Scott."

"That's for your sister to say," Logan replied, looking at Madeline in a way that reminded her of the last time they had shared dinner together . . . and the night of passion that had followed. He seemed to take grim enjoyment in her discomfort.

Thankfully the conversation turned to more mundane matters, but Madeline couldn't keep her mind focused on the subject of their wedding. Thoughts swarmed in her head. One week from now she would become Logan's wife, and if he desired her, they would share a bed again. He had warned her that it wouldn't be as pleasant as before. She supposed that meant he would no longer care about her pleasure. Or perhaps he would even cause her pain—although she couldn't quite believe that of him. Logan was not a cruel man, despite his temper.

Agnes returned to participate in the discussion of wedding details, offering few objections to Logan's plans except when it came to her daughter's attire. There was no way on God's earth, she assured him, that she would allow Madeline to wear white. "It would be the height of hypocrisy," Agnes said firmly. "Madeline has forfeited that right."

Logan met her gaze without blinking. "Madeline was innocent when I met her. She's entitled to wear white during our wedding."

"Not when you take your vows before God, with Madeline dressed in the color of purity. It would be blasphemous. I wouldn't be surprised if a bolt of lightning pierced the roof!"

Logan's mouth twisted sardonically. "Although I don't claim to be a religious man, I suspect that the Lord has other things to worry about besides the color of Maddy's gown."

"Maddy," Agnes repeated, shaking her head in distaste at the nickname. "I'll thank you not to call my daughter by a name that sounds appropriate for a barmaid—"

"Mother," Justine interrupted, placing a restraining hand on Agnes's narrow shoulder. Agnes subsided, her expression as dark as a thundercloud.

Madeline gathered her nerve and touched Logan's shoulder lightly. "Please," she said, her voice soft. "Mother is right . . . I shouldn't wear white."

Although it was clear that Logan would have liked to argue, he scowled and made no reply, letting his silence serve as assent.

"Thank you," Madeline said, relief washing over her.

"I don't give a damn if you go through the ceremony stark naked," he muttered. "I'd like the damned thing to be over with, so I can get on with my work."

Overhearing the comment, Agnes stiffened and glared at Logan, while Justine sought to calm her yet again.

Madeline's gaze fell to her lap. She understood Logan's impatience, knowing that the Capital would always take precedence over everything else in his life. No mere person would ever surpass his beloved theater.

With the matter of the wedding attire agreed upon, the conversation was quickly resolved, and Logan took his leave. After his departure, the mixture of nerves and exhilaration that had seized Madeline began to fade. Feeling slightly depressed, she returned to her room to continue packing, and Justine accompanied her.

"What an extraordinary man!" Justine exclaimed as soon as the bedroom door was closed. "Such a presence—and those blue eyes! However, it's the voice that I find most remarkable. I think he could seduce any woman with that voice—even if he were reciting mathematical equations!"

As she listened to her sister's admiring comments, Madeline was aware of an inward flicker of pride. Justine had always treated her with a mixture of affection and condescension. Now, for the first time, there was an envious tone in Justine's voice.

"What a little minx you turned out to be," Justine said. "Neither Althea nor I could believe it when we heard that you'd run away from school and had an affair with Logan Scott. I think it's delicious. Of course, it is a pity that you're marrying a man so far beneath you."

Madeline stiffened. "I don't consider him beneath me in any way."

"That's the right spirit. You must go on as if you're not even aware of his low birth." Justine leaned forward, her eyes filled with keen interest. "Scott seems a very virile man. I suppose he was very masterful? Do tell me what it was like, Madeline!"

"I couldn't," Madeline protested, startled by the request. "That's private."

"But I'm your sister—you can confide anything in me. Now tell me about Mr. Scott, and in return I'll tell you anything you wish to know about Lord Bagworth."

Madeline pictured Justine's short, round-faced husband and began to smile. "Justine . . . forgive me, but that's hardly an inducement."

"Well." Her older sister sat back and gave her a look of annoyance. "Lord Bagworth may not be as dashing as Mr. Scott, but he has entrées in society that far surpass your husband's."

"I'm sure you're right," Madeline replied, suppressing a laugh. She had not expected such a reaction from her sister. Justine had always been so satisfied, even smug, about landing a titled husband with an expansive country estate, a fine London home, and a score of servants to attend her. But Logan Scott had even greater wealth—and as Justine had admitted, he was very dashing. Madeline didn't care that he hadn't even a drop of blue blood in his veins. Logan was the most fascinating and accomplished man she had ever met, and she could ask for no worthier husband. In fact, she only hoped that she could become worthy of him.

They were married a week later in Logan's drawing room, with its richly colored paintings and shining parquet floor. Madeline was vaguely conscious of her family standing behind them: her parents, her sister Justine, and Lord Bagworth.

The only people Logan had invited to the ceremony were the Duke and Duchess of Leeds, and, strangely, Mrs. Florence. It puzzled Madeline that Logan had desired the elderly woman's presence at his wedding, when he had never met her until recently. They treated each other with polite wariness, but Madeline sensed that they shared some secret that no one else was privileged to know. Perhaps she would find out later what confidence had occurred between them, and why they each seemed to have some greater knowledge of the situation than anyone else present.

In response to the clergyman's inquiries, Logan spoke in monosyllables. His face was hard, yet composed—the look of an actor expertly masking his emotions. Madeline was certain that Logan's pride was revolted by the entire situation. He had never dreamed that he would someday be compelled to marry a woman he actively resented— but she had inadvertently forced him to this. Truly, she had intended to bear the responsibility for the baby alone . . . but in some part of her heart, she had known that Logan wouldn't be able to ignore his child's existence, once he found out. Regret and shame made her eyes sting with unshed tears.

As the clergyman exhorted them to love and honor each other and guided them through the vows that would bind them eternally, Logan glanced at Madeline's face, and he saw her tears. His jaw tautened until the muscles twitched. They were pronounced man and wife, and he pressed a cool kiss against her lips to seal the ceremony.

Afterward, the guests sat down to an eight-course meal in the spectacular dining hall, a circular room lined with marble and gilded Corinthian columns. The ceiling was painted with a scene from *The Tempest*, with ornate sheaves of Italian plasterwork trailing down the walls.

Seated at the opposite end of the long table, Madeline could barely see her husband through the crystal and gold candelabra between them. It was clear that her relatives were amazed by the luxury and beauty of their surroundings. The atmosphere lightened considerably as expensive wines flowed into crystal glasses and platters of French cuisine were brought around.

Justine's husband, Lord Bagworth, exclaimed with pleasure over the selection of exquisite vintages. "I must say, Scott, for a man who never entertains at his own home, you play the role of host to perfection."

Before Logan could reply, Madeline's mother chose that moment to look up from her gold-rimmed plate and comment acerbically, "One can only hope that Mr. Scott will perform the role of dutiful husband with equal skill."

Spoken in a lighter tone, the remark could easily have been taken as a friendly jest—but Agnes's disapproval couldn't have been more clear.

Madeline tensed as she waited for Logan's reply. To her relief, he answered evenly. "I trust you'll have no complaints on that score, Lady Matthews—and neither will my wife."

"No, indeed," Madeline said. Since she had been quiet for most of the day, her remark caused many at the table to look at her in surprise. She continued in a meaningful tone. "I'm certain my mother meant that she believes her high expectations of you will be entirely justified, Mr. Scott."

"I know what she meant," Logan assured her, his blue eyes touched with a flicker of amusement, the first she had seen from him that day.

The meal concluded with a course of cheese, wine, and fruit, and then the men enjoyed glasses of port and thick cigars while the ladies withdrew for tea and conversation. The Duchess of Leeds took the opportunity to speak to Madeline privately, as they occupied chairs slightly removed from the others. It was the first time they had seen each other since Madeline had left the Capital.

"Congratulations, Maddy," Julia said. "I hope you'll both find a great deal of happiness in your marriage."

Madeline responded with a wan smile. "Considering how it began, I don't see how that will be possible."

Julia clucked in sympathy. "Yours isn't the first marriage to begin under less-than-perfect circumstances—nor will it be the last. I believe that having a wife and child will benefit Logan in ways he doesn't begin to suspect."

"He'll never forgive me for what I did," Madeline said. "And I don't blame him."

"Nonsense. I'm certain you must realize that Logan still loves you, Maddy. It's only that he's afraid to trust you again. I hope you'll be patient with him. I don't expect it will be easy. He's stubborn enough to try a saint, you know." Her manner became brisk and encouraging as she continued. "I don't know if Logan has told you yet, but he has asked me to help you plan a ball, to be held no later than a month from now."

"But why?"

"To show you off to all of London, of course."

Madeline was dismayed, the blood draining from her face. "But everyone will be looking at me and whispering—"

"It doesn't matter what they say," Julia assured her. "Believe me, I've been the subject of gossip and rumors for years, and now that you are married to a man as well-known as Logan, so will you. You'll become accustomed to it after a while."

Mrs. Florence approached them and seated herself, declining Julia's offer of assistance. She looked queenly in a dark-blue gown trimmed in tiers of lace, with ropes of heavy pearls twined around her throat and wrists. They exchanged a few pleasant remarks about the service, as well as the splendor of Logan's estate.

"Actors are notoriously helpless when it comes to financial matters," Mrs. Florence remarked, glancing at their luxurious surroundings with an inexplicable flash of pride. "It seems your husband is an exception to that rule, Maddy. You're a very fortunate woman."

"I'm fortunate for many reasons," Madeline replied with a forced smile that didn't deceive her two companions.

"Yes, you are," Mrs. Florence said softly, the lines at the corners of her eyes deepening in affectionate amusement. "And this will all become easier in time, child. I promise you that."

Madeline took a deep breath and relaxed a little. Strange, that the two were able to give her the comfort that her own mother and sister hadn't even attempted to offer. Impulsively her hand sought Mrs. Florence's. "Thank you for coming to my wedding, ma'am. Your presence has made the day easier for me."

"I must say, I wouldn't have missed your wedding to Mr. Scott for all the world. You've opened many doors for me, child, ones I'm certain you can't even begin to guess." Mrs. Florence seemed pleased by the younger women's puzzled expressions.

"What doors?" Julia asked, and laughed as she shook an admonishing finger at her friend. "You look like a cat who found the cream-pot. I must know why."

"Perhaps someday," came the placid reply. Mrs. Florence would say no more after that; she only drank a cup of tea and continued to glance around the room with obvious satisfaction.

Madeline wasn't conscious of when the guests departed, only that they seemed to drift away until there was no one left but servants efficiently whisking away all traces of the wedding . . . and Logan, who was disturbingly matter-of-fact about her presence in his home. Leisurely he sat at the dining table and finished a cigar, stretching out his legs. Madeline occupied a chair nearby, still dressed in her wedding attire, a pale pink gown adorned at the throat and waist with roses of a deeper shade.

Were it not for her strained nerves, she would have enjoyed sitting there with the earthy scent of his cigar drifting to her. The house was blessedly quiet now, and the ordeal of making small talk was over. However, there was another ordeal yet to come, and when or if it would happen was completely up to Logan.

His gaze moved over her with detached interest, in the same way he might regard a painting or sculpture. Madeline felt certain that Julia's assurance that he still loved her was completely untrue. No man could look at a woman he loved as if she were merely a belonging that he could pick up or set aside at will. She thought up a hundred different conversational openings and discarded each one. How odd, that the silences between them had once been so comfortable, when now they were so stiff and strained.

"A room has been prepared for you," Logan finally said, flicking the tip of the cigar into a molded bronze dish. "Have one of the servants show you upstairs."

"Then we won't be sharing—"

"No. We'll occupy separate rooms. As you know, I tend to come and go at unconventional hours. I won't disturb your rest if we sleep in different beds."

*And I won't disturb your privacy*, Madeline thought, but held her tongue. "That is very considerate," she murmured, standing up. Logan stood as well, every inch the courteous host.

"Naturally I reserve the right to visit you from time to time," he remarked.

Madeline nodded with hard-won composure. "What about tonight?" she asked, her voice shaking a little.

His blue eyes held no expression as they gleamed through a thin haze of smoke. "Come to my room when you're ready for bed."

Madeline swallowed hard. "Very well."

Logan occupied his chair again as soon as she reached the threshold. Madeline felt his gaze on her even after she was out of sight, as if the heat of it had left a brand on the middle of her back.

The extra bedroom in Logan's private suite had been enlarged, one wall having been removed to double its size. Gleaming white and gold brocade covered the walls, while oil paintings framed in gold had been hung in artful groupings. There was a scene of children at play, and several others of women and children in domestic settings.

Taking pleasure in the feminine decor, Madeline wandered about the room, noting every change, including the gold clock on the fireplace mantel, the intricate lace on the cream silk counterpane, and the sewing workbox in the corner, inlaid with mother of pearl.

Although she hadn't yet rung for a maid, one appeared to help her change out of her wedding gown. Madeline sat before the dressing table in her high-necked nightgown, lost in her thoughts as the servant brushed her long golden-brown locks.

The maid said something, and Madeline looked up with a flustered smile. "What?" she asked. "I'm afraid I wasn't paying attention."

"I asked if there was anything else you needed, Mrs. Scott."

"Mrs. Scott," Madeline repeated with a faltering smile. "You're the first one who's called me that."

The housemaid returned her smile and bobbed a curtsy before leaving the room.

Madeline stared at her own ashen complexion and automatically pinched and patted her cheeks to bring color to them. Surely there was no reason to be afraid of Logan. He wouldn't harm her, if for no other reason than her carrying his child. On the other hand, he could make things very unpleasant for her. He was her husband now, and she was completely at his mercy. No one would intervene on her behalf, whether he chose to be cruel or kind.

Madeline stood and checked the long row of buttons that fastened the front of her white linen robe. Lifting her chin resolutely, she left her room.

Logan's room was only a few doors away, filled with the flickering light from the fireplace. He was half-reclining on the bed, leaning against the headboard with his hands clasped behind his dark head. He was naked beneath the sheet, every angle of his aroused body clearly defined. The fireglow made his face gleam like freshly cast metal. Approaching the bed, Madeline stopped a few yards away as she heard the deep rumble of his voice.

"Take off your robe."

She looked at him in confusion.

"Go on," he murmured, his eyes glittering like those of a stalking beast.

Understanding what he wanted, Madeline tried to comply, but her fingers were stiff. Logan waited with unnatural patience, silent and watchful. Madeline fumbled with the long row of tiny buttons, freeing them from the silk loops. When the task was completed, she drew her arms from the long sleeves and let the robe drop to the floor. She was dressed only in her thin gown. Her skin seemed to burn as she realized that the light from the fire shone through the garment, illuminating every detail of her body.

"The rest," Logan said inexorably.

She stared at his taut face and reached for the fastenings at the back of her neck. The sense of being a possession, an object on display, was over-whelming. If Logan meant to humiliate her, he was succeeding. Grasping handfuls of the delicate fabric, she began to lift it over her head and hesitated. She couldn't.

"Now," came her husband's suddenly thick voice.

Holding her breath, Madeline obeyed in a decisive motion, lifting off the nightgown and casting it to the floor. The cold air seemed to penetrate every inch of her skin, raising goosebumps on her naked flesh and shrinking her nipples into hard points. Dry-mouthed, she stood before him with her hands clenched at her sides, while he stared at her.

"I . . . I'm cold," she whispered desperately, longing for something, anything, that she could use to cover herself.

"So I see," Logan replied, his gaze lingering at her breasts. Unfolding his hands from behind his head, he turned back the sheet and gestured for her to come to him.

Madeline couldn't keep from covering herself as she walked toward him, one arm clasped across her breasts, the other hand protecting the shadowed place between her thighs.

The gesture seemed to amuse Logan, his breath deepening audibly as she reached the bed.

"There's no need for modesty, my sweet. You'll have no secrets left before the night is through."

Her teeth chattered as she crawled onto the mattress and lay on the smooth, slick linen. Every muscle in her body was tightly bunched. Logan's huge, warm hand slid over her hip, his touch making her flinch. Contrary to her fears, he was very gentle, almost impersonal, as he pulled her

against him. He traced the lines of her body with
the expertise of a sculptor, his fingertips light and
gentle.

But there was a detached quality in the way he
touched her, and Madeline realized that the impas-
sioned lover she remembered from before had
been replaced by a calculating stranger. He made
love to her in a purely physical sense, with his
emotions locked firmly away. If only she could be
similarly unaffected . . . but she couldn't hold back
a whimper of pleasure as his mouth found the
aching tip of her breast, while at the same time his
hand slid between her thighs. His fingers delved
through a thatch of silken curls, parted the tender
lips and skimmed through gathering moisture.

Madeline writhed beneath his caress, arching
her breast up to the persistent tugging of his mouth
while the sensations climbed higher and higher.
Words trembled on the edge of her lips, and it took
all her power to keep them from spilling out . . . *I
love you . . . love you . . .* but he didn't want her
love.

Just as the piercing ecstasy began to sweep over
her, Logan pulled away. Filled with an intolerable
ache, Madeline gasped out a protest and reached
for him, only to find herself being pushed back to
the mattress. She saw the outline of his head and
shoulders above her, and for a moment she feared
that he intended to leave her like this, shamed and
trembling with need. "Please—" she began, her
voice not sounding like her own.

"Hush." He touched her lips with fingers that
carried her own intimate scent.

Madeline bit her lip and lay still, her lungs rising
and falling rapidly. She jerked as she felt Logan's
warm mouth just below her breasts, drifting to her

stomach. Unsteadily she touched his head, her fingers curling in his rich dark locks. Logan pushed her hand away and continued his path across her body, investigating with lips, teeth, and tongue . . . finding the sensitive hollow of her navel . . . the rise of her hip . . . the tender crease of her inner thigh.

"No," she gasped as he reached that sensitive area, and she twisted away with a shudder. She had never imagined that he would do such a thing. "No—"

But Logan caught her and pinned her in place, his grip tight on her wrists. "Don't ever say that word to me again," he said, his voice steely. "Not in bed, or out of it."

The statement shocked her. She understood that she had hurt him, and that this was the form of his revenge, to inflict his will on her. "You mustn't," she managed to say, her wrists straining in his grasp. "I don't want that."

Logan laughed, the sound mocking her as he bent his head once more. Madeline's eyes pricked with tears of fury and shame, and she felt his mouth on her, there where she had never imagined it, never thought it possible. Although she tried to close her thighs, her traitorous body disobeyed, spreading wide to receive him. His lips were hot, burning her, his tongue a sleek invasion that made her groan and cry out in mortifying pleasure. She ceased to be herself, reduced to a wanton creature who clung and arched with frantic need until a great rolling wave of climax came over her, leaving her limp and weak in its aftermath.

Before the glow of sensation had faded, Logan moved his body over hers. She felt him enter her, and she tried to protest the massive intrusion,

pushing feebly at his chest. He forced himself
inside her swollen depths until she groaned in
surrender and opened to him. The rhythm began, a
slow, steady thrusting that sent her beleaguered
senses whirling out of control once again.

Madeline turned her face into the hard curve of
his neck and shoulder, feeling somehow that this
act had made her his in a way that their other time
had not. Then, Logan had been a partner, a
teacher, a beloved friend. This time he was her
master, dominating her body and soul.

The pleasure overtook her once again, like fire
dissolving inside her, and she gasped against his
taut throat. Logan drove inside her one final time,
burying himself deeply, his large body shuddering
in release. The perspiration from his skin sealed
them together, arms and legs wrapped in a tight
embrace. Somehow it reassured Madeline to feel
Logan tremble slightly, to feel his breath strike her
skin and his heart pound in his chest. No matter
how he tried, he wasn't able to stay indifferent to
her. He relaxed over her, and she welcomed his
heavy weight until he rolled away with a sigh.

She wished that he would kiss her, caress her,
even hold her hand for a moment, but he refrained
from touching her. Abruptly the room was chilly
again. Madeline reached for the sheet and covers,
pulling them up to her shoulders. Perplexed, she
wondered if he wanted her to leave.

"Shall I go now?" she asked.

Logan took a long time to answer. "No. I may
have need of you again tonight."

Her mouth compressed at the arrogant com-
mand, but she rested back against the pillows. *Be
patient with him,* Julia had advised . . . well, it was
certainly worth the effort. She would try to atone

for the past—she owed that to him. She turned on her side to watch his profile in the firelight. Logan's eyes were closed, but she sensed that it took a long time for him to fall asleep, and she could only guess at the thoughts that occupied him.

In the decade since Logan had started the Capital Theatre, lovingly reconstructing and refurbishing the old set of buildings; assembled a company of actors, musicians, painters, carpenters, costumiers, sceneshifters, property men, stage managers, and the like; and trained the lot of them to his satisfaction . . . he had never been late to rehearsal. Until this morning.

He usually awoke easily, but this morning he had been drowsy and dream-fogged . . . and when he had seen Madeline sleeping beside him, he hadn't been able to stop himself from reaching for her. He had made love to her while she had yawned and purred like a sleepy kitten. Only afterward had he realized how late it was.

Cursing and scowling, Logan had dressed with lightning speed and raced in his carriage to reach the theater as quickly as possible. However, he arrived a full forty-five minutes after the designated hour, and he winced as he strode through the back entrance and headed to the greenroom. The company would doubtless mutter and grumble about his lateness. They were entitled to complain. He had never hesitated to fine any of them for the same offense.

The greenroom was empty save for Jeff, the shopboy. "Mr. Scott!" he exclaimed. "We all wondered if you were coming today—"

"Where is everyone?" Logan interrupted, a scowl pulling at his face.

"Onstage, sir. The duchess took it on herself to rehearse 'em, seeing as how you weren't here."

Logan nodded shortly and went through the door leading to the backstage area. He was aware of a ripple of hasty mutters, and a bit of scuffling as he approached the stage. Squaring his shoulders, he came out of the wing—and stopped short as he saw the entire company waiting in a semicircle with glasses and cups in their hands. There was the sound of corks popping, and the crew grinned like idiots as they confronted him. "Congratulations!" someone shouted, while at the same time another voice laughingly accused, "You're late!"

The scene erupted into a chorus of laughter and cheers, and glasses clinked busily as frothy champagne was poured. A cup of champagne was pressed into Logan's hand, and he felt his mouth pulling into a crooked smile. "Are we celebrating my tardiness or my wedding?" he asked.

Julia came forward as she replied, her lovely face wreathed in amusement. "Let's say that both have been a long time in coming. Take care, Mr. Scott— or we all might begin to think that you're human."

"I believe we can all agree on that point," Logan replied. "And I want it understood that I intend to fine myself for being late."

"Oh, that's all right," Arlyss Barry said cheekily, "we used the cashbox in your office to pay for the champagne."

The crew laughed gustily, and Logan shook his head, the smile remaining on his lips.

"To the Capital Theatre Company!" one of them cried merrily. "A bunch of thieving drunkards."

Amid the general round of amusement, Logan raised his own glass. "To Mrs. Scott," he said, and they all drank and agreed vociferously.

"Hear! Hear!"

"God bless Mrs. Scott!"

"Lord take pity on her!" someone added, and the revelers chuckled into their champagne.

# Twelve

*Perhaps it* had been the champagne, or the will generated by news of his wedding, or merely Logan's own grudging good mood, but the atmosphere at the Capital Theatre was a hundred times improved. Logan couldn't recall when a rehearsal had gone so well. The actors were alert and responsive, and the crew performed their jobs with energy and close attention to detail. As for himself . . . it was as if some vital essence had been restored.

The knowledge that Madeline was waiting at home, that he was free to touch her, see her, make love to her whenever he wished, filled him with a satisfaction that he was hard-pressed to conceal. Not that he was prepared to admit any hint of love or forgiveness . . . he wasn't nearly ready for that. But he was fully aware that her presence in his life was necessary to his very existence. Last night, and today, had been proof of that. In the space of twenty-four hours he had returned to his old self, able once more to take the reins at the Capital with ease.

"Excellent," Julia had said to him during rehearsal—she, who never praised his abilities because she claimed there was no need to inflate his self-opinion any further. They were rehearsing a new piece entitled *The Rose*, the story of an old man reliving the memories of his tumultuous life. "You nearly brought tears to my eyes during your monologue about remembering how it feels to be young," she told him.

"It's a well-written part," Logan replied, walking backstage with her as they headed to their respective offices.

"And you play it brilliantly," Julia said, her turquoise eyes filled with speculation. She smiled slightly. "It seems you've recaptured whatever it was that's been missing. It's because of Maddy, isn't it?"

Although Logan was annoyed by her perceptiveness, he couldn't argue. He responded with a surly grunt.

Julia continued with obvious enjoyment. "You must resent Madeline for proving that you're not invulnerable."

"I never claimed I was invulnerable," he returned evenly. "And if I harbor any resentment toward my wife, it's for a very different reason."

"Really." Julia's gaze mocked him. She entered her office, poking her blond head outside the door to add, "I shall enjoy watching you during the next few months, Logan. It will be interesting to see which part of you will win the battle—the half that wants to be happy, or the half that wants to flee from anyone who might dare to love you."

"Your talents are wasted as an actress, Your Grace," Logan informed her over his shoulder, continuing on his way. "With your imagination, you should have been a writer."

The sound of her laughter trailed down the hall

after him. As soon as Logan reached his office, he saw a familiar dark head above the back of his chair. Andrew, Lord Drake, was enjoying a drink at his desk.

"Jimmy!" he cried, grinning broadly. "What a fine newlywed you look, scowling that way."

"What do you want?" Logan asked, shaking his hand in a firm grip.

Andrew smiled and indicated a crate beside the desk. It contained a dozen brandy bottles, each tied with a jaunty bow. "I brought you a gift, Jimmy. I'll admit, my feelings were wounded that you didn't ask me to stand up for you at the ceremony—but in the face of our long-standing friendship, I decided to let it pass."

Logan took one of the bottles and inspected it admiringly. The vintage was an exquisite thirty-year-old French brandy. "Thank you, Andrew."

"I decided to sample a bottle while I waited for you," Andrew said. "Like nectar of the gods. Care for a glass?"

"I'll get one from the greenroom."

"Don't bother—I brought one for you. Can't drink brandy like this from anything but a proper snifter."

"I should have invited you to the ceremony," Logan said gruffly, sitting on the edge of the desk as Andrew poured. "But it was all done rather quickly."

"So I heard." Andrew slanted him a wicked grin, his blue eyes sparkling. "Word has it that your new wife is carrying a bag pudding." He looked at Logan with mock horror. "Can it be true? Will the Scott household soon be blessed with a little Logan?"

Logan accepted the snifter of brandy and nodded grimly, waiting for further mockery.

"Well done, then," Andrew said abruptly, surprising him. "She's a likely wench, not to mention easy on the eye . . . and you could hardly do better than the daughter of a viscount."

"No remarks about my being 'caught'?" Logan asked. "I was certain you'd have something to say about that." He sipped his brandy slowly, rolling the fine flavor on his tongue.

Andrew smiled. "You weren't caught, Jimmy. I've known you for too long. You wouldn't have married her unless you wanted her."

Andrew was right . . . the only reason he had married Madeline was because he wanted her, needed her. The pregnancy had been a convenient excuse. Strange, that Andrew could have seen that so easily.

"We have no secrets from each other, do we?" Logan asked, staring at the man next to him and realizing that they were indeed brothers. Now he knew why they had remained friends for so long. They had each unknowingly felt the pull of their shared blood for years.

"Not one," Andrew agreed cheerfully.

The urge to tell him . . . *Andrew, I'm your brother* . . . was so strong that Logan bit the insides of his lips to keep from speaking. He drank deeply of the brandy. There was no predicting for certain what Andrew's reaction would be to the revelation. Perhaps he might take a fleeting pleasure in the news, but Logan doubted it. More likely, Andrew would be suspicious, skeptical, bitter. He would turn against his father, and Logan as well and cut himself loose from any kind of steadying influence. Logan had no wish to see his half brother embark on a gambling or drinking spree that could result in ruin.

"Why are you looking at me like that?" Andrew asked, quirking his dark brows. "Just as my father does . . . like a scientist about to dissect a specimen."

"Sorry." Logan relaxed his features. "I was just thinking that you seem a bit fashed, Andrew. Been spending too much time at the hazard tables of late?"

"One night too many," Andrew admitted with a forced laugh. "But my confessions will keep 'til later. I only came by to offer my congratulations."

"If you're in trouble—"

"I'm always in trouble." Andrew rested his boots on the desk, heedless of the books and papers beneath his muddy heels. "But at least life is never boring. Tell me, Jimmy . . . how does it feel to be a married man?"

"I've only been wed for a day," Logan said dryly. "It's too soon to come to any conclusion."

Andrew made a face. "I can't say I'd fancy being served the same supper every night for the rest of my life. But, of course, a man can slip out now and then for a little variety, as long as he's discreet."

"I suppose," Logan murmured, contemplating his brandy absently. Madeline was hardly in a position to object were he to take a mistress. But he had no desire to insult her that way . . . and though he might belie it, the truth was that no woman had ever appealed to him as she did.

Andrew seemed to read his thoughts, reacting with a spurt of incredulous laughter. "Good God—don't tell me you're in love with her?"

"No," Logan said swiftly, his eyes turning hard.

"That's a relief. Love is poison, Jimmy. Just

remember what happened the last time you succumbed to it."

"How could I forget?" Logan said, his voice
tainted with sudden malice, and he stared at Andrew until the latter murmured uncomfortably and
finished his brandy.

"I must be off, Jimmy. Good luck to you, and all
that. By the by, I heard a rumor that you'll soon be
giving a ball for her at your estate. If that's true, I'll
be expecting an invitation." Breezily he waved
good-bye and left the office, his booted feet echo-
ing in the hallway.

"There's no reason for Logan to host such a
grand affair . . . not for my sake." Madeline stared
in distress at samples of hand-painted invitations,
trying to envision the prospect of six hundred
guests pouring through Logan's elegant London
mansion.

"It's not all for your sake, dear," Julia replied
dryly, sitting nearby as she worked on the guest
list. "It's partly to assuage Logan's all-important
pride. Rather than handle the circumstances of
your marriage with discretion, he wants to make
a show of it, to demonstrate that he couldn't be
more pleased with the situation. No doubt such a
spectacle will dull the point of many a gossip's
arrow—especially the ones who want to receive
invitations." Frowning slightly, Julia crossed out
a few names and inserted others, striving to
achieve the perfect blend.

"But why have it here?" Madeline asked. "Logan
will hate having hundreds of people wandering
through his home, staring at his art collection and
investigating every surface and corner—"

"Of course he will. However, he knows that

hosting the ball at his mysterious mansion will drive people into a frenzy. Everyone of significance is already begging for an invitation, and those who suspect they won't get one are already making plans to leave London the night of the ball."

"He'll lose all his privacy," Madeline said, unable to share Julia's enthusiasm.

"I'm certain Logan knew when he married you that he had to sacrifice most of his privacy. He certainly wouldn't expect a girl of your age to enjoy his reclusive lifestyle. You'll want to dance and attend the opera, travel, join clubs and social groups—" Julia stopped and peered at the list in her lap more closely. "Hmm. I should add a few more international names . . ."

While the duchess labored over the list, Madeline subsided in her chair with a quiet moan. She was beginning to understand what Logan wanted of her, and it would require the performance of her life. Not only was she to hold her head high as people tried to observe if she was showing or not . . . she was also to move among the crowd with confidence and poise—things they would expect of Logan Scott's wife. If she failed, it would reflect badly on Logan as well as herself. Why would he put her to such a test, and so soon after their marriage?

"I don't know if I can do it," she said aloud, her fingers twining tightly in her lap.

Julia's turquoise eyes flickered with friendly sympathy. "Maddy . . . all he expects is that you try."

Madeline nodded. She would do whatever Logan asked, because she loved him. He must never regret having married her. No matter how long it took, she would make him admit someday that he had chosen the right woman to share his life with. "I'll do more than try," she said. "I'm going to succeed."

"Good for you," Julia said with an admiring laugh. "You're made of resilient stuff, aren't you?"

"I hope so."

As the two women worked and talked, a tray of tea and delicate sandwiches was brought in, but Madeline couldn't bring herself to eat anything. Nausea was still a persistent problem. Logan had clearly been annoyed by her lack of appetite and had threatened to send for the doctor if she didn't improve soon.

"I wouldn't worry," Julia reassured her. "Your appetite will return soon enough. You'll regain the weight you've lost, and a great deal more."

Madeline rested a hand on her own flat stomach. "I'm actually looking forward to it. Right now it doesn't seem as if there is a baby at all."

"Wait until it starts moving and kicking," Julia said, smiling. "Then you'll have no doubt."

The afternoon grew late, and Julia departed with the promise that she would return on the morrow to take Madeline calling with her. There were a few young married women whom Madeline must meet. "Not all of my friends are in the theater, you know," Julia said impishly. "Marrying the duke has forced me to associate with respectable people from time to time."

The duchess was being extraordinarily kind, Madeline reflected after she had left. It spoke of Julia's high regard for Logan, that she would go out of her way to be so gracious to his wife. Relaxing in a plush corner of the parlor settee, Madeline occupied herself with reading and needlework until Logan arrived home. He came into the parlor carrying the wintry scent from outside, his dark hair disordered and his cheeks slightly reddened from the cold. "Maddy," he said, coming to stand by the settee.

Madeline tilted her head back to look at him, feeling as if she would drown in his fathomless blue eyes.

"Have you eaten?" Logan asked.

Madeline shook her head. "I was waiting for you."

He extended a hand and helped her from the settee, his grasp warm and hard. "How was the afternoon with Julia?"

"We made some headway, I think. It's quite an undertaking, planning an event this large."

He shrugged indifferently. "It's only a matter of hiring the right people."

As they walked to the circular dining hall, Madeline wanted to slip her hand companionably over his arm, but thought better of it. So far Logan hadn't encouraged any overtures from her, and she thought it likely that he would rebuff her if she tried.

In the few days since their wedding, their relationship had been polite and somewhat strained. They discussed neutral subjects and chose their words carefully. There were no intimate glances, no casual kisses or caresses. It was only at night that the constraints melted away, when Logan would come to her bed and wordlessly remove her gown, and make love to her until she ached with the pleasure of it. Each morning he left for the theater before she awoke.

"Did rehearsal go well?" Madeline asked as he seated her at the table.

Logan amused her with an account of Arlyss

Barry's latest feud with another actress who had upstaged her, and the dissatisfaction of a few actors regarding an agreement he had made with a rival theater. "The Daly has recently lost a pair of its major performers, so I've decided to lend them a few of my actors for their run of *As You Like It*. In return, we'll use two or three of their players for supporting roles in *The Rose*. Unfortunately, my actors are protesting the transfer. They consider themselves too good to perform at the Daly."

"I don't blame them," Madeline commented, watching from the corner of her eye as a pair of footmen brought in silver dishes and trays. "If I were an actor, I would much rather appear at the Capital."

"Nevertheless, they'll do as I tell them."

"But why enter into an agreement that will benefit the Daly far more than the Capital?"

"It's good for the profession as a whole. I don't intend to allow my sense of competition to harm the London stage—*any* stage, not just mine."

"You're quite a statesman," Madeline said with a sudden smile.

"I can afford to be."

Expertly the footmen set the dishes before them and served tender slices of chicken bathed in cream-and-sherry sauce, vegetables that had been mixed with buttered breadcrumbs and molded into artful shapes, and pastry stuffed with truffles and eggs.

As Madeline stared at the array of French cuisine, the cloying aromas began to erode any trace of appetite. Feeling queasy, she averted her gaze from her plate and reached for her water glass. Logan watched her with a sudden scowl.

"You're going to eat," he said.

"I'm not hungry." Madeline swallowed against the rising pressure in her throat, while the smell of rich food filled her nostrils. Pushing her plate away, she closed her eyes and breathed through her mouth.

"Dammit," she heard Logan mutter. "You're not consuming enough to keep yourself healthy, much less provide for the babe."

"I'm trying," she returned, her eyes still closed. "But I feel sick all the time."

Logan summoned a footman and instructed him to bring more food from the kitchen: dry chicken with no seasoning, and boiled potatoes mashed with milk.

"I'll only send it back," Madeline said stubbornly. "I can't eat anything tonight. Perhaps I'll feel better tomorrow."

They exchanged a mutual glare. "You'll eat something if I have to stuff it down your throat," Logan said grimly. "Now that you've gotten yourself in this condition, you have a responsibility to the child."

The accusatory note in his voice stung. "I had some help 'getting myself in this condition,'" Madeline snapped, her own temper flaring. "It was as much your fault as mine!" She leaned her head on her hands, breathing unsteadily and wishing that the waves of nausea would go away.

There was a short silence. "You're right," Logan said abruptly. "I didn't give a thought to the possible consequences of what we did that night. I was too eager to bed you." He sounded distinctly uncomfortable as he added, "Besides, I've never had to bother with that sort of thing. The women I . . . er, knew before you were all in the habit of taking preventative measures."

Madeline peered at him between her fingers. Was it her imagination, or did he look almost contrite? "Preventative measures?" she repeated. "I don't know what you're talking about."

Logan smiled. "We'll discuss it later. After the baby is born." He moved his chair beside hers and slid his arm behind her back. Dipping a napkin into a water glass, he held the cool cloth against her sweat-beaded forehead. "Remember the milk toast you fed me when I was sick?" he murmured. "You promised I could have my revenge someday."

She made a sound somewhere between a laugh and a groan. "I should have left you alone."

"You saved my life," Logan said. "It doesn't matter what your motives were. You took care of me in spite of my bad temper and delirious rantings and sickroom stench." The cool, damp cloth moved over her cheek and down to her throat, soothing her. "The least I can do is return the favor."

The tightness in her throat eased, the sickness receding a little. Madeline opened her eyes and saw Logan's face very close to hers. The way he looked at her made her heart pick up a rapid beat. It wasn't the loving gaze she remembered from before . . . but at least the coldness and distance had been banished. "You can have anything you want," he murmured, as if he were coddling a sick child. "Just tell me."

"Anything?" She laughed shakily. "You're putting yourself at risk, making an offer like that."

His intense blue eyes held hers. "I never say things I don't mean."

She stared at him wonderingly, until the footman returned with a new plate of food and set it before them.

"Thank you, George," Logan said, picking up a fork. "That's all for now." His arm remained behind Madeline's back. Scooping up a tiny morsel of mashed boiled potato, he held it to her lips. "Do you think you could manage one bite, sweet?"

Resignedly she opened her mouth and accepted the offering, despite the roiling of her stomach. The potato was bland and crumbling on her tongue. Chewing slowly, she tried to keep from gagging.

"Once more," Logan coaxed.

He was unexpectedly patient, distracting her with light conversation, supporting her back with his hard arm as he fed her. He could be very gentle, for such a large man. Each bite went down a little easier than the last, until she had consumed half the food on the plate. Finally she shook her head with a sigh. "No more."

He seemed reluctant to withdraw his arm. "Are you certain?"

Madeline nodded. "You should eat now. Your supper is getting cold." She sipped a goblet of water while Logan attended to his own plate. She was fascinated by the movements of his hands, the way his long fingers tore chunks from a hard-crusted roll, the way he held a crystal glass. As he realized that she was watching him, some unvoiced question seemed to hover between them. His expression was arrested . . . he seemed curiously discomforted, as if he wanted something he shouldn't have.

Waving away the offer of dessert with an abrupt gesture, Logan helped Madeline from the table. The past few nights they had spent an hour or two after dinner in a private parlor, reading and conversing before the fire. Tonight, however, Logan seemed disinclined to share her company. "Perhaps I'll see you in the morning," he said, casually flicking her chin with his forefinger. "I have some work to do in the library."

Her brows knit together, and she kept her voice low, mindful of being overheard. "You won't . . . come to me later?"

His expression didn't change. "No. I won't bother you tonight."

Logan started to turn away, but she touched his wrist lightly, and he went very still. Her clear amber eyes looked into his. "I wouldn't mind," she said. It was the closest she could bring herself to inviting him.

An awkward, charged silence came between them. Logan wrestled with temptation, knowing very well what she was offering. It was something he wanted badly indeed. He wanted to laugh in frustration at the way Madeline doggedly refused to protect herself. It was her peculiar strength, that she could take any setdown and still not close herself away. He almost envied her—it was a strength he didn't possess.

He leaned over and touched his lips to her forehead, craving her silken skin, her supple body beneath his mouth and hands . . . but he pulled away after the chaste kiss. "Good night," he said gruffly.

Madeline nodded, forcing an unconcerned smile to her face, and went alone to her room. She would give him all the time he needed. She would be patient with him, just as she would with a wild creature that feared her touch . . . a creature that might be coaxed to eat from her hand or just as likely bite it off.

Changing into a thin long-sleeved gown, she snuggled beneath the heavy silk covers. Gradually the warmth of her body collected in the cocoon of bedclothes. Her bones seemed to ache, especially the lower region of her spine, and she changed position many times until she found a comfortable place on her side.

Sleep was elusive. Madeline listened in vain for the sound of Logan entering his room a few doors away. Gradually she drifted in and out of a fragmented slumber that gave her no peace. Waking from a vivid dream, she discovered that her legs were tight and knotted, and she flexed her calves to ease them. Immediately she was seized with a knifelike pain in her right leg, the muscle cramping and burning. She wasn't aware of making a sound, but she must have, for Logan's voice suddenly broke through the darkness, and she felt his weight as he climbed onto the mattress to reach her.

"Maddy," he said urgently, his hands sliding over her as she gathered herself in a ball of pain. "Maddy, what the hell is wrong? Tell me—"

"My leg," she gasped. It hurt. It paralyzed her so that no movement was possible. "Don't touch me—"

"Let me." Logan pushed her hands away and felt for her leg. "Try to relax."

"I can't." But she leaned back against him and jerked as his hand closed around her calve. He found the cramped muscle and kneaded gently until the agony began to ebb. Madeline let out a sigh of relief, resting against Logan's chest as he continued to work out the soreness. When he moved to her other leg, she managed a soft murmur—"That one's all right"—but he hushed her and massaged it as well.

"What happened?" he asked, pushing her night-gown to the tops of her thighs.

"I woke with leg cramps," Madeline replied, feeling drugged. Logan seemed to know exactly how to touch her, how deeply to ply her muscles without hurting them. "Julia said to expect it sometimes—it's common for women in my condition."

"I never knew that," he said, sounding disgruntled. "How often does it happen?"

"I don't know. This was the first time." Modestly she tugged at the hem of her nightgown where it had ridden too high. "Thank you. I'm sorry to have bothered you." His hands slipped away from her, and Madeline yawned and curled on her side.

There were sounds of him undressing in the darkness, the rustle of clothes dropping to the floor. Madeline opened her eyes and stared at his shadowy figure. "Aren't you going to leave?" she asked hesitantly.

"No, madam." He crawled into the space beside her. "It seems that you're determined to have me in your bed tonight."

"If you're implying that I was trying to trick you—"

"It's clear that my charms are too much for you to resist. I understand." His arm slid around her, and his smiling mouth covered hers.

Realizing that he was teasing her, Madeline pushed at his chest. "You conceited man—" she exclaimed with a laugh, as his hand closed around the back of her head.

"Kiss me." He held her steady as his mouth moved over hers in gentle exploration, his breath burning her cheek. His playful mood vanished, replaced by an intense concentration, a tenderness,

that she had never thought he would show her
again. He touched her body with his fingertips,
brushing across the downy hairs on her spine, the
peaks of her breasts, the creases behind her knees.
Madeline lay still beneath him, floating on a current of pleasure, trembling in anticipation as his
mouth drifted across her chest.

He lingered on her nipples for long minutes,
sucking and stroking with his tongue, bringing
them to acutely hard points. Restlessly she arched
upward, wanting his body over her, inside her,
wanting him to crush her with his weight . . . but
he held back, drawing the smooth pads of his
fingers over her body in long trails of fire.

All shame deserted her, and she found herself
gasping and pleading, opening her legs for him,
until finally his fingers parted her aching flesh,
sliding inside with teasing flicks.

Madeline reached down to grasp the stiff, hot
length of him, her touch inexperienced but ardent.
Logan drew in a sharp breath and held her tightly,
one large hand sliding over hers. His voice was
velvety-rough as he murmured in her ear. "Maddy,
yes . . . sweet . . . this way . . ." Growling with
pleasure, he taught her what he liked, pressing
mingled words and kisses across her skin.

When he had reached his limits, Logan pulled
her to her side and drew her leg high over his hip.
Her small body, so supple and responsive, twined
around him bonelessly, fitting as if she had been
made for him. Entering her by slow degrees, he
savored the feel of her, silk and heat enfolding him
tightly. Her face was transfixed beneath his, her
soft mouth drawn taut, low sounds coming from
her throat. Slowly he rocked against her, pushing
inside her, until Madeline shuddered and moaned,

sensations colliding in a white-hot burst of rapture. Then Logan moved strongly between her thighs, inflamed by her sweet welcoming warmth, letting the tension uncoil and streak through him in exquisite release.

Afterward Logan remained inside her, cupping her body in his hands. Her skin was as delicate and fragrant as the petals of night-blooming jasmine. Lowering his mouth to her throat, he tasted the faint flavor of salt and touched his tongue to her still-rapid pulse. This was a luxury he didn't usually allow himself, to linger with her in the aftermath. Too intimate, and dangerous.

The ticking of the gold mantel clock seemed to mock him. Ignoring the sound, he relaxed beside Madeline, his hands buried in the soft sheaves of her hair. She was his, after all. He could do as he liked with her . . . just as long as she never came to suspect that he loved her.

Faced with the prospect of a morning meeting with a playwright whose new work required extensive editing, Logan decided to see him at Banbury's coffeehouse. He often did such work at the coffeehouse, where he was always shown to the same table located near a large window that provided ample daylight. The atmosphere at Banbury's was relaxed and convivial. Hopefully it would serve to lighten the playwright's mood, since he tended to regard each word he had written as sacred.

"Brew a pot that's extra strong and black," Mr. Banbury called to his daughter, who helped him run the place. "Mr. Scott has just arrived!"

Logan made his way to his usual table, stopping briefly here and there to exchange a few words with friends and acquaintances. Banbury's tended

to attract an intellectual crowd: artists, philoso-
phers, and hordes of writers from Fleet Street.

One of the coffeehouse patrons, a fellow member of the Society of Artists, approached Logan as
he set out the play folio, fresh sheets of parchment,
and writing implements.

"Scott, what luck to see you here this morning!"
the man, Lord Beauchamp, exclaimed heartily.
"I've been meaning to speak to you about a certain
matter . . . pardon, I can see that you're waiting for
someone, but it won't take long to ask you . . ."

"Ask away," Logan said easily, indicating the
chair next to him.

Lord Beauchamp sat and regarded him with an
earnest smile. "I wouldn't trouble you with this,
Scott, but knowing of your close relationship with
the artistic community and the generous patronage
you've given to so many artists—"

Logan interrupted with an inquiring arch of his
brow. "You may as well go straight to the point, my
lord. I'm inured to flattery."

Lord Beauchamp laughed. "I believe you're the
first actor to ever make such a claim. Very well, I'll
be direct—I want a favor for a young artist, a
gentleman by the name of Mr. James Orsini."

"I've heard of him," Logan said, casting a brief
smile at the young woman who placed a tray of
coffee before him. His attention returned to Beauchamp.

"Orsini has a marvelous technique, experiment-
ing with light and texture—remarkable for a man
in his twenties. The problem is, he is in search of a
subject that will earn him an invitation to exhibit
his paintings—"

Logan interrupted with a quiet laugh, lifting a
cup of bitter black coffee to his lips. After taking a

bracing swallow, he looked at Beauchamp with gleaming blue eyes. "I know what you're going to ask, my lord. The answer is no."

"But no artist is considered important until he's painted Logan Scott—and you've allowed at least twenty of them to do so, at my count."

"Twenty-five," Logan said dryly.

"I assure you, Scott, you've never sat for an artist as deserving of the honor as Orsini."

Logan shook his head. "No doubt you're right. However, I've been painted more than any actor you could name—"

"That's because you're so successful," Beauchamp pointed out.

"—and I've had enough of it. I've been represented in oil, mezzotint, metal, marble, and wax . . . busts, medallions, paintings, conversation pieces . . . let's spare the public from yet another portrait of me."

"Orsini will agree to any arrangements you would care to make. There are a score of others in the Society who feel as strongly as I that you must allow this artist the chance to paint you. Good God, man, will you make us all beg?"

Logan regarded him with mock alarm and took another swallow of coffee. While Beauchamp waited tensely for an answer, Logan considered the possibilities. After a moment, he smiled slightly and spoke. "I have an alternate proposition. Tell Orsini that I'll allow him to paint my wife."

"Your wife . . ." Beauchamp sputtered in confusion. "That's right, I'd heard that you were married recently . . . but I'm positive that Orsini would much prefer *you* as a subject—"

"A portrait of Mrs. Scott will be a suitable centerpiece for an exhibition. If Orsini is able to

capture what I see in her, I'll ensure that he is
amply rewarded."

Beauchamp regarded him doubtfully. "Well . . .
Mrs. Scott *is* reputed to be a very attractive
woman—"

"She's damned beautiful." Logan stared into the
silken dark surface of his coffee. "There's a quality
of innocence about her that won't change even if
she lives to be a hundred . . ." Abruptly he recalled
himself from the brief reverie. "To my knowledge,
she's never been painted before. Orsini is fortunate
to have the opportunity."

Lord Beauchamp regarded him with gathering
amusement. "I'll inform Mr. Orsini that he must
paint her, as everyone will be avidly curious about
the woman who's made you so besotted."

"I wouldn't use that word," Logan replied,
scowling faintly.

"Dear fellow, no other word will do. The look on
your face as you described her . . ." Chuckling,
Lord Beauchamp stood and nodded good-bye to
him, returning to his own table.

" 'Besotted,' my arse," Logan grumbled, leafing
through the play folio. "I only said she was beautiful."

Orsini accepted the proposal without hesitation,
forwarding a letter of gratitude that arrived at the
Scotts' London home in the morning. Upon being
informed of the plans for a portrait, Madeline
reacted with dismay.

"I'll be showing before the portrait is done," she
protested, standing before Logan in the library,
nervously crumpling and smoothing a sheet of
paper in her hands.

Logan closed an account book and turned in his

chair to face her. "An appropriate gown will disguise your condition, and Orsini will trim your waistline with a few brush strokes. Besides, it will give you something to do during confinement."

"I can think of many other things worth doing."

"I want a portrait of you. After Orsini uses the work in his exhibition, I intend to purchase it."

"Exhibition!" Madeline exclaimed, flushing. "Logan, I have no wish to be displayed as if I were some object, or a trophy—"

"But you are," he countered. The devilish light in his eyes gave her a chill of apprehension. "You're mine, and I'll flaunt you when and where I choose."

Madeline stared at him with wide eyes, too flustered to speak.

"What is that?" Logan asked, his gaze flickering to the paper in her hand.

"It's a list . . . a-an estimate of the expenses for the ball. Obviously some things must be eliminated, and I would like your advice—"

"Come here and show it to me." He moved his chair back from the desk and patted his knee, wearing an expression that made her uneasy.

Approaching him with caution, Madeline sat gingerly on his lap, her spine held straight. "Perhaps you would be more comfortable if I sat over there—"

"I'm perfectly comfortable," he said, his arm tightening until she reclined against his chest. Taking the paper from her, he glanced down the list of numbers. To Madeline's amazement, he seemed to find nothing untoward. "It's more or less what I expected," he said calmly.

"It's going to cost a *fortune*," Madeline replied. "I kept telling the duchess there was no need to be so extravagant, but she kept ordering the best of everything, and doubling the amounts I asked for, and . . . why are you smiling like that?''

"I had no idea you were so reluctant to spend my money, sweet." Logan discarded the list and resettled Madeline on his chest. "Prudence is a fine thing, but you're hardly a fiddler's wife."

"Of course not, but . . . what will we live on for the rest of the year?"

He toyed with the lace at the neckline of her bodice and pulled gently at the gauzy scarf that covered her throat and collarbone. A smile touched the corners of his mouth. "You can set your mind at ease, Maddy. We could comfortably afford a ball like this every week for the rest of our lives."

Perplexed, she stared at him, her brow wrinkling. "You . . . we . . . have as much as all that?"

"Four estates, not including a hunting lodge in Wiltshire." Noting her interest, he continued casually. "We also own a yacht, a brewery, a building yard and tilery, and holdings in a colonial mining company. In addition, I've invested in railroad and shipping stocks, which are producing excellent revenue. Then, of course, there is the art collection and the theater, as well as other assorted properties." He seemed amused by her thunderstruck expression. "You may open accounts wherever you choose, madam. I have no doubt that I have the means to afford you."

It took a moment for Madeline to gather her wits. It appeared that she had married into a fortune greater than that of her parents or either of her sisters, and larger by far than Lord Clifton's.

Logan watched her expression and laughed suddenly, as if he could read her thoughts. "Before you get too high for your buttons, madam, remember that I'm not a member of the peerage, and none of your children will have titles."

"That doesn't matter to me," Madeline replied, while her heart quickened at the implication that they would have more children.

"It may to them."

"They won't need titles to distinguish them. They'll learn to stand on their own accomplishments, as you have."

"Why, Mrs. Scott." His mouth curved in a mocking smile. "I believe you're trying to flatter me."

As he shifted her on his lap, Madeline felt the hard ridge of his sex straining beneath her, and she flushed. Although his advances were hardly unwelcome, it was improper behavior for the middle of the day. One of the servants might walk in, or someone might pay a call. "Logan," she said faintly as his mouth slid along her throat, "I . . . have so many things to do . . ."

"So do I." He began to unfasten the front of her gown, brushing away her hands as she tried to deter him.

"What if one of the maids comes in?" Madeline asked, quivering as he slid his hand inside her bodice to fondle her breast.

"I'll tell her to leave." He reached beneath her skirts, his fingers delving inside her linen undergarments and searching the most sensitive parts of her body. His eyes narrowed in excitement as he pulled her to straddle him, and there was a rending sound as he tore the delicate fabric of her drawers.

"Not here . . . let's go upstairs," Madeline begged, turning scarlet with distress. His body was hard and powerful between her thighs, sleek muscles flexing as he positioned her to ride him.

"Here," Logan countered, reaching down to unfasten his trousers. A short, breathless laugh escaped him as she squirmed on his lap. "Stop watching the damned door."

"I can't help it." She gasped as she felt him enter her, a hard pressure that slid easily within her moist depths. "Oh, we shouldn't—"

"Put your arms around me," he said, his voice guttural. Muttering instructions, he guided her with his hands as she rode up and down his swollen length.

Madeline's eyes closed with pleasure, her hands clawing over his waistcoat and shirt, groping blindly for his solid shoulders. They strained and arched together, while Logan muffled her soft groans with his mouth. She would never have believed herself capable of it . . . wantonly strad-dling him, thrusting herself on him, discarding every scrap of propriety that had been instilled in her every day of her adult life. But Logan encour-aged, demanded, that she abandon all shame in his arms. He filled her with each downward push, the current of pleasure rising higher and faster, until she shook with spasms of ecstasy. Logan's body went taut beneath her. The crescent of his teeth pressed into her shoulder, the hint of pain some-how intensifying her shivering delight.

Afterward, while Madeline collapsed against his chest, Logan smiled into her disheveled hair. "All those mornings at the Capital, when you helped me with those piles of correspondence . . . I wanted to do this with you."

"This?" Madeline repeated, lifting her head to look at him drowsily. She felt disoriented, giddy, as if she had been drinking. "I had no idea."

"If you would have looked in the right place, madam, you would have seen ample evidence."

"Oh." Raising herself on her elbows, she smiled at him. "In that case, I insist that you have no female secretaries."

"You're the only woman I want," Logan said gruffly, fighting the urge to cuddle her like a kitten and give voice to the endearments that filled his mind. His face hardened, and he heard himself add . . . "For now."

Logan kept his expression blank as he watched the glow fade from her eyes. Carefully Madeline disentangled herself from him and began to straighten her clothes. Although Logan regretted the hurtful words, they had been necessary. Better to spoil the moment between them than to let her think she was important to him. He had made the mistake of trusting her once. There would not be a second time.

# Thirteen

*On the* evening of the ball, Madeline stood before the mirror in her private dressing room while a maid fastened the row of buttons at the back of her gown.

Mrs. Beecham, wearing an elegant black dress with a snowy white apron, had come upstairs to assist in the final preparations. "Splendid," the housekeeper exclaimed, standing back to view her. "You'll be the loveliest woman here tonight, Mrs. Scott. The master won't be able to take his eyes from you."

Madeline smiled, though her heart was beating anxiously. "Have all the flowers been delivered? Has anyone visited the kitchens recently?"

"Everything has been taken care of," Mrs. Beecham assured her. "The house is filled with heavenly flowers, and Cook appears to have outdone herself. The guests will think they're visiting paradise—and when you appear to greet them, Mr. Scott will be the most envied man in London."

Nervously Madeline held a hand to her midriff. The flat surface of her stomach had swelled to a gentle curve, but her scarlet velvet gown had been designed to conceal her condition. A tightly fitted bodice followed the slender outline of her body before flowing into an array of rustling skirts. The gown was startlingly simple, its only adornment three ruby clasps that held the front of the bodice together, above which her breasts rose in creamy white splendor.

The scarlet hue of the ball gown became her, making her skin look like porcelain and complementing the amber color of her eyes. Her golden-brown hair had been pinned at the crown of her head in heavy loops and curls, displaying the slim length of her neck.

Logan entered the room in a few strides and stopped abruptly. He was a magnificent sight in black-and-white formal wear, with a blue-gray waistcoat of richly textured silk. His eyes, the most striking shade of blue Madeline had ever seen, flickered with some disquieting emotion as he stared at her. When he spoke, his voice held a deeper timbre than usual.

"I hope these are to your liking." He held out a black jeweler's box to her. Pleased and surprised by the unexpected gift, Madeline moved forward to receive it.

Smiling, Mrs. Beecham ushered the maid from the room and closed the door, leaving them in privacy.

Madeline gasped in amazement as she opened the box, discovering a ruby-and-gold necklace strung in glittering loops, and matching pendants for her ears. "How beautiful! I didn't expect . . ." Her gaze lifted to his. "You're very generous. Thank you, Logan."

A touch of color burnished his high cheekbones. Taking the necklace from the box, he stood behind Madeline and fastened the heavy creation around her neck. She watched their reflection in the mirror, holding still as she felt his warm fingers brush her nape. It took Logan a long time to fasten the necklace; he fumbled with the intricate catch, his breath filtering through her carefully arranged curls.

Madeline attached the ruby pendants to her ears, enjoying their jaunty swinging as she turned her head. "What do you think of my gown?" she asked, facing Logan.

To her disappointment, he showed neither admiration nor approval. "It's cut too low."

Madeline frowned slightly. "Julia has seen it, and she said it was perfect."

"Only if you're planning to start a riot," he muttered, his gaze pinned on her breasts.

"If you don't approve, I can change into something else—"

"No, wear the bloody thing," he said, attempting an indifferent tone and succeeding only at sounding sullen.

Madeline bit the insides of her lips to suppress a smile. Patiently she waited as Logan continued to stare at her. "You're going to catch cold, dressed like that," he said curtly.

"The house is very warm," she pointed out. "I'll be perfectly fine." She saw his fingers twitch at his side, as if he were struggling to keep from touching her. "Shall we go downstairs?"

Logan responded with a surly grunt and gave her his arm, escorting her to the ballroom as if attending the lavish party were an odious duty rather than something to enjoy.

Thankfully, their guests seemed to have no reservations about taking pleasure in the event. Hundreds of people milled through the house, chattering excitedly about Logan's art collection, the sumptuous buffet tables laden with superb cuisine, the lilting music drifting from the ball-room. Massive arrangements of orchids and tiger lilies in Oriental lacquered vases filled the air with exotic perfume.

Inspired by the inescapably romantic atmo-sphere, couples stole away for hasty rendezvous in the mansion's many private nooks, while gossiping women clustered like flocks of animated hens. Julia had apparently selected a perfect cross section of the different worlds Logan had traversed: peers, wealthy commoners, artists, writers, and even a few politicians. It made for a lively mix—in one evening, enough scandal was being created to fill the papers and entertain the public for weeks. Gentlemen enjoyed the host's endless supply of fine liquor and cigars, and occasionally erupted into minor squabbles over the favors of an elusive female. However, no woman attracted attention more than Madeline.

She was nothing short of a revelation, chatting and smiling, drawing conversation from those around her with surprising skill. It was impossible that she could be as relaxed as she seemed. On the other hand, Logan reflected with private irony, this was what she had been trained for her entire life: to act as an accomplished society hostess. Granted, her family had not planned for their daughter to marry a man like him—but Madeline seemed to have no proper embarrassment about being the wife of an actor.

Logan felt a flicker of pride in her performance, mingled with the bitter awareness that he should have been able to offer her better than this. No matter how competent a hostess Madeline was, she would never ascend the social heights that she would have as Lord Clifton's bride. Logan didn't blame her parents for wanting a brilliant marriage for her. In fact, he felt a strange empathy with the Matthewses, especially as he watched them that night.

Madeline's parents had come to the ball with pleasant, polite facades, but underneath they must also be experiencing mingled pride and bitterness. It was obvious that Madeline was far too refined to be the wife of a man with Logan's debauched past. She was impeccably pedigreed, and she was married to a commoner. He was wealthy, to be sure, but he was no thoroughbred.

It came time for them to lead off the dancing, and Logan offered his arm to Madeline, escorting her toward the center of the room. She was more animated than he had ever seen her, her amber eyes glittering with excitement, her cheeks flushed. It was her first ball, Logan realized with a touch of surprise. Madeline had never been taken on the rounds of social events at which she would be introduced to eligible men.

"I've never really danced with a man before," she said breathlessly, tilting her head to look up at him as he settled one hand at her waist and clasped her fingers with the other. "I had lessons at school. An instructor came once a week. I learned with another girl as a partner, and we took turns leading."

Logan smiled at the revelation. "Why don't I lead?" he suggested dryly and nodded to the musicians. They began a lovely waltz, the melody sweeping them across the floor before Madeline realized what was happening. Logan danced as superbly as he did everything else, knowing how to display his partner to her best advantage, expertly guiding her so there was no opportunity for her to hesitate or stumble.

Madeline knew that she danced stiffly at first. She concentrated intently on following him, on not making a misstep, until Logan laughed at her absorbed expression.

"Relax," he murmured.

"I can't—I'm too busy dancing."

"Look up at me."

Obeying, Madeline discovered that everything became much easier. She no longer knew or cared where he was leading her, only that his blue eyes were warm and his arms were strong. He was so powerful, his thighs brushing hers, the muscles of his shoulder hard beneath her fingers. The room dissolved in a giddy rush, and her hand tightened convulsively on his. She knew a moment of exhilaration, and her entire being was consumed with the wish that tonight would last forever.

Other couples joined in the waltz, eager to display their own facility, until the floor became crowded. As the piece concluded and a quadrille began, Logan took Madeline aside and regarded her with a faint smile. "My compliments to your instructor, madam."

"That was wonderful," she exclaimed, reluctant to release his hand. "Please couldn't we—"

"Would you like to—" Logan said at the same time, but they were both interrupted by a coterie of eager men of varying ages, all of whom besieged Madeline for dances. Madeline threw Logan a glance of consternation.

"It would be selfish of me to monopolize you, Mrs. Scott," Logan said, stepping back with a forced smile as his wife was led to the floor and drawn into the quadrille pattern. It was unfashionable for a man to pay too much attention to his wife. Furthermore, it was his duty as host to dance with some of the other women present.

Logan had always enjoyed the company of women, their complexity, their intriguing variety of shapes, scents, movements . . . but somehow they were all lacking now. All he wanted was Madeline. His wife's sensuous appeal in that damned scarlet dress was causing him to unravel. He had never before experienced the taste of jealousy, and suddenly he was wallowing in it. If one more friend offered him meaningful congratulations, he would commit murder. Every man in the place wanted her. They were all leering at her, at her face and figure, and most of all her half-covered breasts.

Grimly Logan recalled why he had never entertained at his home before now. There was no polite way a host could make his guests leave when he wished, and no means of escaping them. If this were someone else's ball he was attending, he would have left by now. He wanted to be alone somewhere, anywhere, with Madeline. Torrid fantasies seethed in his mind. He thought of pulling up her velvet skirts and having her on one of the long tables, of undressing her in the middle of the ballroom floor and watching their reflection in the massive column-framed mirrors.

His lurid thoughts were interrupted by the appearance of his comanager. Having briefly separated herself from her husband's company, Julia came to Logan and tapped him on the shoulder. She looked as pleased as a mother hen over the progress of her chick. "Congratulations," she said brightly. "You were fortunate to acquire a wife like Madeline."

"So I've been told," he growled. "A hundred times, at least."

Julia smiled, following his gaze to Madeline, who stood several yards away in a circle of admirers. "She has a quality that you and I lack, Logan. She likes people. She takes a genuine interest in them, and they can't help responding to her."

"I like people," Logan muttered defensively, making Julia laugh.

"Only if you think they can be of some use to you."

A reluctant smile twitched at the corner of his mouth. "Why is it that you've always been able to see me exactly for what I am, Julia?"

"I would never make that claim," she countered, her turquoise eyes gleaming with amusement. "After all these years you still manage to surprise me. Your behavior where Madeline is concerned, for example. It betrays a deeply buried romantic streak I hadn't suspected."

"Romantic," Logan scoffed, having always prided himself on being a cynic.

"Deny it all you like," Julia said. "It's only a matter of time until you admit that Madeline has wrapped you around her little finger."

"Only a hundred years or so." He scowled as she walked away. His attention returned to his distant wife, who was still surrounded by a group of admirers. Logan began to stride in her direction when he was beset by a few of the partners in his investment trust. Fidgeting inwardly, he smiled at their effusive compliments and traded a few opinions on subjects of masculine interest.

To Logan's relief, rescue arrived in the form of
Andrew, Lord Drake. Clapping a hand on one of
Logan's tense shoulders, Andrew greeted him
heartily and dragged him away from the group on
the pretext of asking advice on an art acquisition.

"Good God, how do you stand those dullards?"
Andrew asked *sotto voce.* "All that talk about
interest rates and dividends is as exciting as a visit
to the morgue."

"Those 'dullards,' as you call them, are some of
the most brilliant financial minds in England,"
Logan said dryly. "You'd do well to spend time
with them." As he spoke, his glance returned to
Madeline. She stood in the light cast by a chandelier, her pale shoulders like velvet, her piled-up
hair containing every shade from gold to maple
brown.

Following his gaze, Andrew grinned. "For
shame, Jimmy. I thought you above such bourgeois
behavior as lusting after your own wife . . . but as
they say, blood will tell."

Logan looked at him sharply, searching for some
hidden meaning to the comment, but Andrew's
blue eyes were devoid of guile. "I've never claimed
to be anything but bourgeois," Logan replied.
"And one look at my wife is explanation enough."

"I won't dispute that. After tonight, every amateur poet in London will be laboring on an ode to
her. The face of an angel, the hint of scandal about
your hasty nuptials . . . she has everything necessary to drive the public wild with curiosity."

"And to drive me insane," Logan muttered,
making his friend chuckle.

"You've done well for yourself, Jimmy," Andrew
said, sipping from a crystal wine glass. Clearly it
was not his first drink of the evening, nor would it

be his last. "A most enviable life. Wealth, a fine home, a beautiful young wife—and you started out with nothing. Whereas I was given every advantage: a name, a fortune, land—and I've squandered most of it. Lately my chief occupation has been waiting for the old man to die and leave me with a nicely endowed title. With my unfortunate luck, he'll hang on 'til I'm too damned old to enjoy any of it."

Logan arched his brow, surprised by the touch of bitterness in Andrew's tone. "What is the problem, Andrew?" he asked, in the blunt manner he would address a younger brother.

Andrew hesitated, and laughed. "Don't worry about me—just enjoy your bloody wonderful life and your little honeypot of a wife."

Logan stared at him with a mixture of exasperation and concern. Obviously Andrew was in trouble again. The last thing Logan wanted to do tonight was wrest a confession from Andrew and solve his problems once again. However, it was an impulse he had never been—and would never be—free of, especially now that he knew about their secret kinship.

Casting a last longing glance at Madeline, Logan sighed inwardly and turned his full attention to Andrew. "I've been saving a box of exceptional cigars," he said casually. "This seems like an occasion to enjoy them. Care to have a smoke?"

Andrew's moodiness seemed to ease. "Yes, bring them to the billiards room, and we'll visit with some of the fellows."

Logan made his way out of the ballroom, stopping several times to converse with clusters of guests who beckoned to him. As he finally reached the door, he noticed Madeline's sister Justine and her husband, Lord Bagworth. They appeared to be having some kind of spat, edging to the corner of the room and talking tensely. Justine's eyes were narrowed with fury.

Logan exited the ballroom, suppressing a pitying grin. He suspected that Justine must lead Bagworth on a merry dance. As the spoiled beauty of the Matthews family, Justine appeared to insist on being the center of attention at all times. The Matthewses had done no service to their eldest daughter by pampering and spoiling her to the exclusion of their other two children. Having made Justine's acquaintance, Logan wondered how it was that Madeline could have been so overlooked. An ironic smile touched his lips, and he shook his head as he went to the library in search of his private stock of cigars.

Pleading for respite from the dancing, Madeline extricated herself from the crowd of gentlemen surrounding her. She caught sight of her brother-in-law, Lord Bagworth, standing near the long windows that lined the room. He didn't seem to notice her approach, his attention focused on the formal garden outside, his round face shadowed with a frown. He was a kind, pleasant-looking gentleman, though short in stature and not possessed of an imposing physique.

"Mrs. Scott," Lord Bagworth said, smiling as he took her hand and bowed over it. "Congratulations on a splendid evening. I must say I've never seen you look more lovely."

"Thank you, my lord. I hope you and my sister are enjoying yourselves."

"Indeed," Bagworth said automatically, though his expression remained troubled. He paused for a long time, his thoughtful brown eyes staring into hers. "I must admit," he said slowly, "that to my regret, your sister and I have just had a bit of a quarrel."

Puzzled as to why he would make such a confession, Madeline frowned. "My lord . . . is there anything I can do?"

"Perhaps there is." Uneasily he cupped one of his hands over the other and twisted them together. "I'm afraid, Mrs. Scott, that Justine is somewhat distressed by your success this evening."

"By *my*—" Madeline said in astonishment. It was inconceivable that Justine should be jealous of her. Justine had always been the most beautiful, admired, and sought-after sister. "I'm sure I don't understand why, my lord."

He looked distinctly embarrassed. "As we both are aware, Justine is possessed of a rather mercurial nature. She seems to fear that your triumph tonight will somehow detract from her accomplishments."

"But that could never be true," Madeline protested.

"Nevertheless, in her unhappiness I fear she may have taken it in mind to do something . . . drastic."

"Such as?"

Lord Bagworth cast a worried glance around the room. "Where is your husband, Mrs. Scott?"

Madeline's eyes widened. What could Logan have to do with this? Could it be that Justine, in a fit of envy, would actually try to throw herself at Logan, merely to assure herself of her own attractiveness? "Are you suggesting that I go in search of him?"

"I think that is an excellent idea," Lord Bagworth replied at once.

Madeline shook her head with a disbelieving

laugh. "But Justine would never try to . . . there's no reason for . . ."

"It is only a suspicion," Lord Bagworth said quietly. "One that I trust will be quickly proven unfounded."

"If Justine is worried that she will be eclipsed . . . there is no one capable of competing with her, least of all me."

Lord Bagworth managed to smile through his worry. "From a long acquaintance with your family, Mrs. Scott, I've observed how you have always stood in the shadow of your older sisters. You deserve to be recognized as an attractive and accomplished woman in your own right."

Madeline smiled distractedly, thinking only of Logan and where he might be. "Thank you, my lord. If you'll excuse me—"

"Yes, of course." He bowed to her and remained at the windows, sighing deeply.

Logan went to the library and rummaged through the sideboard near his desk. He was unaware that someone had followed him until he heard a provocative voice ask, "What are you looking for, Mr. Scott? Or perhaps I should call you Logan. We're family now, after all."

Logan straightened with the box of cigars in hand, watching sardonically as Madeline's sister Justine entered the room and closed the door. "Is there something I can help you with, Lady Bagworth?" he asked, his expression unreadable.

"I would like to have a private discussion with you."

"I don't have time," he said brusquely. "I have guests to attend to."

"And their needs are more important than those of your family?"

Logan regarded her with a cool gaze, knowing exactly what kind of game Justine was attempting to play. In his life there had been no end of married women who had pursued him for various reasons. "What do you want?" he asked curtly, making no attempt at politeness.

His terse manner didn't seem to bother her. Justine smiled provocatively and came toward him with a slow, suggestive walk. "I want to know if you are making my sister happy. It's a matter of great concern to me."

"You'll have to ask her, Lady Bagworth."

"She wouldn't tell me the truth, I fear. To Madeline, the facade is everything."

"Do you have reason to suspect that my wife is discontented?"

"Only the obvious fact that you're a mismatch, Mr. Scott. A man like you . . . and my little sister . . . I'm sure she has no idea how to handle you. Why, she must be absolutely terrified of you."

"She doesn't give me that impression," Logan replied sardonically, concealing his growing contempt. "Tell me, Lady Bagworth, what kind of woman *do* you envision as a suitable match for a man like me?"

"Someone beautiful . . . confident . . . experienced . . ." Justine shrugged her shoulders in a practiced manner, letting her puffed sleeves drop to her elbows, the front of her blue silk gown drooping over her breasts until the tips were nearly exposed. She leaned back against a table, pushing her cleavage together, and slanted a look from beneath her lashes.

The pose was so blatant that Logan nearly laughed. "A charming invitation," he said, his dry tone implying the opposite. "However, I have no interest in any woman but my wife."

Justine's eyes glinted with jealous fury. "That can't be true," she said baldly. "You can't prefer that timid, plain mouse over me!"

Logan stared at her with a mocking smile. Of all the words that could be used to describe the rebellious girl who had enthusiastically invaded his life and changed everything, "timid" and "plain" were not among them. "I suggest that you pull up your dress, Lady Bagworth, and return to the ball."

His flat refusal only seemed to fuel her determination. "I can make you want me," she said, and launched herself at him.

Logan's mockery evaporated as he tried to separate himself from the woman who was suddenly tangled around him. The box fell to the floor, perfect blended cigars spilling over the carpet. Logan let out a breath of mingled amusement and disbelief. It was like performing in a bad farce. In the brief struggle, he barely heard the opening of the library door. All of a sudden he heard his wife's voice, and he felt a stab of dismay. *Bloody hell*, he thought, glancing in Madeline's direction.

"I've been looking for you, Justine," Madeline said, staring at her sister rather than Logan. For once it was impossible to see what she was thinking, her face still and guarded.

Logan's jaw bunched tightly. With Justine's dress in disarray, the proximity of their bodies . . . he was well aware of how it looked. If there was anything he couldn't stand, it was being manipulated by a woman.

Shooting Justine a murderous glance, he shoved her away and turned to face Madeline. One part of his mind suggested slyly that he should have made use of the opportunity to humble Madeline once and for all. But he instantly rejected the idea. Whatever else Madeline thought of him, it was paramount that she know he had no designs on her sister. He had no desire to be unfaithful to her.

"Maddy . . ." he started, and for the first time in his life realized that he was at a loss for words. Sweating, furious, he thought of a dozen ways to explain the situation but couldn't seem to produce a sound.

Justine gave Madeline a defiant glance, her lips curving triumphantly. "Your husband couldn't seem to help himself," she said. "All I wanted was to talk to him, but he—"

"I know what happened," Madeline said calmly. "And I would appreciate it if in the future you would refrain from throwing yourself at my husband. It's a nuisance he doesn't deserve . . . and neither do I."

Justine straightened her dress and pulled up her sleeves. "Tell her whatever you like," she said to Logan, her voice turning shrill. "I'm sure you'll paint yourself as the innocent victim—she may even be naive enough to believe you." Angrily she swept from the room, the door slamming in her wake.

Logan stared at his wife, feeling as awkward as he had in his boyhood years, when he had been caught in a bit of mischief. "Maddy, I didn't invite her—"

"I know," she said matter-of-factly. "You would never try to seduce your wife's sister, even if you were attracted to her."

"I'm not," Logan muttered, raking his hands through his hair until it stood up wildly.

"Here . . . don't do that." Madeline approached him and reached up to smooth the dark locks with her gloved hand. Her gentle touch soothed his aggravated temper. "Justine wouldn't have gone through with it, in any event. She just wanted some attention."

"She nearly got more than she bargained for. I was ready to kill her."

"I'm sorry you were put in such a situation."

He caught at her stroking hand and held it, staring into her small face. "You have every reason to be suspicious, Maddy."

"I'm not," she said softly, making him shake his head in frustration.

"If our positions had been reversed, I would have believed the worst of you."

A faint, wry smile came to her lips. "I've no doubt you would have."

Her words seemed to inflame him. "Then how the hell can you stand there and claim you trust me, when you know I wouldn't have done as much for you?"

"Why shouldn't I trust you?" she asked calmly. "You've been nothing but honorable and generous to me."

"Honorable?" Logan repeated, staring at her as if she had lost her wits. "I took your virginity, got you with child out of wedlock—"

"When I first started work at the Capital, you made every effort to avoid me, despite the way I threw myself at you. You made love to me only when it was clear that I was more than willing, and when I became pregnant, you married me in spite of your resentment. I deceived you, and in return you've been honest and fair—"

"That's enough." His face was taut with annoyance. "I've been a bastard to you, and I don't intend to stop any time soon, so I'd advise you to dispense with the flattery and the doe-eyed glances, because they're not going to work. Do you understand?" He didn't realize he had seized her until he felt the tender skin of her upper arms beneath his hands, the tantalizing strip of bareness between the short sleeves of her gown and the top edge of her gloves.

"I understand," Madeline said. Her soft mouth was close to his, and Logan longed violently to kiss the hint of a smile from her lips and plunge his hands into the velvet sheath of her bodice. All he wanted from her was physical pleasure. Not her trust. Not affection.

He reached over the back of her dress, found the outline of her buttocks, and pulled her hips hard against his. "I want you," he muttered, staring into the valley of her cleavage, nuzzling his mouth and nose into the fragrant hollow at the base of her throat. "Come upstairs with me."

"Now?" she asked, her breath catching as he urged his aroused loins against hers.

"Now."

"But our guests . . ."

"Let them take care of themselves."

Madeline laughed shakily. "Later," she said. "They'll notice we're gone, and they'll talk—"

"I want them to talk." Every rational thought had left Logan's head. He no longer cared about Andrew's problems, his guests' well-being, or social appearances. "I want them to know that I'm taking my pleasure of you upstairs while they're all down here . . . that you're mine." Hungrily he crushed her mouth beneath his, drinking in her taste, driven wild by the scent and feel of her. His fingers tangled in her carefully arranged coiffure, beginning to pull the pins from the golden-brown curls, and Madeline pulled back with a gasp.

"All right," she said unsteadily, her face pink and glowing. "I'll be more than happy to . . . accommodate you . . . but the guests will stop us before we ever reach the stairs."

Logan smiled and stole a short, hard kiss from her. "I pity anyone who gets in my way," he said, and pulled her toward the door.

# Fourteen

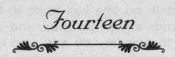

*As the* next month progressed, Madeline's condition became more obvious, making it necessary for her to limit her outings. When she went shopping or drove or walked through the park, she was always escorted by at least two servants, to whom Logan had given specific instructions. She was not to overtire herself, he had said, or venture into less than safe areas, and she was to eat regularly.

"I can't stand being treated like a child," Madeline told Logan one morning as she sat at her dressing table. She couldn't help resenting her loss of freedom. Having once experienced what it was like to do as she pleased and go anywhere she liked, it was difficult to lead the sheltered life of the usual woman in her position. "No matter what I do, there's always someone trying to help me or take care of me . . . or *feed* me something."

Rather than mock or belittle her, Logan listened with apparent seriousness. "You're not being treated like a child," he replied, "but as someone whose well-being I value above all else."

"I feel as if I'm in prison," she said sullenly. "I want to go somewhere, do something . . ."

"Such as?"

Madeline sighed and picked up a brush, dragging it vigorously through her long, loose hair.

"Since the ball, no one has come to the house. I
have no friends except for Julia, and she's always
busy at the theater, as you are. And even though
we receive a dozen invitations every day, we never
accept any of them."

As Logan stared at her small, tense face, a frown
settled on his own brow. He recognized that this
was more or less what he had expected. His years
of carefully maintained seclusion were coming to
an end. Madeline was a young, vibrant woman
who needed to be active in society, to have friends,
to experience the varied amusements London offered.

"I understand," he said, taking the brush from
her and setting it aside. He sank to his haunches
beside her, bringing their faces to the same level.
"I've no desire to keep you like a bird in a golden
cage, sweet. I'll see what I can do to enliven your
days a bit." His mouth quirked with a teasing
smile. "I assume you have no complaints about the
nights."

"No," she said, blushing and returning his smile,
lifting her mouth willingly for his kiss.

True to his word, Logan began to escort Madeline to art exhibitions, auctions, suppers, and musical evenings. When they attended plays at Drury
Lane or the Royal Opera House, they sat in an
elegant private box. To Madeline's delight, they
accepted invitations to weekend parties in the
country, where she was able to meet other young
matrons with whom she had much in common.
She knew that Logan didn't relish such occasions,
as he was constantly an object of attention, speculation, and excitement. The fact that he was willing
to sacrifice his treasured privacy for her sake was
both puzzling and flattering.

Madeline knew that many women envied her having Logan as a husband. He was charming, intelligent, generous, and dashing in a way that other husbands were not. She enjoyed being married to him, took pleasure in his companionship, his ready sense of humor, and of course his skilled lovemaking.

However, no matter how close or comfortable their relationship seemed, Madeline was aware that it was a far cry from the way it could be. Logan never looked at her now as he had once before, never kissed her with feverish love and longing. He maintained a small, crucial distance between them. It was clear that he did not trust her, and he intended they would never be emotionally intimate. Madeline tried to contain her own feelings for him, knowing that her love would only be thrown back in her face, no matter how much he might have wanted it.

As Julia had predicted, Madeline's appetite returned, and she gained back the weight she had lost, as well as a few more pounds. Any private anxiety she might have had about whether or not Logan approved of her altered figure was quickly allayed.

"You may as well sleep here from now on," he said one evening after he had carried her to his bed and made love to her. Sweeping a hand over her naked hip, he added gruffly, "It's more convenient than sending for you every time I want you—or having to dash to your room when your legs cramp."

Stirring in his arms, Madeline smiled sleepily. "I wouldn't want to bother you. I know how you like to sleep alone."

"You don't take up that much room," he observed, his hand drifting to her stomach. "Yet."

Madeline turned on her side. "Soon I'll be wide enough to cover half the bed. Oh, how I wish I were taller! Women of my height don't carry children well—they look like ducks."

Logan drew her back against his long body. "Madam," he said, his voice warm and tickling in her ear, "I've spent every night demonstrating how desirable you are. By now I hardly think you have reason to doubt your attractiveness."

"You've acquired a taste for women with large stomachs?" Madeline asked skeptically, and felt him smile against her neck.

"Only one in particular." Logan pushed her to her back. "Now I suppose you'll want me to prove it. Again."

She turned away from him with feigned reluctance. "If it's no trouble—"

"I insist," he murmured, turning her over once more, and he covered her mouth with his.

He was an unpredictable man, sometimes indulging and teasing her, sometimes treating her with a maddening coolness. Most evenings after a theater performance, he rushed home to be with her, though when he strode through the door it was without the least appearance of haste. He was so adept at concealing his feelings that Madeline wondered if he loved her at all, or if he regarded her more as an amusing pet. There were times, however, when she had reason to hope.

Three afternoons a week Madeline sat for the portrait Logan had commissioned. The artist, Mr. Orsini, was a talented and pleasant man, without the wild temperament that she had expected of an artist.

"Your wife is one of the greatest beauties I have painted," Orsini informed Logan, who had come to watch a sitting in progress.

"Mr. Orsini," Madeline protested from where she was posing, "you mustn't embarrass me—"

"She has an unusual quality," Orsini continued earnestly. "Sensuousness mingled with purity. A bewitching child-woman."

Unused to such lavish compliments, Madeline fixed her gaze on the floor. "Yes," she heard Logan say softly. "That's exactly what I see in her."

When Madeline was able, she visited the Capital for an afternoon, watching rehearsals and even helping with line readings. Logan didn't seem to mind her presence. In fact, he readily admitted that he liked knowing she was within his reach. "It saves me from having to imagine what trouble you might be getting into elsewhere," he told her dryly.

Madeline enjoyed spending time with the theater company, who were not offended by the sight of an expectant woman. Accustomed as they all were to pregnant actresses who continued performing on stage until their sixth or seventh month, the employees of the Capital treated Madeline with a relaxed attitude that made her feel accepted and comfortable.

Best of all were the evenings when she and Logan would relax together after supper. They spent hours reading and talking until Logan finally carried her to bed. It seemed that the fragile bond between them was growing stronger. Madeline began to think that she was slowly winning the battle, regaining Logan's trust . . . until the day that her illusions of happiness seemed to shatter.

* * *

Sunday morning proceeded in the usual fashion, with a lavish breakfast and coffee, followed by Madeline's solitary attendance at church and then a few hours spent with Logan in the private family parlor. Logan pored over a play folio, making notes and corrections, while Madeline warmed herself near the tiled stove and did needlework.

Glancing at her husband's dark head, Madeline was unable to resist going to him. She dropped the bit of embroidery to the floor and stood behind his chair, her hands resting on his broad shoulders. "I despise needlework," she said, bending over to nuzzle the warm space behind his ear.

"Then don't do it," Logan replied, turning a page of the folio.

"I have no choice. All respectable married women do needlework."

"Who wants you to behave respectably?" he asked absently, trying to focus on his work. "Don't read over my shoulder, sweet. I can't concentrate."

Undeterred, she slid her arms around his chest. "You shouldn't work on Sunday. It's a sin." She pressed two or three soft kisses where the column of his throat met his hard jaw, and felt the sudden throb of his pulse against her lips.

"I'm about to commit a worse one," Logan replied, dropping the folio and twisting in the chair to snatch her into his arms. Madeline shrieked with laughter as he pulled her into his lap. His hands roamed intimately over her body. "What do you consider an appropriate activity for Sunday, madam? . . . This? . . . Or perhaps this . . ."

Their play was interrupted by a knock at the door. Madeline struggled from Logan's lap, pulling hastily at her skirts and retreating to the pool of heat near the tiled stove. A footman entered the room and brought a note on a silver tray to Logan. Grinning at Madeline's attempt to appear composed, Logan took the note and dismissed the servant.

"Who is it from?" Madeline asked, returning to Logan as he broke the seal.

"Apparently an acquaintance I met through Lord Drake." Frowning, Logan read aloud, ". . . I am distressed to relay some news concerning our friend Lord Drake. Knowing of your close friendship with him, I felt certain you would wish to be informed at once . . ." His voice faded, and his gaze continued to move rapidly across the page.

Madeline stared at him while he finished reading silently and sat like a statue. "Logan?" she asked tentatively. He didn't seem to hear her. Reaching for the half-crumpled note in his hand, she pried it away. A soft, pitying exclamation escaped her lips as she read the letter. It seemed that Andrew, Lord Drake, had attended a water-party on the Thames the previous night.

Sometime during the revelry, Lord Drake had fallen overboard, but no one had noticed until early morning. Although the private yacht had been thoroughly searched, there had been no sign of him. The Thames would be dragged, but often in such drowning cases the body wasn't discovered for days.

Gently Madeline touched her husband's stiff shoulder. "Was—is—he a strong swimmer? Perhaps he managed to reach shore—"

"No, he couldn't swim well," Logan said, his voice hoarse. "He was probably too damned drunk to even try."

Her hand settled on the nape of his neck. "Logan, I'm sorry—"

He jerked away from her, his breath hissing between his teeth. "Don't." A visible tremor ran along his back. "I want to be alone."

Every impulse in her body prompted her to stay, to comfort him, but Logan didn't want her. He was shutting her out of his grief. It was the worst hell imaginable to love someone who didn't want it. If he did have feelings for her, he fought them at every turn. Madeline stared at his dark head and couldn't stop herself from touching his hair. "Logan, what can I do?" she whispered.

"Just leave."

Madeline's hand fell away, and she left the room without looking back.

For the rest of that day, and most of the next, Logan closed himself in his room and drank. The only time he spoke to Madeline was to tell her to notify the Capital that he wouldn't be coming to work. His understudy would take his place in the performance the following evening.

"When will you return?" Madeline asked, staring into his set face and liquor-glazed eyes. She was met with a stony silence in reply, and he shut himself away in his room once more. He didn't want her company, nor anyone else's. In spite of Madeline's pleas and the trays of food she sent upstairs, he refused to eat.

Worriedly Madeline asked Mrs. Beecham if Logan had ever behaved like this before, and the housekeeper hesitated before replying. "Only when you left him, Mrs. Scott."

Madeline colored with guilt and remorse. "How long did it last?"

"It took one week for him to drink himself insensible, and another before he would begin to eat properly again." Mrs. Beecham shook her head in sincere puzzlement. *"That* I could understand, as we all knew how he felt about you . . . but this . . . I wouldn't have guessed that he cared so much about Lord Drake. I don't like to speak ill of the dead, but the man was a ne'er-do-well, may he rest in peace."

"It must be because they grew up together. For some reason Logan felt responsible for him."

The housekeeper shrugged. "Whatever the cause, the master has taken his passing very hard." Her sympathetic gaze touched on Madeline's strained face. "He'll put himself to rights eventually. Don't distress yourself, Mrs. Scott. It's not good for a woman in your condition to worry."

That, of course, was easier said than done. How could she not worry when her husband seemed determined to drink himself to death? Late in the evening of the second day, Madeline gathered her nerve and went to his door, turning the heavy brass knob and discovering that it was locked. "Logan?" she asked, knocking quietly. As she had expected, there was no reply. She knocked a little harder and heard a muffled snarl from within.

"Stop scratching at the damn door and leave me in peace." His voice was filled with ugly undertones that raised the hairs on the back of her neck.

"Unlock it, please," Madeline said, trying to sound composed, "or I'll get a key from Mrs. Beecham."

"Then I'll wring your neck like a Christmas goose," he returned, sounding as if he would relish the process.

"I'm going to wait here until I see you. I'll stand here all night if necessary." When there was no reply, she added in a moment of inspiration, "And if something happens to the baby, let it be on your conscience!"

Madeline braced herself as she heard his heavy footsteps. All of a sudden the door was unlocked, and she was snatched into the room with a violent jerk.

"There's nothing left of my conscience," Logan said, slamming the door, closing her inside the shadowed bedroom with him. He loomed over her, huge and dark, his hair rumpled, his breath rank with liquor. He wore a pair of astonishingly wrinkled trousers; his feet were bare, and his muscular chest and shoulders, naked. Madeline couldn't help shrinking back, alarmed by his appearance. He seemed capable of almost anything. His mouth twisted with a sneer and there was a wild, desperate gleam in his bloodshot eyes.

"You want to play the dutiful wife," Logan said thickly, "and pat my shoulder while whispering platitudes in my ear. Well, I don't want comfort from you. I don't need it. All I need is *this*." His hand caught in her bodice, his fingers delving into the hollow of her cleavage, and he pulled her hard against him. His hot mouth, surrounded by wiry bristle, scoured the tender skin of her throat.

Madeline sensed that he expected her to protest his crude fondling, but she slid her arms around his neck and relaxed against him. The gentle yielding seemed to be Logan's undoing. "Damn you," he groaned. "Don't you have the sense to be afraid of me?"

"No," she said, her face pressed against his hot, smooth shoulder.

Abruptly he let go of her, breathing in unsteady gulps.

"Logan," she said softly, "you're behaving as if you're somehow to blame for your friend's death. I don't understand why."

"You don't need to."

"I do, when you seem bent on destroying yourself. There are many people who need you . . . and I happen to be one of them."

His anger seemed to drain away, and he suddenly appeared weary and full of self-hatred. "Andrew needed me," he muttered. "I failed him."

Her gaze searched his ravaged face. "Is that what this is about?"

"Partly." Logan picked up a half-empty bottle of brandy and sat on the edge of the unmade bed. There were liquor stains on the sheets and the Aubusson carpet, evidence of the last thirty-six hours of drinking. He raised the bottle to his lips, but before he could take a swallow, Madeline approached and took it from him. He made an unsteady swipe for the bottle and braced himself to keep from toppling over.

Madeline set the brandy aside and stood before him. "Tell me," she said, aching to touch him. "Please."

Looking like an exhausted child, he closed his eyes and hung his dark head between his shoulders. He choked out a few names . . . Lord Drake . . . the Earl of Rochester . . . Mrs. Florence . . . and then, in a halting stream of words, an incredible story emerged.

Madeline stood unmoving as she tried to understand what he was telling her. Logan said that he was the illegitimate child of Rochester and Mrs. Florence's daughter . . . that Andrew had been his half brother. She listened in amazement while he unburdened himself with the bitter honesty of a condemned man. It was clear that his grief and love for Andrew were mixed with devastating guilt.

"Why didn't you tell me before?" Madeline finally asked, when he had fallen silent.

"No need . . . you were better off not knowing. So was Andrew."

"But you wanted to tell him, didn't you?" she murmured, daring to reach out to him, smoothing his disheveled hair. "You regret not having said anything when you had the chance."

Logan's head dropped to her chest, and he rested his forehead against the fragrant softness of her breasts. "I'm not sure. I . . . Christ. It's too late now." Sighing, he blotted his eyes against her velvet-covered bodice. "I should have done more for him."

"You did as much as you could. You paid his debts, and you never turned him away. You even forgave him for taking Olivia from you."

"I should have thanked him for that," he said hoarsely. "Olivia was a deceitful bitch."

Madeline winced inwardly, reflecting that her own behavior hadn't been much better than Olivia's. "Will you go to Rochester?" she asked, and she felt him stiffen.

"I wouldn't trust myself to keep from killing him. More than anyone, Rochester is responsible for Andrew's death. For making his life such hell that Andrew's only escape was inside a bottle." A harsh laugh escaped him. "The cockneys have a word for a drunkard. They call him a 'bloat.' The same thing they call a drowned body. Poor Andrew—it suits him either way, doesn't it?"

Ignoring the macabre observation, Madeline continued to caress his dark head. "Come to my bed, and sleep," she said after a moment. "Let the servants clean this room and air it out."

Logan didn't respond for a long moment. Madeline knew that he was contemplating whether or not to go back to his brandy. "You don't want me in your bed," he muttered. "I'm drunk, and God knows I need a bath."

Madeline smiled faintly. "You're welcome there in any condition." Her fingertips trailed down his bare, hard arm until she took his lax hand. "Come," she whispered. "Please."

She thought Logan would refuse. To her surprise, he stood and followed her from the room. The small victory eased some of her worry, but she was far from relieved. She was just beginning to understand the burden Logan had been carrying. No wonder he was suffering over Lord Drake's death. How utterly betrayed he must have felt, to have learned that the wealthy boy he had grown up with had actually been his brother. Neither of them had ever had a real home or a loving family . . . neither of them had ever known happiness.

Her hand slipped to her stomach, as if to protect the tiny life inside. Surely Logan would be able to love an innocent child. If he wouldn't accept her heart . . . at least she could give him that.

Logan slept heavily, occasionally twitching or murmuring in the midst of a dream. Each time he began to stir, Madeline soothed him back to sleep, guarding him through the night. In the morning, she tiptoed from the room and made certain that no one would disturb his continuing slumber. She bathed and donned a dark blue morning gown trimmed with white lace. After breakfasting alone, she spent an hour or two at her desk answering correspondence.

"Pardon, Mrs. Scott . . ." The voice of the butler intruded on her thoughts. He brought a calling card on a small silver tray. "A personal call from the Earl of Rochester. When I informed him that Mr. Scott is not 'at home,' the earl asked if you would receive him, in spite of the unusual hour."

Thrown into consternation, Madeline stared blankly at the calling card. Sharp curiosity mingled with worry. What could the earl possibly have to say to her? Silently she thanked God that Logan was still sleeping soundly upstairs. There was no predicting how he would react if he learned that Rochester was here. "I . . . I'll speak to him briefly," she said, replacing her pen in its engraved silver holder with undue care. "I'll go to the entrance hall."

"Yes, Mrs. Scott."

Her heart pounded heavily as she walked to the entrance hall. All through the night she had wondered what kind of man Rochester was to manipulate his own sons and lie to them for years . . . to deny Logan and allow him to suffer abuse at the hands of a brutish tenant farmer. Without even knowing the earl, she despised him . . . and yet there was a part of her that felt a trace of sympathy. After all, Andrew had been his acknowledged son, and his death must cause the earl no small amount of pain.

Her steps slowed as she saw the iron-haired elderly man standing in the hall, his tall frame slightly stooped, his face hard-angled and utterly devoid of warmth or humor. Although there was no great likeness between him and Logan, Madeline could well believe that the earl was his father. Like Logan, the earl seemed solitary, invincible, full of banked intensity. He wore the evidence of his recent grief: a gray cast to his skin and a certain deadness of the eyes.

"Lord Rochester," Madeline said, declining to extend a hand, merely nodding cautiously.

The earl seemed vaguely amused by her lack of deference. "Mrs. Scott," he said in a rusty voice, "it is gracious of you to receive me."

"I'm sorry for your loss," she murmured.

They studied each other in the following silence. "You know about me," he said. "I can see it in your face."

Madeline nodded. "Yes, he told me."

One haughty brow arched inquisitively. "I suppose he painted me as a black-hearted monster?"

"He merely relayed the facts, my lord."

"You're a cut above what I would have expected Scott to marry," Rochester observed. "A young woman of obvious breeding. What must it have taken to persuade your family to allow such a match?"

"They were quite pleased at the prospect of having such an accomplished gentleman in the family," Madeline lied coolly.

Rochester's sharp gaze rested on her, and he seemed to detect the falsehood, but he smiled in grudging admiration. "My son is fortunate in his choice of a wife."

"Your son?" Madeline repeated. "I was under the impression that you had declined to acknowledge him."

"That is something I intend to discuss with him."

Before Madeline could question him further, they heard someone approaching, and they turned in unison. Logan's face was emotionless as he came to stand beside Madeline, his cold blue eyes fastened on the elderly man.

Logan seemed to have benefitted from the long night's sleep. His hair was still damp from a fresh washing, his face gleamed from a shave, and he was dressed in a white shirt, dark trousers, and a patterned green-and-gray vest. In spite of his well-groomed appearance, there were shadows beneath his eyes and a pallor beneath his tan.

He spoke to Rochester in a dry monotone. "I can't imagine what brings you here."

"You're all I have left," Rochester said simply.

A venomous smile touched Logan's mouth. "I hope to hell you're not suggesting that I serve as a second-rate replacement for Andrew?"

The elderly man flinched visibly. "I made many mistakes with Andrew—I won't deny it. Perhaps I wasn't an ideal parent—"

*'Perhaps?"* Logan repeated with a harsh laugh.

"—but I did have hopes for Andrew. Plans for him. I . . ." Rochester swallowed hard and finished with difficulty. ". . . I did love him, no matter what you may think."

"You might have told him," Logan muttered.

Rochester shook his head as if the conversation were becoming too painful, yet he was driven to continue. "I had high expectations for Andrew. His mother was a woman of refinement, with a delicate nature and the bluest of blood. I chose her to ensure that my son would have impeccable lineage."

"Unlike your first one," Logan said.

"Yes," Rochester admitted readily. "You didn't fit in with my plans. I convinced myself that it was best if I set you aside and started afresh. I intended that my son—the legitimate one—should have the best of everything. I gave him a fortune, the best schools, entry to the highest social circles. There was no reason Andrew shouldn't have been a great success . . . but he failed miserably at everything he attempted. No discipline, no ambition, no talent, no interest in anything but drinking and gambling. Whereas *you* . . . " He cracked an ironic laugh. "I gave you nothing. Your bloodlines are those of a mongrel. Yet somehow you managed to amass a fortune and establish a place for yourself in society. You've even managed to marry the kind of woman Andrew should have had."

Logan regarded him sardonically. "Tell me what you want, Rochester; then leave."

"Very well. I want to end the war between us."

"There is no war," Logan said flatly. "Now that Andrew is gone, I don't give a damn about what happens to you. You'll have nothing to do with me, my wife, or my children. As far as I'm concerned, you don't exist."

The earl seemed unsurprised by Logan's coldness. "That is, of course, your decision. But there is much I could do for your family if you would allow it. To begin with, I could use my influence to have you created a peer, especially in light of the property and land you have amassed. And although there are a few restrictions on what I am able to bequeath to illegitimate issue, there is still a generous patrimony I can leave you."

"I don't want a shilling of your money. It should have been Andrew's."

"Then don't accept it for yourself. However, you might consider your children's interests. I want to make them my heirs. Would you deny them their birthright?"

"I won't take—" Logan began, but the earl interrupted.

"I've never asked you for anything until now. All I want is for you to consider what I've said. You needn't give me an answer right away. These days it seems I have nothing to do but wait."

"You'll wait a long time," Logan said grimly.

Rochester smiled in bitter understanding. "Of course. I'm aware of how stubborn you are."

Logan was silent, watching with a granite-hard face as Rochester bid them good-bye and took his leave.

Unfortunately, either Rochester or one of his associates must have confided the secret of Logan's parentage to someone, for in the space of a few days, the news was all over London. Their home was beseiged with callers and letters, all inquiring if it was true, while the Capital was also inundated.

Logan's performances, always heavily attended, became so popular that there were wild fights over tickets outside the theater. It seemed that the public was fascinated by the romantic notion of a celebrated commoner discovering that he was actually the by-blow of a wealthy aristocrat. The peerage was also shocked and enthralled with every detail of the scandalous story.

Logan had become the most talked-about figure in London, a position he neither wanted nor enjoyed. He grieved over Andrew's death, working himself to exhaustion each day, then taking solace in Madeline's arms at night. His lovemaking was different than before—gentle and prolonged, as if he wanted to lose himself, stay inside her forever. He wasn't satisfied until he had brought them both to piercing ecstasy that left them limp and satiated.

"I never expected to feel such things," Madeline whispered to him one evening. "I didn't know I would find such pleasure in the marriage bed."

Logan laughed quietly, smoothing his large hand over her body. "Neither did I. With my former penchant for women of experience, I never expected to be so captivated by an innocent."

"I'm not an innocent," Madeline said, her breath catching as he settled between her thighs. "After all we've done—"

"There's much more you have to learn, sweet," he said, positioning himself and sliding gently inside her.

"There couldn't be," she protested, gasping as he filled her completely.

"Then we'll continue with your next lesson," Logan murmured with a smile, proceeding to make love to her until she was consumed in a blaze of passion.

Visiting the theater after the day's rehearsal had concluded, Madeline found Logan alone onstage, making notes as he paced through some blocking that had been arranged earlier. At first he was too absorbed to notice her standing in the wings, but soon he turned to look at her. A smile flickered in his blue eyes. "Come here," he said, and Madeline complied gladly.

Logan set his notes aside on a nearby set piece. His hands slid to Madeline's thickening waist, and his gaze traveled over her soft amber-hued gown. "You look like a drop of honey," he murmured, urging her up to her toes. "Give me a taste."

Madeline blushed and glanced around the empty stage, wondering if their embrace would be witnessed by a stray employee or two.

Logan laughed. "No one is going to object, madam," he mocked, and lowered his head. He stole a kiss from her, and then another, his mouth warm and searching.

Smiling and breathless, Madeline drew away from him. "Are you almost finished here?"

"Yes." Logan pulled her back against him and fondled her hips. "I'll require only five more minutes. Why don't you wait for me in my office? We'll have a private meeting there—with the door closed."

"I don't feel like working," she said provocatively, making him grin.

"You won't be, madam." Patting her familiarly on the buttocks, he gave her a gentle push toward the wing.

As Madeline departed, Logan picked up his notes and returned his attention to the final points of choreography. A rueful smile pulled at his lips as he found it difficult to pick up his former train of thought. The only thing on his mind was to get to his office as quickly as possible and seduce his wife. Forcing himself to concentrate, he scribbled a few sentences, using the set piece as a makeshift table.

As he worked, he was aware of a shadowy figure moving through the rows of seats along the side of the theater, gradually approaching the proscenium. "Who is that?" he asked, squinting in the stage light, unable to recognize the intruder. There was no reply. Suspecting that the stranger was a curiosity-seeker who had barged into the theater, Logan sighed shortly. "The Capital is closed to the public. There will be a performance tonight if you wish to return later."

The visitor moved closer, seeming hesitant to leave the shadows.

Logan straightened and continued to stare at the stranger's dark outline. "Who the hell are you?" he demanded abruptly.

The man answered in a drunken, familiar voice that sent Logan's world reeling. "Don't say you've already forgotten me . . . brother."

Andrew emerged from the shadows, his face bloated and brilliant with hatred, cheeks burning with a high flush. Logan stared at him uncomprehendingly. He wasn't aware of moving until he felt the edge of the set piece pressing hard against his spine and realized he had staggered backward a step or two. His lips formed Andrew's name, and for an insane moment he thought he was seeing a ghost . . . until he saw the pistol in Andrew's hand.

"I thought you were dead," Logan said hoarsely, trying to gather his wits.

"You must be disappointed," Andrew replied. "All set to take my place, were you?"

"No, I . . ." Logan shook his head, inhaling a few deep breaths to restore himself. "Damn you, Andrew, what in God's name happened? Everyone thinks you drowned during that bloody water-party—"

"That's what I wanted them to think. I had to do something. I had sharks from a gambling-hell following my every footstep, with every intention of ending my miserable life if I couldn't repay my debts. I had to have some time . . . had to fool them, until I could get my hands on some money."

"You put me through hell," Logan snapped, his shock fading.

"It didn't last long, did it?" Andrew asked softly.

"You recovered sufficiently to announce to the world that you're my half brother. A fact that no one bothered to tell me."

"I didn't know about it until recently." Logan's gaze fell to the gun in Andrew's wavering hand. "You're drunk, Andrew. Put that damn thing aside, and we'll talk."

"I intend to use it," came the unsteady reply. "On you, or myself . . . perhaps both of us. My life isn't worth a shilling. And only think how your career would benefit. You would become the greatest legend in theater history."

Logan showed no reaction, but his heart beat unpleasantly fast. Andrew had always been an unpredictable drunk. He could very well carry out his threat.

"I've never ended someone's life before," Andrew muttered, shaking like a tree in a storm— only the storm wasn't from outside; it was his own inner upheaval. "But you deserve it, Jimmy."

"Why?"

Andrew's mouth twisted in a spasm of bitterness. "I always knew what to expect from you. Even though the rest of the world was filled with liars, I could depend on you. Now it turns out you're the worst of them all. Keeping Rochester's dirty secret, stepping into my shoes when you thought I was gone . . . well, you can't have what's mine. I'll kill you first."

As Andrew spoke, he ventured closer, waving the gun agitatedly. Rapidly Logan considered making a grab for the weapon and forcing it from him. Out of the corner of his eye, he saw Madeline standing in the nearby wing, and his heart skipped several beats. *Dammit,* he thought in sudden terror. *Leave, Maddy. Get out of here!* But she didn't move. It was incomprehensible that she would place herself in such danger. She could be hit by a stray shot . . . she could unwittingly provoke Andrew into a fit of deadly rage. Logan broke out into a sweat, not daring to look at her.

"I don't want anything of yours," Logan said to Andrew, finding it hard to speak. "All I want is to help you." His throat felt as if it had been lined with barrel stays. He realized that Madeline was moving, walking noiselessly behind the set piece and flats for God knew what purpose. Locked in agony, he waited for her to stumble, to bump into something. Pregnancy had made her clumsy of late.

"Help me?" Andrew scoffed, swaying before him. "What a fine show of brotherly concern . . . I could almost believe you."

"Put down the damned pistol and talk to me," Logan said curtly.

"God, I despise you." Andrew's hand shook as he trained the gun at Logan's midriff. "I never realized before how much like my father you are. Superior bastards with your filthy secrets, manipulating everyone around you—"

"I never treated you that way."

Andrew shook his head in torment. "Jimmy . . . how could we not have known? All those years . . ."

"Andrew, wait," Logan said, the blood draining from his face as his half brother cocked the pistol. "Andrew—"

There was a startling crack as the nearby flat collapsed, the hinged pieces snapping downward as if pushed by an unseen hand. Without any anchoring braces, the reinforced timber frame fell on Andrew before he had time to react. The gun

went off with an ear-splitting explosion, a way-
ward bullet instantly burying itself in the side of
the proscenium.

Madeline stood in the space where the flat had
been, staring at the results of her efforts.

Logan gazed at her, frozen for a few seconds,
registering that she was all right. He bent to shove
the collapsed flat aside and crouched on the floor to
grab his dazed half brother by the collar. Andrew
reeked of wine, gin, and countless other distilla-
tions. His dazed eyes opened to stare into Logan's
downturned face. As Logan had expected, the flat
hadn't been heavy enough to hurt him. "What
happened—" Andrew began.

Logan clipped him on the jaw, knocking him out
cold. Subsiding peacefully onto the stage boards,
Andrew began to snore.

Madeline hurried over to them. "Is he all right?"

Logan stood slowly. He resorted to the tactic of
counting to ten, but it did nothing to stem the flood
of panicked rage. He was afraid to touch her, afraid
he might throttle her.

"What the hell was going through your mind?"
he heard himself ask raggedly. "Did you give a
thought to the safety of our child?"

'No, I . . ." Her bewildered gaze met his. "All I
could think about was you."

"I can damn well look after myself," he roared,
unable to keep from snatching her shoulders and
shaking her. "By God, madam, you've finally managed to make me insane! I'm going to relive the
past minute every day from now on until I'm a
raving lunatic."

"I could hardly stand by and watch him shoot
you. There's no need to be angry. No one was hurt,

and everything's all right now." Her gaze traveled to Andrew's slumbering form. "For the most part."

"Everything is *not* all right," Logan said savagely, letting go of her. His heart still thundered in his chest. Half of him wanted to continue shaking her until her teeth rattled, while the other half wanted to crush her against him and cover every inch of her with violent kisses. The thought that she could have been hurt, even killed, filled him with sheer panic. He fought to shut away the tide of emotion, gritting his teeth and clenching his fists in the effort.

Madeline stared at him in obvious bewilderment. "I don't understand."

"Then let me explain," he replied, his voice turning ugly. "Your only value to me is the child you're carrying. All I've asked of you is to take care of him—and you're too damned impulsive and reckless to do even that."

Madeline's face drained of blood. She looked blank except for a stricken expression in her eyes. "I . . ." She was strangely out of breath. "I'm sorry if you find me so lacking."

They were interrupted by the company members who came rushing to the scene, having heard the gunshot as they worked in other parts of the theater.

"Mr. Scott—"

"What happened?"

"Who is that, and why—"

"Some bastard tried to shoot Mr. Scott!"

Logan crouched by Andrew once more. "It was an accident. No harm was done. Gather up Lord Drake and have him sent to my home, in my carriage. And be careful with him. He's ill."

"Stinking bloody soused is what he is," someone muttered as they obeyed his directives.

Logan threw a hard glance at Madeline. "He'll stay in our guest quarters. Do you have any objections?"

She shook her head briefly, her face suddenly infused with scarlet. "Why bother to ask? You've made it clear that my opinion means nothing to you."

She sounded and looked different than he had ever seen her. Without thinking, he placed a hand on her back to guide her from the stage, and she jerked away from him. It was the first time she had ever rejected his touch.

"I don't need your help," Madeline said stiffly. "All I need from you is the one thing you're determined never to give." She walked away before he could reply, her spine rigid with an anger that disconcerted him. Had he ever seen her angry before? Damn her for making him feel somehow that he was in the wrong, when she was the one who had put herself in danger!

There was silence between them on the way home. Once there, Andrew slept soundly as the servants assisted Logan in assuring that he was clean and comfortable in the guest quarters. After sharing a hasty supper with Madeline, Logan prepared to return to the Capital for the scheduled performance that evening.

"Will you be all right?" he asked her tersely. "I can send for one of your family or friends to keep you company while I'm gone—"

"I'll be fine," she replied, not meeting his eyes. "The servants will be here if I require anything, and I don't expect Lord Drake will awaken before tomorrow."

"If he does, don't go near him."

"Very well. When will you notify Lord Rochester that his son is still alive?"

"I'll let Andrew make that decision when he's able." He stared at her assessingly. "Go to bed early. You've had a shock today. You need to rest."

"You needn't be concerned," Madeline said coolly, determined to match his brusqueness with her own. "The baby is fine."

Scowling, he left without another word.

Madeline tried to summon her usual patience, remembering the wrong she had done him, her vow to earn his love slowly over time . . . but instead she experienced a new burst of anger. It seemed that her love and patience had gotten her nowhere. If this was how Logan wanted things between them, so be it! She was tired of being a martyr, tired of waiting and hoping. Clenching her fists, she went upstairs for a lengthy bath, hoping to soak away her tension in the hot, scented water.

Before retiring, Madeline went to her bedroom window and pushed the velvet curtain aside to glance out at the formal garden and the guest quarters in the other wing of the house. There was a light in the window of Lord Drake's room, and a flicker of movement within.

Lord Drake was awake, she surmised with a frown. No doubt he was guilt-ridden, drunk, and in pain. Madeline thought of ignoring the light in the window and letting him suffer alone. After what he had done that day, threatening her husband's life, he didn't deserve compassion. Moreover, Logan's edict to stay away from him still rang in her ears.

On the other hand, she wasn't a child or a servant to be ordered about. She was an adult, with the right to follow the promptings of her own conscience. Troubled, she rang for her maid and went to her armoire.

The maid appeared in a minute or two. "Yes, Mrs. Scott?" she asked, seeming perplexed by the sight of Madeline pulling a day gown from the armoire.

"Please help me change." Madeline said. "I believe Lord Drake is awake. If so, I would like to speak with him."

"But Mrs. Scott, the master told everyone—"

"Yes, he made his wishes clear. But there's no need to worry. I will be perfectly safe, as I intend to have someone accompany me to his quarters.

"Yes, Mrs. Scott," the maid said doubtfully. "Though I don't think the master will be happy once he hears of this."

As it was, Madeline was escorted to the guest quarters by a footman, Mrs. Beecham, and the butler, all of whom made their disapproval quite clear. "There's no need for such a crowd," Madeline protested, but they were determined to protect her from a man they considered dangerous.

Lord Drake was rummaging through the cabinets of a mahogany sideboard in the guest parlor when they arrived. Swaying unsteadily, blinking like a child who had been awakened too soon, he stared at the four of them, his bloodshot gaze fastening on Madeline's small face.

She was amazed by the contrast between his usual appearance and the way he looked now. The mocking, carefree degenerate had been replaced by a stranger with matted hair and a sickly gray complexion. He had dressed himself in the fresh clothes that had been set out for him: a pair of trousers, a shirt, and a vest that had been tailored for Logan's leaner frame. Buttons and fabric strained to contain his bloated waistline.

"If it's alcohol you're looking for," Madeline said softly, "Logan made certain that it was removed from the guest rooms. Would you like me to send for coffee?"

He gave her a look of horrified shame and seemed to slink to the corner of the room. "Please go," he muttered. "I can't bear to face you. What I did today—"

"You weren't yourself," she replied, her earlier condemnation changing to pity.

"Oh, I was," he assured her. "That was definitely me, cowardly raving bastard that I am." He shook his head as Madeline instructed the footman to bring coffee and sandwiches. "Don't send for anything. I'll be gone within the hour."

"You must stay, Lord Drake. For my husband's sake."

There was a humorous twitch at the corner of his mouth. "I'm sure you don't want him to be deprived of the pleasure of beating me to a pulp."

"You know him better than that," she said quietly, sitting in an armchair while Mrs. Beecham and the butler lit the lamps and stirred the fire. "Do sit and talk to me, Lord Drake."

He complied reluctantly, half-sitting, half-collapsing in a chair near the fire and resting his disheveled head in his hands. Eventually coffee was brought, and Lord Drake downed three cups of the bitter brew, seeming to gain a measure of lucidity. When it seemed that there was no apparent danger from him, the servants acceded to Madeline's murmured request and withdrew to the next room.

Lord Drake spoke before Madeline was able. "I'd

been drinking for three days straight before the water-party," he mumbled. "I was half-crazed with fear, knowing that some bastards I owed a fortune to had put a price on my head. I had devised some idiotic scheme to make it look as if I had drowned, hoping that would throw them off the trail for a while. After my ruse succeeded, I disguised myself in order to play at a gambling-hell on the east side. It was there that I heard the gossip about Logan. Everyone was talking about it, that he was Rochester's bastard son. I went insane. I've never felt such hatred as I did in that moment."

"Toward Logan?" Madeline asked, bewildered.

The dark, disheveled head moved in a weary nod. "Yes . . . although most of it was directed at my father. Between the two of them, they've made me into a fraud. Logan was the first son, and I took his place. I was given the life he should have had . . . and it was always bloody obvious that he was the better man. Look at what he's made of himself. I've always compared myself to him and come off lacking, but at least I could comfort myself with the knowledge that I had the Drake blood flowing through my veins. Now it seems he has that too."

"You are Lord Rochester's only legitimate heir," Madeline said. "Nothing will change that."

Lord Drake wrapped his fingers around the delicate china cup and clasped it until Madeline feared the porcelain might crack. "But it should be Logan, don't you see? Instead he got nothing. Worse than nothing. My God, you couldn't know how he lived, the punishment he took at Jennings's hands, the countless days he went cold and hungry. While I lived in the mansion nearby—"

"You couldn't have done anything to change that," Madeline interrupted softly.

"My father could have—and knowing that is pure hell. I can't stand being his son. And I can't stand having Logan as my brother, when all I've done is take from him since the day I was born." He stood up from his chair and set the china cup aside with hands that shook. "The only thing I can do for Logan in return is to make certain he never sets eyes on me again."

"You're wrong." Madeline remained in her chair, staring at him with a clear gaze that seemed to pin him in place. Her voice trembled with conviction. "At least have the courage to face Logan tomorrow. I think in his heart he believes that everyone he cares about will leave him eventually. If you have any brotherly feeling for Logan, you'll stay and find a way to help him come to terms with the past. He'll never be at peace unless you do. You're the only link that Logan has to Lord Rochester. I don't believe he'll ever come to love or even like Lord Rochester, but he must learn to accept that he is his father."

"And you think I can do that for him?" Lord Drake inquired with a sardonic laugh that sounded startlingly like Logan's. "Good God, I can't even do it for myself."

"Then you'll have to help each other," Madeline replied stubbornly.

Lord Drake sat down again, chuckling unsteadily. "There's more to you than meets the eye, isn't there? You're a persistent little wench—but I suppose you would have to be, married to my brother."

They shared a gaze of silent amusement until

they became aware of a large, shadowy form in the doorway. Logan . . . his face contorted, his voice hoarse as he spoke to Madeline. "Get out of here."

Madeline blinked in confusion. "I was merely talking to Lord Drake—"

"I told you to stay away from him. Is it too much to ask you to obey the simplest instructions?"

"Look here," Lord Drake said, sounding weary and bitterly amused, "nothing illicit has occurred, Jimmy. Don't blame your wife for something that happened long before you met her."

Logan ignored him and stared coldly at Madeline. "In the future, madam, you will not interfere in matters that are none of your business."

Something inside her seemed to wither. For months she had deliberately left herself vulnerable to him, tried to earn his affection by giving him the best of herself . . . and it hadn't been enough. She was tired of trying and failing, repeatedly losing and gaining the same ground. She stood and replied without emotion. "Very well. I won't be a burden to you any longer. From now on you're welcome to your privacy—as much of it as you want." She left the room without a glance.

Logan took his gaze from the empty doorway and sent Andrew a glance rife with hatred. "If you laid one filthy finger on her—"

"My God," Andrew said, shaking his head, "you can't possibly think I'm capable of seducing your wife—or any woman, for that matter—in this condition. I have more pressing matters to worry about. Besides, she wouldn't tolerate my advances. She's not like Olivia."

"I'll kill you if I ever find you alone with her again."

"You're a bigger fool than I am," Andrew observed, sitting and rubbing his aching head. "I didn't think it possible, but you are. You've actually found a woman who loves you, though I can't fathom how or why, and you have no damn idea of how to react."

Logan regarded him icily. "You're drunk, Andrew."

"Of course I am. It's the only time I can bring myself to tell the truth."

"I'll be damned if I'll discuss my wife with you."

"You're damned anyway, brother—you're a Drake. Eventually you'll manage to drive away everyone who cares about you. The Drakes are solitary creatures. We destroy anyone who dares to get too close. We have contempt for the poor idiots who try to love us. It happened to your mother, and it's happening now to your wife."

Logan stared at his half brother in stunned silence. Denial seethed inside him. "I'm not like him," he said in a raw whisper.

"How many people have you sacrificed because of your ambition? How many have you kept at arm's length until they drifted away? You've convinced yourself that you're more comfortable alone. Life is damned safe and convenient that way, isn't it? You've been cursed with an amazing autonomy, Jimmy—just like Rochester and me." He smiled bleakly at whatever it was he saw in Logan's eyes. "Do you want to hear something strange? She asked me to help you."

"Help *me?*" Logan heard himself ask incredulously. "I'm not the one who needs help."

"That's a debatable point," Andrew mocked, laboring to produce a smile. "Let's talk in the morning, brother . . . I'm damned exhausted and drunk. In the meanwhile, you might consider going to your wife and begging her not to leave you."

# *Fifteen*

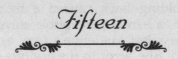

*Logan wandered* to his private suite in a daze, feeling as if his safe, comfortable world had been turned upside down. There had been too many surprises of late . . . the news of his own impending fatherhood, the discovery that he was Rochester's bastard, Andrew's death and subsequent reappearance. Nothing but such an onslaught would have been able to break his defenses. In the middle of it all, only one thing had remained steady and unchanging. Madeline . . . generous, affectionate, resilient, showing him in every way possible that she loved him.

He needed her, but he could hardly bear to admit it, even to himself. Madeline would have to content herself with what he could give, and not ask for more. Summoning his reserves of weary determination, he entered the bedroom. He found his wife sitting on the edge of the mattress, her small hand clasped to her stomach. The odd expression on her face made his heart lurch in sudden panic.

"What is it?" he asked, coming to her swiftly.

"I felt the baby move," she said in wonder.

Startled, Logan could only stand and stare at her. His fingers twitched at his side, and suddenly he wanted badly to touch her, to feel the minute vibrations of his child moving within her. The effort of holding back caused a tremor to run through him, a barely perceptible shiver.

The softness left Madeline's face, and she rose from the bed. She went to the armoire, and it was then that he saw the valise she had pulled from the lower shelf.

"What is that for?" he asked sharply.

Her voice was taut and low. "I've decided I don't want to live here anymore."

Incredulous anger surged through him, and he replied with jeering softness. "You don't have a choice, madam."

"Yes, I do. Unless you physically restrain me, you have no way of keeping me here."

"I had no idea this was so unpleasant for you," he said, gesturing to their luxurious surroundings. "If you haven't been happy, you've given a damned convincing imitation."

"You seem to have a way of making me happy and miserable at the same time." Madeline pulled out a pair of gloves, an armload of linens, and a lace scarf, jamming the articles into the valise. "Obviously I've been a terrible inconvenience to you. However, once I learn to stop loving you, everything will be much easier for both of us."

Logan strode to her and stood in front of the armoire. "Maddy," he said gruffly, "I shouldn't have snapped at you earlier. I was worried about you. Now set that thing aside and come to bed."

She shook her head, her eyes prickling with impatient tears. "I've finally given up, Logan. You'll never stop punishing me for having hurt you. You wait for every opportunity to show me that you can walk away without a backward glance—you've made your point often enough. I admit I've been a fool for hoping you might change. Now all I want is to get away from you and find some peace."

Her quiet stubbornness infuriated him. "Dammit, you're not going anywhere." He took hold of her shoulders and was shocked to feel the quick sting of her hand on his cheek. She had slapped him.

"Let go of me," she said, breathing fast and glaring at him.

It was as unexpected as being bitten by a butterfly. Bewildered, outraged, Logan bent his head to kiss her, trying to soften her the only way he knew how. Instead of offering her usual sweet response, she was stiff in his arms, her mouth cold beneath his. For the first time he discovered the streak of iron that Madeline hadn't revealed until now. Staring at the small, unyielding stranger before him, he let his hands fall away.

"What the hell do you want from me?" he asked roughly.

"I would like the answers to a few questions." Her amber eyes searched his. "Was it true, what you said this afternoon? That my only value is the baby I'm carrying?"

He felt his face darken with a flush. "I was angry with you for putting yourself in danger."

"Did you marry me only because of the baby?" she persisted.

Logan felt as if she were systematically chipping away at him, weakening his foundations with the intention of making him crumble. "Yes, I . . . no. I still wanted you."

"And still loved me?" she half-whispered.

Logan scrubbed his hands through his hair until it was in wild disarray. "Dammit, I won't discuss this."

"All right." Calmly she turned away and re-sumed packing.

Logan made an infuriated sound and took hold of her from behind, ignoring the way she stiffened. He breathed in her scent, rubbing his mouth at the nape of her neck. His raw voice was muffled in her flowing hair. "I don't want to lose you, Maddy."

She strained to break free. "But you don't want to love me, either."

He released her abruptly and paced in the room like a caged wild animal.

"You said it to me once," Madeline burst out angrily. "Why is it so impossible now? Are you really so cold and unforgiving?"

He stopped, facing away from her, and replied in a tortured voice. "I forgave you a long time ago. I understood why you did what you did. Part of me even admired you for it."

"Then why are there still walls between us?" she asked with incredulous despair.

A shudder moved across his shoulders. Madeline bit her lip, waiting, sensing that if she were quiet she might hear the words that would bring her understanding.

"You know that I love you," he said hoarsely. "Everyone knows it. No matter what I do, I can't stop it." He went to the window and flattened his hands on the cold, icy glass, staring fiercely at the wintry garden outside. "But I can't let it happen again. There will be nothing left of me if I lose you this time."

"But you won't lose me," she said in pained confusion. "Logan, you must believe that!"

Logan shook his head. "Rochester told me . . ." He paused and swallowed convulsively. "My mother died while giving birth to me. I was too large—her death was my fault."

Madeline made a sound of protest. "My God, how can you believe that?"

"It's a fact," he said doggedly. "It was my fault. And I can't take any joy in our baby when I think about how it might . . ." He couldn't finish the sentence. There was no need.

"You're afraid that I won't survive the birth," Madeline said, her features wiped clean with astonishment. "Is that what you're trying to say?"

"Any child of mine is bound to be large . . . and you . . ."

"I'm not so frail as that," she said, staring up at his shadowed face. "Logan, look at me! I promise that nothing will happen to me or the babe."

"You can't make such a promise," he said roughly.

Madeline opened her mouth to argue but suddenly recalled that her own mother had experienced many problems with childbirth. Logan was right—she couldn't guarantee that everything would be all right. "What if your fears are justified and the worst happens?" she asked. "Will it be any easier, having kept yourself apart from me?"

He turned to look at her then, his face tormented, his blue eyes shimmering with moisture. "Damn you, I don't know."

"Aren't you ever tired of keeping yourself separate from everyone?" she murmured, staring at him with love and compassion. "Come to me, Logan. We have each other. There's no need for either of us to be lonely."

The words were his undoing. His stiff jaw trembled, and he reached her in a few strides, wrapping her in a painfully tight embrace. "I can't live without you," he said, his voice muffled.

"You won't have to." She clenched her fingers in his hair and kissed his damp cheek, while her body went weak with overwhelming relief.

Logan shuddered, and his hard mouth found hers in a bruising kiss that seemed to last forever. "You'll stay?" he asked.

"Yes, yes . . ." Her lips sought his, clinging sweetly, and he groaned with aching desire.

He would take the risk of loving her. It wasn't as if he had a choice, anyway. Carrying her to the bed, he undressed them both and made love to her with wild tenderness, trembling with the effort to be gentle.

Afterward, Madeline lay replete in his arms, too weary to move as she felt Logan rise on his elbow to look down at her. He bent and pressed his mouth to her stomach, a gesture of hard-won hope that made her eyes sting with the piercing joy she felt. "It will be all right," Madeline whispered, pulling his head to hers. "Trust me." And she kissed him while her heart brimmed with love.

# Epilogue

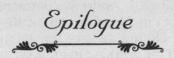

*The labor* had lasted ten hours so far. Having been banished from the bedroom where Madeline was giving birth to their child, Logan sat in the private family parlor nearby, gripping his skull more tightly with each indistinct sound that came through the door. He took some comfort in the fact that Julia was in there with Madeline, lending encouragement and friendship, as well as being available to assist the doctor and midwife. But nothing pierced the haze of worry that surrounded him.

He had stayed with Madeline for the first few hours, the sight of her pain unnerving him unbearably, until Dr. Brooke had ordered him from the room. "I suggest that you find a bottle of brandy," Brooke had told him with a reassuring smile. "This may take several hours yet."

Logan had downed half a bottle so far, and there was no relief from the gnawing fear inside him. He couldn't stand the memory of his wife in pain, the way she gripped a knotted rag during each contraction, the way she had bitten her lips until they were bruised—

"Good God, Jimmy." Andrew walked into the parlor and sat beside him, smiling quizzically. "You're not holding up very well, are you?"

Logan sent him a wretched glare.

"How strange," Andrew commented lightly, "that for once I'm the sober one, while you're half-seas under." During the past few months Andrew had curtailed his drinking to an occasional glass of wine. The alcoholic ruddiness had left his cheeks, and he had dropped a great deal of weight, looking fit and lean for the first time since his teenaged years. He had also given up gambling and had arranged to pay back his debts, with interest. It even seemed that he had managed to build a new, closer relationship with Rochester, who had softened a bit since the scare of his son's "death."

"I'm not drunk enough yet," Logan muttered, flinching as he heard a smothered cry from within the room.

Andrew looked uncomfortably at the door. "You're wound as tight as a watch," he said. "Cheer up, Jimmy. Women survive this sort of thing every day. Why don't you come downstairs with me? I don't mind telling you that I'm tired of trying to make small talk with your in-laws, respectable souls that they are. You should distract yourself by playing host for a little while."

"I'd rather crawl through an acre of broken glass."

A wry, wondering smile crossed Andrew's face. "The great Logan Scott, wearing his heart on his sleeve. That's a sight I never expected to see."

Logan was too miserable to reply. He lifted his gaze to the portrait on the wall, the Orsini painting of Madeline that had earned adulation and rapturous reviews from every notable critic in London. The artist had portrayed her seated before a window, an elbow resting lightly on a walnut table as she stared dreamily into the distance. The white gown she wore was circumspect, except for a sleeve that dipped coyly to reveal the curve of one pale shoulder.

By painting Madeline in profile, Orsini had revealed the delicate purity of her features, yet he had given the bare length of her throat, arms, and shoulder a lush quality that made the viewer aware of the velvety texture of her skin. The portrait was a disturbing study in contrasts: innocent yet sensuous, her face serene and her eye touched with a mischievous glint . . . Madeline as a fallen angel.

"Lovely," Andrew remarked, following Logan's gaze. "One would never suspect from looking at this painting that she can be as stubborn as a goat." He smiled at Logan. "She'll pull through this in good form, Jimmy. If I were still a betting man, I'd put all my chips on it."

Logan nodded slightly, his gaze locked on the painting. The past few months had been filled with the most intense happiness he had ever known. Madeline had become everything to him, filling every empty space in his life, banishing all the bitterness and pain and replacing them with joy. As much as he had loved her before, it was nothing compared to now. He would have walked through hell to spare her one moment's suffering. The knowledge that she had to endure the agony of childbirth alone, that he could do nothing for her, was driving him mad.

All at once he heard a baby crying. The shrill noise caused Logan to shoot to his feet. Chalk-white, he waited for what seemed like an hour, though in reality less than a minute passed.

The door opened, and Julia stood there wearing an expression of weary happiness. "Both mother and child are doing splendidly. Come in, Papa, and have a look at your beautiful daughter."

Logan stared at her uncomprehendingly. "Is Maddy . . ." He stopped and tried to moisten his lips; his mouth was too dry.

Julia smiled and gently touched his cheek. "She did very well, Logan. She's fine. "

"Congratulations, brother," Andrew said, taking the brandy bottle from Logan's nerveless grip. "Give that to me. You don't need it anymore."

Scarcely aware of what was happening, Logan strode into the room.

Wistfully Andrew stared at the half-empty brandy bottle in his hand and gave it to Julia. "Here," he muttered. "I don't trust myself with it. Thank God I still have plenty of other vices to indulge in."

Barely aware of the hearty congratulations of the doctor and midwife, Logan went to the bed and sat beside Madeline. Her eyes half-opened, and she smiled at him.

"Maddy," he said, his voice cracking. He took her free hand and brought it to his mouth, fervently pressing his lips into her palm.

Reading the anguished relief on his face, Madeline murmured soothingly and pulled him down to her. He pressed his face to her breasts and made an inarticulate sound.

"I'm all right," she murmured, stroking his hair. "It wasn't nearly as bad as I thought it would be."

His lips found hers, and as he tasted her familiar sweet warmth, his panic faded. "I've been as scared as hell," he said when their lips parted. "I don't ever want to go through this again."

"I'm afraid you'll have to, darling. You'll want her to have a brother someday."

Logan stared at the tiny form held in the crook of Madeline's arm. The baby was wrapped in linen and cotton, her small pink face wearing a perplexed pucker. There was a patch of downy chest-nut hair on her head. Logan touched the silken strands wonderingly. "Hello," he whispered, brushing his lips over the baby's forehead.

"She's beautiful, isn't she?" Madeline asked.

"Exquisite," he said, staring at the miraculous creation, and his gaze returned to Madeline. "But she doesn't eclipse her mother."

In spite of her discomfort and exhaustion, Madeline managed a chuckle. "Silly man. No woman looks beautiful immediately after childbirth."

"I could stare at you for hours . . . weeks . . . months . . . and never get tired."

"You'll have to do it while I'm sleeping," she said with a yawn, blinking like a small owl.

"Rest," Logan said. "Both of you." His caressing gaze moved over his wife and infant daughter. "I'll watch over you."

"Love me?" Madeline asked with a faint smile, and yawned again.

"It used to be love." He brushed his lips over her closed eyelids. "Now there's no word for it."

"You once told me that you thought love was a weakness."

"I was wrong," he whispered, kissing the corners of her mouth. "I've discovered it's my only strength."

Madeline fell asleep with a smile still on her lips, her hand curled around his.

Hearing a quiet tap at the door, Logan went to answer it and found Mrs. Florence at the threshold. Of late she had been a frequent visitor to the household, ostensibly to call on Madeline, but she and Logan had both found unexpected enjoyment in their time together. They had a great deal in common, after all. They had shared many long,

entertaining conversations about the theater . . .
and sometimes they discussed his mother, Elizabeth. There was still much Logan wanted to know
about her, as well as the man who had sired her.
Piece by piece Mrs. Florence was providing the
truth about his past, giving him a sense of whole-
ness he had never expected to find.

His grandmother was dressed as if for a grand
occasion, her throat and wrists adorned with
pearls, her faded red hair stylishly arranged.

"They're sleeping," Logan said, protective of his
wife and child's need for rest.

Imperiously Mrs. Florence pointed her silver
cane at him. "Don't even think of turning me away
after I ascended all those confounded stairs. I'll
only stay a moment—I must have a look at my
great-grandchild."

"Very well," he muttered, allowing her to pass.
"Apparently there's no stopping you."

As Mrs. Florence approached the bedside, she
appeared enchanted by the sight of the infant in
Madeline's arms. "My great-granddaughter," she
remarked softly, glancing back at Logan. "A gor-
geous creature, and no less than I expected. Have
you decided on a name?"

"Elizabeth," Logan replied.

The elderly woman contemplated him with eyes
that had grown suspiciously moist. She gestured
for him to lean down to her and kissed him on the
cheek. "Your mother would have liked that, dear
boy. She would have liked it very much."